Even with burning lamps lining all the walls and the paths clear and well marked, it took Drizzt and Regis the better part of three hours to cross the miles of the great Mithril Hall complex to the new tunnel areas. They passed through the wondrous, tiered Undercity, with its many levels of dwarven dwellings that resembled gigantic steps on two sides of the huge cavern. The dwellings overlooked a central work area on the cavern floor that bustled with the activities of the industrious race.

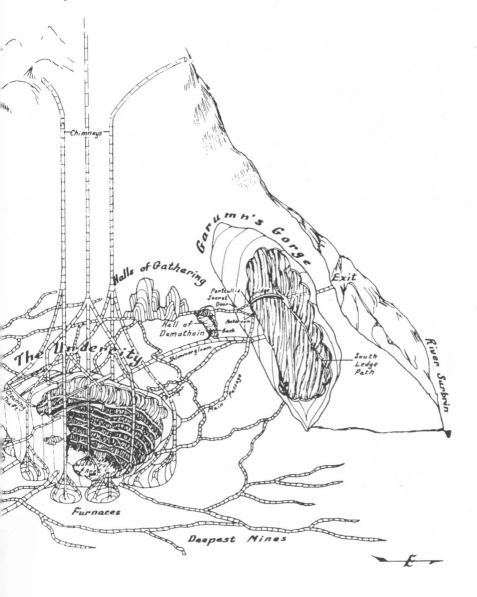

FANTASY ADVENTURE

The LEGACY

R. A. Salvatore

TSR Inc.

To Diane—share this with me.

THE LEGACY

First Printing: September 1992
Printed in the United States of America
Library of Congress Number: 91-67658

9 8 7 6 5 4 3 2 1

ISBN: 1-56076-529-1

TSR, Inc.   TSR Ltd.
P.O. Box 756   120 Church End, Cherry Hinton
Lake Geneva, WI 53147   Cambridge CB1 3LB
U.S.A.   United Kingdom

PRELUDE

T he rogue Dinin made his way carefully through the dark avenues of Menzoberranzan, the city of drow. A renegade, with no family to call his own for nearly twenty years, the seasoned fighter knew well the perils of the city, and knew how to avoid them.

He passed an abandoned compound along the two-mile-long cavern's western wall and could not help but pause and stare. Twin stalagmite mounds supported a blasted fence around the whole of the place, and two sets of broken doors, one on the ground and one beyond a balcony twenty feet up the wall, hung

1

open awkwardly on twisted and scorched hinges. How many times had Dinin levitated up to that balcony, entering the private quarters of the nobles of his house, House Do'Urden?

House Do'Urden. It was forbidden even to speak the name in the drow city. Once, Dinin's family had been the eighth-ranked among the sixty or so drow families in Menzoberranzan; his mother had sat on the ruling council; and he, Dinin, had been a Master at Melee-Magthere, the School of Fighters, at the famed drow Academy.

Standing before the compound, it seemed to Dinin as if the place were a thousand years removed from that time of glory. His family was no more, his house lay in ruins, and Dinin had been forced to take up with Bregan D'aerthe, an infamous mercenary band, simply to survive.

"Once," the rogue drow mouthed quietly. He shook his slender shoulders and pulled his concealing *piwafwi* cloak around him, remembering how vulnerable a houseless drow could be. A quick glance toward the center of the cavern, toward the pillar that was Narbondel, showed him that the hour was late. At the break of each day, the Archmage of Menzoberranzan went out to Narbondel and infused the pillar with a magical, lingering heat that would work its way up, then back down. To sensitive drow eyes, which could look into the infrared spectrum, the level of heat in the pillar acted as a gigantic glowing clock.

Now Narbondel was almost cool; another day neared its end.

Dinin had to go more than halfway across the city, to a secret cave within the Clawrift, a great chasm running out from Menzoberranzan's northwestern wall. There Jarlaxle, the leader of Bregan D'aerthe, waited in one of his many hideouts.

The drow fighter cut across the center of the city, passed right by Narbondel, and beside more than a hundred hollowed stalagmites, comprising a dozen separate family compounds, their fabulous sculptures and gargoyles glowing in multicolored faerie fire. Drow soldiers, walking posts along house walls or along the bridges connecting multitudes of leering stalactites, paused and regarded the lone stranger carefully, handcrossbows or poisoned javelins held ready until Dinin was far beyond them.

That was the way in Menzoberranzan: always alert, always distrustful.

Dinin gave one careful look around when he reached the edge of the Clawrift, then slipped over the side and used his innate powers of levitation to slowly descend into the chasm. More than a hundred feet down, he again looked into the bolts of readied handcrossbows, but these were withdrawn as soon as the mercenary guardsmen recognized Dinin as one of their own.

Jarlaxle has been waiting for you, one of the guards signaled in the intricate silent hand code of the dark elves.

Dinin didn't bother to respond. He owed commoner soldiers no explanations. He pushed past the guardsmen rudely, making his way down a short tunnel that soon branched into a virtual maze of corridors and rooms. Several turns later, the dark elf stopped before a shimmering door, thin and almost translucent. He put his hand against its surface, letting his body heat make an impression that heat-sensing eyes on the other side would understand as a knock.

"At last," he heard a moment later, in Jarlaxle's voice. "Do come in, Dinin, my *Khal'abbil.* You have kept me waiting far too long."

Dinin paused a moment to get a bearing on the unpredictable mercenary's inflections and words. Jarlaxle had called him *Khal'abbil,* "my trusted friend," his nickname for Dinin since the raid that had destroyed House Do'Urden (a raid in which Jarlaxle had played a prominent role), and there was no obvious sarcasm in the mercenary's tone. There seemed to be nothing wrong at all. But, why, then, had Jarlaxle recalled him from his critical scouting mission to House Vandree, the Seventeenth

House of Menzoberranzan? Dinin wondered. It had taken Dinin nearly a year to gain the trust of the imperiled Vandree house guard, a position, no doubt, that would be severely jeopardized by his unexplained absence from the house compound.

There was only one way to find out, the rogue soldier decided. He held his breath and forced his way into the opaque barrier. It seemed as if he were passing through a wall of thick water, though he did not get wet, and, after several long steps across the flowing extraplanar border of two planes of existence, he forced his way through the seemingly inch-thick magical door and entered Jarlaxle's small room.

The room was alight in a comfortable red glow, allowing Dinin to shift his eyes from the infrared to the normal light spectrum. He blinked as the transformation completed, then blinked again, as always, when he looked at Jarlaxle.

The mercenary leader sat behind a stone desk in an exotic cushioned chair, supported by a single stem with a swivel so that it could rock back at a considerable angle. Comfortably perched, as always, Jarlaxle had the chair leaning way back, his slender hands clasped behind his clean-shaven head (so unusual for a drow!).

Just for amusement, it seemed, Jarlaxle lifted one foot onto the table, his high black boot hitting the stone with a resounding thump, then lifted the other, striking the stone just as hard, but this boot making not a whisper.

The mercenary wore his ruby-red eye patch over his right eye this day, Dinin noted.

To the side of the desk stood a trembling little humanoid creature, barely half Dinin's five-and-a-half-foot height, including the small white horns protruding from the top of its sloping brow.

"One of House Oblodra's kobolds," Jarlaxle explained casually. "It seems the pitiful thing found its way in, but cannot so easily find its way back out."

The Legacy

The reasoning seemed sound to Dinin. House Oblodra, the Third House of Menzoberranzan, occupied a tight compound at the end of the Clawrift and was rumored to keep thousands of kobolds for torturous pleasure, or to serve as house fodder in the event of a war.

"Do you wish to leave?" Jarlaxle asked the creature in a guttural, simplistic language.

The kobold nodded eagerly, stupidly.

Jarlaxle indicated the opaque door, and the creature darted for it. It had not the strength to penetrate the barrier, though, and it bounced back, nearly landing on Dinin's feet. Before it even bothered to get up, the kobold foolishly sneered in contempt at the mercenary leader.

Jarlaxle's hand flicked several times, too quickly for Dinin to count. The drow fighter reflexively tensed, but knew better than to move, knew that Jarlaxle's aim was always perfect.

When he looked down at the kobold, he saw five daggers sticking from its lifeless body, a perfect star formation on the scaly creature's little chest.

Jarlaxle only shrugged at Dinin's confused stare. "I could not allow the beast to return to Oblodra," he reasoned, "not after it learned of our compound so near theirs."

Dinin shared Jarlaxle's laugh. He started to retrieve the daggers, but Jarlaxle reminded him that there was no need.

"They will return of their own accord," the mercenary explained, pulling at the edge of his bloused sleeve to reveal the magical sheath enveloping his wrist. "Do sit," he bade his friend, indicating an unremarkable stool at the side of the desk. "We have much to discuss."

"Why did you recall me?" Dinin asked bluntly as he took his place beside the desk. "I had infiltrated Vandree fully."

"Ah, my *Khal'abbil*," Jarlaxle replied. "Always to the point. That is a quality I do so admire in you."

"*Uln'hyrr*," Dinin retorted, the drow word for "liar."

Again, the companions shared a laugh, but Jarlaxle's did

5

not last long, and he dropped his feet and rocked forward, clasping his hands, ornamented by a king's hoard of jewels—and how many of those glittering items were magical? Dinin often wondered—on the stone table before him, his face suddenly grave.

"The attack on Vandree is about to commence?" Dinin asked, thinking he had solved the riddle.

"Forget Vandree," Jarlaxle replied. "Their affairs are not so important to us now."

Dinin dropped his sharp chin into a slender palm, propped on the table. Not important! he thought. He wanted to spring up and throttle the cryptic leader. He had spent a whole year . . .

Dinin let his thoughts of Vandree trail away. He looked hard at Jarlaxle's always calm face, searching for clues, then he understood.

"My sister," he said, and Jarlaxle was nodding before the word had left Dinin's mouth. "What has she done?"

Jarlaxle straightened, looked to the side of the small room, and gave a sharp whistle. On cue, a slab of stone shifted, revealing an alcove, and Vierna Do'Urden, Dinin's lone surviving sibling, swept into the room. She seemed more splendid and beautiful than Dinin remembered her since the downfall of their house.

Dinin's eyes widened as he realized the truth of Vierna's dressings; Vierna wore her robes! The robes of a high priestess of Lloth, the robes emblazoned with the arachnid and weapon design of House Do'Urden! Dinin did not know that Vierna had kept them, had not seen them in more than a decade.

"You risk . . ." he started to warn, but Vierna's frenzied expression, her red eyes blazing like twin fires behind the shadows of her high ebony cheekbones, stopped him before he could utter the words.

"I have found again the favor of Lloth," Vierna announced.

Dinin looked to Jarlaxle, who only shrugged and quietly shifted his eye-patch to his left eye instead.

"The Spider Queen has shown me the way," Vierna went on, her normally melodic voice cracking with undeniable excitement.

Dinin thought the female on the verge of insanity. Vierna had always been calm and tolerant, even after House Do'Urden's sudden demise. Over the last few years, though, her actions had become increasingly erratic, and she had spent many hours alone, in desperate prayer to their unmerciful deity.

"Are you to tell us this way that Lloth has shown to you?" Jarlaxle, appearing not at all impressed, asked after many moments of silence.

"Drizzt." Vierna spat the word, the name of their sacrilegious brother, with a burst of venom through her delicate lips.

Dinin wisely shifted his hand from his chin to cover his mouth, to bite back his retort. Vierna, for all her apparent foolhardiness, was, after all, a high priestess, and not one to anger.

"Drizzt?" Jarlaxle calmly asked her. "Your brother?"

"No brother of mine!" Vierna cried out, rushing to the desk as though she meant to strike Jarlaxle down. Dinin didn't miss the mercenary leader's subtle movement, a shift that put his dagger-launching arm in a ready position.

"Traitor to House Do'Urden!" Vierna fumed. "Traitor to all the drow!" Her scowl became a smile suddenly, evil and conniving. "With Drizzt's sacrifice, I will again find Lloth's favor, will again . . ." Vierna broke off abruptly, obviously desiring to keep the rest of her plans private.

"You sound like Matron Malice," Dinin dared to say. "She, too, began a hunt for our broth— for the traitor."

"You remember Matron Malice?" Jarlaxle teased, using the implications of the name as a sedative on overexcited Vierna. Malice, Vierna's mother and Matron of House Do'Urden, had ultimately been undone by her failure to recapture and kill the traitorous Drizzt.

Vierna did calm down, then she began a fit of mocking

laughter that went on for many minutes.

"You see why I summoned you?" Jarlaxle remarked to Dinin, taking no heed of the priestess.

"You wish me to kill her before she can become a problem?" Dinin replied equally casually.

Vierna's laughter halted; her wild-eyed gaze fell over her impertinent brother. "*Wishya!*" she cried, and a wave of magical energy hurled Dinin from his seat, sent him crashing into the stone wall.

"Kneel!" Vierna commanded, and Dinin, when he regained his composure, fell to his knees, all the while looking blankly at Jarlaxle.

The mercenary, too, could not hide his surprise. This last command was a simple spell, certainly not one that should have worked so easily on a seasoned fighter of Dinin's stature.

"I am in Lloth's favor," Vierna, standing tall and straight, explained to both of them. "If you oppose me, then you are not, and with the power of Lloth's blessings for my spells and curses against you, you will find no defense."

"The last we heard of Drizzt placed him on the surface," Jarlaxle said to Vierna, to deflect her rising anger. "By all reports, he remains there still."

Vierna nodded, grinning weirdly all the while, her pearly white teeth contrasting dramatically with her shining ebony skin. "He does," she agreed, "but Lloth has shown me the way to him, the way to glory."

Again, Jarlaxle and Dinin exchanged confused glances. By all their estimates, Vierna's claims—and Vierna herself—sounded insane.

But Dinin, against his will and against all measures of sanity, was still kneeling.

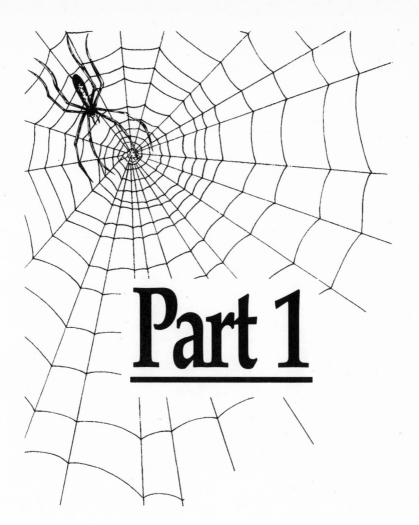

Part 1

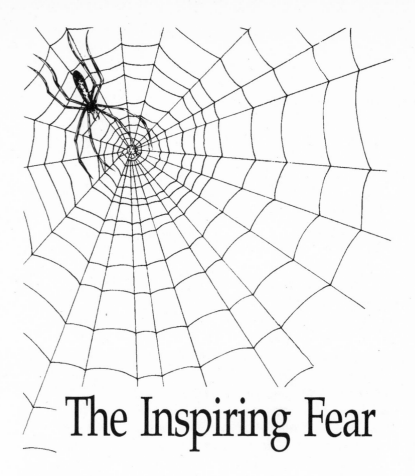

The Inspiring Fear

Nearly three decades have passed since I left my homeland, a small measure of time by the reckoning of a drow
elf, but a period that seems a lifetime to me. All that I
desired, or believed that I desired, when I walked out of
Menzoberranzan's dark cavern, was a true home, a place of friendship
and peace where I might hang my scimitars above the mantle of a warm
hearth and share stories with trusted companions.

I have found all that now, beside Bruenor in the hallowed halls of
his youth. We prosper. We have peace. I wear my weapons only on my
five-day journeys between Mithril Hall and Silverymoon.

Was I wrong?

I do not doubt, nor do I ever lament, my decision to leave the vile world of Menzoberranzan, but I am beginning to believe now, in the (endless) quiet and peace, that my desires at that critical time were founded in the inevitable longing of inexperience. I had never known that calm existence I so badly wanted.

I cannot deny that my life is better, a thousand times better, than anything I ever knew in the Underdark. And yet, I cannot remember the last time I felt the anxiety, the inspiring fear, of impending battle, the tingling that can come only when an enemy is near or a challenge must be met.

Oh, I do remember the specific instance—just a year ago, when Wulfgar, Guenhwyvar, and I worked the lower tunnels in the cleansing of Mithril Hall—but that feeling, that tingle of fear, has long since faded from memory.

Are we then creatures of action? Do we say that we desire those accepted cliches of comfort when, in fact, it is the challenge and the adventure that truly give us life?

I must admit, to myself at least, that I do not know.

There is one point that I cannot dispute, though, one truth that will inevitably help me resolve these questions and which places me in a fortunate position. For now, beside Bruenor and his kin, beside Wulfgar and Catti-brie and Guenhwyvar, dear Guenhwyvar, my destiny is my own to choose.

I am safer now than ever before in my sixty years of life. The prospects have never looked better for the future, for continued peace and continued security. And yet, I feel mortal. For the first time, I look to what has passed rather than to what is still to come. There is no other way to explain it. I feel that I am dying, that those stories I so desired to share with friends will soon grow stale, with nothing to replace them.

But, I remind myself again, the choice is mine to make.

—Drizzt Do'Urden

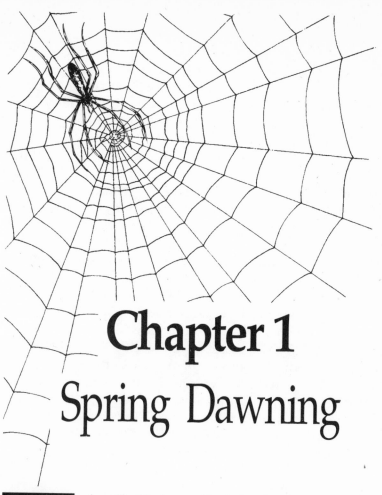

Chapter 1
Spring Dawning

Drizzt Do'Urden walked slowly along a trail in the jutting southernmost spur of the Spine of the World Mountains, the sky brightening around him. Far away to the south, across the plain to the Evermoors, he noticed the glow of the last lights of some distant city, Nesme probably, going down, replaced by the growing dawn. When Drizzt turned another bend in the mountain trail, he saw the small town of Settlestone, far below. The barbarians, Wulfgar's kin from faraway Icewind Dale, were just beginning their morning routines, trying to put the ruins back in order.

Drizzt watched the figures, tiny from this distance, bustle about, and he remembered a time not so long ago when Wulfgar and his proud people roamed the frozen tundra of a land far to the north and west, on the other side of the great mountain range, a thousand miles away.

Spring, the trading season, was fast approaching, and the hardy men and women of Settlestone, working as dealers for the dwarves of Mithril Hall, would soon know more wealth and comfort than they ever would have believed possible in their previous day-by-day existence. They had come to Wulfgar's call, fought valiantly beside the dwarves in the ancient halls, and would soon reap the rewards of their labor, leaving behind their desperate nomadic ways as they had left behind the endless, merciless wind of Icewind Dale.

"How far we have all come," Drizzt remarked to the chill emptiness of the morning air, and he chuckled at the double-meaning of his words, considering that he had just returned from Silverymoon, a magnificent city far to the east, a place where the beleaguered drow ranger never before dared to believe that he would find acceptance. Indeed, when he had accompanied Bruenor and the others in their search for Mithril Hall, barely two years before, Drizzt had been turned away from Silverymoon's decorated gates.

"Ye've done a hundred miles in a week alone," came an unexpected answer.

Drizzt instinctively dropped his slender black hands to the hilts of his scimitars, but his mind caught up to his reflexes and he relaxed immediately, recognizing the melodic voice with more than a little of a Dwarvish accent. A moment later, Cattibrie, the adopted human daughter of Bruenor Battlehammer came skipping around a rocky outcropping, her thick auburn mane dancing in the mountain wind and her deep blue eyes glittering like wet jewels in the fresh morning light.

Drizzt could not hide his smile at the joyous spring in the young girl's steps, a vitality that the often vicious battles she had faced over the last few years could not diminish. Nor could Drizzt deny the wave of warmth that rushed over him whenever he saw Catti-brie, the young woman who knew him better than any. Catti-brie had understood Drizzt and accepted him for his heart, and not the color of his skin, since their first meeting in a rocky, wind-swept vale more than a decade before, when she was but half her present age.

The dark elf waited a moment longer, expecting to see Wulfgar, soon to be Catti-brie's husband, follow her around the bluff.

"You have come out a fair distance without an escort," Drizzt remarked when the barbarian did not appear.

Catti-brie crossed her arms over her chest and leaned on one foot, tapping impatiently with the other. "And ye're beginning to sound more like me father than me friend," she replied. "I see no escort walking the trails beside Drizzt Do'Urden."

"Well spoken," the drow ranger admitted, his tone respectful and not the least bit sarcastic. The young woman's scolding had pointedly reminded Drizzt that Catti-brie could take care of herself. She carried with her a short sword of dwarven make and wore fine armor under her furred cloak, as fine as the suit of chain mail that Bruenor had given to Drizzt! Taulmaril the Heartseeker, the magical bow of Anariel, rested easily over Catti-brie's shoulder. Drizzt had never seen a mightier weapon. And, even beyond the powerful tools she carried, Catti-brie had been raised among the sturdy dwarves, by Bruenor himself, as tough as the mountain stone.

"Is it often that ye watch the rising sun?" Catti-brie asked, noticing Drizzt's east-facing stance.

Drizzt found a flat rock to sit upon and bade Catti-brie to join him. "I have watched the dawn since my first days on the surface," he explained, throwing his thick forest-green cloak back over his shoulders. "Though back then, it surely stung my eyes, a reminder of where I came from, I suppose. Now, though, to my relief, I find that I can tolerate the brightness."

"And well that is," Catti-brie replied. She locked the drow's marvelous eyes with her intense gaze, forced him to look at her, at the same innocent smile he had seen those many years before on a windswept slope in Icewind Dale.

The smile of his first female friend.

"Tis sure that ye belong under the sunlight, Drizzt Do'Urden," Catti-brie continued, "as much as any person of any race, by me own measure."

Drizzt looked back to the dawn and did not answer. Catti-brie went silent, too, and they sat together for a long while, watching the awakening world.

"I came out to see ye," Catti-brie said suddenly. Drizzt regarded her curiously, not understanding.

"Now, I mean," the young woman explained. "We'd word that ye'd returned to Settlestone, and that ye'd be coming back to Mithril Hall in a few days. I've been out here every day since."

Drizzt's expression did not change. "You wish to talk with me privately?" he asked, to prompt a reply.

Catti-brie's deliberate nod as she turned back to the eastern horizon revealed to Drizzt that something was wrong.

"I'll not forgive ye if ye miss the wedding," Catti-brie said softly. She bit down on her bottom lip as she finished, Drizzt noted, and sniffled, though she tried hard to make it seem like the beginnings of a cold.

Drizzt draped an arm across the beautiful woman's strong shoulders. "Can you believe for an instant, even if all the trolls of the Evermoors stood between me and the ceremony hall, that I would not attend?"

Catti-brie turned to him—fell into his gaze—and smiled widely, knowing the answer. She threw her arms around Drizzt for a tight hug, then leaped to her feet, pulling him up beside her.

Drizzt tried to equal her relief, or at least to make her believe that he had. Catti-brie had known all along that he would not miss her wedding to Wulfgar, two of his dearest friends. Why, then, the tears, the sniffle that was not from any budding cold? the perceptive ranger wondered. Why had Catti-brie felt the need to come out and find him only a few hours from the entrance to Mithril Hall?

He didn't ask her about it, but it bothered him more than a little. Anytime moisture gathered in Catti-brie's deep blue eyes, it bothered Drizzt Do'Urden more than a little.

* * * * *

Jarlaxle's black boots clacked loudly on the stone as he made his solitary way along a winding tunnel outside of Menzoberranzan. Most drow out alone from the great city, in the wilds of the Underdark, would have taken great care, but the mercenary knew what to expect in the tunnels, knew every creature in this particular section.

Information was Jarlaxle's forte. The scouting network of Bregan D'aerthe, the band Jarlaxle had founded and taken to greatness, was more intricate than that of any drow house. Jarlaxle knew everything that happened, or would soon happen, in and around the city, and, armed with that information, he had survived for centuries as a houseless rogue. So long had Jarlaxle been a part of Menzoberranzan's intrigue that none in the city, with the possible exception of First Matron Mother Baenre, even knew the sly mercenary's origins.

He was wearing his shimmering cape now, its magical colors cascading up and down his graceful form, and his wide-brimmed hat, hugely plumed with the feathers of a *diatryma*, a great flightless Underdark bird, adorned his clean-shaven head. A slender sword dancing beside one hip and a long dirk on the other were his only visible weapons, but those who knew the sly mercenary realized that he possessed many more than that, concealed on his person, but easily retrieved if the need arose.

Pulled by curiosity, Jarlaxle picked up his pace. As soon as he realized the length of his strides, he forced himself to slow

R. A. Salvatore

down, reminding himself that he wanted to be fashionably late for this unorthodox meeting that crazy Vierna had arranged.

Crazy Vierna.

Jarlaxle considered the thought for a long while, even stopped his walk and leaned against the tunnel wall to recount the high priestess's many claims over the last few weeks. What had seemed initially to be a desperate, fleeting hope of a broken noble, with no chance at all of success, was fast becoming a solid plan. Jarlaxle had gone along with Vierna more out of amusement and curiosity than any real beliefs that they would kill, or even locate, the long-gone Drizzt.

But something apparently was guiding Vierna—Jarlaxle had to believe it was Lloth, or one of the Spider Queen's powerful minions. Vierna's clerical powers had returned in full, it seemed, and she had delivered much valuable information, and even a perfect spy, to their cause. They were fairly sure now where Drizzt Do'Urden was, and Jarlaxle was beginning to believe that killing the traitorous drow would not be such a difficult thing.

The mercenary's boots heralded his approach as he clicked around a final bend in the tunnel, coming into a wide, low-roofed chamber. Vierna was there, with Dinin, and it struck Jarlaxle as curious (another note made in the calculating mercenary's mind) that Vierna seemed more comfortable out here in the wilds than did her brother. Dinin had spent many years in these tunnels, leading patrol groups, but Vierna, as a sheltered noble priestess, had rarely been out of the city.

If she truly believed that she walked with Lloth's blessings, however, then the priestess would have nothing to fear.

"You have delivered our gift to the human?" Vierna asked immediately, urgently. Everything in Vierna's life, it seemed to Jarlaxle, had become urgent.

The sudden question, not prefaced by any greeting or even a remark that he was late, caught the mercenary off guard for a moment, and he looked to Dinin, who responded with only a

18

helpless shrug. While hungry fires burned in Vierna's eyes, defeated resignation lay in Dinin's.

"The human has the earring," Jarlaxle replied.

Vierna held out a flat, disc-shaped object, covered in designs to match the precious earring. "It is cool," she explained as she rubbed her hand across the disc's metallic surface, "thus our spy has already moved far from Menzoberranzan."

"Far away with a valuable gift," Jarlaxle remarked, traces of sarcasm edging his voice.

"It was necessary, and will further our cause," Vierna snapped at him.

"If the human proves to be as valuable an informant as you believe," Jarlaxle added evenly.

"Do you doubt him?" Vierna's words echoed through the tunnels, causing Dinin further distress and sounding clearly as a threat to the mercenary.

"It was Lloth who guided me to him," Vierna continued with an open sneer, "Lloth who showed me the way to regain my family's honor. Do you doubt—"

"I doubt nothing where our deity is concerned," Jarlaxle promptly interrupted. "The earring, your beacon, has been delivered as you instructed, and the human is well on his way." The mercenary swept into a respectfully low bow, tipping his wide-brimmed hat.

Vierna calmed and seemed appeased. Her red eyes flashed eagerly, and a devious smile widened across her face. "And the goblins?" she asked, her voice thick with anticipation.

"They will soon make contact with the greedy dwarves," Jarlaxle replied, "to their dismay, no doubt. My scouts are in place around the goblin ranks. If your brother makes an appearance in the inevitable battle, we will know." The mercenary hid his conniving smile at the sight of Vierna's obvious pleasure. The priestess thought to gain only the confirmation of her brother's whereabouts from the unfortunate goblin tribe, but . Jarlaxle had much more in mind. Goblins and dwarves shared a mutual hatred as intense as that between the drow and their surface elf cousins, and any meeting between the groups would ensure a fight. What better opportunity for Jarlaxle to take an accurate measure of the dwarven defenses?

And the dwarven weaknesses?

For, while Vierna's desires were focused—all that she wanted was the death of her traitorous brother—Jarlaxle was looking at the wider picture, of how this costly exploration up near the surface, perhaps even onto the surface, might become more profitable.

Vierna rubbed her hands together and turned sharply to face her brother. Jarlaxle nearly laughed aloud at Dinin's feeble attempt to imitate his sister's beaming expression.

Vierna was too obsessed to notice her less-than-enthusiastic brother's obvious slip. "The goblin fodder understand their options?" she asked the mercenary, but she answered her own question before Jarlaxle could reply. "Of course, they have no options!"

Jarlaxle felt the sudden need to burst her eager bubble. "What if the goblins kill Drizzt?" he asked, sounding innocent.

Vierna's face screwed up weirdly and she stammered un-successfully at her first attempts at a reply. "No!" she decided at length. "We know that more than a thousand dwarves inhabit the complex, perhaps two or three times that number. The goblin tribe will be crushed."

"But the dwarves and their allies will suffer some casual-ties," Jarlaxle reasoned.

"Not Drizzt," Dinin unexpectedly answered, and there was no compromise in his grim tone, and no argument forthcoming from either of his companions. "No goblin will kill Drizzt. No goblin weapon could get near his body."

Vierna's approving smile showed that she did not under-stand the sincere terror behind Dinin's claims. Dinin alone among the group had faced off in battle against Drizzt.

"The tunnels back to the city are clear?" Vierna asked

Jarlaxle, and, on his nod, she swiftly departed, having no more time for banter.

"You wish this to end," the mercenary remarked to Dinin when they were alone.

"You have not met my brother," Dinin replied evenly, and his hand instinctively twitched near the hilt of his magnificent drow-made sword, as though the mere mention of Drizzt put him on the defensive. "Not in combat, at least."

"Fear, *Khal'abbil*?" The question went straight to Dinin's sense of honor, sounded more like a taunt.

Still, the fighter made no attempt to deny it.

"You should fear your sister as well," Jarlaxle reasoned, and he meant every word. Dinin donned a disgusted expression.

"The Spider Queen, or one of Lloth's minions, has been talking with that one," Jarlaxle added, as much to himself as to his shaken companion. At first glance, Vierna's obsession seemed a desperate, dangerous thing, but Jarlaxle had been around the chaos of Menzoberranzan long enough to realize that many other powerful figures, Matron Baenre included, had held similar, seemingly outrageous fantasies.

Nearly every important figure in Menzoberranzan, including members of the ruling council, had come to power through acts that seemed desperate, had squirmed their way through the barbed nets of chaos to find their glory.

Might Vierna be the next to cross that dangerous terrain?

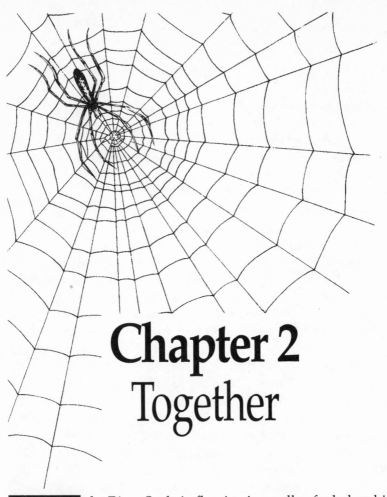

Chapter 2
Together

The River Surbrin flowing in a valley far below him, Drizzt entered the eastern gate of Mithril Hall early that same afternoon. Catti-brie had skipped in some time before him to await the "surprise" of his return. The dwarven guards welcomed the drow ranger as though he were one of their bearded kin. Drizzt could not deny the warmth that flowed through him at their open welcome, though it was not unexpected since Bruenor's people had accepted him as a friend since their days in Icewind Dale.

Drizzt needed no escort in the winding corridors of Mithril

Hall, and he wanted none, preferring to be alone with the many emotions and memories that always came over him when he crossed this section of the upper complex. He moved across the new bridge at Garumn's Gorge. It was a structure of beautiful, arching stone that spanned hundreds of feet across the deep chasm. In this place Drizzt had lost Bruenor forever, or so he had thought, for he had seen the dwarf spiral down into the lightless depths on the back of a flaming dragon.

He couldn't avoid a smile as the memory flowed to completion; it would take more than a dragon to kill mighty Bruenor Battlehammer!

As he neared the end of the long expanse, Drizzt noticed that new guard towers, begun only ten days before, were nearly completed, the industrious dwarves having gone at their work with absolute devotion. Still, every one of the busy dwarven workers looked up to regard the drow's passing and give Drizzt a word of greeting.

Drizzt headed for the main corridors leading out of the immense chamber south of the bridge, the sound of even more hammers leading the way. Just beyond the chamber, past a small anteroom, he came into a wide, high corridor, practically another chamber in itself, where the best craftsmen of Mithril Hall were hard at work, carving into the stone wall the likeness of Bruenor Battlehammer, in its appropriate place beside sculptures of Bruenor's royal ancestors, the seven predecessors of his throne.

"Fine work, eh, drow?" came a call. Drizzt turned to regard a short, round dwarf with a short-clipped yellow beard barely reaching the top of his wide chest.

"Well met, Cobble," Drizzt greeted the speaker. Bruenor recently had appointed the dwarf Holy Cleric of the Halls, a valued position indeed.

"Fitting?" Cobble asked as he indicated the twenty-foot-high sculpture of Mithril Hall's present king.

"For Bruenor, it should be a hundred feet tall," Drizzt

23

replied, and the good-hearted Cobble shook with laughter. The continuing roar of it echoed behind Drizzt for many steps as he again headed down the winding corridors.

He soon came to the upper level's hall area, the city above the wondrous Undercity. Catti-brie and Wulfgar roomed in this area, as did Bruenor most of the time, as he prepared for the spring trading season. Most of the other twenty-five hundred dwarves of the clan were far below, in the mines and in the Undercity, but those in this region were the commanders of the house guard and the elite soldiers. Even Drizzt, so welcomed in Bruenor's home, could not go to the king unannounced and unescorted.

A square-shouldered rock of a dwarf with a sour demeanor and a long brown beard that he wore tucked into a wide, jeweled belt, led Drizzt down the final corridor to Bruenor's upper-level audience hall. General Dagna, as he was called, had been a personal attendant of King Harbromme of Citadel Adbar, the mightiest dwarven stronghold in the northland, but the gruff dwarf had come in at the head of Citadel Adbar's forces to help Bruenor reclaim his ancient homeland. With the war won, most of the Adbar dwarves had departed, but Dagna and two thousand others had remained after the cleansing of Mithril Hall, swearing fealty to clan Battlehammer and giving Bruenor a solid force with which to defend the riches of the dwarven stronghold.

Dagna had stayed on with Bruenor to serve as his adviser and military commander. He professed no love for Drizzt, but certainly would not be foolish enough to insult the drow by allowing a lesser attendant to escort Drizzt to see the dwarf king.

"I told ye he'd be back," Drizzt heard Bruenor grumbling from beyond the open doorway as they approached the audience hall. "Th' elf'd not be missing such a thing as yer wedding!"

"I see they are expecting me," Drizzt remarked to Dagna.

"We heared ye was about from the folks o' Settlestone," the gruff general replied, not looking back to Drizzt as he spoke. "Figerred ye'd come in any day."

Drizzt knew that the general—a dwarf among dwarves, as the others said—had little use for him, or for anyone, Wulfgar and Catti-brie included, who was not a dwarf. The dark elf smiled, though, for he was used to such prejudice and knew that Dagna was an important ally for Bruenor.

"Greetings," Drizzt said to his three friends as he entered the room. Bruenor sat on his stone throne, Wulfgar and Catti-brie flanking him.

"So ye made it," Catti-brie said absently, feigning disinterest. Drizzt smirked at their running secret; apparently Catti-brie hadn't told anyone that she had met him just outside the eastern door.

"We had not planned for this," added Wulfgar, a giant of a man with huge, corded muscles, long, flowing blond locks, and eyes the crystal blue of the northland's sky. "I pray that there may be an extra seat at the table."

Drizzt smiled and bowed low in apology. He deserved their chiding, he knew. He had been away a great deal lately, for weeks at a time.

"Bah!" snorted the red-bearded Bruenor. "I told ye he'd come back, and back to stay this time!"

Drizzt shook his head, knowing he soon would go out again, searching for . . . something.

"Ye hunting for the assassin, elf?" he heard Bruenor ask.

Never, Drizzt thought immediately. The dwarf referred to Artemis Entreri, Drizzt's most hated enemy, a heartless killer as skilled with the blade as the drow ranger, and determined— obsessed!—to defeat Drizzt. Entreri and Drizzt had battled in Calimport, a city far to the south, with Drizzt luckily winning the upper hand before events drove them apart. Emotionally Drizzt had brought the unfinished battle to its conclusion and had freed himself from a similar obsession against Entreri.

R. A. Salvatore

Drizzt had seen himself in the assassin, had seen what he might have become had he stayed in Menzoberranzan. He could not stand the image, hungered only to destroy it. Catti-brie, dear and complicated Catti-brie, had taught Drizzt the truth, about Entreri and about himself. If he never saw Entreri again, Drizzt would be a happier person indeed.

"I've no desire to meet that one again," Drizzt answered. He looked to Catti-brie, who sat impassively. She shot Drizzt a sly wink to show that she understood and approved.

"There are many sights in the wide world, dear dwarf," Drizzt went on, "that cannot be seen from the shadows, many sounds more pleasant than the ring of steel, and many smells preferable to the stench of death."

"Cook another feast!" Bruenor snorted, hopping up from his stone seat. "Suren the elf has his eyes fixed on another wedding!"

Drizzt let the remark pass without reply.

Another dwarf rushed into the room, then exited, pulling Dagna out behind him. A moment later, the flustered general returned.

"What is it?" Bruenor grumbled.

"Another guest," Dagna explained and, even as he spoke, a halfling, round in the belly, bopped into the room.

"Regis!" cried a surprised Catti-brie, and she and Wulfgar rushed over to greet their friend. Unexpectedly, the five companions were together again.

"Rumblebelly!" Bruenor shouted his customary nickname for the always hungry halfling. "What in the Nine Hells—"

What indeed, Drizzt thought, curious that he had not spotted the traveler on the trails outside Mithril Hall. The friends had left Regis behind in Calimport, more than a thousand miles away, at the head of the thieves guild the companions had all but decapitated in rescuing the halfling.

"Did you believe I would miss this occasion?" Regis huffed, acting insulted that Bruenor even doubted him. "The wedding of two of my dearest friends?"

Catti-brie threw a hug on him, which he seemed to enjoy immensely.

Bruenor looked curiously at Drizzt and shook his head when he realized that the drow had no answers for this surprise. "How'd ye know?" the dwarf asked the halfling.

"You underestimate your fame, King Bruenor," Regis replied, gracefully dipping into a bow that sent his belly dropping over his thin belt.

The bow made him jingle as well, Drizzt noted. When Regis dipped, a hundred jewels and a dozen fat pouches tinkled. Regis had always loved fine things, but Drizzt had never seen the halfling so garishly bedecked. He wore a gem-studded jacket and more jewelry than Drizzt had ever seen in one place, including the magical, hypnotic ruby pendant.

"Might ye be staying long?" Catti-brie asked.

"I am in no hurry," Regis replied. "Might I have a room," he asked Bruenor, "to put my things and rest away the weariness of a long road?"

"We'll see to it," Catti-brie assured him as Drizzt and Bruenor exchanged glances once more. They both were thinking the same thing: that it was unusual for a master of a backstabbing, opportunistic thieves' guild to leave his place of power for any length of time.

"And for yer attendants?" Bruenor asked, a loaded question.

"Oh," stammered the halfling. "I . . . came alone. The Southerners do not take well to the chill of a northern spring, you know."

"Well, off with ye, then," commanded Bruenor. "Suren it be me turn to set out a feast for the pleasure of yer belly."

Drizzt took a seat beside the dwarf king as the other three scooted out of the room.

"Few folk in Calimport have ever heared o' me name, elf," Bruenor remarked when he and Drizzt were alone. "And who south o' Longsaddle would be knowing of the wedding?"

Bruenor's sly expression showed that the experienced dwarf agreed exactly with Drizzt's feeling. "Suren the little one brings a bit of his treasure along with him, eh?" the dwarf king asked.

"He is running," Drizzt replied.

"Got himself into trouble again—" Bruenor snorted "—or I'm a bearded gnome!"

* * * * *

"Five meals a day," Bruenor muttered to Drizzt after the drow and the halfling had been in Mithril Hall for a week. "And helpings bigger than a half-sized one should hold!"

Drizzt, always amazed by Regis's appetite, had no answer for the dwarf king. Together they watched Regis from across the hall, stuffing bite after bite into his greedy mouth.

"Good thing we're opening new tunnels," Bruenor grumbled. "I'll be needing a fair supply o' mithril to keep that one fed."

As if Bruenor's reference to the new explorations had been a cue, General Dagna entered the dining hall. Apparently not interested in eating, the gruff, brown-bearded dwarf waved away an attendant and headed straight across the hall, toward Drizzt and Bruenor.

"That was a short trip," Bruenor remarked to Drizzt when they noticed the dwarf. Dagna had gone out just that morning, leading the latest scouting group to the new explorations in the deepest mines far to the west of the Undercity.

"Trouble or treasure?" Drizzt asked rhetorically, and Bruenor only shrugged, always expecting—and secretly hoping for—both.

"Me king," Dagna greeted, coming in front of Bruenor and pointedly not looking at the dark elf. He dipped in a curt bow, his rock-set expression giving no clues about which of Drizzt's suppositions might be accurate.

"Mithril?" Bruenor asked hopefully.

Dagna seemed surprised by the blunt question. "Yes," he said at length. "The tunnel beyond the sealed door intercepted a whole new complex, rich in ore, from what we can tell. The legend of yer gem-sniffing nose'll continue to grow, me king." He dipped into another bow, this one even lower than the first.

"Knew it," Bruenor whispered to Drizzt. "Went down that way once, afore me beard even came out. Killed me an ettin . . ."

"But we have trouble," Dagna interrupted, his face still expressionless.

Bruenor waited, and waited some more, for the tiresome dwarf to explain. "Trouble?" he finally asked, realizing that Dagna had paused for dramatic effect, and that the stubborn general probably would stand quietly for the remainder of the day if Bruenor didn't offer that prompt.

"Goblins," Dagna said ominously.

Bruenor snorted. "Thought ye said we had trouble?"

"A fair-sized tribe," Dagna went on. "Could be hundreds."

Bruenor looked up to Drizzt and recognized from the sparkle in the drow's lavender eyes that the news had not disturbed his friend any more than it had disturbed him.

"Hundreds of goblins, elf," Bruenor said slyly. "What do ye think o' that?"

Drizzt didn't reply, just continued to smirk and let the gleam in his eye speak for itself. Times had become uneventful since the retaking of Mithril Hall; the only metal ringing in the dwarven tunnels was the miner's pick and shovel and the craftsman's sledge, and the trails between Mithril Hall and Silverymoon were rarely dangerous or adventurous to the skilled Drizzt. This news held particular interest for the drow. Drizzt was a ranger, dedicated to defending the good races, and he despised spindly-armed, foul-smelling goblins above all the other evil races in the world.

Bruenor led the two over to Regis's table, though every other table in the large hall was empty. "Supper's done," the red-bearded dwarf king huffed, sweeping the plates from in front of the halfling to land, crashing, on the floor.

"Go and get Wulfgar," Bruenor growled into the halfling's dubious expression. "Ye got a count of fifty to get back to me. Longer than that, and I put ye on half rations!"

Regis was through the door in an instant.

On Bruenor's nod, Dagna pulled a hunk of coal from his pocket and sketched a rough map of the new region on the table, showing Bruenor where they had encountered the goblin sign, and where further scouting had indicated the main lair to be. Of particular interest to the two dwarves were the worked tunnels in the region, with their even floors and squared walls.

"Good for surprising stupid goblins," Bruenor explained to Drizzt with a wink.

"You knew the goblins were there," Drizzt accused him, realizing that Bruenor was more thrilled, and less surprised, by the news of potential enemies than of potential riches.

"Figured there might be goblins," Bruenor admitted. "Seen 'em down there once, but with the coming of the dragon, me father and his soldiers never got the time to clean the vermin out. Still, it was a long, long time ago, elf"—the dwarf stroked his long red beard to accentuate the point—"and I couldn't be sure they'd still be there."

"We are threatened?" came a resonant baritone voice behind them. The seven-foot-tall barbarian moved to the table and leaned low to take in Dagna's diagram.

"Just goblins," Bruenor replied.

"A call to war!" Wulfgar roared, slapping Aegis-fang, the mighty warhammer Bruenor had forged for him, across his open palm.

"A call to play," Bruenor corrected, and he exchanged a nod and chuckle with Drizzt.

"By me own eyes, don't ye two seem eager to be killing," Catti-brie, standing behind with Regis, put in.

"Bet on it," Bruenor retorted.

"Ye found some goblins in their own hole, not to bothering anybody, and ye're planning for their slaughter," Catti-brie went on in the face of her father's sarcasm.

"Woman!" Wulfgar shouted.

Drizzt's amused smile evaporated in the blink of an eye, replaced by an expression of amazement as he regarded the towering barbarian's scornful mien.

"Be glad for that," Catti-brie answered lightly, without hesitation and without becoming distracted from the more important debate with Bruenor. "How do ye know the goblins want a fight?" she asked the king. "Or do ye care?"

"There's mithril in those tunnels," Bruenor replied, as if that would end the debate.

"Would that make it the goblins' mithril?" Catti-brie asked innocently. "Rightfully?"

"Not for long," Dagna interjected, but Bruenor had no witty remarks to add, taken aback by his daughter's surprising line of somewhat incriminating questions.

"The fight's more important to ye, to all of ye," Catti-brie went on, turning her knowing blue eyes to regard all four of the group, "than any treasures to be found. Ye hunger for the excitement. Ye'd go after the goblins if the tunnels were no more than bare and worthless stone!"

"Not me," Regis piped in, but nobody paid much attention.

"They are goblins," Drizzt said to her. "Was it not a goblin raid that took your father's life?"

"Aye," Catti-brie agreed. "And if ever I find that tribe, then be knowing that they'll fall in piles for their wicked deed. But are they akin to this tribe, a thousand miles and more away?"

"Goblins is goblins!" Bruenor growled.

"Oh?" Catti-brie replied, crossing her arms before her. "And are drow drow?"

"What talk is this?" Wulfgar demanded as he glowered at his soon-to-be bride.

"If ye found a dark elf wandering yer tunnels," Catti-brie said to Bruenor, ignoring Wulfgar altogether—even when he stormed over to stand right beside her—"would ye draw up yer plans and cut the creature down?"

Bruenor gave an uncomfortable glance Drizzt's way, but Drizzt was smiling again, understanding where Catti-brie's reasoning had led them—and where it had trapped the stubborn king.

"If ye did cut him down, and if that drow was Drizzt Do'Urden, then who would ye have beside ye with the patience to sit and listen to yer prideful boasts?" the young woman finished.

"At least I'd kill ye clean," Bruenor, his blustery bubble popped, muttered to Drizzt.

Drizzt's laughter came straight from his belly. "Parley," he said at length. "By the well-spoken words of our wise young friend, we must give the goblins at least a chance to explain their intentions." He paused and looked wistfully at Catti-brie, his lavender eyes sparkling still, for he knew what to expect from goblins. "Before we cut them down."

"Cleanly," Bruenor added.

"She knows nothing of this!" Wulfgar griped, bringing the tension back to the meeting in an instant.

Drizzt silenced him with a cold glare, as threatening a stare as had ever passed between the dark elf and the barbarian. Catti-brie looked from one to the other, her expression pained, then she tapped Regis on the shoulder and together they left the room.

"We're gonna talk to a bunch o' goblins?" Dagna asked in disbelief.

"Aw, shut yer mouth," Bruenor answered, slamming his hands back to the table and studying the map once more. It took him several moments to realize that Wulfgar and Drizzt had not finished their silent exchange. Bruenor recognized the confusion underlying Drizzt's stare, but in looking at the barbarian, he found no subtle undercurrents, no hint that this particular incident would be easily forgotten.

* * * * *

Drizzt leaned back against the stone wall in the corridor outside Catti-brie's room. He had come to talk to the young woman, to find out why she had been so concerned, so adamant, in the conference about the goblin tribe. Catti-brie had always brought a unique perspective to the trials facing the five companions, but this time it seemed to Drizzt that something else was driving her, that something other than goblins had brought the fire to her speech.

Leaning on the wall outside the door, the dark elf began to understand.

"You are not going!" Wulfgar was saying—loudly. "There will be a fight, despite your attempts to put it off. They are goblins. They'll take no parley with dwarves!"

"If there is a fight, then ye'll be wanting me there," Catti-brie retorted.

"You are not going."

Drizzt shook his head at the finality of Wulfgar's tone, thinking that never before had he heard Wulfgar speak this way. He changed his mind, though, remembering when he first had met the rough young barbarian, stubborn and proud and talking nearly as stupidly as now.

Drizzt was waiting for the barbarian when Wulfgar returned to his own room, the drow leaning against the wall casually, wrists resting against the angled hilts of his magical scimitars and his forest-green cloak thrown back from his shoulders.

"Bruenor sends for me?" Wulfgar asked, confused as to why Drizzt would be in his room.

Drizzt pushed the door closed. "I am not here for Bruenor," he explained evenly.

Wulfgar shrugged, not catching on. "Welcome back, then," he said, and there was something strained in his greeting. "Too oft you are out of the halls. Bruenor desires your company—"

"I am here for Catti-brie," Drizzt interrupted.

The barbarian's ice-blue eyes narrowed immediately and he squared his broad shoulders, his strong jaw firm. "I know she met with you," he said, "outside on the trails before you came in."

A perplexed look crossed Drizzt's face as he recognized the hostility in Wulfgar's tone. Why would Wulfgar care if Catti-brie had met with him? What in the Nine Hells was going on with his large friend?

"Regis told me," Wulfgar explained, apparently misunderstanding Drizzt's confusion. A superior look came into the barbarian's eye, as though he believed his secret information had given him some sort of advantage.

Drizzt shook his head and brushed his thick white mane back from his face with slender fingers. "I am not here because of any meeting on the trails," he said, "or because of anything Catti-brie has said to me." Wrists still comfortably resting against his weapon hilts, Drizzt strolled across the wide room, stopping opposite the large bed from the barbarian.

"Whatever Catti-brie does say to me, though," he had to add, "is none of your affair."

Wulfgar did not blink, but Drizzt could see that it took all of the barbarian's control to stop from leaping over the bed at him. Drizzt, who thought he knew Wulfgar well, could hardly believe the sight.

"How dare you?" Wulfgar growled through gritted teeth. "She is my—"

"Dare I?" Drizzt shot back. "You speak of Catti-brie as if she were your possession. I heard you tell her, command her, to remain behind when we go to the goblins."

"You overstep your bounds," Wulfgar warned.

"You puff like a drunken orc," Drizzt returned, and he

thought the analogy strangely fitting.

Wulfgar took a deep breath, his great chest heaving, to steady himself. A single stride took him the length of the bed to the wall, near the hooks holding his magnificent warhammer.

"Once you were my teacher," Wulfgar said calmly.

"Ever was I your friend," Drizzt replied.

Wulfgar snapped an angry glare on him. "You speak to me like a father to a child. Beware, Drizzt Do'Urden, you are not the teacher anymore."

Drizzt nearly fell over, especially when Wulfgar, still eyeing him dangerously, pulled Aegis-fang, the mighty warhammer, from the wall.

"Are you the teacher now?" the dark elf asked.

Wulfgar nodded slowly, then blinked in surprise as the scimitars suddenly appeared in Drizzt's hands. Twinkle, the magical blade the wizard Malchor Harpel had given Drizzt, glowed with a soft blue flame.

"Remember when first we met?" the dark elf asked. He moved around the bottom of the bed, wisely, since Wulfgar's longer reach would have given him a distinct advantage with the bed between them. "Do you remember the many lessons we shared on Kelvin's Cairn, looking out over the tundra and the campfires of your people?"

Wulfgar turned slowly, keeping the dangerous drow in front of him. The barbarian's knuckles whitened for lack of blood as he tightly clutched his weapon.

"Remember the verbeeg?" Drizzt asked, the thought bringing a smile to his face. "You and I fighting together, winning together, against an entire lair of giants?"

"And the dragon, Icingdeath?" Drizzt went on, holding his other scimitar, the one he had taken from the defeated wyrm's lair, up before him.

"I remember," Wulfgar replied quietly, calmly, and Drizzt started to slide his scimitars back into their sheaths, thinking he had sobered the young man.

"You speak of distant days!" the barbarian roared suddenly, rushing forward with speed and agility beyond what could be expected from so large a man. He launched a roundhouse punch at Drizzt's face, clipping the surprised drow on the shoulder as Drizzt ducked.

The ranger rolled with the blow, coming to his feet in the far corner of the room, the scimitars back in his hands.

"Time for another lesson," he promised, his lavender eyes gleaming with an inner fire that the barbarian had seen many times before.

Undaunted, Wulfgar came on, putting Aegis-fang through a series of feints before turning it down in an overhead chop that would have crushed the drow's skull.

"Has it been too long since last we saw battle?" Drizzt asked, thinking this whole incident a strange game, perhaps a ritual of manhood for the young barbarian. He brought his scimitars up in a blocking cross above him, easily catching the descending hammer. His legs nearly buckled under the sheer force of the blow.

Wulfgar recoiled for a second strike.

"Always thinking of offense," Drizzt scolded, snapping the flat sides of his scimitars out, one-two, against the sides of Wulfgar's face.

The barbarian fell back a step and wiped a thin line of blood from his cheek with the back of one hand. Still he did not blink.

"My apology," Drizzt said when he saw the blood. "I did not mean to cut—"

Wulfgar came over him in a rush, swinging wildly and calling out to Tempus, his god of battle.

Drizzt sidestepped the first strike—it took out a fair-sized chunk from the stone wall beside him—and stepped forward toward the warhammer, locking his arm around it to hold it in place.

Wulfgar let go of the weapon with one hand, grabbed Drizzt by the front of the tunic, and easily lifted him from the floor. The muscles on the barbarian's bare arm bulged as he pressed his arm straight ahead, crushing the drow against the wall.

Drizzt could not believe the huge man's strength! He felt as if he would be pushed right through the stone and into the next chamber—at least, he hoped there was a next chamber! He kicked with one leg. Wulfgar ducked back, thinking the kick aimed for his face, but Drizzt hooked the leg over the barbarian's stiffened arm, inside the elbow. Using the leg for leverage, Drizzt slammed his hand against the outside of Wulfgar's wrist, bending the arm and freeing him from the wall. He punched out with his scimitar hilt as he fell, connecting solidly on Wulfgar's nose, and let go his lock on the barbarian's warhammer.

Wulfgar's snarl sounded inhuman. He took up the hammer for a strike, but Drizzt had dropped to the floor by then. The drow rolled onto his back, planted his feet against the wall, and kicked out, slipping right between Wulfgar's wide-spread legs. Drizzt's foot snapped up once, stinging the barbarian's groin, and then, when he was behind Wulfgar, snapped both feet straight out, kicking the barbarian behind the knees.

Wulfgar's legs buckled and one of his knees slammed into the wall.

Drizzt used the momentum to roll again. He came back to his feet and leaped, grabbing the overbalanced Wulfgar by the back of his hair and tugging hard, toppling the man like a cut tree.

Wulfgar groaned and rolled, trying to get up, but Drizzt's scimitars came whipping in, hilts leading, to connect heavily on the big man's jaw.

Wulfgar laughed and slowly rose. Drizzt backed away.

"You are not the teacher," Wulfgar said again, but the line of blood-filled spittle rolling from the edge of his torn mouth weakened the claim considerably.

"What is this about?" Drizzt demanded. "Speak it now!"

Aegis-fang came hurling at him, end over end.

Drizzt dove to the floor, narrowly avoiding the deadly hit.

He winced when he heard the hammer hit the wall, no doubt blasting a clean hole in the stone.

He was up again, amazingly, by the time the charging barbarian got anywhere near him. Drizzt ducked under the lumbering man's reach, spun, and kicked Wulfgar in the rump. Wulfgar roared and spun about, only to get hit again in the face with the flat of Drizzt's blade. This time the line of blood was not so thin.

As stubborn as any dwarf, Wulfgar launched another round-house punch.

"Your rage defeats you," Drizzt remarked as he easily avoided the blow. He couldn't believe that Wulfgar, so finely trained in the art—and it was an art!—of battle had lost his composure.

Wulfgar growled and swung again, but recoiled immediately, for this time, Drizzt put Twinkle, or more particularly, put Twinkle's razor-edged blade, in line to catch the blow. Wulfgar retracted the swing too late and clutched his bloodied hand.

"I know your hammer will return to your grasp," Drizzt said, and Wulfgar seemed almost surprised, as though he had forgotten the magical enchantment of his own weapon. "Would you like to have fingers remaining so you might catch it?"

On cue, Aegis-fang came into the barbarian's grasp.

Drizzt, stunned by the ridiculous tirade and tired of this whole episode, slipped his scimitars back into their sheaths. He stood barely four feet from the barbarian, well within Wulfgar's reach, with his hands out wide, defenseless.

Somewhere in the fight, when he had realized that this was no game, perhaps, the gleam had flown from his lavender eyes.

Wulfgar remained very still for a long moment and closed his eyes. To Drizzt, it seemed as if he was fighting some inner battle.

He smiled, then opened his eyes, and let the head of his mighty warhammer dip to the floor.

"My friend," he said to Drizzt. "My teacher. It is good you

have returned." Wulfgar's hand reached out toward Drizzt's shoulder.

His fist balled suddenly and shot for Drizzt's face.

Drizzt spun, hooked Wulfgar's arm with his own, and pulled along the path of the barbarian's own momentum, sending Wulfgar headlong. Wulfgar got his other hand up in time to grab the drow, though, and took Drizzt along for the tumble. They came up together, propped side by side against the wall, and shared a heartfelt laugh.

For the first time since before the meeting in the dining hall, it seemed to Drizzt that he had his old fighting companion beside him again.

Drizzt left soon after, not mentioning Catti-brie again—not until he could sort out what, exactly, had just happened in the room. Drizzt at least understood the barbarian's confusion about the young woman. Wulfgar had come from a tribe dominated by men, where women spoke only when they were told to speak, and did as their masters, the males, bade. It appeared as if, now that he and Catti-brie were to be wed, Wulfgar was finding it difficult to shake off the lessons of his youth.

The thought disturbed Drizzt more than a little. He now understood the sadness he had detected in Catti-brie, out on the trails beyond the dwarven complex.

He understood, too, Wulfgar's mounting folly. If the stubborn barbarian tried to quench the fires within Catti-brie, he would take from her everything that had brought him to her in the first place, everything that he loved—that Drizzt, too, loved, in the spirited young woman.

Drizzt dismissed that notion summarily; he had looked into her knowing blue eyes for a decade, had seen Catti-brie turn her stubborn father in submissive circles.

Neither Wulfgar, nor Drizzt, nor the gods themselves could quench the fires in Catti-brie's eyes.

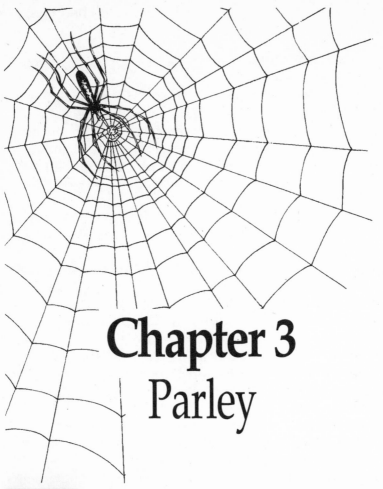

Chapter 3
Parley

T he Eighth King of Mithril Hall, leading his four friends and two hundred dwarven soldiers, was more appropriately arrayed for battle than for parley. Bruenor wore his battered, one-horned helmet, the other horn having long ago been broken away, and a fine suit of mithril armor, vertical lines of the silvery metal running the length of his stout torso and glittering in the torchlight. His shield bore the foaming mug standard of Clan Battlehammer in solid gold, and his customary axe, showing the nicks of a thousand battle kills (and a fair number of them goblins!) was ready in a loop on his belt, within easy reach.

Wulfgar, in a suit of natural hide, a wolf's head set in front of his great chest, walked behind the dwarf, with Aegis-fang, his warhammer, angled out across the crook of his elbow in front of him. Catti-brie, Taulmaril over her shoulder, walked beside him, but the two said little, and the tension between them was obvious.

Drizzt flanked the dwarf king on his right, Regis scampering to keep up beside him, and Guenhwyvar, the sleek, proud panther, muscles rippling with every stride, moved to the right of the two, darting off into the shadows whenever the low and uneven corridor widened. Many of the dwarves marching behind the five friends carried torches, and the flickering light created monsterlike shadows, keeping the companions on their guard—not that they were likely to be surprised marching beside Drizzt and Guenhwyvar. The dark elf's black panther companion was all too adept at leading the way.

And nothing would care to surprise this group. The whole of the force was bedecked for battle, with great, sturdy helms and armor and fine weapons. Every one of the dwarves carried a hammer or axe for distance shots and another nasty weapon in case any enemies got in close.

Four dwarves in a line near the middle of the contingent supported a great wooden beam across their stocky shoulders. Others near them carried huge, circular slabs of stone with the centers cut out. Heavy rope, long notched poles, chains, and sheets of pliable metal all were evident among this section of the brigade as the tools for a "goblin toy," as Bruenor had explained to his nondwarven companions' curious expressions. In looking at the heavy pieces, Drizzt could well imagine how much fun the goblins would get from this particular contraption.

At an intersection where a wide passage ran to their right they found a pile of giant bones, with two great skulls sitting atop it, each of them large enough for the halfling to crawl completely into.

"Ettin," Bruenor explained, for it was he, as a beardless lad, who had felled the monsters.

At the next intersection they met up with General Dagna and the lead force, another three hundred battle-hardened dwarves.

"Parley's set," Dagna explained. "Goblins're down a thousand feet in a wide chamber."

"Ye'll be flanking?" Bruenor asked him.

"Aye, but so're the goblins," the commander explained. "Four hundred of the things if there's a one. I sent Cobble and his three hundred on a wide course, around the backside o' the room to cut off any escape."

Bruenor nodded. The worst that they could expect was roughly even odds, and Bruenor would put any one of his dwarves against five of the goblin scum.

"I'm going straight in with a hundred," the dwarf king explained. "Another hundred're going to the right, with the toy, and the left's for yerself. Don't ye let me down if I'm needin' ye!"

Dagna's chuckle reflected supreme confidence, but then his expression turned abruptly grave. "Should it be yerself doing the talking?" he asked Bruenor. "I'm not for trusting goblins."

"Oh, they've got a trick for me, or I'm a bearded gnome," Bruenor replied, "but this goblin crew ain't seen the likes o' dwarves in hunnerds o' years, unless I miss me guess, and they're sure to think less of us than they should."

They exchanged a heavy handshake, and Dagna stormed off, the hard boots of his three hundred soldiers echoing through the corridors like the rumbling of a gathering thunderstorm.

"Stealth was never a dwarven strong point," Drizzt remarked dryly.

Regis let his stare linger for many moments on the departing host's crack formations, then turned the other way to regard the other group, bearing the beam, stone disks, and other items.

"If ye've not got the belly for it . . ." Bruenor began, interpreting the halfling's interest as fear.

"I am here, aren't I?" Regis came back sharply, rudely actually, and the uncustomary edge to his voice made his friends regard him curiously. But then, in a peculiarly Regis-like movement, the halfling straightened his belt under his prominent paunch, squared his shoulders, and looked away.

The others managed a laugh at Regis's expense, but Drizzt continued to stare at him curiously. Regis was indeed "here," but why he had come, the drow did not know. To say that Regis was not fond of battle was as much an understatement as to say that the halfling was not fond of missing meals.

A few minutes later the hundred soldiers remaining behind their king entered the appointed chamber, coming in through a large archway onto a raised section of stone, several feet up from the wide floor of the huge main area, wherein stood the goblin host. Drizzt noted with more than passing curiosity that this particular raised section held no stalagmite mounds, which seemed to be common throughout the rest of the chamber. Many stalactites leered down from the not-too-high ceiling above Drizzt's head; why hadn't their drippings left the commonplace stone mounds?

Drizzt and Guenhwyvar moved to one side, out of the range of the torches which the drow, with his exceptional vision, did not need. Slipping into the shadows of a grouping of low-hanging stalactites, the two seemed to disappear.

So did Regis, not far behind Drizzt.

"Gave up the high ground afore we ever started," Bruenor whispered to Wulfgar and Catti-brie. "Ye'd think even goblins'd be smarter than that!" That notion gave the dwarf pause, and he glanced around to the edges of the raised section, taking note that this slab of stone had been worked—worked with tools—to fit into this section of the cavern. His dark eyes narrowed with suspicion as Bruenor looked to the area where Drizzt had disappeared.

"I'm thinking that it's a good thing we're up high for the parley," Bruenor said, too loudly.

Drizzt understood.

"The whole section is trapped," Regis, right behind the drow, remarked.

Drizzt nearly jumped, amazed that the halfling had gotten so close to him and wondering what magical item Regis carried to make his movements so silent. Following the halfling's leading gaze, Drizzt regarded the nearest edge of the platform and a pillar half out from under the stone, a slender stalagmite that had been recently decapitated.

"A good hit would bring it down," Regis reasoned.

"Stay here," Drizzt instructed, agreeing with the crafty halfling's estimate. Perhaps the goblins had spent some time in preparing this battlefield. Drizzt moved out into view of the dwarves, gave Bruenor some signals to indicate that he would check it out, then slipped away, Guenhwyvar moving parallel to him, not far to the side.

All the dwarves had entered the chamber by then, with Bruenor cautiously keeping them back, lined end to end against the back edge of the semicircular platform.

Bruenor, with Wulfgar and Catti-brie flanking him, came out a few steps to regard the goblin host. There were well over a hundred—maybe two hundred—of the smelly things in the darker area of the chamber, judging from the many sets of red-shining eyes staring back at the dwarf.

"We came to talk," Bruenor called out in the guttural goblin tongue, "as agreed."

"Talk," came a goblin reply, surprisingly in the Common tongue. "Whats will dwarfses offer to Gar-yak and his thousands?"

"Thousands?" Wulfgar remarked.

"Goblins cannot count beyond their own fingers," Catti-brie reminded him.

"Get on yer toes," Bruenor whispered to them both. "This group's looking for a fight. I can smell it."

Wulfgar gave Catti-brie a positively superior look, but his

juvenile bluster was lost, for the young woman was paying him no heed.

* * * * *

Drizzt slipped from shadow to shadow, around boulders, and, finally, over the lip of the raised platform. As he and Regis had expected, this section, supported along its front end by several shortened stalagmite pillars, was not a solid piece, but a worked slab propped in place. And, as expected, the goblins planned to drop the front end of the platform and spill the dwarves. Great iron wedges had been driven partway through the front supporting line of pillars, waiting for a hammer to drive them through. It was no goblin poised underneath the stone to spring the trap, however, but another two-headed giant, an ettin. Even lying flat it was nearly as tall as Drizzt; he guessed it would tower at least twelve feet high if it ever got upright. Its arms, as thick as the drow's chest, were bare, a great spiked club in either hand, and its two huge heads stared at each other, apparently holding a conversation.

Drizzt didn't know whether the goblins intended to honestly parley, dropping the stone slab only if the dwarves made move to attack, but with the appearance of the dangerous giant, he wasn't willing to take any chances. Using the cover of the farthest pillar, he rolled under the lip and disappeared into the blackness behind and to the side of the waiting giant.

When a cat's green eyes stared back at Drizzt from across the breadth of the prone giant, he knew that Guenhwyvar, too, had moved silently into position.

* * * * *

A torch went up among the goblin ranks, and three of the four-foot-tall, yellow-skinned creatures ambled forward.

"Well," Bruenor grumbled, already tired of this meeting.

45

R. A. Salvatore

"Which one of ye dogs is Gar-yak?"

"Gar-yak back with others," the tallest of the group answered, looking over his sloping shoulder to the main host.

"A sure sign there's to be trouble," Catti-brie muttered, unobtrusively slipping her great bow from her shoulder. "When the leader's safely back, the goblins mean to fight."

"Go tell yer Gar-yak that we don't have to kill ye," Bruenor said firmly. "Me name's Bruenor Battlehammer—"

"Battlehammer?" The goblin spat, apparently recognizing the name. "Yous is king dwarf?"

Bruenor's lips did not move as he mumbled to his companions, "Be ready." Catti-brie's hand came to rest on the quiver at her side.

Bruenor nodded.

"King!" the goblin hooted, looking back to the monster host and pointing excitedly Bruenor's way. The ready dwarves understood the cue for the onslaught faster than the stupid goblins, and the next calls from the chamber were dwarven battle cries.

* * * * *

Drizzt took the call to action faster than the dim-witted ettin. The creature swung its clubs back, then yelped in pain and surprise as the six-hundred-pound panther clamped onto one wrist and a wickedly edged scimitar dove into its armpit on the other side.

The monster's huge heads turned outward in a weird, synchronous movement, one to regard Drizzt, one toward Guenhwyvar.

Before the ettin ever knew what was happening, Drizzt's second scimitar slashed across its bulging eyes. The giant tried to squirm about to get to the stinging elf, but the agile Drizzt slipped under its arm and came in hard and fast at the monster's vulnerable heads.

46

Across the way, Guenhwyvar dug teeth into flesh and set claws into stone, holding fast the monster's arm.

* * * * *

"Drizzt got him!" Bruenor reasoned when the floor bucked beneath him. With the failure of the simple, if not clever, trap, the goblins had indeed surrendered the favorable high ground. The stupid creatures hooted and whooped and came on anyway, launching crude spears, most of which never reached their targets.

More effective was the dwarven response. Catti-brie led it, putting the Heartseeker up in an instant and loosing a magical, silver-shafted arrow that seemed to trail lightning in its deadly flight. It blasted a clean, smoking hole through one goblin, did likewise to a second farther back, and drove into the chest of a third. All three dropped to the floor.

A hundred dwarves roared and charged forward, heaving axes and warhammers into the charging goblin throng.

Catti-brie fired again, and then again, and, with just the three shots, her kill count was up to eight. Now it was her turn to give Wulfgar a superior stare, and the barbarian, humbled, promptly looked away.

The floor bucked wildly; Bruenor heard the roars of the wounded giant beneath him.

"Down!" the dwarf king commanded above the sudden roar of battle.

The ferocious dwarves needed little encouragement, for the leading goblins were close to the platform by then. Out came living dwarven missiles, crushing into the goblin ranks, flailing away with fists and boots and weapons before they even stopped bouncing.

* * * * *

A supporting pillar cracked in half as the ettin inadvertently struck it, trying to bring its club around to get at Drizzt. Down came the platform, pinning the stupid beast.

Drizzt, crouched safely below the level of the giant's girth, could not believe how badly the goblins—and the ettin— had thought out their plan. "How did you ever mean to get out of here?" he asked, though, of course, the ettin could not understand him.

Drizzt shook his head, almost in pity, then his scimitars went to work on the monster's face and throat. A moment later, Guenhwyvar sprang onto the other head, claws raking deep gouges.

In mere seconds, the ranger and his feline companion sprinted out from under the low-riding platform, their business finished. Knowing that his unique talents could be of better use in other ways, Drizzt avoided the wild melee of battle and moved to the side along the cavern wall.

A dozen corridors led into this main chamber, he could see, and goblins were pouring in through nearly every one. Of more concern were the unexpected allies of the goblin forces, though, for, to Drizzt's surprise, he noticed several more gigantic ettins standing still and quiet behind stalagmites, waiting for the moment when they might join the fray.

* * * * *

Catti-brie, still on the platform and firing into the goblin horde, was the first to spot Drizzt, halfway up a stalagmite mound to the left-hand side of the cavern and motioning back for her and Wulfgar.

A goblin came up out of the fighting mass and charged the young woman, but Wulfgar stepped in front of her and whaled on it with his great hammer, sending it flying a dozen feet over the edge. The barbarian spun about as fast as he could, trying to ready a defense, for another goblin had come up to the side, closing with a spear point leading the way.

It nearly got the spear in for a strike, but its head exploded under the impact of a silver-streaking arrow.

"Drizzt is needing us," Catti-brie explained, and she led the barbarian to their left along the tilting platform, Wulfgar running along the edge and pounding any goblins that tried to scramble up.

When they were clear of the main fighting, Drizzt motioned for Catti-brie to hold her position and for Wulfgar to come forward cautiously.

"He has found some giants," Regis, hidden below the pair, explained to them, "behind those mounds."

Drizzt leaped down around the stalagmite, then came diving back out, turning defensive somersaults with an ettin in close pursuit, twin clubs ready to squash the drow.

The giant jerked upright when Catti-brie's arrow thudded into its chest, scorching the filthy animal hide it wore.

A second arrow knocked it off balance, then Wulfgar's hurled hammer, flying to the barbarian's resounding cries of "Tempus!", blasted the creature away.

Guenhwyvar, still on the side of the mound, leaped atop the second ettin as it came barreling out, muscled claws raking viciously, blinding both the monster's heads until Drizzt got in close enough to put his scimitars to work.

The next giant came around the other side of the mound, but Catti-brie was ready for it, and arrow after arrow slammed it, spun it around, and finally dropped it, dead, to the ground.

Wulfgar charged forward, catching his magical warhammer back in his grasp. Drizzt had finished with the giant by the time the barbarian caught up to him, and the dark elf joined his friend as they met the next of the charging monsters side by side.

"Like old times," Drizzt remarked. He didn't wait for an answer, but dove into a roll in front of Wulfgar.

Both of them winced, blinded for an instant, as Catti-brie's next arrow sliced between them, slamming into the nearest giant's belly.

"She did that to make a point, you know," Drizzt remarked, and he didn't wait for an answer, but dove into a roll in front of Wulfgar.

Understanding Drizzt's diversionary tactics, the barbarian heaved Aegis-fang right over the rolling form, and the ettin, stooping for a hit at Drizzt, caught the warhammer squarely on the side of one head. The other head remained alive, but dazed and disoriented for the split second it took to take control of the entire body.

A split second was far too long when dealing with Drizzt Do'Urden. The agile drow came up in a leap, easily avoiding a lumbering swing, and sent his scimitars in a crossing swipe that drew two parallel lines along the giant's throat.

The ettin dropped both its clubs and clutched at the mortal wound.

An arrow blew it to the ground.

Two more ettins remained behind the mound, but they—all four heads—had seen quite enough of the fighting companions. Out a side tunnel the beasts went.

Right into Dagna's rambling force.

One wounded ettin stumbled back into the main chamber, a dozen hurled hammers bouncing off its stooped back for every lumbering step it took. Before Drizzt, Wulfgar, or even Catti-brie with her bow, could make a move at the beast, a multitude of dwarves rushed out of the tunnel and leaped upon it, bore it to the ground, and hacked and pounded away with battle-crazed abandon.

Drizzt looked at Wulfgar and shrugged.

"Fear not, my friend," the barbarian replied, smiling. "There are many more enemies to hit!" With another bellow to his battle god, Wulfgar turned about and charged for the main fight, trying to pick out Bruenor's one-horned helmet amidst a writhing sea of tangled goblins and dwarves.

Drizzt didn't follow, though, for he preferred single combat to the wildness of general melee. Calling Guenhwyvar to his side, the drow made his way along the wall, eventually exiting the main chamber.

After only a few steps and a warning growl from his trusted panther ally, he came to realize that Regis wasn't far behind.

* * * * *

Bruenor's estimates of the dwarven prowess seemed on target as the battle soon became a rout. In trading hits with the armored dwarves, the goblins found their crude swords and puny clubs to be no match against the tempered weapons of their enemies. Bruenor's people, too, were better trained, holding tight formations and keeping their nerves, which was difficult amidst all the chaos and the cries of the dying.

Goblins fled by the dozen, most finding the line of Dagna and his charges eagerly waiting to kill them.

With all the confusion, Catti-brie had to pick her shots carefully, particularly since she couldn't be certain that a skinny goblin torso would stop her flying arrows. Mostly, the young woman concentrated on those goblins breaking ranks, fleeing into the open ground between the main fight and Dagna's line.

For all her talk of parley and all the accusations she had leveled at Bruenor and the others, the young woman could not deny the tingle, the adrenaline rush, that swept over her every time she lifted Taulmaril the Heartseeker.

Wulfgar's eyes, too, gleamed with a luster that indicated the fine edge of survival. Raised among a warlike people, he had learned the battle-lust at an early age, a rage that had been tempered only when Bruenor and Drizzt had taught him the worth of his perceived enemies and the many sorrows his tribe's wars had caused.

There was no guilt in this fight, though, not against evil goblins, and Wulfgar's charge from the dead ettins to the larger battle was accompanied by a hearty song to Tempus. Wulfgar found no target clear enough for him to chance a throw with his hammer, but he was not dismayed, particularly when a group of several goblins broke clear of the fighting and fled his way.

The leading three hardly realized that the barbarian was there when Wulfgar's first sidelong cut with Aegis-fang swept them aside, killing two. The goblins behind stumbled in surprise, but came on anyway, flowing around the barbarian like a river around a rock.

A goblin head exploded under Aegis-fang's next heavy blow; Wulfgar snapped the hammer across one-handed to deflect a sword, then followed with a punching left hook that shattered his would-be attacker's jaw and sent the creature flying.

The barbarian felt a sting in his side, and he flinched before the sword could dig in deeply. His free hand whipped back across, clamping atop his attacker's head and lifting the squirming creature from the ground. It still had its sword, and Wulfgar realized that he was vulnerable. He found his only possible defense in sheer savagery, jerking the lifted goblin back and forth so violently that the creature could not get its bearings for a strike.

Wulfgar spun around to drive his many attackers back, using his momentum to aid in his one-handed hammer swipe. An advancing goblin tried to backtrack, and lifted its arm in a pitiful defense, but the warhammer blasted through the skinny limb and crushed on, knocking the creature's head so powerfully that when the goblin fell to the ground, it landed on its back. Its face, too, was squarely against the stone.

The stubborn, stupid goblin in the air nicked Wulfgar's huge biceps. The barbarian brought the creature down hard, squeezed and twisted, and heard the satisfying crack of neck bone. Seeing a coming charge from the corner of his eye, he hurled the dead thing at its companions, scattering them.

"Tempus!" the barbarian roared. He took up his warhammer in both hands and rushed into the bulk of the surrounding group, whipping Aegis-fang back and forth repeatedly. Any goblin that could not flee that furious charge, could not get out of deadly range, found a piece of its body utterly destroyed.

Wulfgar pivoted and came back at the group he knew was behind him. The goblins had indeed begun an advance, but when the mighty warrior spun about, his face contorted in wild-eyed frenzy, the goblins turned about and ran away. Wulfgar heaved his hammer, crushing one, then pivoted again and rushed back the other way, at the other group.

These, too, fled, apparently not caring that the wild human was unarmed.

Wulfgar caught one of them by the elbow, spun it about to face him, and clamped his other hand over its face, bending it over backward to the ground. Aegis-fang reappeared in his hand, and the barbarian's fury doubled.

* * * * *

Bruenor had to plant a boot solidly to free his many-notched axe from the chest of his latest victim. When the blade pulled free, a burst of blood followed it, showering the dwarf. Bruenor didn't care, sure that the goblins were evil things, that the results of his savage attacks bettered the world.

Smiling with abandon, the dwarf king darted this way and that in the tight press, finally finding another target. The goblin swung first, its club smashing apart when it connected with Bruenor's fine shield. The stupid goblin stared at its broken weapon in disbelief, then looked at the dwarf just in time to see the axe dive between its eyes.

A flash cut right by the dwarf, frightening the pleasure from him. He realized it was Catti-brie's doing, though, and saw the victim a dozen feet away, pinned to the stone floor by the quivering silver-shafted arrow.

"Damn good bow," the dwarf muttered, and in looking back to his daughter, he noticed a goblin scrambling up onto the platform.

"No, ye don't!" the dwarf cried, rushing to the slab and diving into a roll atop it. He came up beside the creature, ready to exchange blows, when another flash forced him to jump back.

The goblin still stood, looking down to its chest as though it expected to find an arrow sticking there. It found a hole instead, right through both lungs.

The goblin poked a finger in, in a ridiculous attempt to stem the blood flow, then it fell dead.

Bruenor planted his hands on hips and stared hard at his daughter. "Hey, girl," he scolded. "Ye're stealing all me fun!"

Catti-brie's fingers began to pull on her bowstring, but she relaxed it immediately.

Bruenor considered the woman's curious action, then understood as a goblin club connected heavily with the back of his head.

"I left that one for yerself," Catti-brie said with a shrug, a lame movement when weighed against the glower of Bruenor's dark eyes.

Bruenor wasn't listening. He threw his shield up, blocking the next predictable attack, and whirled, his axe leading the way. The goblin sucked in its belly and hopped back to its tiptoes.

"Not far enough," the dwarf told it, politely using its own tongue, and his words were proven true as the goblin's guts spilled out.

The horrified creature regarded them in disbelief.

"Ye shouldn't be hitting me when I'm not looking," was all the apology it would get from Bruenor Battlehammer, and his second swipe, angled in at the goblin's neck, took the creature's head from its shoulders.

With the platform clear of enemies, both Bruenor and Catti-brie turned to regard the general battle. Catti-brie brought her bow up, but then didn't see the point of releasing any more arrows. Most of the goblins were in flight, but with Dagna's troops lined across the chamber, they had nowhere to go.

Bruenor leaped down and put his forces into an organized pursuit, and, like a great, snapping maw, the dwarven hosts closed over the goblin horde.

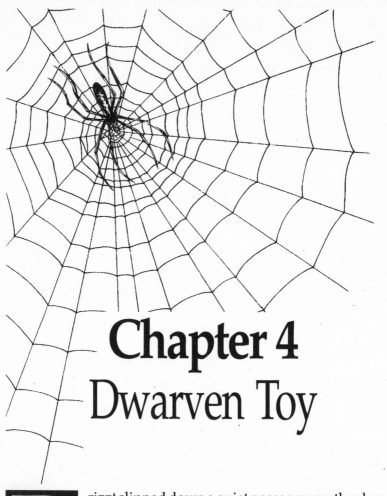

Chapter 4
Dwarven Toy

rizzt slipped down a quiet passageway, the clamor of the wild battle lost behind him. The drow was not worried, for he knew that his shadow, his Guenhwyvar, was padding along silently not too far ahead. Of more concern to Drizzt was Regis, still stubbornly close to his back. Fortunately, the halfling moved as silently as the drow, keeping equally well to the shadows, and did not seem to be a liability to Drizzt.

The need for silence was the only thing that kept Drizzt from questioning the halfling then and there, for if they stumbled on a number of goblins, Drizzt did not know how Regis, who was not skilled in battle, would keep out of harm's way.

Ahead, the black panther paused and looked back at Drizzt. The cat, darker than the darkness, then slipped through an opening and moved to the side into a chamber. Beyond the opening Drizzt heard the unmistakable snarling voices of goblins.

Drizzt looked back to Regis, to the red dots that showed the halfling's heat-sensing infravision. Halflings, too, could see in the dark, but not nearly as well as drow or goblins. Drizzt held one hand up, motioned for Regis to wait in the corridor, then slipped ahead to the entrance.

The goblins, at least six or seven, were huddled near the center of the small chamber, milling about many natural, tooth-like pillars.

To the right, along the wall, Drizzt sensed a slight movement and knew it was Guenhwyvar, patiently waiting for him to make the first move.

How wondrous a fighting companion that panther was, Drizzt reminded himself. Always, Guenhwyvar let Drizzt determine the course of battle, then discerned the best way to fit in.

The drow ranger moved to the nearest stalagmite, belly-crawled to another, and rolled behind yet another, ever closer to his prey. He made out nine goblins now, apparently discussing their best course of action.

They had no guard posted, had no clue that danger was near.

One rolled around to put its back against a stalagmite, separated from the others by a mere five feet. A scimitar sliced up through its belly, into its lungs before it could utter a sound.

Eight remained.

Drizzt eased the corpse to the ground and took its place, putting his back to the stone.

A moment later, one of the goblins called to him, thinking he was the dead goblin. Drizzt grunted in reply. A hand reached around to pat his shoulder, and the drow couldn't hide his smile.

The goblin tapped him once, then again, more slowly, then the thing began feeling around the drow's thick cloak, apparently noticing Drizzt's taller stature.

A curious expression on its ugly face, the goblin peeked around the mound.

Then there were seven, and Drizzt leaped out into their midst, scimitars flashing in a flurry that took the two nearest goblins down in the blink of an eye.

The remaining five shrieked and ran about, some colliding with stalagmites, others slapping and falling all over each other.

A goblin came straight for Drizzt, its mouth flapping a steady stream of undiscernible words and its hands held wide, as though in a gesture of friendship. Apparently the evil creature only then recognized this dark elf was no potential comrade, for it began to frantically back away. Drizzt's scimitars crossed in a downward slash, drawing an X of hot blood on the creature's chest.

Guenhwyvar streaked beside the drow and attacked a goblin fleeing toward the far side of the cavern. With a single swipe of the panther's huge claw, the count was down to three.

Finally, two goblins regained their senses enough to come at the drow in a coordinated fashion, weapons drawn. One launched its club in a roundhouse swing, but Drizzt slapped the weapon wide before it ever got close.

His scimitar, the same he had used to deflect the blow, darted left, then right, left and right, and again a third time, leaving the stunned creature with six mortal wounds. It stared dumbfounded as it fell backward to the floor.

All the while, Drizzt's second scimitar easily parried the other goblin's many desperate attacks.

When the drow turned to face this creature fully, it knew it was doomed. It hurled its short sword at Drizzt, again with little effect, and darted behind the nearest stone pillar.

The last of the confused creatures crossed behind it, startling the drow, and securing the other's escape. Drizzt cursed
the goblin's apparent luck. He wanted none to get away, but
these two were, either wisely or fortunately, fleeing in opposite
directions. A split second later, though, the drow heard a
resounding crack from behind the pillar, and the goblin that
had thrown its short sword toppled back out from behind the
mound, its skull shattered.

Regis, holding his little mace, peeked around the pillar and
shrugged.

Drizzt was at a loss and simply returned the stare, then spun
about to pursue the remaining goblin, which was fast weaving
its way around the cavern teeth toward a corridor at the
chamber's far end.

The drow, faster and more agile, gained steadily. He noticed Guenhwyvar, the panther's maw glowing hot with the
blood of a fresh kill, loping along a parallel course and gaining
on the goblin with every long stride. Drizzt was confident then
that the creature had no chance of escape.

At the corridor's entrance, the goblin jolted to a stop. Drizzt
skidded aside, as did Guenhwyvar, both diving for the cover of
pillars, as a series of snapping and sparking explosions ignited
all about the goblin's body. It shrieked and jerked wildly, this
way and that; pieces of its clothing and its flesh blew away.

The continuing explosions held the goblin up long after it
was dead. Finally, they ended and the creature fell to the floor,
trailing thin lines of smoke from several dozen blasted wounds.

Drizzt and Guenhwyvar held steady, perfectly silent, not
knowing what new monster had arrived.

The chamber lit up suddenly with a magical light.

Drizzt, fighting hard to bring his eyes into focus, clutched
his scimitars tightly.

"All dead?" he heard a familiar dwarven voice say. He
blinked his eyes open just in time to see the cleric Cobble enter
the room, one hand in a large belt pouch, the other holding a

shield out before him.

Several soldiers came in behind, one of them muttering, "Damn good spell, priest."

Cobble moved to inspect the shattered body, then nodded his agreement. Drizzt slipped out from behind the mound.

The surprised cleric's hand came whipping out, launching a score of small objects—pebbles?—at the drow. Guenhwyvar growled, Drizzt dove, and the pebbles hit the rock where he had been standing, initiating another burst of small explosions.

"Drizzt!" Cobble cried, realizing his mistake. "Drizzt!" He rushed to the drow, who was looking back to the many scorch marks on the floor.

"Are you all right, dear Drizzt?" Cobble cried.

"Damn good spell, priest," Drizzt replied in his best imitation-dwarf voice, his smile wide and admiring.

Cobble clapped him hard on the back, nearly knocking him over. "I like that one, too," he said, showing Drizzt that he had a pouch full of the bomblike pebbles. "Ye want to carry some?"

"I do," replied Regis, coming around a stalagmite, closer to the tunnel entrance than Drizzt had been.

Drizzt blinked his lavender orbs in amazement at the halfling's prowess.

* * * * *

Another force of goblins, more than a hundred strong, had been positioned in corridors to the right of the main chamber, to come in at the flank after the fighting had begun. With the trap's failure and Bruenor's ensuing charge (led by the horrible, silver-streaking arrows), the ettin force's miserable failure and Dagna's dwarven troops' subsequent arrival, even the stupid goblins had been wise enough to turn the other way and run.

"Dwarfses," one of the front-running goblins cried out, and the others soon echoed him in calls that shifted from terror to hunger when the creatures came to believe they had stumbled on a small band of the bearded folk, perhaps a scouting party.

Whatever the case, these dwarves apparently had no intentions of stopping to fight, and the chase was on.

A few twists and turns put the fleeing dwarves and the goblins near a wide, smoothly worked, torchlit tunnel, one that had been cut by the dwarves of Mithril Hall several hundred years before.

For the first time since that long-ago day, the dwarves were there again, waiting.

Powerful dwarven hands eased great disks onto a wooden beam, one after another until the whole resembled a solid, cylindrical wheel as tall as a dwarf and nearly as wide as the worked corridor, weighing well over a ton. Completing the structure's main frame were a few well-placed pegs, a wrapping of sheet metal (with sharp, nasty ridges hammered into it), and two notched handles that ran from the wheel's side to behind the contraption, where dwarves could man them and push the thing along.

A cloth with the full-sized likenesses of charging dwarves painted on it was hung out in front as a finishing touch that would keep the goblins in line until it was too late to retreat.

"Here they come," one of the forward scouts reported, returning to the main battle group. "They'll turn the corner in a few minutes."

"Are the baiters ready?" asked the dwarf in charge of the toy brigade.

The other dwarf nodded, and the haulers took up the poles, setting their hands firmly behind the appropriate notches. Four soldiers got out in front of the contraption, ready for their wild run, while the rest of the hundred-dwarf contingent fell into lines behind the haulers.

"The cubbies are a hunnerd feet down," the boss dwarf reminded the lead soldiers. "Don't ye miss the mark! Once we get this thing a-rolling, we're not likely to be stopping it!"

Feigned cries of fear came from the fleeing dwarves at the other end of the long corridor, followed by the whooping of the pursuing goblins.

The boss dwarf shook his bearded face; it was so easy to bait goblins. Just let them believe they had the upper hand, and on they'd come.

The lead soldiers began a slow trot, the haulers behind them took up the easy pace, and the army plodded along behind the thunder of the slow-rolling wheel.

Another series of shouts sounded, and mixed in was the unmistakable cry of "Now!"

The lead soldiers roared and broke into a run. The massive toy came right behind, pumping dwarven legs setting the devilish wheel into a great roll. Above the thunder, the dwarves began their growling song:

Tunnel's too tight,
Tunnel's too low,
Better run goblin,
'Cause here we go!

Their charge sounded like an avalanche, rumbling undertones to the goblins' cries. The baiters waved to their approaching kin, then stopped beside the cubbies and turned to hurl insults at their goblin pursuers.

The boss dwarf smiled grimly at the knowledge that he, that the toy, would pass the small alcoves, the only safe places in front of the contraption, a split second before the goblin hosts arrived there.

Just as the dwarves had planned.

With no way to turn back, thinking that they had encountered a simple dwarven expedition, the long lines of goblins hooted their battle cries and continued their charge.

The leading dwarven soldiers joined the baiters; together they dove aside into the alcoves, and the toy rumbled by, its disguising canopy making the front goblins slow their pace and wonder.

Howls of terror replaced battle cries and echoed down the goblin line. The closest goblin bravely hacked at the bouncing dwarven image, taking the painted canopy down and revealing the disaster an instant before the creature was squashed.

The fearsome dwarves called their war toy, "the juicer," and the puddle of goblin fluid that came out the back side of the crushing wheel showed it was a fitting title.

"Sing, my dwarves!" commanded the boss, and they took their chant to great crescendos, their rumbling voices echoing above the goblin howls.

Every bump's a goblins head,
Pools of blood from the goblin dead.
Run, good dwarves, push that toy,
Squish the little goblin boys!

The brutal contraption bounced and bumped; the haulers stumbled on goblin piles. But if any dwarf fell away, a dozen more were ready to take up his part of the pole, powerful legs pumping feverishly.

The army behind the contraption began to stretch out, dwarves stopping to finish off those broken goblins that still squirmed. The main host stayed close to the bouncing contraption, though, for as it came farther along the tunnel, it began to pass side tunnels. Predetermined brigades of dwarven soldiers turned down these, right behind the passing toy, slaughtering any goblins still in the area.

"Tight turn!" the boss dwarf yelled, and sparks flew from the side of the steel-covered outer stone wheels as they screeched along. The dwarves had counted on this region to stop the rolling monstrosity.

It didn't, and around the bend loomed the end of the corridor, a dozen goblins scratching at the unyielding stone, trying to find escape.

"Let it go!" cried the boss, and the wild-rushing dwarves did, falling all over each other as they continued to bounce along.

With a tremendous explosion that shook the bedrock, the juicer collided with the wall. It wasn't hard for the cheering dwarves to figure out what had happened to the unfortunate creatures caught in between.

"Oh, good work!" the boss dwarf said to his charges as he looked back around the bend to the long line of crushed goblins. The dwarven soldiers were still battling, but now they badly outnumbered their enemies, for more than half the goblin force had been squashed.

"Good work!" the boss reiterated heartily, and by a goblin-hating dwarf's estimation, it certainly was.

* * * * *

Back in the main chamber, Bruenor and Dagna exchanged victorious and wet hugs, "sharing the blood of their enemies," as the brutal dwarves called it. A few dwarves had been killed and many others lay wounded, but neither of the leaders had dared to hope that the rout would be so complete.

"What do ye think o' that, me girl?" Bruenor asked Cattibrie when she came over to join him, her long bow comfortably over one shoulder.

"We did as we had to do," the woman replied. "And the goblins were, as expected, a treacherous bunch. But I'll not back down on me words. We did right in trying to talk first."

Dagna spat on the floor, but Bruenor, the wiser of the two, nodded his agreement with his daughter.

"Tempus!" they heard Wulfgar cry in victory, and the barbarian, spotting the group, began bounding over to them, his mighty warhammer held high above his head.

"I'm still for thinking that ye're all taking a bit too much pleasure in it all," Catti-brie remarked to Bruenor. Apparently not wanting to talk with Wulfgar, she moved away, back to help the wounded.

"Bah!" Bruenor snorted behind her. "Suren ye set yer own bow to some sweet singing!"

Catti-brie brushed her auburn locks out of her face and did not look back. She didn't want Bruenor to see her smile.

The juicer brigade entered the main chamber a half hour later, reporting the right flank clear of goblins. Only a few minutes after them, Drizzt, Regis, and Guenhwyvar came in, the drow telling Bruenor that Cobble's forces were finishing up in the corridors to the left and the rear.

"Did ye get a few for yerself?" the dwarf asked. "After the ettins, I mean?"

Drizzt nodded. "I did," he replied, "as did Guenhwyvar . . . and Regis." Both Drizzt and the dwarf turned curious eyes on the halfling, who stood easily, his bloodied mace in hand. Noticing the looks, Regis slipped the weapon behind his back as though he were embarrassed.

"I did not even expect ye to come, Rumblebelly," Bruenor said to him. "I thought ye'd be staying up, helping yerself to more food, while the rest of us did all the fighting."

Regis shrugged. "I figured that the safest place in all the world would be beside Drizzt," he explained.

Bruenor wasn't about to argue with that logic. "We can set to digging in a few weeks," he explained to his ranger friend. "After some expeditionary miners come through and name the place safe."

By this point, Drizzt was hardly listening to him. He was more interested in the fact that Catti-brie and Wulfgar, moving about the ranks of wounded, obviously were avoiding each other.

"It's the boy," Bruenor told him, noticing his interest.

"He did not think a woman should be at the battle," Drizzt replied.

"Bah!" snorted the red-bearded dwarf. "She's as fine a fighter as we've got. Besides, five dozen dwarf women came along, and two of 'em even got killed."

Drizzt's face twisted with surprise as he regarded the dwarf king. He shook his white shock of hair helplessly and started away to join Catti-brie, but stopped and looked back after only a few steps, shaking his head yet again.

"Five dozen of 'em," Bruenor reiterated into his doubting expression. "Dwarf women, I tell ye."

"My friend," Drizzt answered, moving off once more, "I never could tell the difference."

* * * * *

Cobble's forces joined the other dwarves two hours later, reporting the rear areas clear of enemies. The rout was complete, as far as Bruenor and his commanders could discern, with not a single enemy left alive.

None of the dwarven forces had noticed the slender, dark forms—dark elves, Jarlaxle's spies—floating among the stalactites near critical areas of battle, watching the dwarven movements and battle techniques with more than passing interest.

The goblin threat was ended, but that was the least of Bruenor Battlehammer's problems.

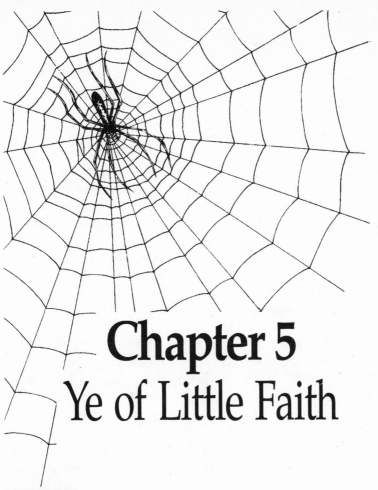

Chapter 5
Ye of Little Faith

Dinin watched Vierna's every move, watched how his sister went through the precise rituals to honor the Spider Queen. The drow were in a small chapel Jarlaxle had secured for Vierna's use in one of the minor houses of Menzoberranzan. Dinin remained faithful to the dark deity Lloth and willingly had agreed to accompany Vierna to her prayers this day, but, in truth, the male drow thought the whole thing a senseless facade, thought his sister a ridiculous mockery of her former self.

"You should not be so doubting," Vierna remarked to him,

still going about her ritual and not bothering to look over her shoulder to regard Dinin.

At the sound of Dinin's disgusted sigh, though, Vierna did spin about, an angry red glower in her narrow-set eyes.

"What is the purpose?" Dinin demanded, facing her wrath bravely. Even if she was out of Lloth's favor, as Dinin stubbornly believed, Vierna was larger and stronger than he and armed with some clerical magic. He gritted his teeth, firmed his resolve, and did not back down, fearful that Vierna's mounting obsession again would lead those around him down a path to destruction.

In answer, Vierna produced a curious whip from under the folds of her clerical robes. While its handle was unremarkable black adamantite, the instrument's five tendrils were writhing, living snakes. Dinin's eyes widened; he understood the weapon's significance.

"Lloth does not allow any but her high priestesses to wield these," Vierna reminded him, affectionately petting the heads.

"But we lost favor . . ." Dinin started to protest, but it was a lame argument in the face of Vierna's demonstration.

Vierna eyed him and laughed evilly, almost purred, as she bent to kiss one of the heads.

"Then why go after Drizzt?" Dinin asked her. "You have regained the favor of Lloth. Why risk everything chasing our traitorous brother?"

"That is how I regained the favor!" Vierna screamed at him. She advanced a step, and Dinin wisely backed away. He remembered his younger days at House Do'Urden, when Briza, his oldest and most vicious sister, often tortured him with one of those dreaded, snake-headed whips.

Vierna calmed immediately, though, and looked back to her dark, (both live and sculpted) spider-covered altar. "Our family fell because of Matron Malice's weakness," she explained. "Malice failed in the most important task Lloth ever gave her."

"To kill Drizzt," Dinin reasoned.

"Yes," Vierna said simply, looking back over her shoulder to regard her brother. "To kill Drizzt, wretched, traitorous Drizzt. I have promised his heart to Lloth, have promised to right the family's wrong, so that we—you and I—might regain the favor of our goddess."

"To what end?" Dinin had to ask, looking around the unremarkable chapel with obvious scorn. "Our house is no more. The name of Do'Urden cannot be spoken anywhere in the city. What will be the gain if we again find Lloth's favor? You will be a high priestess, and for that I am glad, but you will have no house over which to preside."

"But I will!" Vierna retorted, her eyes flashing. "I am a surviving noble of a destroyed house, as are you, my brother. We have all the Rights of Accusation."

Dinin's eyes went wide. Vierna was technically correct; the Rights of Accusation was a privilege reserved for surviving noble children of destroyed houses, wherein the children named their attackers and thus brought the weight of drow justice upon the guilty party. In the continuing back-room intrigue of chaotic Menzoberranzan, though, justice was selectively meted out.

"Accusation?" Dinin stammered, barely able to get the word out of his suddenly dry mouth. "Have you forgotten which house it was that destroyed our own?"

"It is all the sweeter," purred his stubborn sister.

"Baenre!" Dinin cried. "House Baenre, First House of Menzoberranzan! You cannot speak against Baenre. No house, alone or in alliance, will move against them, and Matron Baenre controls the Academy. Where will your force of justice be garnered?

"And what of Bregan D'aerthe?" Dinin reminded her. "The very band of mercenaries that took us in helped defeat our house." Dinin stopped abruptly, considering his own words, ever amazed by the paradox, the cruel irony, of drow society.

"You are a male and cannot understand the beauty of

Lloth," Vierna replied. "Our goddess feeds from this chaos, considers this situation all the sweeter simply because of the many furious ironies."

"The city will not wage war against House Baenre," Dinin said flatly.

"It will never come to that!" Vierna snapped back, and again came that wild flash in her red-glowing orbs. "Matron Baenre is old, my brother. Her time has long past. When Drizzt is dead, as the Spider Queen demands, I will be granted an audience in House Baenre, wherein I . . . we will make our accusation."

"Then we will be fed to Baenre's goblin slaves," Dinin replied dryly.

"Matron Baenre's own daughters will force her out so that the house might regain the Spider Queen's favor," the excited Vierna went on, ignoring her doubting brother. "To that end, they will place me in control."

Dinin could hardly find the words to rebut Vierna's preposterous claims.

"Think of it, my brother," Vierna went on. "Envision yourself standing beside me as I preside over the First House of Menzoberranzan!"

"Lloth has promised this to you?"

"Through Triel," Vierna replied, "Matron Baenre's oldest daughter, herself Matron Mistress of the Academy."

Dinin was beginning to catch on. If Triel, much more powerful than Vierna, meant to replace her admittedly ancient mother, she certainly would claim the throne of House Baenre for herself, or at least allow one of her many worthy sisters to take the seat. Dinin's doubts were obvious as he half-sat on one bench, crossing his arms in front of him and shaking his head slowly, back and forth.

"I have no room for disbelievers in my entourage," Vierna warned.

"Your entourage?" Dinin replied.

"Bregan D'aerthe is but a tool, provided to me so that I

might please the goddess," Vierna explained without hesitation.

"You are insane," Dinin said before he could find the wisdom to keep the thought to himself. To his relief, though, Vierna did not advance toward him.

"You shall regret those sacrilegious words when our traitorous Drizzt is given to Lloth," the priestess promised.

"You'll never get near our brother," Dinin replied sharply, his memories of his previous disastrous encounter with Drizzt still painfully clear. "And I'll not go along with you to the surface—not against that demon. He is powerful, Vierna, mightier than you can imagine."

"Silence!" The word carried magical weight, and Dinin found his next planned protests stuck in his throat.

"Mightier?" Vierna scoffed a moment later. "What do you know of power, impotent male?" A wry smile crossed her face, an expression that made Dinin squirm in his seat. "Come with me, doubting Dinin," Vierna bade. She started for a side door in the small chapel, but Dinin made no move to follow.

"Come!" Vierna commanded, and Dinin found his legs moving under him, found himself leaving the single stalagmite mound of the lesser house, then leaving Menzoberranzan altogether, faithfully following his insane sister's every step.

* * * * *

As soon as the two Do'Urdens walked from view, Jarlaxle lowered the curtain in front of his scrying mirror, dispelling the image of the small chapel. He thought he should speak with Dinin soon, to warn the obstinate fighter of the consequences he might face. Jarlaxle honestly liked Dinin and knew that the drow was heading for disaster.

"You have baited her well," the mercenary remarked to the priestess standing beside him, giving her a devious wink with his left eye—the uncovered one this day.

71

The female, shorter than Jarlaxle but carrying herself with an undeniable strength, snarled at the mercenary, her contempt obvious.

"My dear Triel," Jarlaxle cooed.

"Hold your tongue," Triel Baenre warned, "or I will tear it out and give it to you, that you might hold it in your hand."

Jarlaxle shrugged and wisely shifted the conversation back to the business at hand. "Vierna believes your claim," he remarked.

"Vierna is desperate," Triel Baenre replied.

"She would have gone after Drizzt on the simple promise that you would take her into your family," the mercenary reasoned, "but to bait her with delusions of replacing Matron Baenre . . ."

"The greater the prize, the greater Vierna's motivation," Triel replied calmly. "It is important to my mother that Drizzt Do'Urden be given to Lloth. Let the fool Do'Urden priestess think what she will."

"Agreed," Jarlaxle said with a nod. "Has House Baenre prepared the escort?"

"A score and a half will slip out beside the fighters of Bregan D'aerthe," Triel replied. "They are only males," she added derisively, "and expendable." The first daughter of House Baenre cocked her head curiously as she continued to regard the wily mercenary.

"You will accompany Vierna personally with your chosen soldiers?" Triel asked. "To coordinate the two groups?"

Jarlaxle clapped his slender hands together. "I am a part of this," he answered firmly.

"To my displeasure," the Baenre daughter snarled. She uttered a single word and, with a flash, disappeared.

"Your mother loves me, dear Triel," Jarlaxle said to the emptiness, as if the Matron Mistress of the Academy were still beside him. "I would not miss this," the mercenary continued, thinking out loud. By Jarlaxle's estimation, the hunt for Drizzt could be only a good thing. He might lose a few soldiers, but they were replaceable. If Drizzt was indeed brought to sacrifice, Lloth would be pleased, Matron Baenre would be pleased, and Jarlaxle would find a way to be rewarded for his efforts. After all, on a simpler level, Drizzt Do'Urden, as a traitorous renegade, carried a high bounty on his head.

Jarlaxle chuckled wickedly, reveling in the beauty of it all. If Drizzt managed somehow to elude them, then Vierna would take the fall, and the mercenary would continue on, untouched by it all.

There was another possibility that Jarlaxle, removed from the immediate situation and wise in the ways of the drow, recognized, and if, by some remote chance, it came to pass, he again would be in a position to profit greatly, simply from his favorable relationship with Vierna. Triel had promised Vierna an unbelievable prize because Lloth had instructed her, and her mother, to do so. What would happen if Vierna fulfilled her part of the agreement? the mercenary wondered. What ironies did conniving Lloth have in store for House Baenre?

Surely Vierna Do'Urden seemed insane for believing Triel's empty promises, but Jarlaxle knew well that many of Menzoberranzan's most powerful drow, Matron Baenre included, had seemed, at one time in their lives, equally crazy.

* * * * *

Vierna pressed through the opaque doorway to Jarlaxle's private chambers later that day, her crazed expression revealing the anxiety for the coming events.

Jarlaxle heard a commotion in the outer corridor, but Vierna merely continued to smile knowingly. The mercenary rocked back in his comfortable chair, tapping his fingers together in front of him and trying to discern what surprise the Do'Urden priestess had prepared for him this time.

"We will need an extra soldier to complement our party,"

Vierna ordered.

"It can be arranged," Jarlaxle replied, beginning to catch on. "But why? Will Dinin not be accompanying us?"

Vierna's eyes flashed. "He will," she said, "but my brother's role in the hunt has changed."

Jarlaxle didn't flinch, just continued to sit back and tap his fingers.

"Dinin did not believe in Lloth's destiny," Vierna explained, casually taking a seat on the edge of Jarlaxle's desk. "He did not wish to accompany me in this critical mission. The Spider Queen has demanded this of us!" She hopped back to the floor, suddenly ferocious, and stepped back toward the opaque door.

Jarlaxle made no move, except to flex the fingers on his dagger-throwing hand, as Vierna's tirade continued. The priestess swept about the small room, praying to Lloth, cursing those who would not fall to their knees before the goddess, and cursing her brothers, Drizzt and Dinin.

Then Vierna calmed again suddenly, and smiled wickedly. "Lloth demands fealty," she said accusingly.

"Of course," replied the unshakable mercenary.

"Justice is for a priestess to deal."

"Of course."

Vierna's eyes flashed—Jarlaxle quietly tensed, fearing that the unsteady female would lash out at him for some unknown reason. She instead went back to the door and called loudly for her brother.

Jarlaxle saw the unremarkable, veiled silhouette beyond the portal, saw the opaque material bend and stretch as Dinin started in from the other side.

A huge spider leg slipped into the room, then another, then a third. The mutated torso came through next, Dinin's unclothed and bloated body transmuted from the waist down into the lower torso of a giant black spider. His once fair face now seemed a dead thing, swollen and expressionless, his eyes showing no luster.

The mercenary fought hard to keep his breathing steady. He removed his great hat and ran a hand over his bald, sweating head.

The disfigured creature moved into the room fully and stood obediently behind Vierna, the priestess smiling at the mercenary's obvious discomfort.

"The quest is critical," Vierna explained. "Lloth will not tolerate dissent."

If Jarlaxle had held any doubts about the Spider Queen's involvement with Vierna's quest, they were gone now.

Vierna had exacted the ultimate punishment of drow society on troublesome Dinin, something only a high priestess in the highest favor of Lloth could ever accomplish. She had replaced Dinin's graceful drow body with this grotesque and mutated arachnid form, had replaced Dinin's fierce independence with a malevolent demeanor that she could bend to her every whim.

She had turned him into a drider.

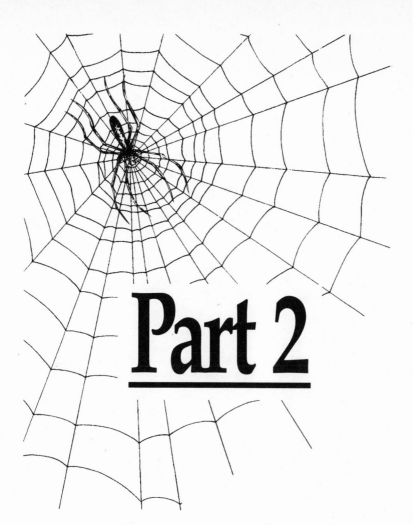

Part 2

Perceptions

There is no word in the drow language for love. The closest word I can think of is ssinssrigg, but that is a term better equated with physical lust or selfish greed. The concept of love exists in the hearts of some drow, of course, but true love, a selfless desire often requiring personal sacrifice, has no place in a world of such bitter and dangerous rivalries.

The only sacrifices in drow culture are gifts to Lloth, and those are surely not selfless, since the giver hopes, prays, for something greater in return.

Still, the concept of love was not new to me when I left the Under-

dark. I loved Zaknafein. I loved both Belwar and Clacker. Indeed, it was the capacity, the need, for love that ultimately drove me from Menzoberranzan.

Is there in all the wide world a concept more fleeting, more elusive? Many people of all the races seem simply not to understand love, burden its beauteous simplicity with preconceived notions and unrealistic expectations. How ironic that I, walking from the darkness of loveless Menzoberranzan, can better grasp the concept than many of those who have lived with it, or at least with the very real possibility of it, for all of their lives.

Some things a renegade drow will not take for granted.

My few journeys to Silverymoon in these past weeks have invited good-hearted jests from my friends. "Suren the elf has his eyes fixed on another wedding!" Bruenor has often crooned, regarding my relationship with Alustriel, the Lady of Silverymoon. I accept the taunts in light of the sincere warmth and hopes behind them, and have not dashed those hopes by explaining to my dear friends that their notions are misguided.

I appreciate Alustriel and the goodness she has shown me. I appreciate that she, a ruler in a too-often unforgiving world, has taken such a chance as to allow a dark elf to walk freely down her city's wondrous avenues. Alustriel's acceptance of me as a friend has allowed me to draw my desires from my true wishes, not from expected limitations.

But do I love her?

No more than she loves me.

I will admit, though, I do love the notion that I could love Alustriel, and she could love me, and that, if the attraction were present, the color of my skin and the reputation of my heritage would not deter the noble Lady of Silverymoon.

I know now, though, that love has become the most prominent part of my existence, that my bond of friendship with Bruenor and Wulfgar and Regis is of utmost importance to any happiness that this drow will ever know.

My bond with Catti-brie runs deeper still.

The Legacy

Honest love is a selfless concept, that I have already said, and my own selflessness has been put to a severe test this spring.

I fear now for the future, for Catti-brie and Wulfgar and the barriers they must, together, overcome. Wulfgar loves her, I do not doubt, but he burdens his love with a possessiveness that borders on disrespect.

He should understand the spirit that is Catti-brie, should see clearly the fuel that stokes the fires in her marvelous blue eyes. It is that very spirit that Wulfgar loves, and yet he will undoubtedly smother it under the notions of a woman's place as her husband's possession.

My barbarian friend has come far from his youthful days roaming the tundra. Farther still must he come to hold the heart of Bruenor's fiery daughter, to hold Catti-brie's love.

Is there in all the world a concept more fleeting, more elusive?

—Drizzt Do'Urden

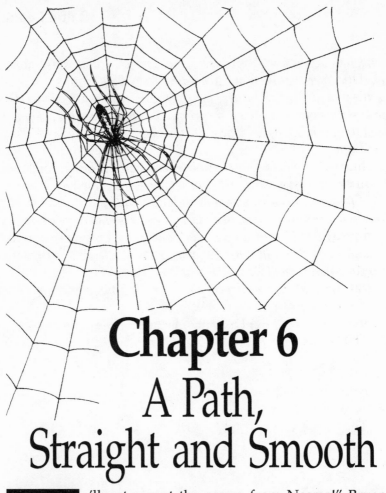

Chapter 6
A Path, Straight and Smooth

I'll not accept the group from Nesme!" Bruenor growled at the barbarian emissary from Settlestone.

"But, king dwarf..." the large, red-haired man stammered helplessly.

"No!" Bruenor's severe tone silenced him.

"The archers of Nesme played a role in reclaiming Mithril Hall," Drizzt, who stood at Bruenor's side in the audience hall, promptly reminded the dwarf king.

Bruenor shifted abruptly in his stone seat. "Ye forgotten the treatment the Nesme dogs gave ye when first we passed through their land?" he asked the drow.

Drizzt shook his head, the notion actually bringing a smile to his face. "Never," he replied, but his calm tones and expression revealed that, while he had not forgotten, he apparently had forgiven.

Looking at his ebon-skinned friend, so at peace and content, the huffy dwarf's rage was soon deflated. "Ye think I should let them come to the wedding, then?"

"You are a king now," answered Drizzt, and he held out his hands as though that simple statement should explain everything. Bruenor's expression showed clearly that it did not, though, and so the equally stubborn dark elf promptly elaborated. "Your responsibilities to your people lie in diplomacy," Drizzt explained. "Nesme will be a valuable trading partner and a worthwhile ally. Besides, we can forgive the soldiers of an oft-imperiled town for their reaction to the sight of a dark elf."

"Bah, ye're too soft-hearted, elf," Bruenor grumbled, "and ye're taking me along with ye!" He looked to the huge barbarian, obviously akin to Wulfgar, and nodded. "Send out me welcome to Nesme, then, but I'll be needing a count o' them that's to attend!"

The barbarian cast an appreciative look at Drizzt, then bowed and was gone, though his departure did little to stop Bruenor's grumbling.

"A hunnerd things to do, elf," the dwarf complained.

"You try to make your daughter's wedding the grandest the land has ever seen," Drizzt remarked.

"I try," Bruenor agreed. "She's deserving it, me Catti-brie. I've tried to give her what I could all these years, but..." Bruenor held his hands out, inviting a visual inspection of his stout body, a pointed reminder that he and Catti-brie were not even of the same race.

Drizzt put a hand on his friend's strong shoulder. "No human could have given her more," he assured Bruenor.

The dwarf sniffled; Drizzt did well to hide his chuckle.

R. A. Salvatore

"But a hunnerd damned things!" Bruenor roared, his fit of sentimentality predictably short-lived. "King's daughter has to get a proper wedding, I say, but I'm not for getting much help in doing the damned thing right!"

Drizzt knew the source of Bruenor's overblown frustration. The dwarf had expected Regis, a former guildmaster and undeniably skilled in etiquette, to help in planning the huge celebration. Soon after Regis had arrived in the halls, Bruenor had assured Drizzt that his troubles were over, that "Rumblebelly'll see to what's needin' seein' to."

In truth, Regis had taken on many tasks, but hadn't performed as well as Bruenor had expected or demanded. Drizzt wasn't sure if this came from Regis's unexpected ineptitude or Bruenor's doting attitude.

A dwarf rushed in, then, and handed Bruenor twenty different scrolls of possible layouts for the great dining hall. Another dwarf came in on the first one's heels, bearing an armful of potential menus for the feast.

Bruenor just sighed and looked helplessly to Drizzt.

"You will get through this," the drow assured him. "And Catti-brie will think it the grandest celebration ever given." Drizzt meant to go on, but his last statement gave him pause and a concerned expression crossed his brow that Bruenor did not miss.

"Ye're worried for the girl," the observant dwarf remarked.

"More for Wulfgar," Drizzt admitted.

Bruenor chuckled. "I got three masons at work to fixing the lad's walls," he said. "Something put a mighty anger in the boy."

Drizzt only nodded. He had not revealed to anyone that he had been Wulfgar's target on that particular occasion, that Wulfgar probably would have killed him blindly if the barbarian had won.

"The boy's just nervous," Bruenor said.

Again the drow nodded, though he wasn't certain he could

84

bring himself to agree. Wulfgar was indeed nervous, but his behavior went beyond that excuse. Still, Drizzt had no better explanations, and since the incident in the room, Wulfgar had become friendly once more toward Drizzt, had seemed more his old self.

"He'll settle down once the day gets past," Bruenor went on, and it seemed to Drizzt that the dwarf was trying to convince himself more than anyone else. This, too, Drizzt understood, for Catti-brie, the orphaned human, was Bruenor's daughter in heart and soul. She was the one soft spot in Bruenor's rock-hard heart, the vulnerable chink in the king's armor.

Wulfgar's erratic, domineering behavior had not escaped the wise dwarf, it seemed. But, while Wulfgar's attitude obviously bothered Bruenor, Drizzt did not believe the dwarf would do anything about it—not unless Catti-brie asked him for help.

And Drizzt knew that Catti-brie, as proud and stubborn as her father, would not ask—not from Bruenor and not from Drizzt.

"Where ye been hiding, ye little trickster?" Drizzt heard Bruenor roar, and the dwarf's sheer volume startled Drizzt from his private contemplations. He looked over to see Regis entering the hall, the halfling looking thoroughly flustered.

"I ate my first meal of the day!" Regis shouted back, and he got a sour look on his cherubic face and put a hand on his grumbling tummy.

"No time for eating!" Bruenor snapped back. "We got a—"

"Hunnerd things to do," Regis finished, imitating the dwarf's rough accent and holding up his chubby hand in a desperate plea for Bruenor to back off.

Bruenor stomped a heavy boot and stormed over to the pile of potential menus. "Since ye're so set on thinking about food, . . ." Bruenor began as he gathered up the parchments and heaved them, showering Regis. "There'll be elves and humans aplenty at the feast," he explained as Regis scrambled to put the pile in order. "Give 'em something their sensitive innards'll take!"

Regis shot a pleading look at Drizzt, but when the drow only shrugged in reply, the halfling picked up the parchments and shuffled away.

"I'd've thought that one'd be better at this wedding planning stuff," Bruenor remarked, loudly enough for the departing halfling to hear.

"And not so good at fighting goblins," Drizzt replied, remembering the halfling's remarkable efforts in the battle.

Bruenor stroked his thick red beard and looked to the empty doorway through which Regis had just passed. "Spent lots of time on the road beside the likes of us," the dwarf decided.

"Too much time," Drizzt added under his breath, too quietly for Bruenor to hear, for it was obvious to the drow that Bruenor, unlike Drizzt, thought the surprising revelations about their halfling friend a good thing.

* * * * *

A short while later, when Drizzt, on an errand for Bruenor, neared the entrance to Cobble's chapel, he found that Bruenor was not the only one flustered by the hectic preparations for the upcoming wedding.

"Not for all the mithril in Bruenor's realm!" he heard Catti-brie emphatically shout.

"Be reasonable," Cobble whined back at her. "Yer father's not asking too much."

Drizzt entered the chapel to see Catti-brie standing atop a pedestal, hands resolutely on her slender hips, and Cobble down low before her, holding out a gem-studded apron.

Catti-brie regarded Drizzt and gave a curt shake of her head. "They're wanting me to wear a smithy's apron!" she cried. "A damned smithy's apron on the day o' me wedding!"

Drizzt prudently realized that this was not the time to smile. He walked solemnly to Cobble and took the apron.

"Battlehammer tradition," the cleric huffed.

86

"Any dwarf would be proud to wear the raiment," Drizzt agreed. "Must I remind you, though, that Catti-brie is no dwarf?"

"A symbol of subservience is what it is," the auburn-haired woman spouted. "Dwarven females are expected to labor at the forge all the day. Not ever have I lifted a smithy's hammer, and . . ."

Drizzt calmed her with an outstretched hand and a plaintive look.

"She's Bruenor's daughter," Cobble pointed out. "She has a duty to please her father."

"Indeed," Drizzt, the consummate diplomat, agreed once more, "but remember that she is not marrying a dwarf. Catti-brie has never worked the forge—"

"It's symbolic," Cobble protested.

"—and Wulfgar lifted the hammer only during his years of servitude to Bruenor, when he was given no choice," Drizzt finished without missing a beat.

Cobble looked to Catti-brie, then back to the apron, and sighed. "We'll find a compromise," he conceded.

Drizzt threw a wink Catti-brie's way and was surprised to realize that his efforts apparently had not brightened the young woman's mood.

"I have come from Bruenor," the drow ranger said to Cobble. "He mentioned something about testing the holy water for the ceremony."

"Tasting," Cobble corrected, and he hopped all about, looking this way and that. "Yes, yes, the mead," he said, obviously flustered. "Bruenor's wanting to settle the mead issue this day." He looked up at Drizzt. "We're thinking that the dark stuff'll be too much for the soft-bellied group from Silverymoon."

Cobble rushed about the large chapel, scooping buckets from the various fonts that lined the walls. Catti-brie offered Drizzt an incredulous shrug as he silently mouthed the words,

87

R. A. Salvatore

"Holy water?"

Priests of most religions prepared their blessed water with exotic oils; it should have come as no surprise to Drizzt, after many years beside rowdy Bruenor, that the dwarven clerics used hops.

"Bruenor said you should bring a generous amount," Drizzt said to Cobble, instructions that were hardly necessary given that the excited cleric already had filled a small cart with flasks.

"We're done for the day," Cobble announced to Catti-brie. The dwarf ambled quickly to the door, his precious cargo bouncing along. "But don't ye be thinking that ye've had the last word in all of this!" Catti-brie snarled again, but Cobble, rambling along at top speed, was too far gone to notice.

Drizzt and Catti-brie sat side by side on the small pedestal in silence for some time. "Is the apron so bad?" the drow finally mustered the nerve to ask.

Catti-brie shook her head. "'Tis not the garment, but the meaning of the thing I'm not liking," she explained. "Me wedding's in two weeks. I'm thinking that I've seen me last adventure, me last fight, except for those I'm doomed to face against me own husband."

The blunt admission struck Drizzt profoundly and alleviated much of the weight of keeping his fears private.

"Goblins across Faerun will be glad to hear that," he said facetiously, trying to bring some levity to the young woman's dark mood. Catti-brie did manage a slight smile, but there remained a profound sadness in her blue eyes.

"You fought as well as any," Drizzt added.

"Did ye not think I would?" Catti-brie snapped at him, suddenly defensive, her tone as sharp as the edges of Drizzt's magical scimitars.

"Are you always so filled with anger?" Drizzt retorted, and his accusing words calmed Catti-brie immediately.

"Just scared, I'm guessing," she replied quietly.

Drizzt nodded, understanding and appreciating his friend's

growing dilemma. "I must go back to Bruenor," he explained, rising from the pedestal. He would have left it at that, but he could not ignore the pleading look Catti-brie then gave him. She turned away immediately, staring straight ahead under the cowl of her thick auburn locks, and that despondence struck Drizzt even more profoundly.

"It is not my place to tell you how you should feel," Drizzt said evenly. Still the young woman did not look back to him. "My burden as your friend is equal to the one you carried in the southern city of Calimport, when I had lost my way. I say to you now: The path before you turns soon in many directions, but that path is yours to choose. For all our sakes, and mostly yours, I pray that you consider your course carefully." He bent low, pushed back the side of Catti-brie's hair and kissed her gently on the cheek.

He did not look back as he left the chapel.

* * * * *

Half of Cobble's cart was already empty by the time the drow entered Bruenor's audience hall. Bruenor, Cobble, Dagna, Wulfgar, Regis, and several other dwarves argued loudly over which pail of the "holy water" held the finest, smoothest taste— arguments that inevitable produced further taste tests, which in turn created further arguments.

"This one!" Bruenor bellowed after draining a pail and coming back up with his red beard covered in foam.

"That one's good for goblins!" Wulfgar roared, his voice dull. His laughter ended abruptly, though, when Bruenor plopped the pail over his head and gave it a resounding backhand.

"I could be wrong," Wulfgar, suddenly sitting on the floor, admitted, his voice echoing under the metal bucket.

"Tell me what ye think, drow," Bruenor bellowed when he noticed Drizzt. He held out two sloshing buckets.

Drizzt put up a hand, declining the invitation. "Mountain springs are more to my liking than thick mead," he explained.

Bruenor threw the buckets at him, but the drow easily stepped aside, and the dark, golden liquid oozed slowly across the stone floor. The sheer volume of the ensuing protests from the other dwarves at the waste of good mead astounded Drizzt, but not as much as the fact that this probably was the first time he had ever seen Bruenor scolded without finding the courage to fight back.

"Me king," came a call from the door that ending the argument. A rather plump dwarf, fully arrayed in battle gear, entered the audience hall, the seriousness of his expression deflating the mirth in the tasting chamber.

"Seven kin have not returned from the newer sections," the dwarf explained.

"Taking their time, is all," Bruenor replied.

"They missed their supper," said the guard.

"Trouble," Cobble and Dagna said together, suddenly solemn.

"Bah!" snorted Bruenor as he waved his thick hand unsteadily in front of him. "There be no more goblins in them tunnels. The groups down there now're just hunting mithril. They found a vein o' the stuff, I tell ye. That'd keep any dwarf, even from his supper."

Cobble and Dagna, even Regis, Drizzt noted, wagged their heads in agreement. Given the potential danger whenever traveling the tunnels of the Underdark (and the deepest tunnels of Mithril Hall could be considered nothing less), the wary drow was not so easily convinced.

"What're ye thinking?" Bruenor asked Drizzt, seeing his plain concern.

Drizzt considered his response for a long while. "I am thinking that you are probably right."

"Probably?" Bruenor huffed. "Ah, well, I never could convince ye. Go on, then. It's what ye want. Take yer cat and go find me overdue dwarves."

Drizzt's wry smile left no doubt that Bruenor's instructions had been his intention all along.

"I am Wulfgar, son of Beornegar! I will go!" Wulfgar proclaimed, but he sounded somewhat ridiculous with his head still under the bucket. Bruenor leveled another backhand to silence his spouting.

"And elf," the king called, turning Drizzt back to him. Bruenor offered a wicked smile to all of those about him, then dropped it fully over Regis. "Be taking Rumblebelly with ye," the dwarf king explained. "He's not doing me much good about here."

Regis's big, round eyes got even bigger and rounder. He ran plump, soft fingers through his curly brown hair, then tugged uncomfortably at the one dangling earring he wore. "Me?" he asked meekly. "Go back down there?"

"Ye went once," Bruenor reasoned, making his argument more to the other dwarves than to Regis. "Got yerself a few goblins, if me memory's right."

"I have too much to—"

"Get ye going, Rumblebelly," Bruenor growled, leaning forward in his seat and nearly overbalancing in the process. "For the first time since ye come running back to us—and know that we're knowing ye're running!—do what I ask of ye without yer back talk and excuses!"

The seriousness of Bruenor's grim tone surprised everyone in the room, apparently even Regis, for the halfling offered not another word, just got up and walked obediently to stand beside Drizzt.

"Can we stop by my room?" Regis quietly asked the drow. "I would like my mace and pack, at least."

Drizzt draped an arm over his three-foot-tall companion's slumping shoulders and turned him about. "Fear not," he said under his breath, and to accentuate the point he dropped the onyx figurine of Guenhwyvar into the halfling's eager hands.

Regis knew he was in fine company.

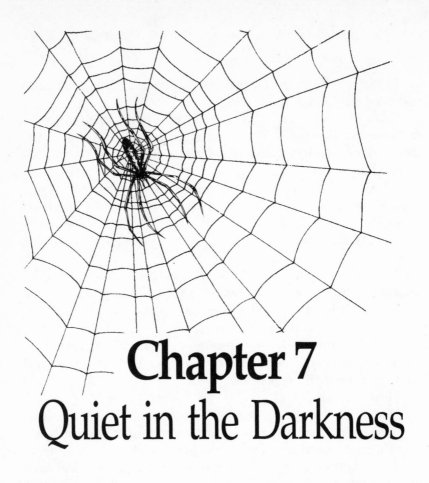

Chapter 7
Quiet in the Darkness

Even with burning lamps lining all the walls and the paths clear and well marked, it took Drizzt and Regis the better part of three hours to cross the miles of the great Mithril Hall complex to the new tunnel areas. They passed through the wondrous, tiered Undercity, with its many levels of dwarven dwellings that resembled gigantic steps on two sides of the huge cavern. The dwellings overlooked a central work area on the cavern floor that bustled with the activities of the industrious race. This was the hub of the entire complex; here the majority of Bruenor's people lived and worked. Great furnaces roared all day, every day. Dwarven hammers rang out in a continual song, and, though the mines had been opened for only a couple of months, thousands of finished products—everything from finely crafted weapons to beautiful goblets—already filled many pushcarts, which waited along the walls for the onset of the trading season.

Drizzt and Regis entered from the eastern end on the top tier, crossed the cavern along a high bridge, and weaved down the many stairways to exit the city's lowest level, heading west into Mithril Hall's deepest mines. Low-burning lamps lined the walls, though these were fewer now and farther between, and every now and then the companions came to a dwarven work crew, bleeding precious silvery mithril from the tunnel wall.

Then they came to the outer tunnels, where there were no lamps and no dwarves. Drizzt pulled off his pack, thinking to light a torch, but noticed the halfling's eyes glowing with the telltale red of infravision.

"I do prefer the light of a torch," Regis commented when the drow started to replace the pack without striking a light.

"We should save them," Drizzt answered. "We do not know how long we will have to remain in the new areas."

Regis shrugged; Drizzt took amusement in the fact that the halfling was already holding his small but undeniably effective mace, though they hadn't yet passed beyond the secured regions of the complex.

They took a short break, then started on again, putting another two or three miles behind them. Predictably, Regis soon began to complain about his sore feet and quieted only when they heard the sound of dwarven chatter somewhere up ahead.

A few twists and turns in the tunnel took them to a narrow stair that emptied into the final guardroom of this section. Four dwarves were in there, playing bones (grumbling with every throw) and paying little attention to the great, iron-barred stone door that sealed off the new areas.

"Well met," Drizzt said, interrupting the game.

"We got some kin down there," a stocky, brown-bearded dwarf replied as soon as he noticed Drizzt. "King Bruenor sending yerselves to find them?"

"Lucky us," Regis remarked.

Drizzt nodded. "We are to remind the missing dwarves that the mithril will be gotten in proper time," he said, trying to keep this encounter lighthearted, wanting to not alarm the dwarven guards that he believed there might be trouble in the new section.

Two of the dwarves took up their weapons while the other two walked over to remove the heavy iron bar that locked the door.

"Well, when ye're ready to come back out, tap the door three, then two," the brown-bearded dwarf explained. "We're not for opening it unless the signal's right!"

"Three, then two," Drizzt agreed.

The bar came off and the door fell inward with a great sucking sound. Nothing but the blackness of an empty tunnel was apparent beyond it.

"Easy, my little friend," Drizzt said, seeing the sudden gleam in the halfling's eye. They had been down here just a couple of weeks before, for the goblin fight, but, though they had seen that threat eradicated, the hushed tunnel seemed no less imposing.

"Hurry ye up," the brown-bearded dwarf said to them, obviously not happy with keeping the door open.

Drizzt lighted a torch, and led the way into the gloom, Regis close on his heels. The dwarves shut the door immediately when the companions were clear, and Drizzt and Regis heard the clanging of the iron bar being set back into place.

Drizzt handed Regis the torch and drew out his scimitars, Twinkle glowing a soft blue. "We should get done as quickly as we can," the drow reasoned. "Bring in Guenhwyvar and let the cat lead us."

Regis set down his mace and torch and fumbled around to find the onyx figurine. He placed it on the ground before him and took up his other items, then looked to Drizzt, who had moved a few steps farther down the tunnel.

"You may call the panther," Drizzt said, somewhat surprised, when he looked back to see the halfling waiting for him, a curious sight given Regis's close relationship with the great cat. Guenhwyvar was a magical entity, a denizen of the Astral Plane, that came to the summons of the figurine's possessor. Bruenor always had been a bit shy around the cat (dwarves didn't generally like magic other than the magic of fine weapons), but Regis and Guenhwyvar had been close friends. Guenhwyvar had even saved the halfling's life once by taking Regis along on an astral ride, getting the halfling out of a collapsing tower in the process.

Now, though, Regis stood above the figurine, torch and mace in hand, apparently unsure of how to proceed.

Drizzt walked back the few steps to join his diminutive friend. "What is the problem?" he asked.

"I . . . I just think you should call Guenhwyvar," the halfling replied. "It's your panther, after all, and yours is the voice Guenhwyvar knows best."

"Guenhwyvar would come to your call," Drizzt assured Regis, patting the halfling's shoulder. Not wanting to delay and argue the point, though, the drow softly called out the panther's name. A few seconds later, a grayish mist, seeming darker in the dim light, gathered about the figurine and gradually shaped itself into the panther form. The mist subtly transformed, became something more substantial, then it was gone, leaving in its stead Guenhwyvar's muscled feline form. The panther's ears went flat immediately—Regis took a prudent step back— then Drizzt grabbed Guenhwyvar by a jowl and gave a playful shake.

"Some dwarves are missing," Drizzt explained to the cat, and Regis knew that Guenhwyvar understood every word.

"Find their scent, my friend. Lead me to them."

Guenhwyvar spent a long moment studying the immediate area, turned back to stare at Regis for a bit, then issued a low growl.

"Go on," Drizzt bade the cat, and the sleek muscles flexed, propelling Guenhwyvar easily and in perfect silence into the darkness beyond the torchlight.

Drizzt and Regis followed at an easy pace, the drow confident that the panther would not outdistance them and Regis glancing nervously, this way and that, with every passing inch. They came through the intersection with the giant ettin's bones, Bruenor's first kill, a short while later, and Guenhwyvar joined them once more when they entered the low cavern where the main goblin force had been routed.

Little evidence remained of that recent battle, save the many bloodstains and a diminishing pile of goblin bodies in the center of the place. Ten-foot-long wormlike creatures swarmed all about these, long tendrils feeling the way as they feasted on the bloated corpses.

"Keep close," Drizzt warned, and Regis didn't have to be told twice. "Those are carrion crawlers," the drow ranger explained, "the vultures of the Underdark. With food so readily available, they likely will leave us alone, but they are dangerous foes. A sting from their tendrils can steal the strength from your limbs."

"Do you think the dwarves got too close to them?" Regis asked, squinting in the dim light to see if he could make out any nongoblin bodies among the pile.

Drizzt shook his head. "The dwarves know the crawlers well," he explained. "They welcome the beasts to be rid of the stench of goblin corpses. I would hardly expect seven veteran dwarves to be taken down by crawlers."

Drizzt started down from the angled platform, but the halfling grabbed his cloak to stop him. "There's a dead ettin under here," Regis explained. "Lots of meat."

Drizzt cocked his head curiously as he regarded the quick-thinking halfling, the drow thinking that maybe Bruenor had been wise in sending the little one along. They skirted the lip of the raised stone and came down far to the side. Sure enough, several carrion crawlers worked over the huge ettin body; Drizzt's original course would have taken him dangerously close to the beasts.

They were into the empty tunnels again in a few seconds, Guenhwyvar drifting silently into the darkness to lead them.

The torch soon burned low; Regis shook his head when Drizzt reached for another one, reminding Drizzt that they should save their light sources.

They went on, in the quiet, in the dark, with only the soft glow of Twinkle to mark their passing. To the drow it seemed like old times, traversing the Underdark with his feline companion, his senses heightened in the knowledge that danger might well lurk around any bend.

* * * * *

"The disk is warm?" Jarlaxle asked, seeing Vierna's pleasurable expression as she rubbed her delicate fingers across the metallic surface. She sat atop the drider, her mount for the journey, Dinin's bloated face expressionless and unblinking.

"My brother is not far," the priestess replied, her eyes closed in concentration.

The mercenary leaned against the wall, peering down the long tunnel filled with flattened goblin corpses. All about him dark forms, his quiet band of killers, slipped silently about their way.

"Can we know that Drizzt is here at all?" the mercenary dared to ask, though he was not anxious to dispel volatile Vierna's anticipation—especially not with the priestess sitting atop so poignant a reminder of her wrath.

"He is here," Vierna replied calmly.

97

"And you are sure our friend will not kill him before we find him?" the mercenary asked.

"We can trust this ally," Vierna replied calmly, her tone a relief to the edgy mercenary leader. "Lloth has assured me."

So ends any debate, Jarlaxle told himself, though he hardly felt secure in trusting any human, particularly the wicked one to whom Vierna had led him. He looked back to the tunnel, back to the shifting forms as the mercenary band cautiously made its way.

What Jarlaxle did trust was his soldiers, drow-for-drow as fine a force as any in the dark elf world. If Drizzt Do'Urden was indeed wandering about these tunnels, the skilled killers of Bregan D'aerthe would get him.

"Should I dispatch the Baenre force?" the mercenary asked Vierna.

Vierna considered the words for a moment, then shook her head, her indecision revealing to Jarlaxle that she was not as certain of her brother's whereabouts as she claimed. "Keep them close a while longer," she instructed. "When we have found my brother, they will serve to cover our departure."

Jarlaxle was all too glad to comply. Even if Drizzt was down here, as Vierna believed, they did not know how many of his friends might have accompanied him. With fifty drow soldiers about them, the mercenary was not too worried.

He did wonder, though, how Triel Baenre might welcome the news that her soldiers, even if they were only males, had been used as no more than fodder.

* * * * *

"These tunnels are endless," Regis moaned after two more hours of unremarkable twists and turns in the goblin-enhanced natural passageways. Drizzt allowed a break for supper—even lit a torch—and the two friends sat in a small natural chamber on a flat rock, surrounded by leering stalactites and monsterlike mounds of piled stone.

Drizzt understood just how unintentionally perceptive the halfling's words might prove. They were far underground, several miles, and the caverns continued aimlessly, connecting chambers large and small and meeting with dozens of side passages. Regis had been in the dwarven mines before, but he had never entered that next lower realm, the dreaded Underdark, wherein lived the drow elves, wherein Drizzt Do'Urden had been born.

The stifling air and inevitable realizations of thousands of tons of rock over his head inevitably led the dark elf to thoughts of his past life, of the days when he had lived in Menzoberranzan, or walked with Guenhwyvar in the seemingly endless tunnels of Toril's subterranean world.

"We'll get lost, just like the dwarves," Regis grumbled, munching a biscuit. He took tiny bites and chewed them a thousand times to savor each precious crumb.

Drizzt's smile didn't seem to comfort him, but the ranger was confident that he and, more particularly, Guenhwyvar knew exactly where they were, making a systematic circuit with the chamber of the main goblin battle as their hub. He pointed behind Regis, his motion prompting the halfling to half-turn in his rocky seat.

"If we went back through that tunnel and branched at the first right-hand passage, we would come, in a matter of minutes, to the large chamber where Bruenor defeated the goblins," Drizzt explained. "We were not so far from this spot when we met Cobble."

"Seems like farther, that's all," Regis mumbled under his breath.

Drizzt did not press the point, glad to have Regis along, even if the halfling was in a particularly grumpy mood. Drizzt hadn't seen much of Regis in the weeks since he had returned to Mithril Hall; no one had, actually, except perhaps the dwarven cooking staff in the communal dining halls.

"Why have you returned?" Drizzt asked suddenly, his question making Regis choke on a piece of biscuit. The halfling stared at him incredulously.

"We are glad to have you back," Drizzt continued, clarifying the intentions of his rather blunt question. "And certainly all of us are hoping you will stay here for a long time to come. But, why, my friend?"

"The wedding . . ." Regis stammered.

"A fine reason, but hardly the only one," Drizzt replied with a knowing smile. "When last we saw you, you were a guildmaster and all of Calimport was yours for the taking."

Regis looked away, ran his fingers through his curly brown hair, fiddled with several rings, and slipped his hand down to tug at his one dangling earring.

"That is the life the Regis I know always desired," Drizzt remarked.

"Then maybe you really didn't understand Regis," the halfling replied.

"Perhaps," Drizzt admitted, "but there is more to it than that. I know you well enough to understand that you would go to great lengths to avoid a fight. Yet, when the goblin battle came, you remained beside me."

"Where safer than with Drizzt Do'Urden?"

"In the higher complex, in the dining halls," the drow replied without hesitation. Drizzt's smile was one of friendship; the luster in his lavender eyes showed no animosity for the halfling, whatever falsehoods Regis might be playing. "Whatever the reason you have come, be sure that we are all glad you are here," Drizzt said honestly. "Bruenor more than any, perhaps. But if you have found some trouble, some danger, you would be well advised to state it openly, that we might battle it together. We are your friends and will stand beside you, without blame, against whatever odds we are offered. By my experience, those odds are always better when I know the enemy."

"I lost the guild," Regis admitted, "just two weeks after you left Calimport."

The news did not surprise the drow.

"Artemis Entreri," Regis said grimly, lifting his cherubic face to stare at Drizzt directly, studying the drow's every movement.

"Entreri took the guild?" Drizzt asked.

Regis nodded. "He didn't have such a hard time of that. His network reached to my most trusted colleagues."

"You should have expected as much from the assassin," Drizzt replied, and he gave a small laugh, which made Regis's eyes widen with apparent surprise.

"You find this funny?"

"The guild is better in Entreri's hands," Drizzt replied, to the halfling's continued surprise. "He is suited for the double-dealing ways of miserable Calimport."

"I thought you . . ." Regis began. "I mean, don't you want to go and . . ."

"Kill Entreri?" Drizzt asked with a soft chuckle. "My battle with the assassin is ended," he added when Regis's eager nod confirmed his guess.

"Entreri might not think so," Regis said grimly.

Drizzt shrugged—and noticed that his casual attitude seemed to bother the halfling more than a little. "As long as Entreri remains in the southland, he is of no concern to me." Drizzt knew that Regis didn't expect Entreri to remain in the south. Perhaps that was why Regis would not stay in the upper levels during the goblin fight, Drizzt thought. Perhaps Regis feared that Entreri might sneak into Mithril Hall. If the assassin found both Drizzt and Regis, he probably would go after Drizzt first.

"You hurt him, you know," Regis went on, "in your fight, I mean. He's not the type to forgive something like that."

Drizzt's look became suddenly grave; Regis shifted back, putting more distance between himself and the fires in the drow's lavender eyes. "Do you believe he has followed you north?" Drizzt asked bluntly.

Regis shook his head emphatically. "I arranged things so it would look like I had been killed," he explained. "Besides, Entreri knows where Mithril Hall is. He could find you without having to follow me here.

"But he won't," Regis went on. "From all I have heard, he has lost the use of one arm, and lost an eye as well. He would hardly be your fighting equal anymore."

"It was the loss of his heart that stole his fighting ability," Drizzt remarked, more to himself than to Regis. Despite his casual attitude, Drizzt could not easily dismiss his long-standing rivalry with the deadly assassin. Entreri was his opposite in many ways, passionless and amoral, but in fighting ability he had proven to be Drizzt's equal—almost. Entreri's philosophy maintained that a true warrior be a heartless thing, a pure, efficient killer. Drizzt's beliefs went in exactly the opposite direction. To the drow, who had grown up among so many warriors holding similar ideals as the assassin, the passion of righteousness enhanced a warrior's prowess. Drizzt's father, Zaknafein, was unequaled in Menzo–berranzan because his swords rang out for justice, because he fought with the sincere belief that his battles were morally justified.

"Do not doubt that he will ever hate you," Regis remarked grimly, stealing Drizzt's private contemplations.

Drizzt noted a sparkle in the halfling's eye and took it as an indication of Regis's burning hatred of Entreri. Did Regis want, expect, him to go back to Calimport and finish his war with Entreri? the drow wondered. Did Regis expect Drizzt to deliver the thieves' guild back to him, deposing its assassin leader?

"He hates me because my way of life shows his to be an empty lie," Drizzt remarked firmly, somewhat coldly. The drow would not go back to Calimport, would not go back to do battle with Artemis Entreri, for any reason. To do so would put him on the assassin's moral level, something the drow, who had turned his back on his own amoral people, feared more than anything in all the world.

Regis looked away, apparently catching on to Drizzt's true feelings. Disappointment was obvious in his expression; the drow had to believe that Regis really did hope he would regain his precious guild at the end of Drizzt's scimitars. And Drizzt didn't really take much hope in the halfling's claims that Entreri would not come north. If the assassin, or at least agents of the assassin, would not be about, then why had Regis remained tight to Drizzt's side when they went down to fight the goblins?

"Come," the drow bade, before his mounting anger could take hold of him. "We have many more miles to cover before we break for the night. We must soon send Guenhwyvar back to the Astral Plane, and our chances of finding the dwarves are better with the panther beside us."

Regis stuffed his remaining food in his small pack, doused the torch, and fell in step behind the drow. Drizzt looked back at him often, somewhat amazed, somewhat disappointed, by the angry glow in the red dots that were the halfling's eyes.

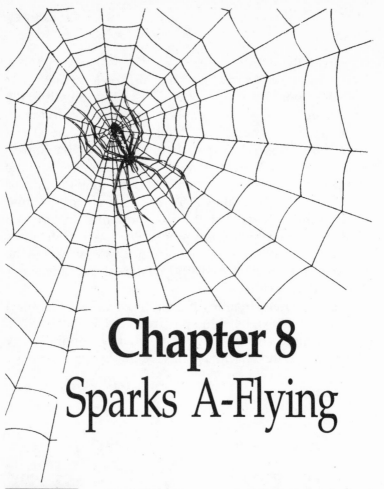

Chapter 8
Sparks A-Flying

Beads of glistening sweat rolled along the barbarian's sculpted arms; shadows of the flickering hearth drew definitive lines along his biceps and thick forearms, accentuating the enormous, corded muscles.

With astounding ease, as though he were swinging a tool made for slender nails, Wulfgar brought a twenty-pound sledge down repeatedly on a metal shaft. Bits of molten iron flew with every ringing hit and spattered the walls and floor and the thick leather apron he wore, for the barbarian had carelessly overheated the metal. Blood surged in Wulfgar's great shoulders, but he did not blink and he did not tire. He was driven by the certainty that he had to work out the demon emotions that had grabbed his heart.

He would find solace in exhaustion.

Wulfgar had not worked the forge in years, not since Bruenor had released him from servitude back in Icewind Dale, a place, a life, that seemed a million miles removed.

Wulfgar needed the iron now, needed the unthinking, instinctual pounding, the physical duress to overrule the confusing jumble of emotions that would not let him rest. The rhythmic banging forced his thoughts into a straight line pattern; he allowed himself to consider only a single complete thought between each interrupting bang.

He wanted to resolve so many things this day, mostly to remind himself of those qualities that initially had drawn him to his soon-to-be bride. At each interval, though, the same image flashed to him: Aegis-fang twirling dangerously close to Drizzt's head.

He had tried to kill his dearest friend.

With suddenly renewed vigor, he sent the sledge pounding home on the metal and again sent lines of sparks flying throughout the small, private chamber.

What in the Nine Hells was happening to him?

Again, the sparks flew wildly.

How many times had Drizzt Do'Urden saved him? How empty would his life have been without his ebon-skinned friend?

He grunted as the hammer hit home.

But the drow had kissed Catti-brie—Wulfgar's Catti-brie!—outside Mithril Hall on the day of his return!

Wulfgar's breathing came in labored gasps, but his arm pumped fiercely, playing his fury through the smithy hammer. His eyes were closed as tightly as the hand that clenched the hammer; his muscles swelled with the strain.

"That one for throwin' around corners?" he heard a dwarf's voice ask.

Wulfgar's eyes popped open and he spun about to see one of Bruenor's kinfolk shuffling past the partly opened doorway, the dwarf's laughter echoing as he made his way along the stone-worked corridor. When the barbarian looked back to his work, he understood the dwarf's mirth, for the metal spear he had been shaping was now badly bowed in the middle from the too-hard slams on the overheated metal.

Wulfgar tossed the ruined shaft aside and let the hammer drop to the stone floor.

"Why did you do it to me?" he asked aloud, though, of course, Drizzt was too far away to hear him. His mind held a conjured image of Drizzt and his beloved Catti-brie embraced in a deep kiss, an image the beleaguered Wulfgar could not let go, even though he had not actually seen the two in the act.

He wiped a hand across his sweaty brow, leaving a line of soot on his forehead, and slumped to a seat on the edge of a stone table. He hadn't expected things to become this complicated, hadn't anticipated Catti-brie's outrageous behavior. He thought of the first time he had seen his love, when she was barely more than a girl, skipping along the tunnels of the dwarven complex in Icewind Dale—carelessly skipping, as though all the ever-present dangers of that harsh region, and all the memories of the recent war against Wulfgar's people simply fell away from her delicate shoulders, bounced off her as surely as did her lustrous auburn tresses.

It didn't take young Wulfgar long to understand that Catti-brie had captured his heart with that carefree dance. He had never met a woman like her; in his male-dominated tribe, women were virtual slaves, cowering to the often unreasonable demands of the menfolk. Barbarian women did not dare to question their men, certainly did not embarrass them, as Catti-brie had done to Wulfgar when he had insisted that she not accompany the force sent to parley with the goblin tribe.

Wulfgar was wise enough now to admit his own shortcomings, and he felt a fool for the way he had spoken to Catti-brie. Still, there remained in the barbarian a need for a woman—a wife—that he could protect, a wife that would allow him his rightful place as a man.

Things had become so very complicated, and then, just to make matters worse, Catti-brie, his Catti-brie, had shared a kiss with Drizzt Do'Urden!

Wulfgar bounced up from his seat and rushed to retrieve the hammer, knowing that he would spend many more hours at the forge, many more hours transferring the rage from his knotted muscles to the metal. For the metal had yielded to him as Catti-brie would not, had complied to the undeniable call of his heavy hammer.

Wulfgar sent the hammer down with all his might, and a newly heated metal bar shuddered with the impact. *Pong*! Sparks whipped across Wulfgar's high cheekbones, one nipping at the edge of his eye.

Blood surging, muscles corded, Wulfgar felt no pain.

* * * * *

"Put up the torch," the drow whispered.

"Light will alert our enemies," Regis argued in similarly hushed tones.

They heard a growl, low and echoing, down the corridor.

"The torch," Drizzt instructed, handing Regis a small tinderbox. "Wait here with the light. Guenhwyvar and I will circle about."

"Now I am bait?" the halfling asked.

Drizzt, his senses tuned outward for signs of danger, did not hear the question. One scimitar drawn, Twinkle and its telltale glow waiting poised in its sheath, he slipped silently ahead and disappeared into the gloom.

Regis, still grumbling, struck flint to steel and soon had the torch blazing. Drizzt was out of sight.

A growl spun the halfling about, mace at the ready, but it was only Guenhwyvar, ever alert, doubling back down a side passage. The panther padded past the halfling, following Drizzt's course, and Regis quickly shuffled behind, though he could not hope to keep pace with the beast.

He was alone again in seconds, his torch casting elongated, ominous shadows along the uneven walls. His back to the stone, Regis inched on, as quiet as death.

The black mouth of a side passage loomed just a few feet away. The halfling continued walking, holding the torch straight out behind him, his mace leading the way. He sensed a presence around that corner, something inching up to the edge at him from the other direction.

Regis carefully laid the torch on the stone and brought his mace in close to his chest, gently sliding his feet to perfectly balance his weight.

He went around the corner in a blinding rush, chopping with the mace. Something blue flashed to intercept; there came the ring of metal on metal. Regis instantly brought his weapon back and sent it whipping in sidelong, lower.

Again came the distinctive ring of a parry.

Out came the mace, and back in, deftly along the same course. The halfling's skilled adversary was not fooled, though, and the blocking blade was still in place.

"Regis!"

The mace twirled above the halfling's head, ready to dart ahead, but Regis swung it down at arm's length instead, suddenly recognizing the voice.

"I told you to remain back there with the light," Drizzt scolded him, stepping out of the shadow. "You are fortunate I did not kill you."

"Or that I did not kill you," Regis replied without missing a beat, and his calm, cold tone made Drizzt's face contort with surprise. "Have you found anything?" the halfling asked.

Drizzt shook his head. "We are close," he replied quietly. "Both Guenhwyvar and I are certain of that."

Regis walked over and picked up his torch, then tucked his mace into his belt, within easy reach.

Guenhwyvar's sudden growl echoed at them from farther down the long corridor, launching them both into a run. "Don't leave me behind!" Regis demanded, and he grabbed hold of Drizzt's cloak and would not let go, his furry feet skipping, jumping, even skidding along as he tried to keep pace.

Drizzt slowed when Guenhwyvar's yellow-green, glassy eyes reflected back at him from just beyond the leading edge of the torchlight, at a corner where the passageway turned sharply.

"I think we found the dwarves," Regis muttered grimly. He handed Drizzt the torch and let go of the cloak, following the drow up to the bend.

Drizzt peeked around—Regis saw him wince—then brought the torch into the open, casting light on the dreadful scene.

They had indeed found the missing dwarves, sliced and slaughtered, some lying, some propped against the walls at irregular intervals along a short expanse of worked stone corridor.

* * * * *

"If ye're not for wearing the apron, then don't ye be wearing it!" Bruenor said in frustration. Catti-brie nodded, finally hearing the concession she had wanted from the beginning.

"But, me king, . . ." protested Cobble, the only other one in the private chamber with Bruenor and Catti-brie. Both he and Bruenor sported severe holy water headaches.

"Bah!" the dwarf king snorted to silence the good-intentioned cleric. "Ye're not knowing me girl as well as meself. If she's saying she won't be wearing it, then all the giants o' the Spine of the World couldn't be changing her mind."

"Bah yerself!" came an unexpected call from outside the

109

room, followed by a tremendous knock. "I know ye're in there, Bruenor Battlehammer, who calls himself king o' Mithril Hall! Now be opening yer door and meet your better!"

"Do we know that voice?" asked Cobble, he and Bruenor exchanging confused glances.

"Open it, says me!" came another cry, followed by a sharp rap. Wood splintered as a glove nail, a large spike set into the face of a specially constructed metal gauntlet, wedged itself through the thick door.

"Aw, sandstone," came a quieter call.

Bruenor and Cobble looked to each other in disbelief. "No," they said in unison, wagging their heads back and forth.

"What is it?" Catti-brie asked, growing impatient.

"It cannot be," Cobble replied, and it seemed to the young woman that he hoped with all his heart that his words were true.

A grunt signaled that the creature beyond the door had finally extracted his spike.

"What is it?" Catti-brie demanded of her father, her hands planted squarely on her hips.

The door burst open, and there stood the most curious-looking dwarf Catti-brie had ever seen. He wore a spiked steel gauntlet, open-fingered, on each hand, had similar spikes protruding from his elbows, knees, and the toes of his heavy boots, and wore armor (custom-fitted to his short, barrellike form) of parallel, horizontal metal ridges half an inch apart and ringing his body from neck to midthigh and his arms from shoulder to forearm. His gray helmet was open-faced, with thick leather straps disappearing under his monstrous black beard, and sported a gleaming spike atop it, nearly half again as tall as the four-foot-high dwarf.

"It," Bruenor answered, his tone reflecting his obvious disdain, "is a battlerager."

"Not just 'a battlerager,' " the curious, black-bearded dwarf put in. "*The* battlerager! The most wild battlerager!" He walked toward Catti-brie and smiled widely with his hand extended toward her. His armor, with every movement, issued grating, scraping noises that made the young woman's hair stand straight up on the back of her neck.

"Thibbledorf Pwent at yer service, me good lady!" the dwarf introduced himself grandly. "First fighter o' Mithril Hall. Yerself must be this Catti-brie I've heared so much tell of back in Adbar. Bruenor's human daughter, so they told me, though still I'm a bit shaken at seeing any Battlehammer woman without a beard to tickle her toes!"

The smell of the creature nearly overwhelmed Catti-brie. Had he taken that armor off anytime this century? she had to wonder. "I'll try to grow one," she promised.

"See that ye do! See that ye do!" Thibbledorf hooted, and he hopped over to stand before Bruenor, the noise of his armor scraping at the marrow of Catti-brie's bones.

"Me king!" Thibbledorf bellowed. He fell to a bow—and nearly halved Bruenor's long, pointy nose with his helmet spike as he did.

"What in the Nine Hells is yerself doing here?" Bruenor demanded.

"Alive, anyway," Cobble added, then he returned Bruenor's incredulous stare with a helpless shrug.

"It was me belief that ye fell when the dragon Shimmergloom took the lower halls," Bruenor went on.

"His breath was death!" Thibbledorf shouted.

Look who's talking, Catti-brie thought, but she kept silent.

Pwent roared on, dramatically waving his arms about and turning a spin on the floor, his eyes staring at nothing in particular, as though he was recalling a scene from his distant past. "Evil breath. A deep blackness that fell over me and stole the strength from me bones.

"But I got out and got away!" Thibbledorf cried suddenly, spinning at Catti-brie, one stubby finger pointing her way. "Out a secret door in the lower tunnels. Even the likes o' that dragon couldn't stop the Pwent!"

"We held the halls for two more days afore Shimmergloom's minions drove us into Keeper's Dale," Bruenor put in. "I heared no words o' yer return to fight beside me father and his father, the then king o' Mithril Hall."

"It was a week afore I got me strength back and got back around the mountain passes to the western door," Pwent explained. "By then the halls were lost.

"Sometime later," Pwent continued, parting his impossibly thick beard with one of his glove nails, "I heared that a bunch of the younger folk, yerself included, had gone to the west. Some said ye were to work the mines o' Mirabar, but when I got there, I heared not a word."

"Two hunnerd years!" Bruenor growled in Pwent's face, stealing his seemingly perpetual smile. "Ye had two hunnerd years to find us, but not once did we hear a word that ye was even alive."

"I came back to the east," Pwent explained easily. "Been living—living well, doing mercenary work, mostly—in Sundabar and for King Harbromme of Citadel Adbar. It was back there, three weeks past—I'd been off to the south for some time, ye see—that I first heared o' yer return, that a Battlehammer had taken back the halls!

"So here I be, me king," he said, dipping to one knee. "Point me at yer enemies." He gave Catti-brie a garish wink and poked a dirty, stubby finger toward the tip of his helmet spike.

"Most wild?" Bruenor asked, somewhat derisively.

"Always been," Thibbledorf replied.

"I'll call ye an escort," Bruenor said, "so ye can get yerself a bath and a meal."

"I'll take the meal," Pwent replied. "Keep yer bath and yer escort. I know me way around these old halls as well as yerself, Bruenor Battlehammer. Better, I say, since ye was but a stubble-chinned dwarfling when we was pushed out." He put his hand out to pinch Bruenor's chin and had it promptly slapped away. His shrieking laughter like a hawk's cry, his armor squealing like talons on slate, the battlerager stomped away.

"Pleasant sort," Catti-brie remarked.

"Pwent alive," Cobble mused, and Catti-brie could not tell if that was good news or not.

"Ye've never once mentioned that one," Catti-brie said to Bruenor.

"Trust me, girl," Bruenor replied. "That one's not worth mentioning."

* * * * *

Exhausted, the barbarian fell into his cot and sought some needed sleep. He felt the dream returning before he had even closed his eyes. He bolted upright, not wanting to see again the images of his Catti-brie entwined with the likes of Drizzt Do'Urden.

They came to him anyway.

He saw a thousand thousand sparkles, a million reflected fires, spiraling downward, inviting him along.

Wulfgar growled defiantly and tried to stand. It took him several moments to realize that the attempt had been futile, that he was still sitting on his cot, and that he was descending, following the undeniable trail of glittering sparkles down to the images.

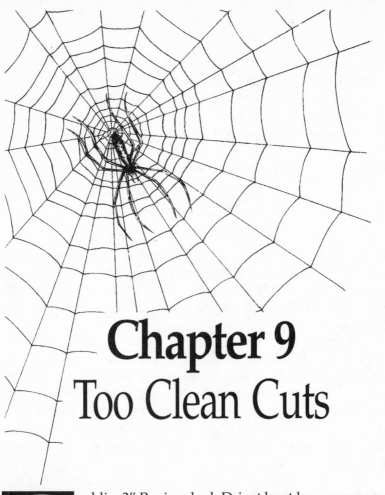

Chapter 9
Too Clean Cuts

oblins?" Regis asked. Drizzt bent low over one of the dwarven corpses, shaking his head even before he got close enough to fully inspect the wounds. Goblins would not likely have left the dwarves in this condition, the drow ranger knew, certainly not with all of their valuable armor and equipment intact. Besides, goblins never recovered the bodies of their own dead, yet the only kills in this corridor were dwarves. No matter how large the goblin force, and how great their advantage of surprise, Drizzt did not think it likely that they could have killed this sturdy party

114

without a single loss.

The wounds on the nearest dwarf seemed to confirm the drow's instincts. Slender and precise, these cuts were not made by crude, jagged goblin weapons. A fine edge, razor sharp and probably enchanted, had sliced this particular dwarf's throat. The line was barely visible, even after Drizzt had wiped away the blood, but ultimately deadly.

"What killed them?" Regis asked, growing impatient. He shifted about from foot to foot, moving the torch alternately from one hand to the other.

Drizzt's mind refused to accept the obvious conclusion. How many times in his years in Menzoberranzan, fighting beside his drow kin, had Drizzt Do'Urden witnessed wounds similar to these? No other race in all the Realms, with the possible exception of the surface elves, used weapons so finely edged.

"What killed them?" Regis asked again, a notable tremor in his voice.

Drizzt shook his white locks. "I do not know," he replied honestly. He moved to the next body, this one slumped, half-sitting against the wall. Despite the abundance of blood, the only wound the drow found was a single clean, diagonal slash along the right side of the unfortunate dwarf's throat, a cut paper thin but very deep.

"It could be Duergar," Drizzt said to Regis, referring to the evil race of gray dwarves. The thought made sense, since Duergar had served as minions to Shimmergloom the dragon, and had inhabited these halls until just a few months before, when Bruenor's forces had chased them out. Still, Drizzt knew that his reasoning was based more in hope than in truth. Greedy Duergar would have stripped these victims clean, particularly of the valuable mining equipment, and Duergar, like mountain dwarves, favored heavier weapons, such as the battle-axe. No such weapon had hit this dwarf.

"You don't believe that," Regis said behind him. Drizzt

didn't turn to regard the halfling; staying in a crouch, he shuffled over to the next unfortunate dwarf.

Regis's voice fell away behind him, but Drizzt heard the halfling's last statement as clearly as he had ever heard anything in his life.

"You think Entreri did it."

Drizzt did not think that, did not think that any lone warrior, however skilled, could possibly have done such a complete and precise job. He glanced back at Regis, standing impassively under his upheld torch, his eyes searching Drizzt for some clue of a reaction. Drizzt thought the halfling's reasoning curious indeed, and the only explanation he could think of was that Regis was terribly frightened that Entreri had followed him out of Calimport.

Drizzt shook his head and turned back to his investigation. On the body of the third dwarf he found a clue that narrowed the list of potential killers to one race.

A tiny dart protruded from the body's side, under its cloak. Drizzt had to take a steadying breath before he mustered the nerve to pull it out, for he recognized it, and it explained the ease with which these toughened dwarves had been slaughtered. The quarrel, made for a hand-held crossbow, undoubtedly had been coated with sleep poison and was a favored missile of dark elves.

Drizzt came up from his low crouch; his scimitars leaped into his slender hands. "We must leave this place," he whispered harshly.

"What is it?" Regis asked.

Drizzt, his keen senses attuned to the darkness farther along the corridor, did not answer.

From somewhere back behind the halfling, Guenhwyvar issued a low growl.

Drizzt eased one foot behind him and slid slowly backward, somehow understanding that any abrupt movement would trigger an attack. Dark elves in Mithril Hall! Of all the horrors

116

Drizzt could think of—and in Faerun, these were countless—not one came near to the disaster of the drow.

"Which way?" Regis whispered.

Twinkle's blue light seemed to flare.

"Go!" Drizzt cried, understanding the scimitar's warning. He spun about and saw Regis for just a moment, then the halfling disappeared under a ball of conjured darkness, the magic snuffing out the light of the halfling's torch in the blink of an eye.

Drizzt rolled to the side of the corridor and spun back around behind the propped body of a dead dwarf. He closed his eyes, forcing them into the infrared spectrum, and felt the dwarf's body jerk slightly, once and then again. Drizzt knew it had been hit with quarrels.

A black streak emerged from the globe of darkness behind him; the corridor brightened just a bit as Regis apparently went out the back side of the darkened area, his torch shedding some light around the edge of the unyielding globe.

The halfling did not cry out, though. This surprised Drizzt and made him fear that Regis had been taken.

Guenhwyvar padded by him and darted left, then right. A poison-coated quarrel skipped off the stone floor, inches from the panther's fast-moving paws. Another struck Guenhwyvar with a thud, but the cat hardly slowed.

Drizzt saw the heated outlines of two slender forms many yards away, each with a single arm extended, as though they were again taking aim with their wicked weapons. Drizzt called upon his own innate magical abilities and dropped a globe of darkness into the corridor ahead of Guenhwyvar, offering some cover. Then he, too, was up and running, following the cat, hoping that Regis somehow had escaped.

He went into his own area of darkness without slowing, sure-footed, remembering the layout of the corridor perfectly and deftly skipping over yet another dwarven body. When he emerged, Drizzt noticed the black mouth of a side passage to his left. Guenhwyvar had flown right past it, and now was bearing down on the two drow forms, but Drizzt, trained in the tactics of the dark elves, knew in his heart that the side passage could not be clear.

He heard a scuttling noise, as of many hard-edged legs, and then he fell back, stunned and afraid, as an eight-legged monstrosity, half drow and half arachnid, clambered around the bend, its legs catching hold with equal ease on both floor and wall. Twin axes waved ominously in its hands, which once had been the delicate hands of a drow.

In all the wide world, there was nothing more repulsive to any dark elf, Drizzt Do'Urden included, than a drider.

Guenhwyvar's roar, accompanied by the sounds of several clicking crossbows, brought Drizzt back to his senses in time to deflect the drider's first attack. The monster came straight in with its front legs raised and kicking—to keep Drizzt off balance—and launched its axes in a quick double chop at Drizzt's head.

Drizzt spun back out of range of the legs in time to avoid the slicing axes, but instead of continuing his retreat, he hooked an arm on one spidery leg and rolled around it, rushing back in. Twinkle whipped across, blasting aside a second leg and giving Drizzt enough of an opening to slide down to his knees, right under the beast.

The drider reared and hissed, both of its axes chopping at Drizzt's backside.

Drizzt's other scimitar was already in place, though, leveled horizontally in back of his vulnerable neck. It deflected one axe harmlessly wide and caught the other where its head met its handle. Drizzt put his feet under him and turned sideways as he rose, both his blades turning point up. With his parrying scimitar, he continued the movement, twisting the trapped axe right over in the drider's hand, then tugging it free. With Twinkle he thrust straight up, finding a ridge in the creature's armored exoskeleton and sinking the blade deep into spidery

118

flesh. Hot fluids gushed over Drizzt's arm; the drider shrieked in agony and twitched violently.

Legs buffeted Drizzt from every side. He nearly lost his grip on Twinkle and had to pull the blade out to keep hold of it. Through his prison bars of spider legs Drizzt noticed more dark forms emerging from the side corridor, drow elves, he knew, each with one arm extended his way.

He spun frantically as the first one fired. His thick cloak luckily floated out behind him and caught the quarrel harmlessly in its heavy folds. When he ended his desperate maneuver, though, Drizzt found that he was half out from under the drider, and the creature had turned about enough to line him up with its remaining axe. Even worse, the second drow had him solidly targeted in crossbow sights.

The axe came down curiously—flat end leading, Drizzt noted—forcing Drizzt to parry. He expected to hear the click of a firing crossbow, but Drizzt heard instead a muffled groan as six hundred pounds of black panther buried his dark elf attacker.

Drizzt slapped the axe aside with one blade, then the other, buying himself enough time to get out the rest of the way. He came up, instinctively spinning away from the drider, just in time to get his weapons up to block a sword thrust from the closest drow enemy.

"Drop your weapons and it will go easier on you!" the drow, holding two fine swords, cried in a language that Drizzt had not heard in more than a decade, a language that sent images of beautiful, twisted, terrible Menzoberranzan flowing back into his mind. How many times had Zaknafein, his father, stood before him, similarly armed, awaiting their inevitable sparring tournament?

A growl that he was not even cognizant of escaped Drizzt's lips; he went into a series of offensive combinations that left his opponent dazzled and off balance in a split second. A scimitar came in low to the side, the second came in high, straight ahead, and the first chopped in again, angled downward at shoulder level.

The enemy drow's eyes widened as if he had suddenly realized his doom.

Guenhwyvar shot by them both, hit the drider full on, and went tumbling in a black ball of raking claws and flailing spider legs.

More dark elves were coming, Drizzt knew, from farther ahead and from the side passage. Drizzt's fury did not relent. Twinkle and his other blade worked fiercely, preventing the other drow from beginning an offensive counter.

He found an opening level with the drow's neck but had no heart for a kill. This was no goblin he faced, but a drow, one of his own race, one like Zaknafein, perhaps. Drizzt remembered a vow he had made when he had left the dark elf city. Ignoring the opening for the drow's neck, he whipped his blade low instead, banging one of his opponent's swords. Twinkle followed the attack immediately, slamming at the same sword, then Drizzt's first blade whipped back the other way, hitting the weapon on the opposite side and sending the battered thing flying away. The evil drow fell back, then came in low, hoping to counter quickly enough with his remaining sword to push Drizzt back, that he might recover his lost weapon.

A blinding backhand from Twinkle sent that remaining sword flying out wide, and Drizzt, never doubting the effectiveness of his strike, was moving forward before Twinkle ever connected.

He could have hit the drow anywhere he chose, including a dozen critical areas, but Drizzt Do'Urden recalled again the vow he had made when he had left Menzoberranzan, a promise to himself and a justification of his departure, that he would never again take the life of one of his people.

His scimitar jabbed downward, angling in above his opponent's kneecap. The evil drow howled and fell back, rolling to the stone and grasping at his torn joint.

Guenhwyvar was under the standing drider, the muscles of the panther's flank exposed from under a loose-hanging piece of the cat's black-furred skin.

"Go, Guenhwyvar!" Drizzt shouted as he ran along the wall, leaping wildly, hacking away, into the jumble of drider legs on that side. He heard the monstrosity shriek again as a scimitar blasted deep into one leg, nearly severing it, and then he tumbled free, out the back side.

Guenhwyvar took another axe hit but did not respond, did not follow Drizzt or counter the attack.

"Guenhwyvar!" Drizzt called, and the panther's head turned slowly to regard him. Drizzt understood the panther's delay when Guenhwyvar flinched several more times from continued crossbow hits.

Drizzt's instincts told him to send the panther away before any more punishment could be leveled upon it—but he did not have the figurine!

"Guenhwyvar!" he cried again, seeing many forms closing quickly from beyond the drider. Truly torn, Drizzt decided to rush back in and fight beside the panther to the bitter end.

The eight-legged creature hissed victoriously as its axe lined up for a stroke on the helpless and quivering panther's neck. Down came the blade, but it hit only insubstantial mist, and the drider's cry turned to one of frustration.

"Come on!" Drizzt heard Regis say behind him. The ranger understood then and was relieved.

But then the drider turned on him fully, and for the first time, with the torchlight returned to this area of the tunnel, Drizzt got a good look at the creature's unnervingly familiar face.

He had not the time to stop to consider it, though. He swept about, exaggerating the movement to send his cloak flying wide (and it took yet another quarrel that had been diving for his back), and rushed away.

The corridor darkened immediately, then lightened a bit,

then darkened again, as Regis went into and through the two globes of darkness. Drizzt dove to the side as soon as he went into the cover of his own globe, and he heard a quarrel skip off the stone not far away. In full stride, he caught Regis just beyond the second globe, and the two flew past the dwarven bodies, cut around the bend in the corridor, and kept on running, Drizzt leading the way.

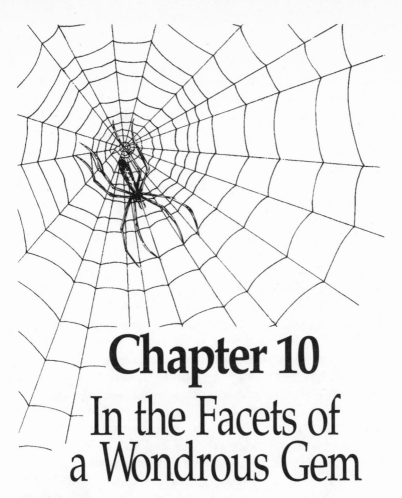

Chapter 10
In the Facets of a Wondrous Gem

Regis and Drizzt pulled up in a small side chamber, its ceiling relatively clear of the persistent stalactites common in this region of caves, and its entryway low and defensible.

"Should I put out the torch?" the halfling asked. He stood behind Drizzt as the drow crouched in front of the entryway, listening for sounds of movement in the main tunnel beyond.

Drizzt thought for a long moment, then shook his head, knowing that it really did not matter, that he and Regis had no chance of escaping these tunnels without further confrontation.

Soon after they had fled the battle, Drizzt discovered other enemies paralleling them down side corridors. He knew the dark elf hunting techniques well enough to understand that the trap would not be set with any obvious openings.

"I fight better in the light than my kin, I would guess," Drizzt reasoned.

"At least it wasn't Entreri," Regis said lightly, and Drizzt thought the reference to the assassin a strange thing indeed. Would that it were Artemis Entreri! the drow mused. At least then he and Regis would not be surrounded by a horde of drow warriors!

"You did well in dismissing Guenhwyvar," Drizzt remarked.

"Would the panther have died?" Regis asked.

Drizzt honestly did not know the answer, but he did not believe that Guenhwyvar had been in any mortal peril. He had seen the panther dragged into the stone by a creature of the elemental plane of earth and plunged into a magically created lake of pure acid. Both times the panther had returned to him and eventually all of Guenhwyvar's wounds had healed.

"If the drow and the drider had been allowed to continue," he added, "it is likely that Guenhwyvar would have needed more time to mend wounds on the Astral Plane. I do not believe the panther can be killed away from its home, however, not as long as the figurine survives." Drizzt looked back to Regis, sincere gratitude on his handsome face. "You did well in sending Guenhwyvar away, though, for certainly the panther was suffering at the hands of our enemies."

"I'm glad Guenhwyvar would not die," Regis commented as Drizzt looked back to the entryway. "It would not do to lose so valuable a magical item."

Nothing Regis had said since his return from Calimport, nothing Regis had ever said to Drizzt, seemed so very out of place. No, it went further than that, Drizzt decided as he crouched there, stunned by his halfling companion's callous remark. Guenhwyvar and Regis had been more than companions, had been friends, for many years. Regis would never refer to Guenhwyvar as a magical item.

Suddenly, it all began to make sense to the dark elf: the halfling's references to Artemis Entreri now, back with the dead dwarves, and back when they had talked of what had happened in Calimport after Drizzt's departure. Now Drizzt understood the eager way in which Regis measured his responses to remarks about the assassin.

And Drizzt understood the viciousness of his fight with Wulfgar—hadn't the barbarian mentioned that it was Regis who had told him about Drizzt's meeting with Catti-brie outside Mithril Hall?

"What else did you tell Wulfgar?" Drizzt asked, not turning around, not flinching in the least. "What else did you convince him of with that ruby pendant that hangs about your neck?"

The little mace skipped noisily across the floor beside the drow, coming to rest several feet to the front and side of him. Then came another item, a mask that Drizzt himself had worn on his journey to the southern empires, a mask that had allowed Drizzt to alter his appearance to that of a surface elf.

* * * * *

Wulfgar eyed the outrageous dwarf curiously, not quite sure what to make of this unorthodox battlerager. Bruenor had introduced Pwent to the barbarian just a minute before, and Wulfgar had gotten the distinct impression that Bruenor wasn't overly fond of the black-bearded, smelly dwarf. The dwarf king, to take his seat between Cobble and Catti-brie, had then rushed across the audience hall, leaving Wulfgar awkwardly standing by the door.

Thibbledorf Pwent, though, seemed perfectly at ease.

"You are a warrior, then?" Wulfgar asked politely, hoping to find some common ground.

Pwent's burst of laughter mocked him. "Warrior?" the

bawdy dwarf bellowed. "Ye mean, one who's for fighting with honor?"

Wulfgar shrugged, having no idea of where Pwent was leading.

"Is yerself a warrior, big boy?" Pwent asked.

Wulfgar puffed out his great chest. "I am Wulfgar, son of Beornegar, . . ." he began somberly.

"I thinked as much," Pwent called across the room to the others. "And if ye was fighting another, and he tripped on his way in and dropped his weapon, ye'd stand back and let him pick it up, knowing that ye'd win the fight anyway," Pwent reasoned.

Wulfgar shrugged, the answer obvious.

"Ye realize Pwent will surely insult the boy," Cobble, leaning on the arm of Bruenor's chair, whispered to the dwarf king.

"Gold against silver on the boy, then," Bruenor offered quietly. "Pwent's good and wild, but he ain't got the strength to handle that one."

"Not a bet I'd take," Cobble replied, "but if Wulfgar lifts a hand against that one, he's to get stung, not to doubt."

"Good," Catti-brie put in unexpectedly. Both Bruenor and Cobble turned incredulous looks on the young woman. "Wulfgar's needing some stinging," she explained with uncharacteristic callousness.

"Well, there ye have it then!" Pwent roared in Wulfgar's face, leading the barbarian across the room as he spoke. "If I was fighting anyone, if I was fighting yerself, and ye dropped yer weapon, I'd let ye bend and pick it up."

Wulfgar nodded in agreement, but jumped back as Pwent snapped his dirty fingers right under Wulfgar's nose. "And then I'd put me spike right through the top o' yer thick head!" the battlerager finished. "I ain't no damned stupid warrior, ye durned fool! I'm a battlerager, *the* battlerager, and don't ye ever forget that the Pwent plays to win!" He snapped his fingers again Wulfgar's way, then stormed past the stunned barbarian, stomping over to stand before Bruenor.

"Ye got some outrageous friends, but I'm not surprised," Pwent roared at Bruenor. He regarded Catti-brie with his broken-toothed smile. "But yer girl'd be a cute one if ye could find a way to put some hair on her chin."

"Take it as a compliment," Cobble quietly offered to Catti-brie, who only shrugged and smiled with amusement.

"Battlehammers always kept a soft spot in their hearts for them that wasn't dwarf-kin," Pwent went on, directing his remarks at Wulfgar as the tall man moved beside him. "And we let 'em be our kings anyway. Never could figure that part out."

Bruenor's knuckles whitened under the strain as he grabbed hard on the arms of his chair, trying to control himself. Catti-brie dropped a hand over his, and when he looked at her tolerant eyes, the storm quickly passed.

"Speaking of that," Pwent went on, "there's an ugly rumor making the rounds that ye've got a drow elf standing beside ye. There be any truth o' that?"

Bruenor's first reaction was one of anger—always the dwarf had been defensive about his oft-maligned drow friend.

Catti-brie spoke first, though, her words directed more to her father than to Pwent, a reminder to Bruenor that Drizzt's skin had thickened and that he could take care of himself. "Ye'll be meeting the drow soon enough," she told the battlerager. "Suren that one's a warrior to fit yer description, if ever there was one."

Pwent roared in derisive laughter, but it faded as Catti-brie continued.

"If ye came at him to start a fight, but dropped yer pointy helm, he'd pick it up for ye and put it back on yer head," she explained. "Of course, then he'd take it back off and stuff it down the back of yer pants, and give ye a few boots, just so ye'd get 'the pwent.'"

The battlerager's lips seemed to tie themselves up in a neat knot. For the first time in many days, Wulfgar seemed to approve completely of Catti-brie's reasoning, and the nod of his head, and of Bruenor's and of Cobble's, was certainly appreciative when Pwent made no move to answer.

"How long will Drizzt be gone?" the barbarian asked, to change the subject before Pwent could find his irritating voice.

"The tunnels are long," Bruenor replied.

"He will return for the ceremony?" Wulfgar asked, and there seemed to Catti-brie to be some ambivalence in his tone, an uncertainty of which answer he would prefer.

"Be sure that he will," the young woman put in evenly. "For be sure that there'll be no wedding until Drizzt is back from the tunnels." She looked at Bruenor, thoroughly squashing his protests before he ever uttered them. "And I'm not for caring if all the kings and queens of the North are kept waiting a month!"

Wulfgar seemed on the verge of an explosion, but he was wise enough to direct his mounting anger away from volatile Catti-brie. "I should have gone with him!" he growled at Bruenor. "Why did you send Regis along? What good might the halfling do if enemies are found?"

The ferocity of the lad's tone caught Bruenor off his guard.

"He's right," Catti-brie snapped in her father's ear, not that she wanted to agree with Wulfgar on any point, but that she, like Wulfgar, saw the opportunity to vent her anger openly.

Bruenor sank back in his chair, his dark eyes darting from one to the other. "Dwarves're lost, is all," he said.

"Even if that is true, what will Regis do but slow down the drow?" Catti-brie reasoned.

"He said he'd find a way to fit in!" Bruenor protested.

"Who said?" Catti-brie demanded.

"Rumblebelly!" shouted her flustered father.

"He did not even wish to go!" Wulfgar shot back.

"Did too!" Bruenor roared, leaping up from his seat and pushing the leaning Wulfgar back two steps with a sturdy forearm slam to the lad's chest. "'Twas Rumblebelly that telled me to send him along with the drow, I tell ye!"

"Regis was here with yerself when ye got the news o' the missing dwarves," Catti-brie reasoned. "Ye didn't say a thing about Regis telling ye to send him."

"He told me before that," Bruenor answered. "He telled . . ." The dwarf stopped suddenly, realizing the illogic of it all. Somehow, somewhere in the back of his mind, he remembered Regis explaining that he and Drizzt should go after the missing dwarves, but how could that be, since Bruenor had made the decision as soon as they all learned that dwarves were missing?

"Have ye been tasting the holy water again, me king?" Cobble asked respectfully but firmly.

Bruenor held his hand out, motioning for them all to be quiet while he sought his recollections. He remembered Regis's words distinctly and knew he was not imagining them, but no images accompanied the memory, no scene where he could place the halfling and thus straighten out the apparent time discrepancy.

Then an image came to Bruenor, a swirling array of shining facets, spiraling down and drawing him with them into the depths of a wondrous ruby.

"Rumblebelly told me that the dwarves'd be missing," Bruenor said slowly and clearly, his eyes closed as he forced the memory from his subconscious. "He told me I should send himself, and Drizzt, to find them, that them two alone'd get me dwarves back to the halls safely."

"Regis could not have known," Cobble reasoned, obviously doubting Bruenor's words.

"And even if he did, the little one would not have wished to go along to find them," Wulfgar added, equally doubtful. "Is this a dream—?"

"Not a dream!" Bruenor growled. "He told me . . . with that ruby of his." Bruenor's face screwed up as he tried to remember, tried to call upon his dwarven resistance to magic to fight past the stubborn mental block.

"Regis would not—" Wulfgar started to say again, but this

time it was Catti-brie, knowing the truth of her father's claims, who interrupted him.

"Unless it wasn't really Regis," she offered, and her own words made her mouth drop open with their terrible implications. The three had been through much beside Drizzt, and they all knew well that the drow had many evil and powerful enemies, one in particular who would have the wiles to create such an elaborate deception.

Wulfgar looked equally stricken, at a loss, but Bruenor was fast to react. He jumped down from the throne and blasted between Wulfgar and Pwent, nearly knocking them both from their feet. Catti-brie went right behind, Wulfgar turning to follow.

"What in the head of a goblin are them three talking about?" Pwent demanded of Cobble as the cleric, too, rambled past.

"A fight," Cobble replied, knowing well how to deflect any of Pwent's demands for a lengthy explanation.

Thibbledorf Pwent dropped to one knee and rolled his burly shoulder, punching his fist triumphantly out in front of him. "Yeeeeeah!" he cried in glee. "Suren it's good to be back serving a Battlehammer!"

* * * * *

"Are you in league with them, or is this all a terrible coincidence?" Drizzt asked dryly, still refusing to turn about and give Artemis Entreri the satisfaction of viewing his torment.

"I do not believe in coincidence," came the predictable answer.

Finally, Drizzt did turn around, to see his dreaded rival, the human assassin Artemis Entreri, standing easily at the ready, fine sword in one hand, jeweled dagger in the other. The torch, still burning, lay at his feet. The magical transformation from halfling to human had been complete, clothing included, and this fact somewhat confused Drizzt. When Drizzt had used the mask, it had done no more than alter the color of his skin and hair, and his amazement now was obvious on his face.

"You should better learn the value of magical items before you so casually toss them aside," the assassin said to him, understanding the look.

There was a note of truth in Entreri's words, apparently, but Drizzt had never regretted leaving the magical mask in Calimport. Under its protective camouflage, the dark elf had walked freely, without persecution, among the other races. But under that mask, Drizzt Do'Urden had walked in a lie.

"You could have killed me in the goblin fight, or a hundred other times since your return to Mithril Hall," Drizzt reasoned. "Why the elaborate games?"

"The sweeter comes my victory."

"You wish me to draw my weapons, to continue the fight we began in Calimport's sewers."

"Our fight began long before there, Drizzt Do'Urden," the assassin chided. He casually poked his blade at Drizzt, who neither flinched nor reached for his scimitars as the fine sword nicked him on the cheek.

"You and I," Entreri continued, and he began to circle to Drizzt's side, "have been mortal enemies from the day we learned of each other, each an insult to the other's code of fighting. I mock your principles, and you insult my discipline."

"Discipline and emptiness are not the same," Drizzt answered. "You are but a shell that knows how to use weapons. There is no substance in that."

"Good," Entreri purred, tapping Drizzt's hip with his sword. "I feel your anger, drow, though you try so desperately to hide it. Draw your weapons and let it loose. Teach me with your skills what your words cannot."

"You still do not understand," Drizzt replied calmly, his head cocked to the side and a smug, sincere grin widening on his face. "I would not presume to teach you anything. Artemis

Entreri is not worth my time."

Entreri's eyes flared in sudden rage and he leaped forward, sword high as if to strike Drizzt down.

Drizzt didn't flinch.

"Draw your weapons and let us continue our destiny," Entreri growled, falling back and leveling his sword at the drow's eye level.

"Fall on your own blade and meet the only end you'll ever deserve," Drizzt replied.

"I have your cat!" Entreri snapped. "You must fight me, or Guenhwyvar will be mine."

"You forget that we are both soon to be captured—or killed," Drizzt reasoned. "Do not underestimate the hunting skills of my people."

"Then fight for the halfling," Entreri growled. Drizzt's expression showed that the assassin had hit a nerve. "Had you forgotten about Regis?" Entreri teased. "I have not killed him, but he will die where he is, and only I know of that place. I will tell you only if you win. Fight, Drizzt Do'Urden, if for no better reason than to save the life of that miserable halfling!"

Entreri's sword made a lazy thrust at Drizzt's face again, but this time it went flying wide to the side as a scimitar leaped out and banged it away.

Entreri sent it right back in, and followed it closely with a dagger strike that nearly found a hole in Drizzt's defenses.

"I thought you had lost the use of an arm and an eye," the drow said.

"I lied," Entreri replied, stepping back and holding his weapons out wide. "Must I be punished?"

Drizzt let his scimitars answer for him, rushing in quickly and chopping repeatedly, left and right, left and right, then right a third time as his left blade twirled up above his head and came straight ahead in a blinding thrust.

Sword and dagger countering, the assassin batted aside each attack.

The fight became a dance, movements too synchronous, too much in perfect harmony for either to gain an advantage. Drizzt, knowing that time was running out for him, and more particularly for Regis, maneuvered near the low-burning torch, then stomped down on it, rolling it about and smothering the flames, stealing the light.

He thought his racial night vision would gain him the edge, but when he looked at Entreri, he saw the assassin's eyes glowing in the telltale red of infravision.

"You thought the mask gave me this ability?" Entreri reasoned. "Not true, you see. It was a gift from my dark elf associate, a mercenary, not so unlike myself." His words ended at the beginning of his charge, his sword coming high and forcing Drizzt to twist and duck to the side. Drizzt grinned in satisfaction as Twinkle came up, the scimitar ringing as it knocked Entreri's dagger aside. A subtle twist put Drizzt back on the offensive, Twinkle coming around Entreri's dagger hand and slicing at the assassin's exposed chest.

Entreri already had begun to roll, straight backward, and the blade never got close.

In the dim light of Twinkle's glow, their skin colors lost in a common gray, they seemed alike, brethren come from the same mold. Entreri approved of that perception, but Drizzt surely did not. To the renegade drow, Artemis Entreri seemed a dark mirror of his soul, an image of what he might have become had he remained in Menzoberranzan beside his amoral kin.

Drizzt's rage led him now in another series of dazzling thrusts and cunning, sweeping cuts, his curved blades weaving tight lines about each other, hitting at Entreri from a different angle with every attack.

Sword and dagger played equally well, blocking and returning cunning counters, then blocking the countering counters that the assassin seemed to anticipate with ease.

Drizzt could fight him forever, would never tire with Entreri standing opposite him. But then he felt a sting in his calf and a burning, then numbing, sensation emanating throughout his leg.

In seconds, he felt his reflexes slowing. He wanted to shout out the truth, to steal the moment of Entreri's victory, for surely the assassin, who so desired to beat Drizzt in honest combat, would not appreciate a win brought on by the poisoned quarrel of hidden allies.

Twinkle's tip dipped to the floor and Drizzt realized he was dangerously vulnerable.

Entreri fell first, similarly poisoned. Drizzt sensed the dark shapes slipping in through the low door and wondered if he had time to bash in the fallen assassin's skull before he, too, slumped to the ground.

He heard one of his own blades, then the other, clang to the floor, but he was not aware that he had dropped them. Then he was down, his eyes closed, his dimming consciousness trying to fathom the extent of this disaster, the many implications for his friends and for him.

His thoughts were not eased with the last words he heard, a voice in the drow language, a voice from somewhere in his past.

"Sleep well, my lost brother."

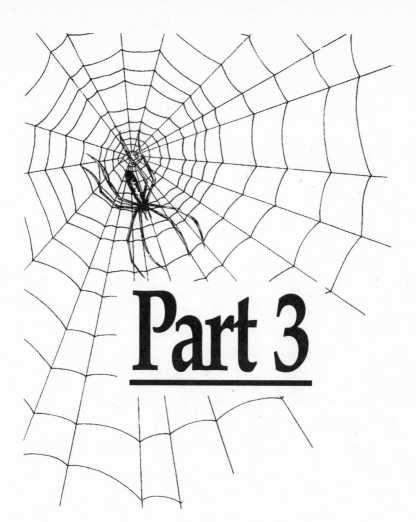

Part 3

Legacy

What dangerous paths I have trod in my life; what crooked ways these feet have walked, in my homeland, in the tunnels of the Underdark, across the surface Northland, and even in the course following my friends.

I shake my head in wonderment—is every corner of the wide world possessed of people so self-absorbed that they cannot let others cross the paths of their lives? People so filled with hatred that they must take up chase and vindicate themselves against perceived wrongs, even if those wrongs were no more than an honest defense against their own encroaching evils?

R. A. Salvatore

I left Artemis Entreri in Calimport, left him there in body and with my taste for vengeance rightfully sated. Our paths had crossed and separated, to the betterment of us both. Entreri had no practical reason to pursue me, had nothing to gain in finding me but the possible redemption of his injured pride.

What a fool he is.

He has found perfection of the body, has honed his fighting skills as perfectly as any I have known. But his need to pursue reveals his weakness. As we uncover the mysteries of the body, so too must we unravel the harmonies of the soul. But Artemis Entreri, for all his physical prowess, will never know what songs his spirit might sing. Always will he listen jealously for the harmonies of others, absorbed with bringing down anything that threatens his craven superiority.

So much like my people is he, and so much like many others I have met, of varied races: barbarian warlords whose positions of power hinge on their ability to wage war on enemies who are not enemies; dwarf kings who hoard riches beyond imagination, while when sharing but a pittance of their treasures could better the lives of all those around them and in turn allow them to take down their ever-present military defenses and throw away their consuming paranoia; haughty elves who avert their eyes to the sufferings of any who are not elven, feeling that the "lesser races" somehow brought their pains unto themselves.

I have run from these people, passed these people by, and heard countless stories of them from travelers of every known land. And I know now that I must battle them, not with blade or army, but by remaining true to what I know in my heart is the rightful course of harmony.

By the grace of the gods, I am not alone. Since Bruenor regained his throne, the neighboring peoples take hope in his promises that the dwarven treasures of Mithril Hall will better all the region. Cattibrie's devotion to her principles is no less than my own, and Wulfgar has shown his warrior people the better way of friendship, the way of harmony.

They are my armor, my hope in what is to come for me and for all the world. And as the lost chasers such as Entreri inevitably find their paths linked once more with my own, I remember Zaknafein, kindred of blood and soul. I remember Montolio and take heart that there are others who know the truth, that if I am destroyed, my ideals will not die with me. Because of the friends I have known, the honorable people I have met, I know I am no solitary hero of unique causes. I know that when I die, that which is important will live on.

This is my legacy; by the grace of the gods, I am not alone.

—Drizzt Do'Urden

139

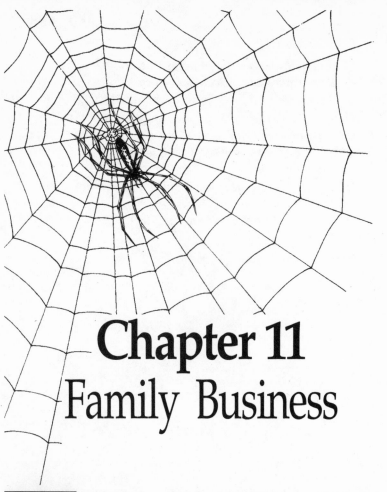

Chapter 11
Family Business

C lothing flew wildly, bric-a-brac smashed against the wall across the room, assorted weapons spun up into the air and twirled back down, some bouncing off Bruenor's back. The dwarf, top half buried in his private locker, felt none of it, didn't even grunt when, as he rose for a moment, the flat side of a throwing axe struck and dislodged his one-horned helmet.

"It's in here!" the dwarf growled stubbornly, and a half-completed suit of chain mail whipped over his shoulder, nearly clobbering the others in the room. "By Moradin, the damned thing's got to be in here!"

"What in the Nine—" Thibbledorf Pwent began, but Brue–
nor's ecstatic cry cut him short.

"I knowed it!" the red-bearded dwarf proclaimed, spinning
up and turning away from the dismantled chest. In his hand he
held a small, heart-shaped locket on a golden chain.

Catti-brie recognized it instantly as the magical gift Lady
Alustriel of Silverymoon had given Bruenor, that he might find
his friends who had gone into the southland. Inside the locket
was a tiny portrait of Drizzt, and the item was attuned to the
drow, would give its possessor general information about
Drizzt Do'Urden's whereabouts.

"This'll lead us to the elf," Bruenor proclaimed, holding the
locket up high before him.

"Then give it over, me king," said Pwent, "and let me find
this strange . . . friend o' yers."

"I can work it well enough," Bruenor growled in reply,
replacing his one-horned helm atop his head and taking up his
many-notched axe and golden shield.

"Ye're king of Mithril Hall!" Pwent protested. "Ye cannot be
running off into the danger of unknown tunnels."

Catti-brie ripped off an answer before Bruenor got the
chance.

"Shut yer mouth, battlerager," the young woman insisted.
"Me Dad'd throw the halls to the goblins afore he'd be letting
Drizzt stay in trouble!"

Cobble grabbed Pwent's shoulder (and got a nasty cut on
one finger from the many-ridged armor in the process) to
confirm the woman's observation and silently warn the wild
battlerager not to press this point.

Bruenor wouldn't have listened to any arguments anyway.
The red-bearded dwarf king, fires aglow in his dark eyes, again
blasted past Pwent and Wulfgar and led the charge out of the
room.

R. A. Salvatore

* * * * *

The image came into focus slowly, surrealistically, and by the time Drizzt Do'Urden fully awakened, he clearly recognized his sister Vierna, bending low to regard him.

"Purple eyes," the priestess said in the drow tongue.

A sense that he had played out this identical scene a hundred times in his youth nearly overwhelmed the trapped dark elf.

Vierna! The only member of his family that Drizzt had ever cared for, besides the dead Zaknafein, stood before him now.

She had been Drizzt's wean-mother, assigned to bring him, as a prince of House Do'Urden, into the dark ways of drow society. But thinking back to those distant memories, to times of which he had few, if any, recollections, Drizzt knew there was something different about Vierna, some underlying tenderness buried beneath the wicked robes of a priestess of the Spider Queen.

"How long has it been, my lost brother?" Vierna asked, still using the language of the dark elves. "Nearly two decades? And how far you have come, and yet so close again to where you began, and where you belong."

Drizzt steeled his gaze, but had no practical retort—not with his hands bound behind him and a dozen drow soldiers milling about the small chamber. Entreri was there, too, talking to a most curious dark elf who wore an outrageously plumed hat and a short, open-front vest that showed the rippling muscles of his slender stomach. The assassin had the magical mask tied to his belt, and Drizzt feared the mischief Entreri might cause if he were allowed to return to Mithril Hall.

"What will you think when you walk again into Menzoberranzan?" Vierna asked Drizzt, and though the question was again rhetorical, it drew his attention fully back to her.

"I will think as a prisoner thinks," Drizzt replied. "And when I am brought before Matr—before wicked Malice—"

"Matron Malice!" Vierna hissed.

"Malice," Drizzt repeat defiantly, and Vierna slapped him hard across the face. Several dark elves turned to regard the incident, then gave quiet chuckles and went back to their conversations.

Vierna, too, erupted in laughter, long and wild. She threw her head back, her flowing white tresses flipping back from her face.

Drizzt regarded her silently, having no idea of what had precipitated the explosive reaction.

"Matron Malice is dead, you fool!" Vierna said suddenly, snapping her head forward to within an inch of Drizzt's face.

Drizzt did not know how to react. He had just been told that his mother was dead, and he had no idea of how the information should affect him. He felt a sadness, distantly, but dismissed it, understanding that it came from a sense of never knowing a mother, not from the loss of Malice Do'Urden. As he settled back, digesting the news, Drizzt came to feel a calmness, an acceptance that brought not an ounce of grief. Malice was his natural parent, never his mother, and by all of Drizzt Do'Urden's estimation, her death was not a bad thing.

"You do not even know, do you?" Vierna laughed at him. "How long you have been gone, lost one!"

Drizzt cocked a curious eye, suspecting that some further, even greater, revelation was yet to be spoken.

"By your own actions House Do'Urden was destroyed, and you do not even know!" Vierna cackled hysterically.

"Destroyed?" Drizzt asked, surprised but, again, not overly concerned. In truth, the renegade drow felt no more for his own house than for any other in Menzoberranzan. In truth, Drizzt felt nothing at all.

"Matron Malice was charged with finding you," Vierna explained. "When she could not, when you slipped through her grasp, so, too, did the favor of Lloth."

"A pity," Drizzt interjected, his voice dripping with sar-

143

casm. Vierna hit him again, harder, but he held firm to his stoic discipline and did not blink.

Vierna spun away from him, clenched her delicate but deceptively strong hands in front of her, and found breath hard to come by.

"Destroyed," she said again, suddenly obviously pained, "taken down by the will of the Spider Queen. They are dead because of you," she cried, spinning back at Drizzt and pointing accusingly. "Your sisters, Briza and Maya, and your mother. All the house, Drizzt Do'Urden, dead because of you!"

Drizzt gave no outward expression, an accurate reflection of his absence of feelings, for the incredible news Vierna had just thrown at him. "And what of our brother?" he asked, more to discern information about this raiding force than for any sincere cares about Dinin's well-deserved demise.

"Why, Drizzt," Vierna said with obviously feigned confusion, "you have met him yourself. You nearly took one of his legs."

Drizzt's confusion was genuine—until Vierna finished the thought.

"One of his eight legs."

Again Drizzt managed to keep his features expressionless, but the stunning information that Dinin had become a drider certainly had caught him by surprise.

"Again the blame is yours!" Vierna snarled, and she watched him for a long moment, her smile gradually fading as he did not react.

"Zaknafein died for you!" Vierna cried suddenly, and, though Drizzt knew she had said it only to evoke a reaction, this time he could not remain calm.

"No!" he shouted back in rage, lurching forward from the floor, only to be easily pushed back to his seat.

Vierna smiled evilly, knowing she had found Drizzt's weak spot.

"Were it not for the sins of Drizzt Do'Urden, Zaknafein

would live still," she prodded. "House Do'Urden would have known its highest glories and Matron Malice would sit upon the ruling council."

"Sins?" Drizzt spat back, finding his courage against the painful memories of his lost father. "Glories?" he asked. "You confuse the two."

Vierna's hand shot up as though to lash out again, but when stoic Drizzt did not flinch, she lowered it.

"In the name of your wretched deity, you revel in the evilness of the drow world," the indomitable Drizzt went on. "Zaknafein died . . . no, was murdered, in pursuit of false ideals. You cannot convince me to accept the blame. Was it Vierna who held the sacrificial dagger?"

The priestess seemed on the verge of an explosion, her eyes glowing intensely and her face flushed hot to Drizzt's heat-seeing eyes.

"He was your father, too," Drizzt said to her, and she winced in spite of her efforts to sustain her rage. It was true enough. Zaknafein had sired two, and only two, children with Malice.

"But you do not care about that," Drizzt reasoned immediately. "Zaknafein was just a male, after all, and males do not count in the world of the drow.

"But he was your father," Drizzt had to add. "And he gave more to you than you will ever accept."

"Silence!" Vierna snarled through gnashing teeth. She slapped Drizzt again, several times in rapid succession. He could feel the warmth of his own blood oozing down his face.

Drizzt remained quiet for the moment, caught in private reflections of Vierna, and of the monster she had become. She now seemed more akin to Briza, Drizzt's oldest and most vicious sister, caught up in the frenzy that the Spider Queen always seemed ready to promote. Where was the Vierna that had secretly shown mercy to young Drizzt? Where was the Vierna who went along with the dark ways, as did Zaknafein, but never seemed to fully accept what Lloth had to offer?

Where was Zaknafein's daughter?

She was dead and buried, Drizzt decided as he regarded that heat-flushed face, buried beneath the lies and the empty promises of twisted glory that perverted everything about the dark world of the drow.

"I will redeem you," Vierna said, calm again, the heat gradually leaving her delicate, beautiful face.

"More wicked ones than you have tried," Drizzt replied, misunderstanding her intent. Vierna's ensuing laughter revealed that she recognized the error of his conclusions.

"I will give you to Lloth," the priestess explained. "And I will accept, in return, more power than even ambitious Matron Malice ever hoped for. Be of cheer, my lost brother, and know that you will restore to House Do'Urden more prestige and power than it ever before knew."

"Power that will wane," Drizzt replied calmly, and his tone angered Vierna more than his insightful words. "Power that will raise the house to another precipice, so that another house, finding the favor of Lloth, might push Do'Urden down once more."

Vierna's smile widened.

"You cannot deny it," Drizzt snarled at her, and it was he who now faltered in the war of words, he who found his logic, however sound, to be inadequate. "There is no constancy, no permanence, in Menzoberranzan beyond the Spider Queen's latest whim."

"Good, my lost brother," Vierna purred.

"Lloth is a damned thing!"

Vierna nodded. "Your sacrilege cannot harm me any more," the priestess explained, her tone deathly calm, "for you are not of me anymore. You are nothing more than a houseless rogue whom Lloth has deemed suitable for sacrifice.

"So do continue to spit your curses at the Spider Queen," Vierna went on. "Do show Lloth how proper this sacrifice will be! How ironic it is, for if you repented your ways, if you came back to the truth of your heritage, then you would defeat me."

Drizzt bit his lip, realizing that he would do well to hold his silence until he better fathomed the depth of this unexpected meeting.

"Do you not understand?" Vierna asked him. "Merciful Lloth would welcome back your skilled sword, and my sacrifice would be no more. Thus would I live as an outcast, like you, a houseless rogue."

"You do not fear to tell me this?" Drizzt asked her coyly.

Vierna understood her renegade brother better than he believed. "You will not repent, foolish, honorable Drizzt Do'Urden," she replied. "You would not utter such a lie, would not proclaim your fealty to the Spider Queen, even to save your very life. What useless commodities are these ideals you hold so precious!"

Vierna slapped him one more time, for no particular reason that Drizzt could discern, and she twirled away, her hot form blurred by the shielding flow of her clerical robes. How fitting that image seemed to Drizzt, that the true outline of his sister should be hidden beneath the garments of the perverting Spider Queen.

The curious-looking drow that had been conversing with Entreri walked over to Drizzt then, his high boots clacking loudly on the stone. He gave Drizzt an almost sympathetic look, then shrugged.

"A pity," he remarked, as he produced the glowing Twinkle from under the folds of his shimmering cape.

"A pity," he said again, and he walked away, this time his boots making not a whisper of sound.

* * * * *

The amazed guards snapped to rigid attention when their king unexpectedly entered their chamber, accompanied by his daughter, Wulfgar, Cobble, and a strangely armored dwarf that they did not know.

"Ye heared from the drow?" Bruenor asked the guards, the dwarf king going straight for the heavy bar on the stone door as he spoke.

Their silence told Bruenor all he needed to know. "Get to General Dagna," he instructed one of the guardsmen. "Tell him to gather together a war party and get down the new tunnels!"

The dwarven guard obediently kicked up his heels and darted away.

Bruenor's four companions came beside him as the bar clanged to the stone, Wulfgar and Cobble bearing blazing torches.

"Three, then two, is the drow's signal," the remaining guard explained to Bruenor.

"Three, then two, it is," Bruenor replied, and he disappeared into the gloom, forcing the others, particularly Thibble–dorf, who still did not think it a good thing that the king of Mithril Hall was even down there, to scamper quickly just to keep pace.

Cobble and even hardy Pwent glanced back and grimaced as the stone door slammed shut, while the other three, bent forward with the weight of their fears for their missing friend, did not even hear the sound.

Chapter 12
The Truth Be Known

B lood," Catti-brie muttered grimly, holding a torch and bending low over the line of droplets in the corridor, near the entryway of a small chamber.

"Could be from the goblin fight," Bruenor said hopefully, but Catti-brie shook her head.

"Still wet," she replied. "The blood from the goblin fight'd be long dried by now."

"Then from them crawlers we seen," Bruenor reasoned, "tearing apart the goblin bodies."

Still Catti-brie was not convinced. Stooping low, torch held far in front of her, she went through the short doorway of the side chamber. Wulfgar clambered in behind and pushed past her as soon as the passage widened again, coming up defensively in front of the young woman.

The barbarian's action did not sit well with Catti-brie. Perhaps, from Wulfgar's point of view, he was merely following a prudent course, getting his battle-ready body in front of one encumbered with a torch and whose eyes were on the floor. But Catti-brie doubted that possibility, felt that Wulfgar had come in so urgently because she had been in the lead, because of his need to protect her and stand between her and any possible danger. Proud and able, Catti-brie was more insulted than flattered.

And worried, for if Wulfgar was so fearful of her safety, then he might well make a tactical mistake. The companions had survived many dangers together because each had found a niche in the band, because each had played a role complementary to the abilities of the others. Catti-brie understood clearly that a disruption of that pattern could be deadly.

She pushed back ahead of Wulfgar, batting aside his arm when he held it out to block her progress. He glared at her, and she promptly returned the unyielding stare.

"What d'ye got in there?" came Bruenor's call, deflecting the imminent showdown. Catti-brie looked back to see the dark form of her father crouched in the low doorway, Cobble and Pwent, who held the second torch, out in the corridor behind him.

"Empty," Wulfgar answered firmly, and turned to go.

Catti-brie kept on crouching and looking about, though, as much to prove the barbarian wrong as in an honest search for clues.

"Not empty," she corrected a moment later, and her superior tone turned Wulfgar back around and lured Bruenor into the chamber.

They flanked Catti-brie, who bent low over a tiny object on

the floor: a crossbow quarrel, but far too small for any of the crossbows Bruenor's fighters carried, or any similar weapon the companions had ever seen. Bruenor picked it up in his stubby fingers, brought it close to his eyes, and studied it carefully.

"We got pixies in these tunnels?" he asked, referring to the diminutive but cruel sprites more common to woodland settings.

"Some type of—" Wulfgar began.

"Drow," Catti-brie interrupted. Wulfgar and Bruenor turned on her, Wulfgar's clear eyes flashing with anger at being interrupted, but only for the moment it took him to understand the gravity of what Catti-brie had announced.

"The elf had a bow that'd fit this?" Bruenor balked.

"Not Drizzt," Catti-brie corrected grimly, "other drow." Wulfgar and Bruenor screwed up their faces in obvious doubt, but Catti-brie felt certain of her guess. Many times in the past, back in Icewind Dale on the empty slopes of Kelvin's Cairn, Drizzt had told her of his homeland, had told her of the remarkable accomplishments and exotic artifacts of the dark elf nation. Among those artifacts was the most favored weapon of the dark elves, hand-held crossbows, with quarrels usually tipped in poison.

Wulfgar and Bruenor looked to each other, each hopeful that the other would find some logic to defeat Catti-brie's grim assertions. Bruenor only shrugged, tucked the quarrel away, and started for the outside passage. Wulfgar looked back to the young woman, his face flushed with concern.

Neither of them spoke—neither had to—for they both knew well the horror-filled tales of marauding dark elves. The implications seemed grave indeed if Catti-brie's guess proved correct, if drow elves had come to Mithril Hall.

There was something more in Wulfgar's expression that troubled Catti-brie, though, a possessive protectiveness that the young woman was beginning to believe would get them all in trouble. She pushed past the huge man, dipping low and exiting the chamber, leaving Wulfgar in the dark with his inner turmoil.

* * * * *

The caravan made its slow but steady way through the tunnels, the passageways becoming ever more natural. Drizzt still wore his armor but had been stripped of his weapons and had his hands tightly bound behind his back by some magical cord that would not loosen in the least, no matter how he managed to twist his wrists.

Dinin, eight legs clicking on the stone, led the troupe, with Vierna and Jarlaxle a short way behind. Several in the twenty-drow party had fallen into formation behind them, including the two keeping watch over Drizzt. They intersected once with the larger, flanking band of House Baenre soldiers, Jarlaxle issuing quiet orders and the second drow force slipping, melting, away into the shadows.

Only then did Drizzt begin to understand the import of the raid on Mithril Hall. By his count, somewhere between two and three score dark elves had come up from Menzoberranzan, a formidable raiding party indeed.

And it had all been for him.

What of Entreri? Drizzt wondered. How did the assassin fit into this? He seemed to mesh so well with the dark elves. Of similar build and temperament, the assassin moved along with the drow ranks easily, inconspicuously.

Too well, Drizzt thought.

Entreri spent some time with the shaven-headed mercenary and Vierna, but then dropped back rank by rank, making his way inevitably toward his most-hated enemy.

"Well met," he said coyly when he at last fell into step beside Drizzt. A look from the human sent the two closest dark elf guards moving respectfully away.

Drizzt eyed the assassin closely for a moment, looking for

clues, then pointedly turned away.

"What?" Entreri insisted, grabbing the obstinate drow's shoulder and turning him back. Drizzt stopped abruptly, drawing concerned looks from the drow flanking him, particularly Vierna. He started moving again immediately, though, not liking the attention and, gradually, the other dark elves settled into their comfortable pace around him.

"I do not understand," Drizzt remarked offhandedly to Entreri. "You had the mask, had Regis, and knew where I could be found. Why then did you ally with Vierna and her gang?"

"You presume that the choice was mine to make," Entreri replied. "Your sister found me—I did not seek her out."

"Then you are a prisoner," Drizzt reasoned.

"Hardly," Entreri replied without hesitation, chuckling as he spoke. "You said it correctly the first time. I am an ally."

"Where my kin are concerned, the two are much the same."

Again Entreri chuckled, apparently seeing the bait for what it was. Drizzt winced at the sincerity in the assassin's laughter, because he then realized the strength in the bonds of his enemies, ties he had hoped, in a fleeting moment of any hope, he might stretch and exploit.

"I deal with Jarlaxle, actually," the assassin explained, "not your volatile sister. Jarlaxle, the pragmatic mercenary, the opportunist. That one, I understand. He and I are much alike!"

"When you are no longer needed—" Drizzt began ominously.

"But I am and shall continue to be!" Entreri interrupted. "Jarlaxle, the opportunist," he reiterated loudly, drawing an approving nod from the mercenary, who apparently understood well the Common tongue of the surface. "What gain would Jarlaxle find in killing me? I am a valuable tie to the surface, am I not? The head of a thieves' guild in exotic Calimport, an ally that might well prove useful in the future. I have dealt with Jarlaxle's kind all my life, guildmasters from a dozen cities along the Sword Coast."

"Drow have been known to kill for the simple pleasure of killing," Drizzt protested, not willing to let go of this one loose strand so easily.

"Agreed," Entreri replied, "but they do not kill when they stand to gain by not killing. Pragmatic. You will not shake this alliance, doomed Drizzt. It is of mutual benefit, you see, to your inevitable loss."

Drizzt paused a long while to digest the information, to find some way to regain that potentially unwinding strand, that loose end that he believed always existed when treacherous individuals came together on any cause.

"Not mutual benefit," he said quietly, noting Entreri's curious glance his way.

"Explain," Entreri bade him after a long moment of silence.

"I know why you came after me," Drizzt reasoned. "It was not to have me killed, but to kill me yourself. And not just to kill me, but to defeat me in even combat. That possibility seems less likely now, in these tunnels beside merciless Vierna and her desires for simple sacrifice."

"So formidable even when all is lost," Entreri remarked, his superior tones pulling that elusive strand from Drizzt's reach once more. "Defeat you in combat, I will—that is the deal, you see. In a chamber not so far from here, your kin and I will part company, but not until you and I have settled our rivalry."

"Vierna would not let you kill me," Drizzt retorted.

"But she would allow me to defeat you," Entreri answered. "She desires that very thing, desires that your humiliation be complete. After I have settled our business, then she will give you to Lloth . . . with my blessings.

"Come now, my friend," Entreri purred, seeing no response coming from Drizzt, seeing Drizzt's face screwed up in an uncharacteristic pout.

"I am not your friend," Drizzt growled back.

"My kindred, then," Entreri teased, his delight absolute when Drizzt turned an angry glower at him.

"Never."

"We fight," Entreri explained. "We both fight so very well, and fight to win, though our purposes for battle may vary. I have told you before that you cannot escape me, cannot escape who you are."

Drizzt had no answer for that, not in a corridor surrounded by enemies and with his hands tied behind his back. Entreri had indeed made these claims before, and Drizzt had reconciled them, had come to terms with the decisions of his life and with the path he had chosen as his own.

But seeing the obvious pleasure on the evil assassin's face disturbed the honorable drow nonetheless. Whatever else he might do in this seemingly hopeless situation, Drizzt Do'Urden determined then not to give Entreri his satisfaction.

They came to an area of many side passages, winding, scalloped tunnels, worm holes, they seemed, meandering and rolling about in every direction at once. Entreri had said that the room, the parting of ways, was close, and Drizzt knew he was running out of time.

He dove headlong to the floor, tucked his feet in tight, and slipped his arms over them, then brought them back in front, as he rolled to a standing position. By the time he turned back, the ever-alert Entreri already had his sword and dagger in hand, but Drizzt charged him anyway. Weaponless, the drow had no practical chance, but he guessed that Entreri would not strike him down, guessed that the assassin would not so impulsively destroy the even challenge he desperately craved, the very moment Entreri had worked so very hard to achieve.

Predictably, Entreri hesitated, and Drizzt was beyond his half-hearted defenses in a moment, leaping into the air and landing a double-footed kick on Entreri's face and chest that sent the man flying away.

Drizzt bounced back to his feet and rushed toward the entrance to the nearest side tunnel, blocked by a single drow guard. Again Drizzt came on fearlessly, hoping that Vierna had

155

promised incredible torments to anyone who stole her sacrifice—a hope that seemed confirmed when Drizzt glanced back to Vierna, to see her hand holding back Jarlaxle's, the mercenary's fingers clutching a throwing dagger.

The blocking drow fighter, as agile as a cat, punched out at the charging Drizzt, hilt first. But Drizzt, quicker still, snapped his hands straight up, and the ties binding his wrists hooked the fighter's weapon hand and threw his sword harmlessly high. Drizzt slammed into him, body to body, lifting his knee as they came together, and connecting cleanly on his opponent's abdomen. The fighter doubled over and Drizzt, with no time to spare, pushed past him, throwing him down to trip up the next soldier, and Entreri, coming in fast.

Around a bend, down a short expanse, then diving into yet another side passage, Drizzt barely managed to keep ahead of the pursuit—so close were his enemies in fact, that as he turned into the next passage, he heard a quarrel skip along the wall to the side.

Even worse, the drow ranger noted other forms slipping in and out of the openings to the sides of the tunnel. There had been no more than seven dark elves in the corridor with him, but he knew that more than twice that number had accompanied Vierna, not to mention the larger force that had been left behind not so long ago. The missing soldiers were all about, Drizzt knew, flanking and scouting, feeding reports along prescribed routes in silent codes.

Around another bend he went, then another, turning back opposite the first. He scrambled up a short wall, then cursed his luck when the branching corridor atop it sloped back down to the previous level.

Around another bend he saw a flash of heat glowing fiercely and knew it was a signal speculum, a metal plate magically heated on one side, which the dark elves used for signaling. The heated side glowed like a mirror in sunlight to beings using infravision. Drizzt cut down a side passage, realizing that the webs were tightening about him, knowing that his desperate attempt would not succeed.

Then the drider reared up in front of him.

Drizzt's revulsion was absolute, and he backpedaled in spite of the dangers he knew were behind him. To see his brother in such a state! Dinin's bloated torso moved in harmony with the eight scrabbling legs, his face an expressionless death mask.

Drizzt quieted his churning emotions, his need to scream out, and looked for a practical way to get past this obstacle. Dinin had turned his twin axes to their blunt sides, waving them wildly, and his eight legs kicked and bucked, giving Drizzt no obvious opening.

Drizzt had no choice; he spun about, intending to flee back the other way. Vierna, Jarlaxle, and Entreri turned the corner to greet him.

They conversed quietly in the Common tongue. Entreri said something about settling his score then and there, but apparently changed his mind.

Vierna advanced instead, her whip of five living snake heads waving ominously before her.

"If you defeat me, then you can have back your freedom," she teased in the drow tongue, as she tossed Twinkle to the floor at Drizzt's feet. He went for the weapon and Vierna struck, but Drizzt had expected as much and he fell back short of his dropped scimitar, leaving Twinkle just out of reach.

The drider scrambled ahead, an axe clipping Drizzt's shoulder, knocking him backwards toward Vierna. The ranger had no other choice now, and dove headlong for his blade, his fingers barely reaching it.

Snake fangs dug into his wrist. Another bite took him on the forearm and three more dove at his face or at his other hand, which was twisted over his grasping hand in a feeble defense. The sting of the bites was vicious, but it was the more insidious poison that defeated Drizzt. He had Twinkle in his grasp, he thought, but he couldn't be certain, since his numbed fingers could no longer feel the weapon's metal.

Vierna's cruel whip lashed out again, five heads biting eagerly into Drizzt's flesh, spreading the waves of numbness throughout his battered form. The merciless priestess of a merciless goddess beat the helpless prisoner a dozen times, her face twisted in absolute, evil glee.

Drizzt stubbornly held consciousness, eyed her with utter contempt, but that only prodded Vierna on, and she would have beaten him to death then and there had not Jarlaxle, and more pointedly, Entreri, come beside her and calmed her.

For Drizzt, his body racked with agony and all hope of survival long flown, it seemed less than a reprieve.

* * * * *

"Aaargh!" Bruenor wailed. "Me kinfolk!"

Thibbledorf Pwent's reaction to the gruesome scene of seven slaughtered dwarves was even more dramatic. The battlerager floundered to the side of the tunnel and began slamming his forehead against the stone wall. Undoubtedly he would have knocked himself cold had not Cobble quietly reminded him that his hammering could be heard a mile away.

"Killed clean and fast," Catti-brie commented, trying to keep rational and make some sense of this newest clue.

"Entreri," Bruenor growled.

"By all our guesses, if he's truly wearing the face and body of Regis, these dwarves were missing afore he went into these tunnels," Catti-brie reasoned. "Seems the assassin might have bringed some helpers along." The image of the small crossbow bolt played in her mind and she hoped her suspicions would prove false.

"Dead helpers when I get me hands around their murdering throats!" Bruenor promised. He fell to his knees then, hunched over a dead dwarf who had been a close friend.

Catti-brie could not bear the sight. She looked away from her father, to Wulfgar, standing quietly and holding the torch.

Wulfgar's scowl, aimed at her, caught her by surprise.

She studied him for a few moments. "Well, say yer thoughts," she demanded, growing uncomfortable under his unrelenting glare.

"You should not have come down here," the barbarian answered calmly.

"Drizzt is not me friend, then?" she asked, and she was surprised again at how Wulfgar's face crinkled in barely explosive rage at her mention of the dark elf.

"Oh, he is your friend, I do not doubt," Wulfgar replied, his tone dripping with venom. "But you are to be my wife. You should not be in this dangerous place."

Catti-brie's eyes opened wide in disbelief, in absolute outrage, showing the reflections of the torchlight as though some inner fire burned within them. "'Tis not yer choice to be making!" she cried loudly—so loudly that Cobble and Bruenor exchanged concerned looks and the dwarf king rose from his dead friend and moved toward his daughter.

"You are to be my bride!" Wulfgar reminded her, his volume equally disturbing.

Catti-brie didn't flinch, didn't blink, her determined stare forcing Wulfgar back a step. The resolute young woman almost smiled in spite of her rage, with the knowledge that the barbarian was finally beginning to catch on.

"You should not be here," Wulfgar said again, renewing his strength in his declaration.

"Get yerself to Settlestone, then," Catti-brie retorted, poking a finger into Wulfgar's massive chest. "For if ye're thinking I should not be here to help in finding Drizzt, then ye cannot call yerself a friend of the ranger!"

"Not as much as you can!" Wulfgar snarled back, his eyes glowing angrily, his face twisted and one fist clenched tightly at his side.

R. A. Salvatore

"What're ye saying?" Catti-brie asked, sincerely confused by all of this, by Wulfgar's irrational words and erratic behavior.

Bruenor had heard enough. He stepped between the two, pushing Catti-brie gently back and turning to squarely face the barbarian who had been like a son to him.

"What are ye saying, boy?" the dwarf asked, trying to keep calm, though he wanted nothing more than to punch Wulfgar in the blabbering mouth.

Wulfgar didn't look at Bruenor at all, just reached over the sturdy but short dwarf to point accusingly at Catti-brie. "How many kisses have you and the drow shared?" he bellowed.

Catti-brie nearly fell over. "What?" she shrieked. "Ye've lost yer senses. I never—"

"You lie!" Wulfgar roared.

"Damn yer words!" howled Bruenor and out came his great axe. He whipped it across, forcing Wulfgar to leap back and slam hard against the corridor wall, then chopped with it, forcing the barbarian to dive aside. Wulfgar tried to block with the torch, but Bruenor slapped it from his hand. Wulfgar tried to get to Aegis-fang, which he had slipped under his backpack when they had found the dead dwarves, but Bruenor came at him relentlessly, never actually striking, but forcing him to dodge and dive, to scramble across the hard stone.

"Let me kill him for ye, me king!" Pwent cried, rushing up and misunderstanding Bruenor's intentions.

"Get ye back!" Bruenor roared at the battlerager, and all the others were amazed, Pwent most among them, at the sheer force of Bruenor's voice.

"I been playing along with yer stupid actions for weeks now," Bruenor said to Wulfgar, "but I've no more time for ye. Ye speak out whatever's got yer hair up here and now, or shut yer stupid mouth and keep it shut until we find Drizzt and get us outta these stinking tunnels!"

"I have tried to remain calm," Wulfgar retorted, and it seemed more a plea since the barbarian was still on his knees from dodging Bruenor's dangerously close swings. "But I cannot ignore the insult to my honor!" As though realizing his subservient appearance, the proud barbarian leaped to his feet. "Drizzt met with Catti-brie before the drow returned to Mithril Hall."

"Who told ye that?" Catti-brie demanded.

"Regis!" Wulfgar shouted back. "And he told me that your meeting was filled with more than words!"

"It's a lie!" Catti-brie cried.

Wulfgar started to respond in kind, but he saw Bruenor's wide smile and heard the dwarf's mocking laughter. The head of the dwarf's axe dropped to the floor, Bruenor placing both hands on his hips and shaking his head in obvious disbelief.

"Ye stupid . . . ," the dwarf muttered. "Why don't ye use whatever part o' yer body's not muscle and think o' what ye just said? We're here because we're guessing that Regis ain't Regis!"

Wulfgar scrunched his face up in confusion, realizing only then that he had not reconsidered the halfling's volatile accusations in light of the recent revelations.

"If ye're feeling as stupid as ye look, then ye're feeling the way ye ought to feel," Bruenor remarked dryly.

The sudden revelations hit Wulfgar as surely as Bruenor's axe ever could. How many times had Regis spoken with him alone these last few days? And what, he considered carefully, had been the content of those many meetings? For the first time, perhaps, Wulfgar realized what he had done in his chamber against the drow, truly realized that he would have killed Drizzt if the drow had not won the battle. "The halfling . . . Artemis Entreri, tried to use me in his evil plans," Wulfgar reasoned. He remembered a swirling myriad of sparkling reflections, the facets of a gemstone, inviting him down into its depths. "He used his pendant on me—I cannot be sure, but I think I remember . . . I believe he used . . ."

"Be sure," Bruenor said. "I knowed ye a long time, lad, and

never have I knowed ye to act so durned stupid. And meself as well. To send the halfling along with Drizzt into this unknown region!"

"Entreri tried to get me to kill Drizzt," Wulfgar went on, trying to fathom it all.

"Tried to get Drizzt to kill yerself, ye mean," Bruenor corrected. Catti-brie snorted, unable to contain her pleasure and her gratitude that Bruenor had put the boastful barbarian in his place.

Wulfgar scowled at her from over Bruenor's shoulder.

"You did meet with the drow," he asked as much as stated.

"That's me own business," the young woman replied, not giving in an inch to Wulfgar's lingering jealousy.

The tension began to mount again—Catti-brie could see that while the revelations about Regis had taken some of the bite from Wulfgar's growl, the protective man still did not wish her there, did not wish his bride-to-be in a dangerous situation. Stubborn and proud, Catti-brie remained more insulted than flattered.

She didn't get the chance to vent her rage, though, not then, for Cobble came shuffling back to the group, begging them all to be silent. Only then did Bruenor and the others notice that Pwent was no longer present.

"Noise," the cleric explained quietly, "somewhere farther along in the deeper tunnels. Let us pray to Moradin that whatever is down there did not hear the clamor of our own stupidity!"

Catti-brie looked to the fallen dwarves, looked to see Wulfgar do likewise, and knew that the barbarian, like her, was reminding himself that Drizzt was in serious danger. How petty their arguments seemed to her then, and she was ashamed.

Bruenor sensed her despair, and he came over to her and draped his arm across her shoulders. "Had to be said," he offered comfortingly. "Had to be brought out and cleared afore the fighting begins."

Catti-brie nodded her agreement and hoped that the fighting, if there was to be any, would begin soon.

She hoped, too, with all her heart, that the next battle would not be fought as vengeance for the death of Drizzt Do'Urden.

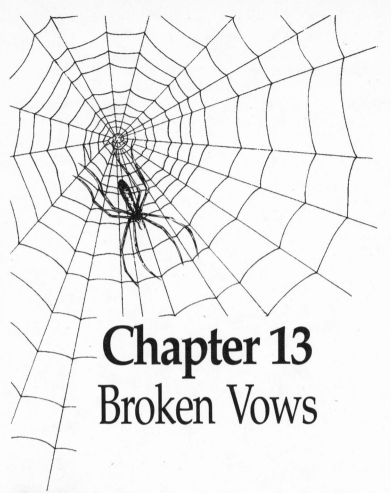

Chapter 13
Broken Vows

A single torch was lit; Drizzt realized it was part of the deal. Entreri probably was not yet comfortable enough with his newly acquired infravision to battle Drizzt without any light source at all.

When his eyes shifted into the normal spectrum of light, Drizzt studied the medium-sized chamber. While its walls and ceiling were quite naturally formed, curving and with jutting angles and small stalactites hanging down, it had two wooden doors—recently constructed, Drizzt believed, most probably arranged by Vierna as part of the deal with Entreri. A drow soldier flanked the doors on each side and a third stood between them, right in front of each portal.

Twelve dark elves were in the room now, including Vierna and Jarlaxle, but the drider was nowhere to be found. Entreri was talking with Vierna; Drizzt saw her give the assassin the belt holding Drizzt's two scimitars.

There also was a curious alcove in the room, a single step in from the back wall of the main area and with a waist-high ledge, the top covered by a blanket and a soldier leaning on it, his sword and dagger drawn.

A chute? Drizzt wondered.

Entreri had said this was the place where he and the dark elves would part company, but Drizzt doubted that the assassin, his business finished, meant to go back the way they had come, anywhere near Mithril Hall. With only one other door apparent in the chamber, perhaps there did indeed loom a chute under that blanket, a way to the open and twisted corridors of the deeper Underdark.

Vierna said something that Drizzt did not hear, and Entreri came over to him, bearing his weapons. A drow soldier moved behind Drizzt and released his bonds, and he slowly brought his hands back in front of him, his shoulders aching from their long stay in the awkward position and from the residual pain of Vierna's vicious beating.

Entreri dropped the scimitar belt at Drizzt's feet and took a cautious step backward. Drizzt looked down to his weapons curiously, unsure of what he should do.

"Pick them up," Entreri instructed.

"Why?"

The question seemed to slap the assassin across the face. A great scowl flashed for just an instant, then was replaced by Entreri's typically emotionless expression.

"That we might learn the truth," he answered.

"I know the truth," Drizzt replied calmly. "You wish to distort it, that you might keep hidden, even from yourself, the folly of your wretched existence."

"Pick them up," the assassin snarled, "or I will kill you where you stand."

Drizzt knew the threat was a hollow one. Entreri would not kill him, not until the assassin had tried to redeem himself in honest battle. Even if Entreri did strike to slay him, Drizzt figured Vierna would intervene. Drizzt was too important to Vierna; sacrifices to the Spider Queen were not readily accepted unless given by drow priestesses.

Drizzt finally did bend and retrieve his weapons, feeling more secure as he belted them on. He knew that the odds in this room were impossible, whether he had the scimitars or not, but he was experienced enough to realize that opportunities were fleeting and often came when least expected.

Entreri drew his slender sword and jeweled dagger, then crouched low, his thin lips widening into an eager smile.

Drizzt stood easily, shoulders slumped, scimitars still in their sheaths.

The assassin's sword cut across, nicking Drizzt on the tip of his nose, forcing his head to flinch to the side. He reached up casually with his thumb and index finger, pinching the flow of blood.

"Coward," Entreri teased, feigning a straightforward lunge and still circling.

Drizzt turned to keep him directly in front, not bothered at all by the ridiculous insult.

"Come now, Drizzt Do'Urden," Jarlaxle intervened, drawing looks from both Drizzt and Entreri. "You know you are doomed, but will you not gain any pleasure in killing this human, this man who has done you and your friends so many wrongs?"

"What have you to lose?" Entreri asked. "I cannot kill you, only defeat you—that is my deal with your sister. But you may kill me. Surely Vierna would not intervene, and might even be amused, at the loss of a simple human life."

Drizzt remained impassive. He had nothing to lose, they claimed. What they apparently did not understand was that Drizzt Do'Urden did not fight when he had nothing to lose, only when he had something to gain, only when the situation necessitated that he fight.

"Draw your weapons, I beg," Jarlaxle added. "Your reputation is considerable and I would dearly love to see you at play, to see if you are truly the better of Zaknafein."

Drizzt, trying to play it calm, trying to hold fast to his principles, could not hide his grimace at the mention of his dead father, reputably the finest weapons master ever to draw swords in Menzoberranzan. In spite of himself, he drew his scimitars, Twinkle's angry blue glow sincerely reflecting the welling rage that Drizzt Do'Urden could not fully suppress.

Entreri came on suddenly, fiercely, and Drizzt reacted with warrior instincts, scimitars ringing against sword and dagger, defeating every attack. Taking the offensive before he even realized what he was doing, acting solely on instinct, Drizzt began turning full circles, his blades flowing around him like the edging of a screw, every turn bringing them in at his opponent from different heights and different angles.

Entreri, confused by the unconventional routine, missed as many parries as he hit, but his quick feet kept him out of reach. "Always a surprise," the assassin admitted grimly, and he winced jealously at the approving sighs and comments from the dark elves lining the room.

Drizzt stopped his spin, ending perfectly squared to the assassin, blades low and ready.

"Pretty, but to no avail," Entreri cried and rushed forward, sword flying low, dagger slicing high. Drizzt twisted diagonally, one blade knocking the sword aside, the other forming a barrier that the dagger could not get through as it cut harmlessly high.

Entreri's dagger hand continued a complete circuit—Drizzt noticed that he flipped the blade over in his fingers—while his sword darted and thrust, this way and that, to keep Drizzt busy.

Predictably, the assassin's dagger hand came about, dipping down to the side, and he whipped the dagger free.

Ringing like a hammer on metal, Twinkle darted into the missile's path and batted it away, knocking it across the room.

"Well done!" Jarlaxle congratulated, and Entreri, too, backed off and nodded his sincere approval. With just a sword now, the assassin came in more cautiously, loosing a measured strike.

His surprise was absolute when Drizzt did not parry, when Drizzt missed not one deflection, but two and the thrusting weapon slipped past the scimitar defense. The sword quickly recoiled, never reaching its vulnerable mark. Entreri came in again, feigning another straightforward thrust, but snapping the weapon back and around instead.

He had Drizzt beaten, could have ripped the drow's shoulder, or neck, apart with that simple feint! Drizzt's knowing smile stopped him, though. He turned his sword to its flat edge and smacked it against the drow's shoulder, doing no real damage.

Drizzt had let him through, both times, was now mocking the assassin's precious fight with a pretense of inability!

Entreri wanted to scream out his protests, let all the other dark elves in on Drizzt's private game. The assassin decided that this battle was too personal, though, something that should be settled between himself and Drizzt, and not through any intervention by Vierna or Jarlaxle.

"I had you," he teased, using the rocky Dwarvish language in the hopes that those drow around him, except, of course, for Drizzt, would not understand it.

"You should have ended it, then," Drizzt replied calmly, in the Common surface language, though he spoke the Dwarvish tongue perfectly well. He wouldn't give Entreri the satisfaction of removing this to a personal level, would keep the fight public and ridicule it openly with his actions.

"You should have fought better," Entreri retorted, reverting to the Common tongue. "For the sake of your halfling friend, if not for yourself. If you kill me, then Regis will be free, but if I walk from here, . . ." He let the threat hang in the air, but it grew less ominous indeed when Drizzt laughed at it openly.

"Regis is dead," the drow ranger reasoned. "Or will be, whatever the outcome of our battle."

"No—" Entreri began.

"Yes," Drizzt interrupted. "I know you better than to fall prey to your unending lies. You have been too blinded by your rage. You did not anticipate every possibility."

Entreri came in again, easily, not making any blatant strikes that would make this continuing charade obvious to the gathered dark elves.

"He is dead," Drizzt asked as much as stated.

"What do you think?" Entreri snapped back, his snarling tone making the answer seem obvious.

Drizzt realized the shift in tactics, understood that Entreri now was attempting to enrage him, to make him fight in anger.

Drizzt remained impassive, let fly a few lazy attack routines that Entreri had little trouble defeating—and that the assassin could have countered to devastating effect if he had so desired.

Vierna and Jarlaxle began to speak in whispers, and Drizzt, thinking they might grow tired of the charade, came on more forcefully, though still with measured and ineffective strikes. Entreri gave a slight but definite nod to show that he was beginning to understand. The game, the subtle and silent undercurrents and communications, were getting personal, and Drizzt, as much as Entreri, did not want Vierna intervening.

"You will savor your victory," Entreri promised uncharacteristically, a leading phrase.

"It will come as no gain," Drizzt replied, a response the assassin was obviously fully beginning to expect. Entreri wanted to win this fight, wanted to win it even more badly because Drizzt did not seem to care. Drizzt knew that Entreri was not stupid, though, and while he and Drizzt were of similar fighting skills, their motivations surely separated them. Entreri would fight with all his heart against Drizzt just to prove something, but Drizzt honestly felt that he had nothing to prove, not to the assassin.

Drizzt's failings in this fight were not a bluff, were not something that Entreri could call him on. Drizzt would lose, taking more satisfaction in not giving Entreri the satisfaction of honest victory.

And, as his actions now revealed, the assassin was not completely surprised by the turn of events.

"Your last chance," Entreri teased. "Here, you and I part company. I leave through the far door, and the drow go back *down* to their dark world."

Drizzt's violet eyes flicked to the side, to the alcove, for just a moment, his movement revealing to Entreri that he had not missed the emphasis on the word "down," had not missed the obvious reference to the cloth-covered chute.

Entreri rolled to the side suddenly, having worked himself around close enough to retrieve his lost dagger. It was a daring maneuver, and again a revealing move to his opponent, for with Drizzt's fighting so obviously lacking, Entreri had no need to take the risk of going for his lost weapon.

"Might I rename your cat?" Entreri asked, shifting his waist to reveal a large belt pouch, the black statuette obvious through the open edges of its bulging top.

The assassin came in fast and hard with a four-strike routine, any of which could have slipped through, had he pressed them, to nick at Drizzt.

"Come now," Entreri said loudly. "You can fight better than that! I have witnessed your skills too many times—in these very tunnels even—to think you might be so easily defeated!"

At first, Drizzt was surprised that Entreri had so obviously let their private communication become so public, but Vierna and the others probably had figured by that point that Drizzt was not fighting with all his heart. Still, it seemed a curious comment—until Drizzt came to understand the hidden meanings of the assassin's words, the assassin's bait. Entreri had referred to their fighting in these tunnels, but those battles had not been against each other. On that unusual occasion, Drizzt Do'Urden and Artemis Entreri had fought together, side by side and back-to-back, out of simple desire to survive against a common enemy.

Was it to be that way again, here and now? Was Entreri so desperate for an honest fight against Drizzt that he was offering to help him defeat Vierna and her gang? If that happened, and they won, then any following battle between Drizzt and Entreri would certainly give Drizzt something to gain, something to honestly fight for. If together he and Entreri could win out, or get away, the ensuing battle between them would dangle Drizzt's freedom before his eyes with only Artemis Entreri standing in his way.

"*Tempus!*" The cry stole the contemplations from both opponents, forced them to react to the obvious forthcoming distraction.

They moved in perfect harmony, Drizzt whipping his scimitar across and the assassin dropping his defenses, falling back and turning his hip to stick out his belt pouch. Twinkle cut through the pouch cleanly, spilling the figurine of the enchanted panther onto the floor.

The door, the same door through which they had entered the chamber, blew apart under the weight of flying Aegis-fang, hurling the drow standing before it to the floor.

Drizzt's first instinct told him to go to the door, to try to link up with his friends, but he saw that possibility blocked by the many scrambling dark elves. The other door, too, offered no hope, for it opened immediately with the onset of commotion, the drider Dinin leading the drow charge into the room.

The chamber flashed bright with magical light; groans erupted from every corner. A silver-streaking arrow sizzled in through the blasted portal, catching the same unfortunate dark elf in midstep as he rose from beneath the blasted door. It hurtled him backwards against the far wall, where he stuck in place, arrow through chest and stone.

"Guenhwyvar!"

Drizzt could not wait and see if his call to the panther had been heard, could not wait for anything at all. He rushed for the alcove, the single drow holding guard near it raising his weapons in surprised defense.

Vierna cried out; Drizzt felt a dagger cut into his wide-flying cloak and knew it was hanging just an inch from his thigh. Straight ahead he ran, dipping one shoulder at the last moment as though he meant to dive sidelong.

The drow guard dipped right along with him, but Drizzt came back up straight before his adversary, his scimitars crossing high, at neck level.

The guarding drow couldn't get his sword and dirk up fast enough to deflect the lightning-fast attack, couldn't reverse his momentum and fall back to the side out of harm's way.

Drizzt's fine-edged weapons crossed over his throat.

Drizzt winced, tucked his bloodied blades in close and dove headlong for the cloth, hoping that there was indeed an opening under it and hoping that it was a chute, not a straight drop.

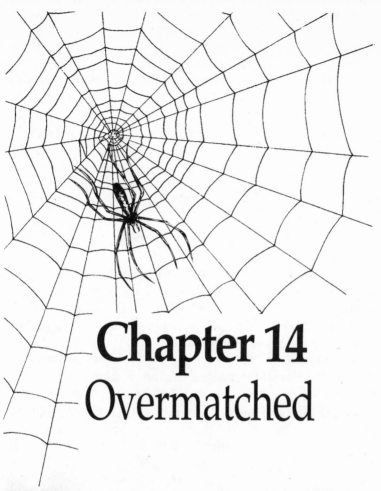

Chapter 14
Overmatched

Thibbledorf Pwent rushed along a side passage, running parallel and twenty feet to the right of the tunnel where he had split from his companions to go out on a prudent flanking maneuver. He heard the crash of the warhammer-blasted door, the sizzle of Catti-brie's arrows, and cries from several places, even a growl or two, and cursed his luck for being caught out of fun's way.

Torch leading, the battlerager eagerly spun around a sharp left-hand corner, hoping to get back with the others before the fighting was through. He pulled up short, considering a curious figure, apparently as surprised to see him as he was to see it.

"Hey, now," the battlerager asked, "is yerself Bruenor's pet drow?"

Pwent watched the slender elf's hand come up and heard the "click" as a hand-held crossbow fired, the quarrel striking Pwent's sturdy armor and slipping through one of the many cracks to draw a drop of blood on the dwarf's shoulder.

"Guess not!" the happy Pwent cried, charging wildly with every word and tossing his torch aside. He dipped his head, putting his helmet spike in line, and the dark elf, seeming amazed at the sheer viciousness of this one's attack, fumbled to get his sword out and ready.

Pwent, barely able to see but fully expecting the defense, whipped his head from side to side as he neared the target, parrying the sword away. He stood up straight again without slowing and launched himself at his opponent, barreling into the stunned dark elf with abandon.

They crashed against the wall, the drow still holding his balance, and holding Pwent up in the air, not knowing what to make of this unusual, hugging battle style.

The dark elf shook his sword hand free, while Pwent simply began to shake, his sharp-ridged armor digging lines in the drow's chest. The elf squirmed frantically, his own desperate actions only aiding the battlerager's convulsive attack. Pwent freed one arm and punched wildly, glove nail poking holes in the smooth ebony skin. The dwarf kneed and elbowed, bit the drow on the nose, and punched him in the side.

"Aaaaaargh!" The growling scream erupted all the way from Pwent's belly, reverberating unsteadily from his flapping lips as he furiously whipped himself about. He felt the warmth of his enemy's flowing blood, the sensation only driving him, driving the most wild battlerager, to further heights of ferocity.

"Aaaaaargh!"

The drow went down in a heap, Pwent atop him, still convulsing wildly. In a few moments, his enemy no longer squirmed, but Pwent did not relinquish his advantage.

"Ye sneaky elven thing!" he roared, repeatedly slamming his forehead into the dark elf's face.

Quite literally, the battlerager, with his sharpened armor and spiked joints, shook the unfortunate drow apart.

Pwent finally let go and hopped to his feet, pulling the limp body to a sitting position and leaving it slumped against the wall. The battlerager felt the pain in his back and realized that the drow's sword had hit him at least once. Of more concern, though, was the numbness flowing down Pwent's arm, poison spreading from the crossbow wound. Rage mounting once more, Pwent dipped his pointy helmet, scraped a boot across the stone several times for traction, and rushed ahead, spearing the already dead foe through the chest.

When he jumped back this time, the dead drow toppled to the floor, warm blood spreading out under the body's ripped torso.

"Hope ye wasn't Bruenor's pet drow," the battlerager remarked, suddenly realizing that the whole incident might have been an honest mistake. "Oh, well, can't be helped now!"

* * * * *

Cobble, magically inspecting for traps ahead, instinctively winced as another arrow zipped past his shoulder, its silver shine diminishing into the brightly lit chamber beyond. The dwarven cleric forced himself back to his work, wanting to be done quickly, that he might loose the charge of Bruenor and the others.

A crossbow quarrel dove into his leg, but the cleric wasn't too concerned about its buglike sting or its poison, for he had placed enchantments upon himself to slow the drug's effects. Let the dark elves hit him with a dozen such bolts; it would be hours before Cobble fell to sleep.

His scan of the corridor complete, with no immediate traps

R. A. Salvatore

discerned, Cobble called back to others, who were impatient and already moving toward him. When the cleric looked back, though, in the dim light emanating from the enemies' chamber, he noticed something curious across the floor: metallic shavings.

"Iron?" he whispered. Instinctively his hand went into his bulging pouch, filled with enchanted pebble bombs, and he went into a defensive crouch, holding his free hand out behind him to warn the others back.

When he focused within the general din of the sudden battle, he heard a female drow voice, chanting, spell-casting.

The dwarf's eyes widened in horror. He turned back, yelling for his friends to be gone, to run away. He, too, tried to run, his boots slipping across the smooth stone, so fast did his little legs begin to move.

He heard the drow spell-caster's crescendo.

The iron shavings immediately became an iron wall, unsupported and angled, and it fell over poor Cobble.

There came a great gush of wind, the great explosion of tons of iron slamming against the stone floor, and flying spurts of pressure-squeezed blood and gore whipped back into the faces of the three stunned companions. A hundred small explosions, a hundred tiny sparkling bursts, rang hollowly under the collapsed iron wall.

"Cobble," Catti-brie breathed helplessly.

The magical light in the distant chamber went away. A ball of darkness appeared just outside the chamber door, blocking the end of the passageway. A second ball of darkness came up, just ahead of the first, and a third after that, covering the back edge of the fallen iron wall.

"Get charging!" Thibbledorf Pwent cried at them, coming back into the corridor and rushing past his hesitating friends.

A ball of darkness appeared right in front of the battlerager, stopping him short. Handcrossbow after handcrossbow clicked unseen behind the blackness, sending stinging little darts whipping out.

176

"Back!" Bruenor cried. Catti-brie loosed another arrow; Pwent, hit a dozen times, began to slump to the stone. Wulfgar grabbed him by the helmet spike and started away after the red-bearded dwarf.

"Drizzt," Catti-brie moaned quietly. She dropped low to one knee, firing another arrow and another after that, hoping that her friend would not come running out of the room into danger's path.

A quarrel, oozing poison, clicked against her bow and bounced harmlessly wide.

She could not stay.

She fired one more time, then turned and ran after her father and the others, away from the friend she had come to rescue.

* * * * *

Drizzt fell a dozen feet, slammed against the sloping side of the chute, and careened along a winding and swiftly descending way. He held tightly to his scimitars; his greatest fear was that one of them would get away from him and wind up cutting him in half as he bounced along.

He did a complete loop, managed to somersault to put his feet out in front of him, but inadvertently got turned back around at the next vertical drop, the ending slam nearly knocking him unconscious.

Just as he thought he was gaining control, was about to turn himself about once more, the chute opened up diagonally into a lower passageway. Drizzt rifled out, though he kept the presence of mind to hurl his scimitars to their respective sides, clear of his tumbling body.

He hit the floor hard, rolled across, and slammed his lower back into a jutting boulder.

Drizzt Do'Urden lay very still.

He did not consider the pain—fast changing to numbness— in his legs; he did not inspect the many scrapes and bruises the tumbling ride had given him. He did not even think of Entreri, and at that agonizing moment, one notion overruled even the loyal dark elf's compelling fears for his friends.

He had broken his vow.

When young Drizzt had left Menzoberranzan, after killing Masoj Hun'ett, a fellow dark elf, he had vowed that he would never again kill a drow. That vow had held up, even when his family had come after him in the wilds of the Underdark, even when he had battled his eldest sister. Zaknafein's death had been fresh in his mind and his desire to kill the wicked Briza as great as any desire he had ever felt. Half mad from grief, and from ten years of surviving in the merciless wilds, Drizzt still had managed to hold to his vow.

But not now. There could be no doubt that he had killed the guardsman at the top of the chute; his scimitars had cut fine lines, a perfect X across the dark elf's throat.

It had been a reaction, Drizzt reminded himself, a necessary move if he meant to be free of Vierna's gang. He had not precipitated the violence, had not asked for it in any way. He could not reasonably be blamed for taking whatever action necessary to escape from Vierna's unjust court, and to aid his friends, coming in against powerful adversaries.

Drizzt could not reasonably be blamed, but as he lay there, the feeling gradually returning to his bruised legs, Drizzt's conscience could not escape the simple truth of the matter.

He had broken his vow.

* * * * *

Bruenor led them blindly through the twisting maze of corridors, Wulfgar right behind and carrying the snoring Pwent (and getting a fair share of cuts from the battlerager's sharp-ridged armor!). Catti-brie slipped along at his side, pausing whenever pursuit seemed close behind to launch an arrow or two.

178

Soon the halls were quiet, save the group's own clamor—too quiet, by the frightened companions' estimation. They knew how silent Drizzt could move, knew that stealth was the dark elves' forte.

But where to run? They could hardly figure out where they were in this little known region, would have to stop and take time to get their bearings before they could make a reasonable guess on how to get back to familiar territory.

Finally, Bruenor came upon a small side passage that branched three ways, each fork branching again just a short way in. Following no predetermined course, the red-bearded dwarf led them in, left then right, and soon they came into a small chamber, goblin worked and with a large slab of stone just inside the low entryway. As soon as they all were in, Wulfgar leaned the slab against the portal and fell back against it.

"Drow!" Catti-brie whispered in disbelief. "How did they come to Mithril Hall?"

"Why, not how," Bruenor corrected quietly. "Why are the elf's kin in me tunnels?

"And what?" Bruenor continued grimly. He looked to his daughter, his beloved Catti-brie, and to Wulfgar, the proud lad he had helped mold into so fine a man, a sincerely grave expression on the dwarf's bristling cheeks. "What have we landed ourself into this time?"

Catti-brie had no answer for him. Together the companions had battled many monsters, had overcome incredible obstacles, but these were dark elves, infamous drow, deadly, evil, and apparently with Drizzt in their clutches, if indeed he still drew breath. The mighty friends had gone in fast and strong to rescue Drizzt, had struck the dark elves by surprise. They had been simply overmatched, driven back without catching more than a fleeting glimpse of what might have been their lost friend.

Catti-brie looked to Wulfgar for support, saw him staring her way with the same helpless expression Bruenor had placed over her.

The young woman looked away, having neither the time nor the inclination to berate the protective barbarian. She knew that Wulfgar continued to be worried more for her than for himself—she could not chastise him for that—but Catti-brie, the fighter, knew, too, that if Wulfgar was looking out for her, his eyes would not be focused on the dangers ahead.

In this situation, she was a liability to the barbarian, not for any lack of fighting skills or survival talents, but because of Wulfgar's own weakness, his inability to view Catti-brie as an equal ally.

And with dark elves all about them, how badly they needed allies!

* * * * *

Using innate powers of levitation, the pursuing drow soldier eased himself out of the chute, his gaze immediately locking on the slumped form under the thick cloak across the corridor.

He pulled out a heavy club and rushed across, crying out with joy for the rewards that certainly would come his way for recapturing Drizzt. The club came down, sounding unexpectedly sharp as it banged off the solid stone under Drizzt's cloak.

As silent as death, Drizzt came down from his perch above the chute exit, right behind his adversary.

The evil drow's eyes widened as he realized the deception, remembered then the stone lying opposite the chute.

Drizzt's first instincts were to strike with the hilt of his scimitar; his heart asked him to honor his vow and take no more drow lives. A well-placed blow might drop this enemy and render him helpless. Drizzt could then bind him and strip him of his weapons.

If Drizzt were alone in these tunnels, if it simply were a matter of his desire to escape Vierna and Entreri, he would have followed the cry of his merciful heart. He could not ignore his friends above, though, no doubt struggling against those enemies he had left behind. He could not chance that this soldier, recovered, would bring harm to Bruenor or Wulfgar or Cattibrie.

Twinkle came in point first, slicing through the doomed drow's backbone and heart, driving out the front of his chest, the blade's blue glow showing a reddish tint.

When he pulled the scimitar back out, Drizzt Do'Urden had more blood on his hands.

He thought again of his imperiled friends and gritted his teeth, determined, if not confident, that the blood would wash away.

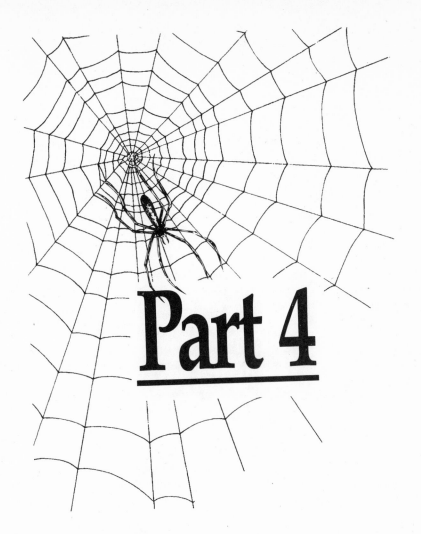

Part 4

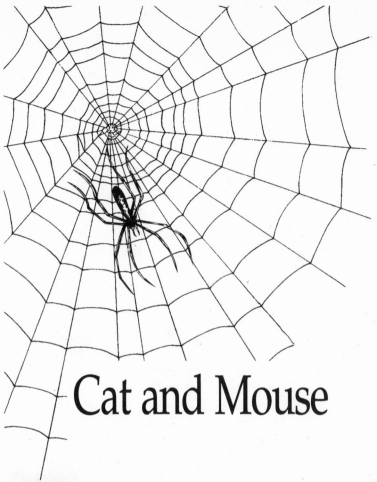

Cat and Mouse

What turmoil I felt when first I broke my most solemn, principle-intentioned vow: that I would never again take the life of one of my people. The pain, a sense of failure, a sense of loss, was acute when I realized what wicked work my scimitars had done.

The guilt faded quickly, though—not because I came to excuse myself for any failure, but because I came to realize that my true failure was in making the vow, not in breaking it. When I walked out of my homeland, I spoke the words out of innocence, the naivete of unworldly youth, and I meant them when I said them, truly. I came to know,

R. A. Salvatore

though, that such a vow was unrealistic, that if I pursued a course in life as defender of those ideals I so cherished, I could not excuse myself from actions dictated by that course if ever the enemies showed themselves to be drow elves.

Quite simply, adherence to my vow depended on situations completely beyond my control. If, after leaving Menzoberranzan, I had never again met a dark elf in battle, I never would have broken my vow. But that, in the end, would not have made me any more honorable. Fortunate circumstances do not equate to high principles.

When the situation arose, however, that dark elves threatened my dearest friends, precipitated a state of warfare against people who had done them no wrong, how could I, in good conscience, have kept my scimitars tucked away? What was my vow worth when weighed against the lives of Bruenor, Wulfgar, and Catti-brie, or when weighed against the lives of any innocents, for that matter? If, in my travels, I happened upon a drow raid against surface elves, or against a small village, I know beyond any doubts that I would have joined in the fighting, battling the unlawful aggressors with all my strength.

In that event, no doubt, I would have felt the acute pangs of failure and soon would have dismissed them, as I do now.

I do not, therefore, lament breaking my vow—though it pains me, as it always does, that I have had to kill. Nor do I regret making the vow, for the declaration of my youthful folly caused no subsequent pain. If I had attempted to adhere to the unconditional words of that declaration, though, if I had held my blades in check for a sense of false pride, and if that inaction had subsequently resulted in injury to an innocent person, then the pain in Drizzt Do'Urden would have been more acute, never to leave.

There is one more point I have come to know concerning my declaration, one more truth that I believe leads me farther along my chosen road in life. I said I would never again kill a drow elf. I made the assertion with little knowledge of the many other races of the wide world, surface and Underdark, with little understanding that many of these myriad peoples even existed. I would never kill a drow, so I said, but what of the svirfnebli, the deep gnomes? Or the halflings, elves, or

186

dwarves? And what of the humans?

I have had occasion to kill men, when Wulfgar's barbarian kin invaded Ten-Towns. To defend those innocents meant to battle, perhaps to kill, the aggressor humans. Yet that act, unpleasant as it may have been, did not in any way affect my most solemn vow, despite the fact that the reputation of humankind far outshines that of the dark elves.

To say, then, that I would never again slay a drow, purely because they and I are of the same physical heritage, strikes me now as wrong, as simply racist. To place the measure of a living being's worth above that of another simply because that being wears the same color skin as I belittles my principles. The false values embodied in that long-ago vow have no place in my world, in the wide world of countless physical and cultural differences. It is these very differences that make my journeys exciting, these very differences that put new colors and shapes on the universal concept of beauty.

I now make a new vow, one weighed in experience and proclaimed with my eyes open: I will not raise my scimitars except in defense: in defense of my principles, of my life, or of others who cannot defend themselves. I will not do battle to further the causes of false prophets, to further the treasures of kings, or to avenge my own injured pride.

And to the many gold-wealthy mercenaries, religious and secular, who would look upon such a vow as unrealistic, impractical, even ridiculous, I cross my arms over my chest and declare with conviction: I am the richer by far!

—Drizzt Do'Urden

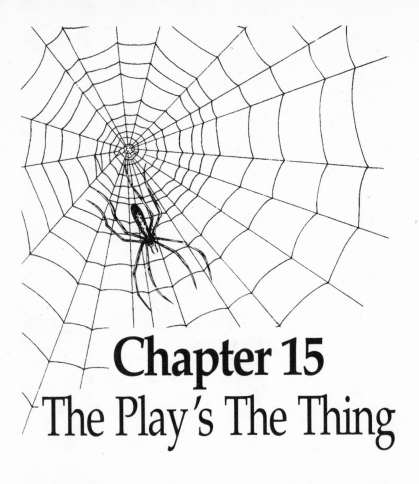

Chapter 15
The Play's The Thing

ilence! Vierna's delicate fingers signaled the command repeatedly in the intricate drow hand code.

Two handcrossbows clicked as their bowstrings locked into a ready position. Their drow wielders crouched low, staring at the broken door.

From behind them, across the small chamber, there came a slight hiss as an arrow magically dissolved, releasing its dark elf victim, who slumped to the floor at the base of the wall. Dinin, the drider, shifted away from the fallen drow, his hard-skinned legs clacking against the stone.

Silence!

Jarlaxle crawled to the edge of the blasted door, cocked an ear to the impenetrable blackness of the conjured globes. He heard a slight shuffling and drew out a dagger, signaling to the crossbowmen to stand ready.

Jarlaxle stood them down when the figure, his scout, crawled out of the darkness and entered the room.

"They have gone," the scout explained as Vierna rushed over to join the mercenary leader. "A small group, and smaller still with one crushed under your most excellent wall." Both Jarlaxle and the guard bowed low in respect to Vierna, who smiled wickedly in spite of the sudden disaster.

"What of Iftuu?" Jarlaxle asked, referring to the guard they had left watching the corridor where the trouble had begun.

"Dead," the scout replied. "Torn and ripped."

Vierna turned sharply on Entreri. "What do you know of our enemies?" she demanded.

The assassin eyed her dangerously, remembering Drizzt's warnings against alliances with his kin. "Wulfgar, the large human, hurled the hammer that broke the door," he answered with all confidence. Entreri looked to the two fast-cooling forms splayed out across the stone floor. "You can blame the deaths of those two on Catti-brie, another human, female."

Vierna turned to Jarlaxle's scout and translated what Entreri had told her into the drow tongue. "Were either of these under the wall?" the priestess asked of the scout.

"Only a single dwarf," the drow replied.

Entreri recognized the drow word for the bearded folk. "Bruenor?" he asked rhetorically, wondering if they had inadvertently assassinated the king of Mithril Hall.

"Bruenor?" Vierna echoed, not understanding.

"Head of Clan Battlehammer," Entreri explained. "Ask him," he bade Vierna, indicating the scout, and he grabbed at his clean-shaven chin with his hand, as though stroking a beard. "Red hair?"

Vierna translated, then looked back, shaking her head. "There was no light out there. The scout could not tell."

Entreri silently cursed himself for being so foolish. He just couldn't get used to this heat-sight, where shapes blurred indistinctly and colors were based on amount of heat, not reflecting hues.

"They are gone and are no longer our concern," Vierna said to Entreri.

"You would let them escape after killing three in your entourage?" Entreri started to protest, seeing where this line of reasoning would take them—and not so sure he liked that path.

"Four are dead," Vierna corrected, her gaze leading the assassin to Drizzt's victim lying beside the revealed chute.

"Ak'hafta went after your brother," Jarlaxle quickly put in.

"Then five are dead," Vierna replied grimly, "but my brother is below us and must get through us to rejoin his friends."

She began talking to the other drow in their native tongue, and, though he had not come close to mastering the language, Entreri realized that Vierna was organizing the departure down the chute in pursuit of Drizzt.

"What of my deal?" he interrupted.

Vierna's reply was to the point. "You have had your fight. We allow you your freedom, as agreed."

Entreri acted pleased by that reply; he was worldly enough to understand that to show his outrage would be to join the other fast-cooling forms on the floor. But the assassin was not about to accept his losses so readily. He looked around frantically, searching for some distraction, some way to alter the apparently done deal.

Entreri had planned things perfectly to this point, except that, in the commotion, he hadn't been able to get into the chute behind Drizzt. Alone down below, he and his arch-rival would have had the time to settle things once and for all, but now the prospect of getting Drizzt alone for a fight seemed remote and moving farther away with every second.

The wily assassin had wormed his way through more precarious predicaments than this—except, he prudently reminded himself, that this time he was dealing with dark elves, the masters of intrigue.

* * * * *

"Shhh!" Bruenor hissed at Wulfgar and Catti-brie, though it was Thibbledorf Pwent, deep in sleep and snoring as only a dwarf can snore, who was making all the noise. "I think I heared something!"

Wulfgar angled the battlerager's helmet point against the wall, slapped one hand under Pwent's chin, closing the battlerager's mouth, then clamped his fingers around Pwent's wide nose. Pwent's cheeks bulged weirdly a couple of times, and a strange squeaky-smacking type of noise came out from somewhere. Wulfgar and Catti-brie exchanged looks; Wulfgar even bent to the side, wondering if the outrageous dwarf had just snored out of his ears!

Bruenor cringed at the unexpected blast, but was too intent to turn and scold his companions. From down the corridor there came another slight shuffling noise, barely perceptible, and then another, still closer. Bruenor knew they soon would be found; how could they escape when both Wulfgar and Catti-brie needed torchlight to navigate the twisting tunnels?

Another scuffle came, just outside the small chamber.

"Well, come on out, ye pointy-eared orc kisser!" the frustrated and frightened dwarf king roared, hopping through the small opening around the slab Wulfgar had used to partially block the passageway. The dwarf lifted his great axe high above his head.

He saw the black form, as expected, and tried to chop, but the form was by him too quickly, springing into the small chamber with hardly a whisper of noise.

"What?" the startled dwarf, axe still high, balked, swinging himself around and nearly spinning to the floor.

"Guenhwyvar!" he heard Catti-brie call from beyond the slab.

Bruenor rambled back into the chamber just as the mighty panther opened its maw wide and let drop the valuable figurine—along with the ebon-skinned hand of the unfortunate dark elf who had grabbed for it when Guenhwyvar had made the break.

Catti-brie gave a sour look and kicked the disembodied hand far from the figurine.

"Damn good cat," Bruenor admitted, and the rugged dwarf was truly relieved that a new and powerful ally had been found.

Guenhwyvar roared in reply, the mighty growl reverberating off the tunnel walls for many, many yards in every direction. Pwent opened his weary eyes at the sound. Wide those dark orbs popped indeed when the battlerager caught sight of the six-hundred-pound panther sitting only three feet away!

Adrenaline soaring to new heights, the wild battlerager flubbed out sixteen words at once as he scrambled and kicked to regain his footing (inadvertently kneeing himself in the shin and drawing some blood). He almost got there, until Guen–hwyvar apparently realized his intent and absently slapped a paw, claws retracted, across his face.

Pwent's helmet rung out a clear note as he rebounded off the wall, and he thought then that another nap might do him good. But he was a battlerager, he reminded himself, and, by his estimation, a most wild battle was about to be fought. He produced a large flask from under his cloak and took a hearty swig, then whipped his head about to clear the cobwebs, his thick lips flapping noisily. Somehow seeming revived, the battlerager set his feet firmly under him for a charge.

Wulfgar grabbed him by the helmet point and hoisted him off the floor, Pwent's stubby legs pumping helplessly.

"What're ye about?" the battlerager snarled in protest, but even Thibbledorf Pwent had his bluster drained, along with the blood in his face, when Guenhwyvar looked to him and growled, ears flattened and pearly teeth bared.

"The panther is a friend," Wulfgar explained.

".The wh—who is . . . the damn cat?" Pwent stuttered.

"Damn good cat," Bruenor corrected, ending the debate. The dwarf king went back to watching the hall then, glad to have Guenhwyvar beside them, knowing that they would need everything Guenhwyvar could give, and perhaps a little bit more.

* * * * *

Entreri noticed one wounded drow propped against the wall, being tended by two others, the bandages they applied quickly growing hot with spilling blood. He recognized the injured dark elf as one that had reached for the statuette soon after Drizzt had called for the cat, and the reminder of Guen—hwyvar gave the assassin a new ploy to try.

"Drizzt's friends will pursue you, even down the chute," Entreri remarked grimly, interrupting Vierna once more.

The priestess turned to him, obviously concerned about his reasoning—as was the mercenary standing beside her.

"Do not underestimate them," Entreri continued. "I know them, and they are loyal beyond anything in the dark elf world—except of course for a priestess's loyalty to the Spider Queen," he added, in deference to Vierna because he didn't want his skin peeled off as a drow trophy. "You plan now to go after your brother, but even if you catch him at once and head with all speed for Menzoberranzan, his loyal friends will chase you."

"They were but a few," Vierna retorted.

"But they will be back with many more, especially if that dwarf under the wall was Bruenor Battlehammer," Entreri countered.

Vierna looked to Jarlaxle for confirmation of the assassin's claims, and the more worldly dark elf only shrugged and shook his head in helpless ignorance.

"They will come better equipped and better armed," Entreri went on, his new scheme formulating, his banter building momentum. "With wizards, perhaps. With many clerics, surely. And with that deadly bow"—he glanced at the body near the wall—"and the barbarian's warhammer."

"The tunnels are many," Vierna reasoned, seemingly dismissing the argument. "They could not follow our course." She turned, as if her argument had satisfied her, to go back to formulating her initial plans.

"They have the panther!" Entreri growled at her. "The panther that is the dearest friend of all to your brother. Guen–hwyvar would pursue you to the Abyss itself if there you carried Drizzt's body."

Again distressed, Vierna looked to Jarlaxle. "What say you?" she demanded.

Jarlaxle rubbed a hand across his pointy chin. "The panther was well known among the scouting groups when your brother lived in the city," he admitted. "Our raiding party is not large—and apparently five fewer now."

Vierna turned back sharply on Entreri. "You who seem to know the ways of these people so well," she prompted with more than a bit of sarcasm, "what do you suggest we do?"

"Go after the fleeing band," Entreri replied, pointing to the blackened corridor beyond the blasted door. "Catch them and kill them before they can get back to the dwarven complex and muster support. I will find your brother for you."

Vierna eyed him suspiciously, a look Entreri most certainly did not like.

"But I am awarded another fight against Drizzt," he insisted, baiting the plan with some measure of believability.

"When we are rejoined," Vierna added coldly.

"Of course." The assassin swept into a low bow and leaped for the chute.

"And you will not go alone," Vierna decided. She gave a

look to Jarlaxle, and he motioned for two of his soldiers to accompany the assassin.

"I work alone," Entreri insisted.

"You die alone," Vierna corrected, "against my brother in the tunnels, I mean," she added in softer, teasing tones, but Entreri knew that Vierna's promise had nothing at all to do with her brother.

He saw little point in continuing to argue with her, so he just shrugged and motioned for one of the dark elves to lead the way.

Actually, having a drow with the levitational powers beneath him made the ride down the dangerous chute much more comfortable for the assassin.

The leading dark elf came out into the lower corridor first, Entreri landing nimbly behind him and the second drow coming in slowly behind the assassin. The first drow shook his head in apparent confusion and kicked lightly at the prone body, but Entreri, wiser to Drizzt's many tricks, pushed the dark elf aside and slammed his sword down onto the apparent corpse. Gingerly, the assassin turned the dead drow over, confirming that it was not Drizzt in a clever disguise. Satisfied, he slipped his sword away.

"Our enemy is clever," he explained, and one of his companions, understanding the surface language, nodded, then translated for the other drow.

"That is Ak'hafta," the dark elf explained to Entreri. "Dead, as Vierna predicted." He led his drow companion toward the assassin.

Entreri was not at all surprised to find the slain soldier right below the chute. He, above anyone else in Vierna's party, understood how deadly their opponent might be, and how efficient. Entreri did not doubt that the two accompanying him, skilled fighters but inexperienced concerning the ways of their enemy, would have little chance of catching Drizzt. By Entreri's estimation, if these unknowing dark elves had come through the chute alone, Drizzt might well have cut them down already.

Entreri smiled privately at the thought, then smiled even more widely as he realized that these two didn't understand their ally, let alone their enemy.

His sword jabbed to the side as the trailing drow passed by him, neatly skewering both of the unfortunate elf's lungs. The other drow, quicker than Entreri had expected, wheeled about, handcrossbow leveled and ready.

A jeweled dagger came first, nicking the drow's weapon hand hard enough to deflect the shot harmlessly wide. Undaunted, the dark elf snarled and produced a pair of finely edged swords.

It never ceased to amaze Entreri how easily these dark elves fought so well with two weapons of equal length. He whipped his thin leather belt from his breeches and looped it double in his free left hand, waving it and his sword out in front to keep his opponent at bay.

"You side with Drizzt Do'Urden!" the drow accused.

"I do not side with you," Entreri corrected. The drow came at him hard, swords crossing, going back out wide, then crossing in close again, forcing Entreri to bat them with his own sword, then promptly retreat. The attack was skilled and deceptively quick, but Entreri immediately recognized the primary difference between this drow and Drizzt, the subtle level of skill that elevated Drizzt—and Entreri, for that matter—from these other fighters. The double crossing attack had been launched as finely as any Entreri had ever seen, but during the few seconds he had taken to execute the maneuver, the dark elf's defenses had not been aligned. Like so many other fine fighters, this drow was a one-way warrior, perfect on the attack, perfect on defense, but not perfect on both at the same time.

It was a minor thing; the drow's quickness compensated so well that most fighters would never have noticed the apparent weakness. But Entreri was not like most fighters.

Again the drow pressed the attack. One sword darted

196

straight for Entreri's face, only to be swatted aside at the last moment. The second sword came in low, right behind, but Entreri reversed his weapon's momentum and batted the thrusting tip to the ground.

Furiously the drow came on, swords flying, diving for any apparent opening, only to be intercepted by Entreri's sword or hooked and pulled wide by the leather belt.

And all the while the assassin willingly retreated, bided his time, waited for the sure kill.

The swords crossed, went out wide, and crossed again as they charged for Entreri's midsection, the dark elf repeating his initial attack.

The defense had changed, the assassin moving with sudden, terrifying speed.

Entreri's belt looped around the tip of the sword in the drow's right hand, which was crossed under the other, and then the assassin jerked back to his left, pulling the swords tightly together and forcing them both to the side.

The doomed dark elf started backing at once, and both swords easily came free of the awkward belt, but the drow, his defensive balance forfeited in the offensive routine, needed a split second to recover his posture.

Entreri's flashing sword didn't take that split second. It dove hungrily into the drow's exposed left flank, tip twisting as it weaved its way into the soft flesh beneath the rib cage.

The wounded warrior fell back, his belly wickedly torn, and Entreri did not pursue, instead falling into his balanced battle stance.

"You are dead," he said matter-of-factly as the drow struggled to stand and keep his swords level.

The drow could not dispute the claim, and could not hope, through the blinding and burning agony, to stop the assassin's impending attack. He dropped his weapons to the floor and announced, "I yield."

"Well spoken," Entreri congratulated him, then the assassin

drove his sword into the foolish dark elf's heart.

He cleaned the blade on his victim's *piwafwi*, retrieved his precious dagger, then turned to regard the empty tunnel, running fairly straight both ways beyond the range of his somewhat limited infravision. "Now, dear Drizzt," he said loudly, "things are as I had planned." Entreri smiled, congratulating himself for so perfectly manipulating such a dangerous situation.

"I have not forgotten the sewers of Calimport, Drizzt Do'Urden!" he shouted, his anger suddenly boiling over. "Nor have I forgiven!"

Entreri calmed at once, reminding himself that his rage had been his weakness on that occasion when he had battled Drizzt in the southern city.

"Take heart, my respected friend," he said quietly, "for now we can begin our play, as it was always meant to be."

* * * * *

Drizzt circled back to the chute area soon after Entreri had departed. He knew at once what had transpired when he saw the two new corpses, and he realized that none of this had occurred by accident. Drizzt had baited Entreri in the chamber above, had refused to play the game the way the assassin had desired. But Entreri apparently had anticipated Drizzt's reluctance and had prepared, or improvised, an alternative plan.

Now he had Drizzt, just Drizzt, in the lower tunnels, one against one. Now, too, if it came to combat, Drizzt would fight with all his heart, knowing that to win was to at least have some chance of freedom.

Drizzt nodded his head, silently congratulating his opportunistic enemy.

But Drizzt's priorities were not akin to Entreri's. The dark elf's main concern was to find his way through, to circle back around, that he might rejoin his friends and aid them in their peril. To Drizzt, Entreri was no more than another piece of the larger threat.

If he happened to encounter Entreri on his way, though, Drizzt Do'Urden meant to finish the game.

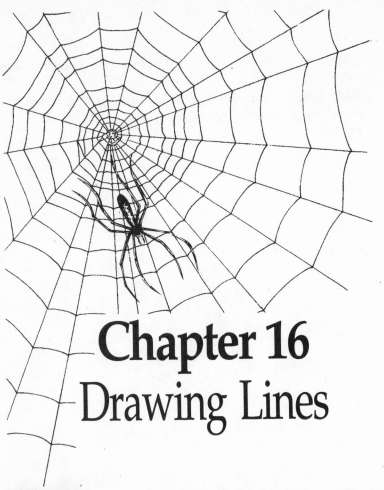

Chapter 16
Drawing Lines

I am not pleased," Vierna remarked, standing with Jarlaxle in the tunnel near the conjured iron wall, with poor Cobble's squashed body underneath.

"Did you believe it would be so easy?" the mercenary replied. "We have entered the tunnels of a fortified dwarven complex with a contingent of barely fifty soldiers. Fifty against thousands.

"You will recapture your brother," Jarlaxle added, not wanting Vierna to get overly anxious. "My troops are well-trained. Already I have dispatched nearly three dozen, the entire

Baenre complement, to the single corridor leading out of Mithril Hall proper. None of Drizzt's allies shall enter that way, and his trapped friends shall not escape."

"When the dwarves learn we are about, they will send an army," Vierna reasoned grimly.

"If they learn," Jarlaxle corrected. "The tunnels of Mithril Hall are long. It will take our adversaries some time to muster a significant force—days perhaps. We will be halfway to Men–zoberranzan, with Drizzt, before the dwarves are organized."

Vierna paused for a long while, considering her next course of action. There were only two ways up from the bottom level: the chute in the nearby room and winding tunnels some distance to the north. She looked to the room and moved into it to regard the chute, wondering if she had done wrong in sending only three after Drizzt. She considered ordering her entire force—a dozen drow and the drider—down in pursuit.

"The human will get him," Jarlaxle said to her, as though he had read her mind. "Artemis Entreri knows our enemy better than we; he has battled Drizzt across the wide expanses of the surface world. Also, he wears still the earring, that you might track his progress. Up here we have Drizzt's friends, only a handful by my scouts' reckoning, to deal with."

"And if Drizzt eludes Entreri?" Vierna asked.

"There are only two ways up," Jarlaxle reminded her again.

Vierna nodded, her decision made, and walked across to the chute. She took a small wand out of a fold in her ornamental robes and closed her eyes, beginning a soft chant. Slowly and deliberately, Vierna traced precise lines across the opening, the tip of the wand spewing sticky filament. Perfectly, the priestess outlined a spiderweb of thin strands, covering the opening. Vierna stepped back to examine her work. From a pouch she produced a packet of fine dust, and, beginning a second chant, she sprinkled it over the web. Immediately the strands thickened and took on a black and silvery luster. Then the shine faded and the warmth of the enchantment's energy cooled to room temperature, leaving the strands practically invisible.

"Now there is one way up," Vierna announced to Jarlaxle. "No weapon can cut the strands."

"To the north, then," Jarlaxle agreed. "I have sent a handful of runners ahead to guard the lower tunnels."

"Drizzt and his friends must not join," Vierna instructed.

"If Drizzt sees his friends again, they will already be dead," the cocky mercenary replied with all confidence.

* * * * *

"There may be another way into the room," Wulfgar offered. "If we could strike at them from both sides—"

"Drizzt is gone from the place," Bruenor interrupted, the dwarf fingering the magical locket and looking to the floor, sensing that his friend was somewhere below them.

"When we've killed all our enemies, yer friend'll find us," Pwent reasoned.

Wulfgar, still holding the battlerager off the ground by his helmet spike, gave him a little shake.

"I've no heart for fighting drow," Bruenor replied, and he gave both Catti-brie and Wulfgar concerned sidelong glances, "not like this. We're to keep away from them if we can, hit at 'em only when we find the need."

"We could go back and get Dagna," Wulfgar offered, "and sweep the tunnels clean of dark elves."

Bruenor looked to the maze of corridors that would bring him back to the dwarven complex, considering the path. He and his friends could lose perhaps an hour in working their roundabout way to Mithril Hall, and several hours more in rounding up a sizable force. Those were several hours that Drizzt probably didn't have to spare.

"We go for Drizzt," Catti-brie decided firmly. "We got yer locket to point us right, and Guenhwyvar will take us to him."

Bruenor knew Pwent would readily agree to anything that

opened the possibility for a fight, and Guenhwyvar's fur was ruffled, the panther anxious, sleek muscles tense. The dwarf looked to Wulfgar and nearly spat at the lad for the worried, condescending expression splayed across his face as he studied Catti-brie.

Without warning, Guenhwyvar froze in place, issuing a low, quiet growl. Catti-brie immediately doused the low-burning torch and crouched low, using the red-glowing dots of dwarven eyes to keep her bearings.

The group came closer together, Bruenor whispering for the others to remain in the side chamber while he went out to see what the cat had sensed.

"Drow," he explained when he returned a moment later, Guenhwyvar at his side, "just a handful, moving fast and to the north."

"Handful o' dead drow," Pwent corrected. The others could hear the battlerager eagerly rubbing his hands together, the shoulder joints of his armor scraping too noisily.

"No fighting!" Bruenor whispered as loudly as he dared, and he grabbed Pwent's arms to stop the motion. "I'm thinking that this group might have an idea of where to find Drizzt, that they're out looking for him, but we got no chance of keeping up with them without light."

"And if we put up the torch, we'll find ourselves fighting soon enough," Catti-brie reasoned.

"Then light the damned torch!" Pwent said hopefully.

"Shut yer mouth," Bruenor answered. "We're going out slow and easy—and ye keep the torch, make it two torches, ready for lighting at the first signs of a fight," he told Wulfgar. Then he motioned to Guenhwyvar to lead them, bidding the cat to keep the pace slow.

Pwent shoved his large flask into Catti-brie's hand as soon as they exited the tunnel. "Take a hit o' this," he instructed, "and pass it about."

Catti-brie blindly moved her hands about the item, finally

discerning it to be a flask. She gingerly sniffed the foul-smelling liquid and started to hand it back.

"Ye'll think the better of it when a drow elf puts a poisoned dart into yer backside," the crude battlerager explained, patting Catti-brie on the rump. "With this stuff flowing about yer blood, no poison's got a chance!"

Reminding herself that Drizzt was in trouble, the young woman took a deep draw on the flask, then coughed and stumbled to the side. For a moment, she saw eight dwarf eyes and four cat eyes staring at her, but the double vision soon went away and she passed the flask on to Bruenor.

Bruenor handled it easily, offering a sigh and a profound, though quiet, belch when he had finished. "Warms yer toes," he explained to Wulfgar when he passed it along.

After Wulfgar had recovered, the group set off, Guenhwyvar's padded paws quietly marking the way, and Pwent's armor squealing noisily with every eager stride.

* * * * *

Forty battle-ready dwarves followed the stomping boots of General Dagna through the lower mines of Mithril Hall to the final guardroom.

"We'll make right for the goblin hall," the general explained to his charges, "and branch out from there." He went on to instruct the door guards, setting up a series of tapping signals and leaving directions for any subsequent troops that came in, explicitly commanding that no dwarves in groups less than a dozen were to be allowed into the new sections.

Then stern Dagna put his soldiers in line, placed himself bravely and proudly at their lead, and moved through the opened door. Dagna really didn't believe that Bruenor was in peril, figured that perhaps a pocket of goblin resistance or some other minor inconvenience remained to be cleared. But the general was a conservative commander, preferring overkill to even odds, and he would take no chances where Bruenor's safety was concerned.

The heavy footsteps of hard boots, clanking armor, and even a grumbling war chant now and then heralded the approach of the force, and every third dwarf held a torch. Dagna had no reason to believe that this formidable force would need stealth, and hoped that Bruenor and any other allies who might be wandering about down here would be able to find the boisterous troupe.

Dagna didn't know about the dark elves.

The dwarves' rolling pace soon got them near the first intersection, in sight of the piled ettin bones from Bruenor's long-ago kill. Dagna called for "side watchers" and started forward, meaning to continue straight ahead, straight for the main chamber of the goblin battle. Before he even reached the side passage, Dagna slowed his troops and called for a measure of quiet.

The general glanced all about curiously, nervously, as he began to cross through the wider intersection. His warrior instincts, honed over three centuries of fighting, told him that something wasn't right; the thick layers of hair on the back of his neck tingled weirdly.

Then the lights went out.

At first, the dwarf general thought something had extinguished the torches, but he quickly realized, from the clamor arising behind him and from the fact that his infravision, when he was able to refocus his eyes, was utterly useless, that something more ominous had occurred.

"Darkness!" cried one dwarf.

"Wizards!" howled another.

Dagna heard his companions jostle about, heard something whistle by his ear, followed by the grunt of one of his undercommanders standing immediately behind him. Instinctively, the general began to backtrack, and, only a few short strides later, he emerged from the globe of conjured darkness to find his charges rushing all around. A second globe of darkness had split the dwarven force almost exactly in half, and those in front of the spell were calling out to those caught within it and to those behind, trying to muster some organization.

"Wedge up!" Dagna cried above the tumult, demanding the most basic of dwarven battle formations. "It's a spell of darkness, nothing more!" Beside the general, a dwarf clutched at his chest, pulled out some small type of dart that Dagna did not recognize, and tumbled to the ground, snoring before he ever hit the stone.

Something nicked at Dagna's shin, but he ignored it and continued his commands, trying to orient the group into a single and unified fighting unit. He sent five dwarves rushing out to the right flank, around the darkness globe and into the beginning of the intersecting passage.

"Find me that damned wizard!" he ordered them. "And find out what in the Nine Hells we're fighting against!"

Dagna's frustration only fueled his ire, and soon he had the remaining dwarven force in a tight wedge formation, ready to punch through the initial darkness globe.

The five flanking dwarves rambled into the side passage. Once convinced that no enemies lurked down that way, they quickly looped about the blackness globe, heading for the narrow opening between the sphere and the entryway farther along the main corridor.

Two dark forms emerged from the shadows, dropping to one knee before the dwarves and leveling small crossbows.

The leading dwarf, hit twice, stumbled but still managed to call for the charge. He and his four companions launched themselves at their enemy in full flight, taking no notice until it was too late that other enemies, other dark elves, were levitating above and dropping down all about them.

"What the . . ." a dwarf gasped as a drow nimbly landed beside him, smashing in the side of his skull with a powerfully enchanted mace.

"Hey, yerself ain't Drizzt!" another dwarf managed to remark a split second before a drow sword sliced his throat.

The group leader wanted to call for a retreat, but even as he started to yell, the floor rushed up and swallowed him. It was a fine bed for a sleeping dwarf, but from this slumber, the vulnerable soldier would never awaken.

In the span of five seconds, only two dwarves remained. "Drow! Drow!" they cried out in warning.

One went down heavily, three arrows in his back. He struggled to get back to his knees, but two dark elves fell over him, hacking with their swords.

The remaining dwarf, rushing back to rejoin Dagna, found himself facing only a single opponent. The drow poked forward with his slender sword; the dwarf accepted the hit and returned it with a vicious axe chop to the side, blasting the drow's arm and rending his fine suit of chain mail.

Past the falling drow and into the darkness the terrified dwarf ran, bursting out the other side of the enchanted globe, right into the front ranks of Dagna's slow-moving wedge.

"Drow!" the frightened dwarf cried once more.

A third globe of darkness came up, connecting the other two. A volley of handcrossbow bolts whipped through, and behind it came the dark elves, skilled at fighting without the use of their eyes.

Dagna realized that clerics would be needed to battle this dark elven magic, but when he tried to call for a retreat, it came out instead as a most profound yawn.

Something hard hit him on the side of the head, and he felt himself falling.

Amidst the chaos and the impenetrable darkness, the wedge could not be maintained, and the surprised dwarves had little chance against a nearly even number of skilled and prepared dark elves. The dwarves wisely broke ranks, many keeping the presence of mind to reach down and grab a fallen kin, and rushed back the way they had come.

The rout was on, but the dwarves were not novices to battle, and there was not a coward among them. As soon as they got out of the darkened areas of tunnel, several took it upon themselves to reorganize the band. Pursuit was hot—there could be no thoughts of turning back to do full battle—but burdened by nearly ten snoozing dwarves, Dagna among them, the slower force could not hope to outrun the quicker drow.

A call went up for blockers and there came no shortage of volunteers. When it sorted out a moment later, the dwarves ran on, leaving six brave soldiers standing shield to shield in the corridor to cover the retreat.

"Run on or those who've fallen will have died in vain!" cried one of the new commanders.

"Run on for the sake of our missing king!" cried another.

Those in the back ranks of the fleeing troupe looked often over their stocky shoulders to view their blocking comrades—until a globe of darkness enveloped the defensive line.

"Run on!" came a common cry, from those fleeing and from the brave blockers alike.

The fleeing dwarves heard the joining of battle as the dark elves hit their stubborn, blocking comrades. They heard the clang of steel against steel, heard the grunts of solid hits and glancing blows. They heard the shriek of a wounded drow and smiled grimly.

They did not look back, but bowed their heads forward and ran on, each vowing silently to toast the lost companions. The blockers would not break ranks and join them in their flight; they would hold the line, hold the enemy back until their lifeless bodies fell to the stone. It was all done in loyalty to their fleeing kin, an act of supreme, valiant sacrifice, dwarf for dwarf.

On ran the dwarves, and if one tripped on the stone, four others paused to help him get back up again. If one's burden of a sleeping kinsman became too cumbersome, another willingly took over the load.

One younger dwarf sprinted ahead of the main host and

began tap-tapping his hammer against the stone walls in the appointed signal for the door guards. By the time he arrived at the tunnel's end, the great barrier was already cracked open, and it spread wide when the truth of the rout became apparent.

The dwarven force piled into the guardroom, some remaining just inside the doorway to coax on any possible stragglers. They kept the door open until the last minute, until a globe of darkness blocked the very end of the tunnel and a handcrossbow quarrel cut through it and took down another soldier.

The tunnel was shut and sealed, and the count showed that twenty-seven of the original forty-one had escaped, with more than a third of them sleeping soundly.

"Get the whole damned army!" one of the dwarves suggested.

"And the clerics," added another, lifting Dagna's limp head to accentuate his point. "We're needing clerics to stop the poisons and to keep the damned lights on!"

The resourceful dwarves soon determined a pecking order and an order of business. Half the force stayed with the sleepers and the guards; the other half ran to the far corners of Mithril Hall, shouting the call to arms.

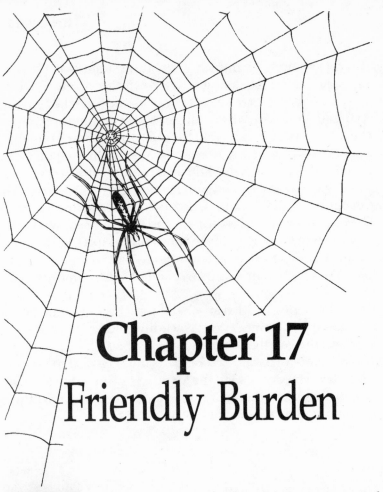

Chapter 17
Friendly Burden

He felt so very vulnerable with his scimitars tucked away, and often paused to tell himself that he was being incredibly foolhardy. The potential cost—the lives of his friends—prodded Drizzt on, though, and he cautiously, quietly, placed hand over hand, inching his way up the winding and treacherous chute. Years ago, when he, too, was a creature of the Underdark, Drizzt had been able to levitate and could have managed the chute much more easily. But that ability, apparently somehow linked to the strange magical emanations of the deepest regions, had flown from

Drizzt soon after he had stepped onto Toril's surface.

He hadn't realized how far he had fallen and silently thanked his goddess, Mielikki, that he had survived the plummet! He put a hundred crawling feet behind him, some of the going easy along sloping stretches, other parts nearly vertical. As nimble as any thief, the drow stubbornly climbed on.

What had happened to Guenhwyvar? Drizzt worried. Had the panther come to his hurried call? Had one of the drow, the opportunistic Jarlaxle, perhaps, simply scooped up the dropped figurine to claim the panther as his own?

Scaling hand over hand, Drizzt neared the chute opening. The blanket had not been replaced, and the room above was eerily quiet. Drizzt knew the silence meant little where his dark elf kin were concerned. He had led drow scouting parties that had covered fifty miles of rough tunnel without a whisper of noise. Rightly fearful, Drizzt imagined a dozen dark elves encircling the small chute, weapons drawn, awaiting their prisoner's foolish return.

But Drizzt had to go up. For the sake of his imperiled friends, Drizzt had to block his fear that Vierna and the others were still in the room.

He sensed danger as his hand inched upward, reaching for the lip. He saw nothing, had no practical, plausible warning, save the silent shouts of his warrior instincts.

Drizzt tried to dismiss them, but his hand inevitably moved more slowly. How many times had his insight—he could call it luck—saved him?

Sensitive fingers slid gingerly up the stone; Drizzt resisted his anxious urge to shoot his hand up, grab the lip and hoist himself over, forcing the play of whatever peril awaited him. He stopped, felt something, barely perceptible, against the tip of his middle digit.

He could not retract his hand!

As soon as the initial moment of fear passed, Drizzt realized the truth of the spiderweb trap and held himself steady. He had witnessed the many uses of magical webs in Menzoberranzan; the First House of the city was actually encircled by a weblike fence of unbreakable strands. And now, though only a single finger was barely touching the magical strands, Drizzt was caught.

He remained perfectly still, perfectly quiet, concentrating his muscle movements so that his weight came more fully against the nearly vertical wall. Gradually he maneuvered his free hand to his cloak, first going for a scimitar, then wisely changing his mind and reaching instead for one of the tiny quarrels he had taken from the dead dark elf in the corridor below.

Drizzt froze at the sound of drow voices above, in the room.

He couldn't make out half their words, but he discerned that they were talking about him—and about his friends! Catti-brie, Wulfgar, and whoever else was with them apparently had escaped.

And the panther was running free; Drizzt heard several remarks, fearful warnings, about the "devil cat."

More determined than ever, Drizzt inched his free hand back toward Twinkle, thinking that he must try to cut through the magical barrier, must get up from the chute and rush to his friends' aid. The moment of desperation was fleeting, however, lasting only as long as it took Drizzt to realize that if Vierna had sealed this chute with the bulk of her force still above it, then there must be another path, not too far, from level to level.

The drow voices receded, and Drizzt took another moment to solidify his precarious perch. He then worked the quarrel free of his cloak, rubbing it against the stone, then against his clothing in an effort to get all of the insidious sleeping poison from its tip. Gingerly he reached his hand up toward the trapped finger, bit his lip to keep from crying out, and jabbed the quarrel under the skin and worked a tear.

Drizzt could only hope he had removed all of the poison, that he would not fall asleep and tumble, probably to his death, back down the chute. Finding a solid grip with his free hand, bracing himself for the jolt and the pain, he jerked his arm hard, tearing the top, trapped skin clean of his finger.

He nearly swooned for the pain, nearly lost his balance, but somehow he held on, brought the finger to his mouth to suck out and spit out the possibly poisoned blood.

He came back into the lower corridor five minutes later, scimitars in hand, eyes darting this way and that in search of his archenemy and in an effort to make some guess about which way he should travel. He knew that Mithril Hall was somewhere back to the east, but realized that his captives had been taking him primarily north. If there was indeed a second way up, it likely was beyond the chute, farther to the north.

He replaced Twinkle in its sheath—not wanting its glow to reveal him—but held his other scimitar out in front of him as he made his stealthy way along the corridor. There were few side passages, and Drizzt was glad for that, realizing that any direction choice he might make at this point, with no feasible landmarks to guide him, would be mere guesswork.

Then he came to an intersection and caught a glimpse of a fleeting, shadowy figure darting along an apparently parallel tunnel to his right flank.

Drizzt knew instinctively that it was Entreri, and it seemed obvious that Entreri would know the other way out of this level.

To the right Drizzt went, in crouched, measured steps, now the pursuer, not the pursued.

He paused when he got to the parallel tunnel, took a deep breath, and peeked around. The shadowy figure, moving quickly, was far ahead, turning unexpectedly right once more.

Drizzt considered this course change with more than a little suspicion. Shouldn't Entreri have kept to the left, kept close to the course he thought Drizzt was taking?

Drizzt suspected then that the assassin knew he was being followed and was leading Drizzt to a place Entreri considered favorable. Drizzt couldn't afford the delay of heeding his suspicions, though, not while the fate of his overmatched friends lay in the balance. To the right he went, quickly, only to find that he had not gained any ground, that Entreri's course had led them both into quite a maze of crisscrossing passageways.

With the assassin no longer in sight, Drizzt concentrated on the floor. To his relief, he was close enough behind so that the residual heat of Entreri's passing footsteps was still visible, though barely, to his superior infravision. He realized that he was vulnerable, head down, with little idea of how many seconds ahead of him the assassin might be, or how many seconds behind, Drizzt knew, for he felt certain that Entreri had led him to this region so that he could double back and come at Drizzt from the back.

His pace barely matched Entreri's as the narrow tunnels gave way to wider natural chambers. The footsteps remained obscure and fast cooling, but Drizzt somehow managed.

A small cry ahead gave him pause. It wasn't Entreri, Drizzt knew, but he believed he was not yet close enough to link up with his friends.

Who had it been, then?

Drizzt used his ears instead of his eyes and sorted through the tiny echoes to follow a barely audible whimpering. He was glad then for his drow warrior training, for years of studying echo patterns in winding tunnels.

The whimpering grew louder; Drizzt knew its source was just around the bend, in what appeared to him from his angle to be a small, oval side chamber.

One scimitar drawn, another hand on Twinkle's hilt, the drow dashed around the corner.

Regis!

Battered and torn, the plump halfling lay sprawled against the far wall, his hands tightly bound, a thin gag pulled tightly across his mouth, and his cheeks caked with blood. Drizzt's first instincts sent him running forward for his injured friend, but he skidded to a halt, fearing another of clever Entreri's many tricks.

Regis noticed him, looked desperately to him.

Drizzt had seen that expression before, recognized its sincerity beyond anything a disguised Entreri, mask or no mask, could hope to duplicate. He was at the halfling's side in a moment, cutting the bonds, tearing free the tight gag.

"Entreri . . ." the halfling began breathlessly.

"I know," Drizzt said calmly.

"No," Regis retorted sharply, demanding the drow's attention. "Entreri . . . was just . . ."

"He passed through here no more than a minute ahead of me," Drizzt finished, not wanting Regis to struggle any more than necessary for his labored breath.

Regis nodded, his round eyes darting about as though he expected the assassin to charge back in and slay them both.

Drizzt was more concerned with an examination of the halfling's many wounds. Taken individually, each of them appeared superficial, but together they added up to a severe condition indeed. Drizzt let Regis take a few moments to get the blood circulating through his recently untied hands and feet, then tried to get the halfling to stand.

Regis shook his head immediately; a great wave of dizziness knocked him from his feet, and he would have hit the stone floor hard had not Drizzt been there to catch him.

"Leave me," Regis said, showing an unexpected measure of altruism.

Indomitable, the drow smiled comfortingly and hoisted Regis to his side.

"Together," he explained casually. "I would not leave you any more than you would leave me."

The assassin's trail was, by then, too cool to follow, so Drizzt had to go on blindly, hoping he would stumble on some clue as to the location of the passage to the higher level. He drew out Twinkle now, instead of his other blade, and used the light to help him avoid any small jags in the floor, that he might keep Regis's walk more comfortable. All measure of stealth had been lost anyway, with the groaning halfling held at his side, Regis's feet more often scraping than stepping as Drizzt pulled him along.

"I thought he would . . . kill . . . me," Regis remarked after he had caught and held enough of his hard-to-find breath to utter a complete sentence.

"Entreri kills only when he perceives it to his advantage," Drizzt replied.

"Why did he . . . bring me along?" Regis honestly wondered. "And why . . . did he let you find me?"

Drizzt looked at his little friend curiously.

"He led you to me," Regis reasoned. "He . . ." The halfling slumped heavily, but Drizzt's strong arm continued to hold him upright.

Drizzt understood exactly why Entreri had led him to Regis. The assassin knew that Drizzt would carry Regis along—by Entreri's measure, that was exactly the difference between him and Drizzt. Entreri perceived that very compassion to be the drow's weakness. In all truth, the stealth had been lost, and now Drizzt would have to play this game of cat and mouse by Entreri's rules, showing as much attention to his burdening friend as to the game. Even if luck showed Drizzt the way up to the next level, he would have a difficult time getting to his friends before Entreri caught up to him.

Even more important than the physical burden, Drizzt realized, Entreri had given Regis back to him to ensure an honest fight. Drizzt would play out their inevitable battle wholeheartedly, with no intention of running away, with Regis lying helpless somewhere nearby.

Regis slipped in and out of consciousness over the next half hour, Drizzt uncomplaining and carrying him along, every now and then switching arms to balance the load. The drow ranger's skill in the tunnels was considerable, and he felt confident that he was making headway in sorting through the maze.

They came into a long, straight passage, a bit higher-roofed and wider than the many they had crossed. Drizzt placed Regis down easily against a wall and studied the patterns in the rock. He noticed a barely perceptible incline in the floor, rising to the south, but the fact that they, traveling north, were going slightly down did not disturb the drow at all.

"This is the main corridor of the region," he decided at length. Regis looked to him, puzzled.

"It once ran fast with water," Drizzt explained, "probably cutting through the mountain to exit at some distant waterfall to the north."

"We're going down?" Regis asked.

Drizzt nodded. "But if there is a passageway back up to the lower levels of Mithril Hall, it will likely lie along this route."

"Well done," came an unexpected reply from somewhere in the distance. A slender form stepped out of a side passage, just a few dozen feet ahead of Drizzt and Regis.

Drizzt's hand went instinctively inside his cloak, but, putting more trust in his scimitars, he retracted it immediately as the assassin approached.

"Have I given to you the hope you so desired?" Entreri teased. He said something under his breath—a call to his weapon probably, for his slender sword began glowing fiercely in bluish-green hues, revealing the assassin's graceful form in dim outline as he sauntered toward his waiting enemy.

"A hope you will come to regret," Drizzt replied evenly.

The whiteness of Entreri's teeth gleamed in the aqua light as he answered through a wide smile. "Let us see."

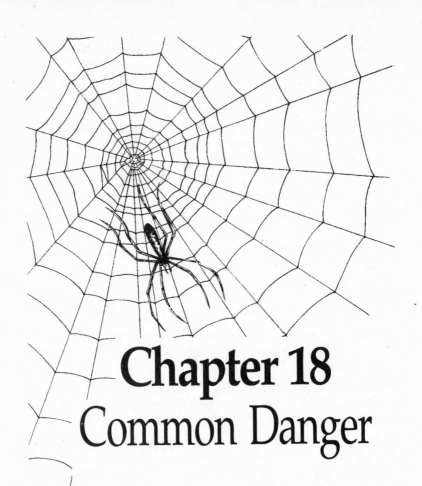

Chapter 18
Common Danger

His noise will bring the whole of the Underdark on our heads," Catti-brie whispered to Bruenor, referring to the battlerager's continually squealing armor. Pwent, realizing the same, had gone far ahead of the others and was gradually outpacing them, for Catti-brie and Wulfgar, human and not blessed with eyes that could see in the infrared spectrum, had to nearly crawl along, one hand on Bruenor at all times. Only Guenhwyvar, sometimes leading, more often moving as a silent emissary between Bruenor and the battlerager, maintained any semblance of communication between the principals of the small troupe.

Another grating squeal from ahead brought a grimace to Bruenor's face. He heard Catti-brie's resigned sigh and agreed with it. Even more so than his daughter, the experienced Bruenor understood the futility of it all. He thought of making Pwent remove the noisy armor but dismissed the notion immediately, realizing that even if all four of them walked naked, their footfalls would sound as clearly as a marching drumbeat to the sensitive ears of the enemy dark elves.

"Put up the torch," he instructed Wulfgar.

"Surely ye cannot," Catti-brie argued.

"They're all about us," Bruenor replied. "I can sense the dogs, and they'll see us as well without the light as with. We've no chance of getting through without another fight—I'm knowing that now—so we might as well fight 'em on terms better suited for our side."

Catti-brie turned her head about, though she could see nothing at all in the pitch blackness. She sensed the truth of Bruenor's observations, though, sensed that dark and silent shapes were moving all about them, closing a noose about the doomed party. A moment later she had to blink and squint when Wulfgar's torch came up in a fiery blaze.

Flickering shadows replaced absolute blackness; Catti-brie was surprised at how uncut this tunnel was, much more natural and rough than those they had left. Soil mixed with the stone along the ceiling and walls, giving the young woman less confidence in the stability of the place. She became acutely aware of the hundreds of tons of earth and rock above her head, aware that a slight shift in the stone could instantly crush her and her companions.

"What're ye about?" Bruenor asked her, seeing her obvious anxiety. He turned to Wulfgar and saw the barbarian growing similarly unnerved.

"Unworked tunnels," the dwarf remarked, coming to understand. "Ye're not so used to the wild depths." He put a gnarly hand on his beloved daughter's arm and felt beads of cold sweat.

"Ye'll get used to it," the dwarf gently promised. "Just remember that Drizzt is alone down here and needing our help. Keep yer mind on that fact and ye'll fast forget the stone above yer head."

Catti-brie nodded resolutely, took a deep breath, and determinedly wiped the sweat from her brow. Bruenor moved ahead then, saying that he was going to the front edge of the torchlight to see if he could locate the leading battlerager.

"Drizzt needs us," Wulfgar said to Catti-brie as soon as the dwarf had gone.

Catti-brie turned to him, surprised by his tone. For the first time in a long while, Wulfgar had spoken to her without a hint of either protective condescension or mounting rage.

Wulfgar walked up to her, put his arm gently against her back to move her along. She matched his slow stride, all the while studying his fair face, trying to sort through the obvious torment in his strong facial features.

"When this is through, we have much to discuss," he said quietly.

Catti-brie stopped, eyeing him suspiciously—and that seemed to wound the barbarian even more.

"I have many apologies to offer," Wulfgar tried to explain, "to Drizzt, to Bruenor, but mostly to you. To let Regis—Artemis Entreri—fool me so!" Wulfgar's mounting excitement flew away when he took the moment to look closely at Catti-brie, to see the stern resolve in her blue eyes.

"What happened over the last few weeks surely was heightened by the assassin and his magical pendant," the young woman agreed, "but I'm fearing that the problems were there afore Entreri ever arrived. First thing, ye got to admit that to yerself."

Wulfgar looked away, considered the words, then nodded his agreement. "We will talk," he promised.

"After we're through with the drow," Catti-brie said.

Again the barbarian nodded.

"And keep yer place in mind," Catti-brie told him. "Ye've a role to play in the group, and it's not a role of looking out for me own safety. Keep yer place."

"And you keep yours," Wulfgar agreed, and his ensuing smile sent a burst of warmth through Catti-brie, a poignant reminder of those special, boyish qualities, innocent and unjudging, that had so attracted her to Wulfgar in the first place.

The barbarian nodded again and, still smiling, started away, Catti-brie at his side—no longer behind him.

* * * * *

"I have given you all of this," Entreri prodded, moving slowly toward his rival, his glowing sword and jeweled dagger held out wide as though he were guiding a tour around some vast treasure hoard. "Because of my efforts, you have hope once more, you can walk these very dark tunnels with some belief that you will again see the light of day."

Drizzt, jaw set firm, scimitars in hand, did not reply.

"Are you not grateful?"

"Please kill him," Drizzt heard the battered Regis whisper, possibly the most pitifully sounding plea the drow ranger had ever heard. He looked to the side to see the halfling trembling with unbridled fright, gnawing his lips and twisting his still-swollen hands about each other. What horrors Regis must have experienced at Entreri's hands, Drizzt realized.

He looked back to the approaching assassin; Twinkle flared angrily.

"Now you are ready to fight," Entreri remarked. He curled his lips up in his customary evil smile. "And ready to die?"

Drizzt flipped his cloak back over his shoulders and boldly strode ahead, for he did not want to fight Entreri anywhere near Regis. Entreri might just flick that deadly dagger of his into the halfling, for no better reason than to torment Drizzt, to raise Drizzt's rage.

The assassin's dagger hand did pump as if he meant to throw, and Drizzt instinctively dropped into a crouch, his blades coming up defensively. Entreri didn't release the blade, though, and his widening smile showed that he never intended to.

Two more strides brought Drizzt within sword's reach. His scimitars began their flowing dance.

"Nervous?" the assassin teased, pointedly slapping his fine sword against Twinkle's reaching blade. "Of course you are. That is the problem with your tender heart, Drizzt Do'Urden, the weakness of your passion."

Drizzt came in a cunning cross, then swiped at a low angle for Entreri's belt, forcing the assassin to suck in his belly and leap back, at the same time snapping his dagger across to halt the scimitar's progress.

"You have too much to lose," Entreri went on, seeming unconcerned for the close call. "You know that if you die, the halfling dies. Too many distractions, my friend, too many items keeping your focus from the battle." The assassin charged as he spoke the last word, sword pumping fiercely, ringing from scimitar to scimitar, trying to open some hole in Drizzt's defenses that he might slip his dagger through.

There were no holes in Drizzt's defenses. Each maneuver, skilled as it might have been, left Entreri back where he had started, and gradually Drizzt worked his blades from defense to offense, driving the assassin away, forcing another break.

"Excellent!" Entreri congratulated. "Now you fight with your heart. This is the moment I have awaited since our battle in Calimport."

Drizzt shrugged. "Please do not let me disappoint you," he said, and came ahead viciously, spinning with his scimitars angled like the edging of a screw, as he had done in the chamber above. Again Entreri had no practical defense against the move—except to keep out of the scimitars' shortened reach.

Drizzt came out of the spin angled slightly to the assassin's left, Entreri's dagger hand. The drow dove ahead and rolled, just out of Entreri's lunging strike, then came back to his feet and reversed momentum immediately, rushing around Entreri's back side, forcing the assassin to spin on his heels, his sword whipping about in a frantic effort to keep the thrusting scimitars at bay.

Entreri was no longer smiling.

He managed somehow to avoid being hit, but Drizzt pressed the attack, kept him on his heels.

They heard the soft click of a handcrossbow from somewhere down the hall. In unison, the mortal enemies jumped back and fell into rolls, and the quarrel skipped harmlessly between them.

Five dark forms advanced steadily, swords drawn.

"Your friends," Drizzt remarked evenly. "It seems our fight will wait once more."

Entreri's eyes narrowed in open hatred as he regarded the approaching dark elves.

Drizzt understood the source of the assassin's frustration. Would Vierna give Entreri another battle, especially with other powerful enemies in the tunnels, searching for Drizzt? And even if she did, Entreri had to realize that, as with the fight before, he would not coax Drizzt into this level of battle, not with Drizzt's hopes for freedom extinguished.

Still, the assassin's next words caught the drow ranger somewhat by surprise.

"Do you remember our time against the Duergar?"

Entreri came in again at Drizzt as the dark elf soldiers continued their advance. Drizzt easily parried the swift but not well aimed attacks.

"Left shoulder," Entreri whispered. His sword came up behind his words, darting for Drizzt's shoulder. Twinkle crossed over from the right to block, but missed, and the assassin's sword nicked in, driving clean holes in the drow's cloak.

Regis cried out; Drizzt dropped one scimitar and lurched to the side, openly revealing his agony. Entreri's sword came tip in, barely five inches from his throat, and Twinkle was too far down for a parry.

"Yield!" the assassin cried. "Drop your weapon!"

Twinkle clanged to the floor and Drizzt continued his exaggerated lean, appearing as though he might tumble over at any moment. From behind, Regis groaned loudly and tried to shuffle away, but his weary, bruised limbs would not support him, would not even afford him the strength to crawl along.

The dark elves came tentatively into the torchlit area, talking among themselves and nodding appreciatively at the assassin's fine work.

"We will take him back to Vierna," one of them said in halting Common.

Entreri began to nod his agreement, then whirled about suddenly, driving his sword right through the speaker's chest.

Drizzt, low to begin with and not at all wounded, snatched up his blades and came up in a spin, one scimitar following the other in a clean slash across the nearest drow's belly. The wounded dark elf tried to fall away, but Drizzt was too quick, reversing his grip on his trailing blade and thrusting it ahead with an upward backhand, its tip cutting under the dark elf's ribs and puncturing his chest cavity.

Entreri was full out against a third drow by this time, the dark elf's twin swords working frantically to keep the assassin's sword and dagger at bay. The assassin wanted the battle over quickly, and his routines were purely offensive, designed to score a fast kill. But this drow, a longtime soldier of Bregan D'aerthe, was no novice to battle and he half-twisted and spun complete circles, fell into a backward roll and pumped his swords hand over hand in a blinding wall of defense.

Entreri growled in dismay but kept up the pressure, hoping his adversary would make even the slightest mistake.

Drizzt found himself squared off against two, and one of these smiled wickedly as he lifted a small crossbow in his free hand. Drizzt proved the quicker, though, angling his scimitar right in front of the weapon so that when the drow fired, the quarrel skipped off the blade and flew harmlessly high.

The drow threw the handcrossbow at Drizzt, forcing the ranger back long enough so that he could draw a dirk to complement the slender sword he carried.

The other drow seized the apparent advantage as Drizzt ducked away, his broadsword and short sword weaving viciously.

Metal rang against metal a dozen times, two dozen, as Drizzt impossibly defeated each attack. Then the second drow joined the melee and Drizzt, as skilled as he was, found himself sorely pressed. Twinkle snapped across to block the short sword, darted farther ahead and low to knock down the tip of the thrusting broadsword, then rifled back the other way, barely deflecting the darting dirk.

So it went for several long and frantic moments, with the two soldiers of Bregan D'aerthe working in harmony, each measuring his attacks in light of the other's, each raising appropriate defenses whenever his companion seemed vulnerable.

Drizzt was not so sure he could win against these two, and knew that even if he did, this battle would take a long time to turn his way. He glanced over his shoulder, to see Entreri beginning to back off from his attack routines, falling into a more mundane rhythm against his skilled opponent.

The assassin noticed Drizzt, and apparently noted Drizzt's predicament. He gave a slight nod, and Drizzt caught a subtle shift in the way Entreri was holding his jeweled dagger.

Drizzt went forward in a sudden burst, driving back the sword and dirk wielder, then spun to the other drow, scimitars starting low and sweeping upward, forcing the drow's broadsword high.

Drizzt released the move immediately, snapped his scimitar from the blade of the broadsword, and skipped two steps backward.

The enemy drow, not understanding, kept his broadsword high for another instant—an instant too long—before he began his countering advance.

The jewels of Entreri's dagger gave a multicolored flicker as the weapon cut through the air, thudding into the vulnerable drow's ribs, below his raised sword arm. He grunted and hopped to the side, crashed against the wall, but kept his balance and kept both his swords defensively out in front.

His comrade came ahead immediately, understanding what Drizzt would do. Long sword darted low, darted high, then came up in a twirl for a high slice.

Drizzt blocked, blocked again, then ducked under the predictably high third attack and veered to the side, both his blades working in sudden, short snaps that opened the defenses of the slumping, wounded drow. One scimitar jabbed into drow flesh just beside the dagger; the other followed at once, sinking deeper, finishing the job.

Instinctively, Drizzt threw his retracted blade out horizontally and up high, the metal singing a perfect note as it stopped the overhead chop from the second drow's descending sword.

The dark elf battling Entreri went on the offensive as soon as the assassin relinquished his dagger. Twin swords worked Entreri's remaining blade high and low, to one side, then the other. When he had prepared the assassin's stance to his liking, thinking the end at hand, the drow came with a straight double-thrust, both swords parallel and knifing in at the assassin.

Entreri's sword hit one, then the other, impossibly fast, knocking both attacks wide. He hit the sword on his right a second time with a backhand, nearly sending the blade from the drow's hand, then a third time, his sword driving his enemy's high.

Drizzt's second scimitar came free of the dead drow's chest, but Drizzt did not bring the blade to bear on his present opponent. Rather, he angled the tip under the crosspiece of the stuck dagger and, when he saw Entreri prepared to receive it, he jerked his blade around, sending the dagger flying across the way.

Entreri caught it with his free hand and redirected its momentum, sticking it into his opponent's exposed ribs under the high-riding swords. The assassin jumped back; the dying drow stared at him in disbelief.

What a pitiful sight, Entreri thought, watching his enemy try to lift swords with arms that no longer had any strength. He shrugged callously as the drow toppled to the floor and died.

One against one, the remaining drow soon realized that he was no match for Drizzt Do'Urden. He kept his movements defensive, angling around to Drizzt's side, then noticed a desperate opportunity. Sword working furiously to keep the darting scimitars at bay, he flipped his dirk over in his hand as if to throw.

Drizzt immediately went into defensive maneuvers, one scimitar flashing across any possible missile path while the other kept the pressure on.

But the enemy warrior glanced to the side, to the halfling, sprawled helpless on the floor not so far away.

"Surrender or I kill the halfling!" the evil dark elf cried in the drow tongue.

Drizzt's lavender eyes flared wickedly.

A scimitar hit the evil drow's wrist, taking the dirk from his grasp; Drizzt's other blade batted the sword once, then darted low, slicing against his enemy's knee. Twinkle came across in a blue flash, batting aside the descending sword, and straight ahead came the free, low-riding scimitar, taking the drow in the thigh.

The doomed dark elf grimaced and wobbled, trying to back away, trying to utter something, some word of surrender, to call off his attacker. But his threat against Regis had put Drizzt past the point of reasoning.

227

R. A. Salvatore

Drizzt's advance was slow and deadly even. Scimitars low to his side, he still got one or the other up to destroy any attempted strikes long before they got near his body.

All that Drizzt's opponent could watch was Drizzt's simmering eyes, and nothing this drow had ever before seen, neither the snake-headed whips of merciless priestesses nor the rage of a matron mother, had promised death so completely.

He ducked his head, screamed aloud, and, giving in to his terror, threw himself forward desperately.

Scimitars hit him alternately in the chest. Twinkle took his biceps cleanly, keeping his sword arm helplessly pinned back, and Drizzt's other blade came up fast under his chin, lifting his face, that he might, at the moment of his death, look once more into those lavender eyes.

Drizzt, his chest heaving with the rush of adrenaline, his eyes burning from inner fires, shoved the corpse away and looked to the side, eager to be done with his business with Entreri.

But the assassin was nowhere to be seen.

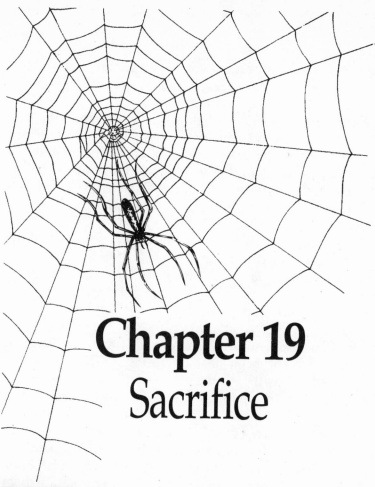

Chapter 19
Sacrifice

Thibbledorf Pwent stood at the end of the narrow tunnel, scanning the wide cavern beyond with his infravision, registering the shifting gradations of heat, that he might better understand the layout of the dangerous area ahead. He made out the many teeth of the ceiling, stalactites long and narrow, and saw two distinctly cooler lines indicating ledges on the high walls—one directly ahead, the other along the wall on his right. Dark holes lined the walls at floor level in several places; Pwent knew that one immediately to his left, two directly across from where he stood, and another diagonally ahead and to the right, under the ledge, likely were long tunnels, and figured several others to be smaller side chambers or alcoves.

Guenhwyvar was at the battlerager's side, the cat's ears flattened, its low growl barely perceptible. The panther sensed the danger, too, Pwent realized. He motioned for Guenhwyvar to follow him—suddenly he was not so upset at having so unusual a companion—and he skittered back down the corridor into the approaching torchlight to stop the others short of the room.

"There be at least three or four more ways in or out," the battlerager told his companions gravely, "and lots of open ground across the place." He went on to give a thorough description of the chamber, paying particular attention to the many obvious hiding spots.

Bruenor, sharing Pwent's dark fears, nodded and looked to the others. He, too, felt that their enemies were near, were all about them, and had been steadily closing in. The dwarf king looked back the way they had come, and it was obvious to the others that he was trying to figure out some other way around this region.

"We can turn their hoped-for surprise against them," Catti-brie offered, knowing the futility of Bruenor's hopes. The companions had precious little time to spare and few of the side tunnels they had passed offered little promise of bringing them to the lower regions, or to wider tunnels where they might find Drizzt.

A sparkle of battle-lust came into Bruenor's dark eyes, but he frowned a moment later when Guenhwyvar plopped down heavily at Catti-brie's feet.

"The cat's been about too long," the young woman reasoned. "Guenhwyvar's needing a rest soon." Wulfgar's and the dwarves' expressions showed that they did not welcome the news.

"More the reason to go straight ahead," Catti-brie said

determinedly. "Guen's got a bit of the fight left, don't ye doubt!"

Bruenor considered the words, then nodded grimly and slapped his many-notched axe across his open palm. "Got to get in close to this enemy," he reminded his friends.

Pwent produced his bitter potion. "Take another hit," he offered to Catti-brie and Wulfgar. "Got to make sure the stuff's fresh in yer belly."

Catti-brie winced, but she did take the flask, then handed it to Wulfgar, who similarly frowned and took a brief draw.

Bruenor and Pwent squatted to the floor between them, Pwent quickly scratching a rough map of the chamber. They had no time for detailed plans, but Bruenor sorted out areas of responsibility, assigning each person the task best suited to his or her battle style. The dwarf could give no specific directions to Guenhwyvar, of course, and didn't bother to include Pwent in much of the discussion, knowing that once the fighting began, the battlerager would go off on his wild, undisciplined way. Catti-brie and Wulfgar, too, realized Pwent's forthcoming role, and neither complained, understanding that, against skilled and precise opponents such as drow elves, a little chaos could well be a good thing.

They kept the torch burning, even lit a second one, and started cautiously ahead, ready to put the fight on their own terms.

As the torchlight breached the room, a darting black form cut through, going into the darkness in full flight. Guenhwyvar broke to the right, cut left toward the center of the chamber, then darted right again, toward the back wall.

From somewhere ahead there came the sound of firing crossbows, followed by the skip of quarrels hitting the stone, always one step behind the dodging, leaping panther.

Guenhwyvar veered again at the last moment, leaped, and turned sidelong, paws running along the vertical wall for several strides before the panther had to come back to the floor. The cat's target, the high ledge on the right-hand wall was now

231

in sight and Guenhwyvar ran full out, speeding for it recklessly.

At the base, in full stride, and apparently soaring toward a headfirst collision, the panther's muscles subtly shifted. Guen–hwyvar's direction change was almost perpendicular, the pan–ther flying, seeming to run, straight up the twenty-foot expanse to the ledge.

The three dark elves atop the ledge could not have expected the incredible maneuver. Two fired their crossbows Guen–hwyvar's way and fell back into a tunnel; the third, having the misfortune to be directly in the leaping panther's path, could only throw his arms up as the panther fell over him.

Torches flew into the room, lighting the battle area, fol–lowed by the leading charge of Bruenor, flanked on his right by Wulfgar and on his left by Thibbledorf Pwent. Catti-brie quietly filtered in behind them, slipping to the side along the same gen–eral course Guenhwyvar had taken, her bow readied and in hand.

Again the crossbows of unseen dark elves clicked, and all of the leading companions took hits. Wulfgar felt the venom streaming into his leg, but felt the tingling burn as Pwent's potent potion counteracted its sleepy effects. A darkness spell fell over one of the torches, defeating its light, but Wulfgar was ready, lighting a third and tossing it far to the side.

Pwent noticed an enemy drow in the tunnel to the left, and off he went, predictably, roaring with every charging stride.

Bruenor and Wulfgar slowed but kept their course straight across the room, for the largest tunnel entrances across the way. The barbarian caught sight of the flicker of drow eyes along the remaining ledge, farther ahead and above the tunnels. He stopped, twirled, and heaved his warhammer with a cry to his god. Aegis-fang went in low, crushing the lip of the walkway, smashing stone apart. One dark elf leaped away to another point on the long ledge; the other tumbled down, his leg blasted, and barely caught the stone halfway down the crumbling wall.

Wulfgar did not follow the throw forward. He got hit again by a stinging quarrel and rushed instead to the side, to the remaining tunnel, along the right-hand wall, wherein crouched a pair of dark elves.

Eager to join in close combat, Bruenor veered behind the barbarian. The dwarf looked back before he had even completed the turn, though, as an eight-legged monster, the drider, came out of the tunnel directly ahead, other dark forms shifting about behind it.

With a whoop of delight, never considering the odds now that he and his friends were committed to the battle, the fiery dwarf veered again to his initial course, determined to meet the enemy, however many there might be, head on.

* * * * *

It took all the discipline Catti-brie could muster to hold her first shot in check. She really didn't have a good angle for either those that Pwent had pursued or the ledge where Guenhwyvar had gone, and she didn't think it worth the trouble to spike the wounded drow hanging helplessly below the blasted ledge—not yet. Bruenor had bade her to make certain that her first shot, the one shot she might get before she was fully noticed, counted.

The eager young woman watched the split between Bruenor and Wulfgar and found her opportunity. A drow, crouching behind a four-foot diagonal jag in the back wall, almost exactly halfway between her rushing companions, leaned out, crossbow in hand. The dark elf fired, then fell back in surprise as a silver arrow streaked past him, skipped off the stone, and left a smoldering scorch in its wake.

Catti-brie's second shot was in the air an instant later. She could no longer see the drow, fully covered by the stone, but she did not believe his cover so thick.

The arrow hit the jutting slab two feet from its edge, two feet from where it joined the wall. There came a sharp crack as the rock split, followed by a grunt as the arrow blasted deep into the dying drow's skull.

233

* * * * *

The prone dark elf on the high ledge scrambled and kicked, kept his buckler above him, and managed, somehow, to get his dagger out with his other hand. Only his fine mesh armor kept Guenhwyvar's raking claws somewhat at bay, kept his mounting wounds serious but not mortal.

He brought the dagger to bear on the panther's flank, but the weapon seemed small against such a foe, seemed only to further enrage the cat. His buckler arm was batted aside, back up over his head with enough force to dislocate his shoulder. He tried to get it back to block but found it would not respond to his mind's frantic call. He scrambled to put his other hand in the great paw's way, a futile defense.

Guenhwyvar's claws hooked his scalp line just above his forehead. The drow plunged the dagger in again, praying for a quick kill.

The panther's claws sheared off his face.

Crossbows clicked again from down the tunnel at the back of the narrow ledge. Not really hurt, the panther came off its victim and loped ahead in pursuit.

The two dark elves summoned globes of darkness between them and the cat, turned, and fled.

If they had looked back, they might have rejoined the fight, for Guenhwyvar's pursuit was not dogged. With the dagger and quarrel wounds, the insidious sleep poison, and the simple duration of the panther's visit to the plane, Guenhwyvar's energy was no more. The cat did not wish to leave, wanted to stay and fight beside the companions, to stay to hunt for its missing master.

The magic of the figurine would not support the desires, though. A few strides into the darkened area, Guenhwyvar stopped, barely holding a tentative balance. Panther flesh dissolved into gray smoke. The planar tunnel opened and beckoned.

* * * * *

He got hit again as he exited the chamber, but the tiny quarrel did no more than bring a smile to the most wild battlerager's contorted face. A darkness globe blocked his flight, but he roared and barreled through, smiling even when he collided full force with the winding wall out the other side.

The amazed dark elf, watching ferocious Pwent's progress, spun away, darting along the tunnel, then turned a sharp corner. Pwent came right behind, armor squealing and drool running from his fat lips in lines down his thick black beard.

"Stupid!" he yelled, ducking his head as he spun the corner right behind the fleeing drow, fully expecting the ambush.

Pwent's darting helmet spike intercepted the sword cut, impaling his enemy through the forearm. The battlerager didn't slow, but hurled himself into the air and lay out flat, body-blocking his opponent across the chest and driving the drow to the ground under him.

Glove nails dug for the dark elf's groin and face; Pwent's ridged armor creased the fine mesh mail as he went into a series of violent convulsions. With each of the battlerager's movements, waves of searing agony ran up the drow's impaled arm.

* * * * *

Bruenor noticed the slender form of a drow, wearing an outrageously wide-brimmed and plumed hat, moving about the entrance to the tunnel. Then came the flicker of objects cutting into the torchlight from behind the monstrous drider, and Bruenor threw his shield up defensively. A dagger banged against the metal, then another, and a third behind that. The fourth throw came in low, scraping the dwarf's shin; the fifth dipped over the leaning shield as Bruenor inevitably bent forward, cutting a line across the dwarf's scalp under the edge of his one-horned helmet.

235

R. A. Salvatore

But minor wounds would not slow Bruenor, nor would the sight of the bloated drider, axes waving, eight legs clacking and scrabbling. The dwarf came in hard, took a hit on the shield, and returned with a smash against the drider's second descending axe. Much smaller than his opponent, Bruenor worked low, his axe smacking the hard exoskeleton of the drider's armored legs. All the while, the dwarf remained a blur of frenzied motion, his shield above him, as fine a shield as was ever forged, deflecting hit after hit from the wickedly edged, drow-enchanted weapons.

Bruenor's axe dove into the wedge between two legs, cracking through to the drider's fleshy interior. The dwarf's smile was short-lived, though, for the drider's responses banged hard on the shield, twisting it about on Bruenor's arm, and the creature put a leg in line and kicked hard into the dwarf's belly, throwing Bruenor back before his axe could do any real damage.

He squared off, his breath lost and his arm aching. Again came a series of dagger throws from the corridor behind the drider, forcing Bruenor off balance. He barely got his shield up to stop the last four. He looked down to the first, jutting from the front of his layered armor, a trickle of blood oozing from behind its tip, and knew he had escaped death by a hair's breadth.

He knew, too, that the distraction would cost him dearly, for he was no longer squared up for melee and the drider was upon him.

* * * * *

Wulfgar's flying hammer led the way to the corridor, his one throw more than matching the crossbow darts that struck the roaring barbarian. He aimed high, for the stalactite teeth hanging above the entryway, and his mighty hammer did its work perfectly, smashing apart several of the hanging rocks.

One dark elf fell back—Wulfgar could not tell if the falling stone had crushed him or not—and the other dove forward, drawing sword and dagger and coming up in the chamber to meet the unarmed barbarian's charge.

Wulfgar skidded to a stop short of the flashing blades, skipped to the side, and kicked out, punched out, doing anything to keep the dangerous and quick opponent at bay for the few seconds the barbarian needed.

The drow, not understanding the magic of Aegis-fang, took his time, seemed in no hurry to chance the grasp of the obviously mighty human. He came with a measured combination, sword, dagger, and dagger again, the last thrust painfully nicking the barbarian's hip.

The drow smiled wickedly.

Aegis-fang appeared in Wulfgar's waiting hands.

With one hand, grasping low on the warhammer's handle, Wulfgar sent the weapon into a flowing circular motion in front of him. The drow took careful measure of the weapon's speed— Wulfgar carefully appraised the drow's examination.

In darted the dagger, behind the flowing hammer. Wulfgar's other hand clapped against the handle just under his weapon's head and abruptly reversed the direction, parrying the drow's attack aside.

The drow was quick, snapping his sword in a downward angle for Wulfgar's shoulder even as his dagger hand was knocked wide. Wulfgar's huge forearm flexed with the strain as he halted the heavy hammer's flow, snapping it back up in front of him. He caught Aegis-fang halfway up the handle with his free hand and jabbed diagonally up, the warhammer's solid head intercepting the sword and driving it harmlessly away.

The end of the parry left the drow with one arm wide and low, the other wide and high, and left Wulfgar standing before his opponent in perfect balance, both hands grasping Aegis-fang. Before the dark elf could recover his wide-flying blades, before he could set his feet to dive away, Wulfgar chopped him, the hammer crunching under his shoulder and driving down toward his opposite hip. The drow fell back from the blow, then, as though the full weight of the incredible hit had not immediately registered, went into an involuntary backward hop that slammed him against the wall.

One leg buckling, one lung collapsed, the drow brought his sword horizontally before his face in a meager defense. Hands low on the handle, Wulfgar brought the hammer up behind him and slammed it home with all his strength, through the blade and into the drow's face. With a sickening crack, the drow's skull exploded, crushed between the unyielding stone of the wall and the unyielding metal of the mighty Aegis-fang.

* * * * *

A blinding streak of silver halted the drider's attacks and saved Bruenor Battlehammer. The arrow didn't hit the drider, however. It soared high, pegging the wounded drow (who had just about climbed back to the blasted ledge) to the stone wall.

The distraction, the moment to recover from the daggers, was all Bruenor needed. He came in hard again, his many-notched axe smashing the drider's closest leg, his shield up high to block the now off-balance axe swipes. The dwarf pressed right into the beast, using its bulk to offer him some cover from the enemies in the corridor, and bulled it backward before it could set its many legs against the charge.

Another of Catti-brie's arrows whipped past him, sparking as it ricocheted along the stone of the corridor.

Bruenor grinned widely, thankful that the gods had delivered to him an ally and friend as competent as Catti-brie.

* * * * *

The first two arrows enraged Vierna; the third, coming down the corridor, nearly took off her head. Jarlaxle raced back from his position near the chamber's entrance to join her.

"Formidable," the mercenary admitted. "I have dead soldiers in the room."

Vierna raced forward, focusing on the dwarf battling her mutated brother. "Where is Drizzt Do'Urden?" she demanded, using magic to focus her voice so that Bruenor would hear her through the drider.

"Ye hit me and ye're meaning to talk?" the dwarf howled, finishing his sentence with an exclamation point in the form of a chopping axe. One of Dinin's legs fell free, and the dwarf barreled on, pushing the unbalanced drider back another few strides.

Vierna hardly had the chance to begin her intended spell before Jarlaxle grabbed her and hauled her down. Her instinctive anger toward the mercenary was lost in the blast of yet another streaking arrow, this one driving a hole into the stone wall where the priestess had been standing.

Vierna remembered Entreri's warning about this group, had the evidence right before her as the battle continued to sour. She trembled with rage, growled indecipherably as she considered what the defeat might cost her. Her thoughts fell inward, followed the path of her faith toward her dark deity, and cried out to Lloth.

"Vierna!" Jarlaxle called from someplace remote.

Lloth could not allow her to fail, had to help her against this unexpected obstacle, that she might deliver the sacrifice.

"Vierna!" She felt the mercenary's hands on her, felt the hands of a second drow helping Jarlaxle put her back on her feet.

"*Wishya!*" came her unintentional cry, then she knew only calm, knew that Lloth had answered her call.

Jarlaxle and the other drow slammed against the tunnel's walls from the force of Vierna's magical outburst. Each looked at her with trepidation.

The mercenary's features relaxed when Vierna bade him to follow her farther along the corridor, out of harm's way.

"Lloth will help us finish what we have started here," the priestess explained.

R. A. Salvatore

Catti-brie put another arrow into the corridor for good measure, then glanced about, searching for a more apparent target. She studied the battle between Bruenor and the monstrous drider, but she knew that any shots she made at the bloated monster would be too risky given the furious melee.

Wulfgar apparently had his situation under control. A drow lay dead at his feet as he peeked about the rubble of the collapsed corridor in search of the enemy who had not come in. Pwent was nowhere to be found.

Catti-brie looked up to the blasted ledge above Bruenor and the drider for the drow who had not fallen, then to the other ledge, where Guenhwyvar had disappeared. In a small alcove below that area the young woman saw a curious sight: a gathering of mists similar to that heralding the panther's approach. The cloud shifted colors, became orange, almost like a swirling ball of flames.

Catti-brie sensed an evil aura, gathering and overwhelming, and put her bow in line. The hairs on the back of her neck tingled; something was watching her.

Catti-brie dropped the Heartseeker and spun about, snapping her short sword from its sheath with her turn, barely in time to bat aside the thrusting sword of a levitating drow that had silently descended from the ceiling.

Wulfgar, too, noticed the mist, and he knew that it demanded his attention, that he must be ready to strike out at it as soon as its nature was revealed. He could not ignore Catti-brie's sudden cry, though, and when he looked at her, he found her hard pressed, nearly sitting on the floor, her short sword working furiously to keep her attacker at bay.

In the shadows some distance behind the young woman and her attacker, another dark shape began its descent.

* * * * *

The warm blood of his torn enemy mingled with the drool on Thibbledorf Pwent's beard. The drow had stopped thrashing, but Pwent, reveling in the kill, had not.

A crossbow quarrel pierced his ear. His head came up as he roared, the impaled helmet spike lifting the dead drow's arm weirdly. There stood another enemy, advancing steadily.

Up leaped the battlerager, snapping his head from side to side, whipping the caught drow back and forth until the ebony skin ripped apart, freeing the helmet spike.

The approaching dark elf stopped his advance, trying to make some sense of the gruesome scene. He was moving again—back the other way—when indomitable Pwent took up the roaring charge.

The drow was truly amazed at the stubby dwarf's frantic pace, amazed that he could not easily outdistance this enemy. He wouldn't have run too far anyway, though, preferring to bait this dangerous one away from the main battle.

They went through a series of twisting corridors, the dark elf ten strides ahead. His graceful steps barely seemed to alter as he leaped, landing and spinning about, sword ready and smile wide.

Pwent never slowed. He merely ducked his head to put his helmet spike in line. With his eyes to the stone, the battlerager realized the trap, too late, as he crossed the rim of a pit the drow had subtly leaped across.

Down went the battlerager, crashing and bouncing, the many points of his battle armor throwing sparks as he skidded along the stone. He cracked a rib against the rounded top of a stalagmite mound some distance down, bounced completely over, and landed flat on his back in a lower chamber.

He lay there for some time, admiring the cunning of his enemy and admiring the curious way the ceiling—tons of solid rock—continued to spin about.

* * * * *

No novice with the sword, Catti-brie worked her blade marvelously, using every defense Drizzt Do'Urden had shown her to gain back some measure of equal footing. She was confident that the drow's initial advantage was fading, confident that she could soon get her feet under her and come back up evenly against this opponent.

Then, suddenly, she had no one to fight.

Aegis-fang twirled by her, its windy wake bringing her thick hair about, and hit the surprised dark elf full force, blasting him away.

Catti-brie spun about, her initial appreciation lost as soon as she recognized Wulfgar's protectiveness. The mist near the barbarian was forming by then, taking on the substantial, corporeal body of a denizen of some vile lower plane, some enemy far more dangerous than the dark elf Catti-brie had been battling.

Wulfgar had come to her aid at the risk of his own peril, had put her safety above his own.

To Catti-brie, confident that she could have taken care of her own situation, that act seemed more stupid than altruistic.

Catti-brie went for her bow—she had to get to her bow.

Before she even had her hands on it, though, the monster, the yochlol, came fully to the plane. Amorphous, it somewhat resembled a lump of half-melted wax, showing eight tentaclelike appendages and a central, gaping maw lined with long, sharp teeth.

Catti-brie sensed danger behind her before she could call out to Wulfgar. She spun, bow in hand, and looked up to her enemy, to a drow's sword fast descending for her head.

Catti-brie shot first. The arrow jolted the drow several inches from the floor and passed right through the dark elf to explode in a shower of sparks against the ceiling. The drow was still standing when he came back to the floor, still holding his sword, his expression revealing that he was not quite sure what had just happened.

Catti-brie grabbed her bow like a club and jumped up to meet him, pressing him fiercely until his mind registered the fact that he was dead.

She looked back once, to see Wulfgar grabbed by one of the yochlol's tentacles, then another. All the barbarian's incredible strength could not keep him from the waiting maw.

* * * * *

Bruenor could see nothing but the black of the drider's torso as he continued to bull in, continued to drive Dinin backward. He could hear nothing except the sounds of flying blades, the clang of metal against metal, or the sound of cracking shell whenever his axe struck home.

He knew instinctively that Catti-brie and Wulfgar, his children, were in trouble.

Bruenor's axe finally caught up with the retreating creature with full force as the drider slammed against the wall. Another spider leg fell away; Bruenor planted his feet and heaved with all his strength, launching himself several feet back.

Dinin, weirdly contorted, two legs lost, did not immediately pursue, glad for the reprieve, but ferocious Bruenor came back in, the dwarf's savagery overwhelming the wounded drider. Bruenor's shield blocked the first axe; his helmet blocked the following strike, a blow that should have dropped him.

Straight across whipped the dwarf's many-notched axe, above the hard exoskeleton to cut a jagged line across the bloated drider's belly. Hot gore spewed out. Fluids ran down the drider's legs and Bruenor's pumping arms.

Bruenor went into a frenzy, his axe smacking repeatedly, incessantly, into the crook between the drider's two foremost legs. Exoskeleton gave way to flesh; flesh opened to spill more gore.

Bruenor's axe struck hard yet again, but he took a hit atop the shoulder of his weapon arm. The drider's awkward angle stole most of the strength from the blow, and the axe did not get through Bruenor's fine mithril mail, but a blast of hot agony assaulted Bruenor.

His mind screamed that Catti-brie and Wulfgar needed him!

Grimacing against the pain, Bruenor whipped his axe in an upward backhand, its flat back cracking against the drider's elbow. The creature howled and Bruenor brought the weapon to bear again, angled up the other way, catching the drider in the armpit and shearing the creature's arm off.

Catti-brie and Wulfgar needed him!

The drider's longer reach got its second axe around the dwarf's blocking shield, its bottom edge drawing a line of blood up the back of Bruenor's arm. Bruenor tucked the shield in close and shoulder-blocked the monster against the wall. He bounced back, drove his axe in hard at the monster's exposed side, then shoulder-blocked again.

Back bounced the dwarf, in chopped his axe, and Bruenor's stubby legs twitched again, sending him hurtling forward. This time, Bruenor heard the drider's other axe fall to the floor, and when he bounced back, he stayed back, chopping wildly with his axe, driving the drider to the stone, splitting flesh and breaking ribs.

Bruenor turned about, saw Catti-brie in command of her situation, and took a step toward Wulfgar.

"*Wishya!*"

Waves of energy hit the dwarf, lifting his feet from the ground and launching him a dozen feet through the air, to slam against the wall.

He rebounded in a redirected run, and he cried a single note of rage as he bore down on the entrance to the distant tunnel, the eyes of several drow watching him from farther within.

"*Wishya!*" came the cry once more, and Bruenor was moving backward suddenly.

"How many ye got?" the tough dwarf roared, shrugging off

this newest hit against the wall.

The eyes, every set, turned away.

A globe of darkness fell over the dwarf, and he was, in truth, glad for its cover, for that last slam had hurt him more than he cared to admit.

* * * * *

A fourth soldier joined Vierna, Jarlaxle, and their one bodyguard as they again moved deeper into the tunnels.

"Dwarf to the side," the newcomer explained. "Insane, wild with rage. I put him down a pit, but I doubt he is stopped!"

Vierna began to reply, but Jarlaxle interrupted her, pointing down a side passage, to yet another drow signaling to them frantically in the silent hand code.

Devil cat! the distant drow signaled. A second form rushed by him, followed by a third a few seconds later. Jarlaxle understood the movements of his troops, knew that these three were the survivors of two separate battles, and understood that both the ledge and the side passage below it had been lost.

We must go, he signaled to Vierna. *Let us find a more advantageous region where we might continue this fight.*

"Lloth has answered my call!" Vierna growled at him. "A handmaiden has arrived!"

"More the reason to be gone," Jarlaxle replied aloud. "Show your faith in the Spider Queen and let us be on with the hunt for your brother."

Vierna considered the words for just a moment, then, to the worldly mercenary's relief, nodded her agreement. Jarlaxle led her along at a great pace, wondering if it could be true that only seven of his skilled Bregan D'aerthe force, himself and Vierna included, remained.

* * * * *

Wulfgar's arms slapped wildly at the waving tentacles; his hands clasped over those appendages wrapping him, trying to break free of their iron grip. More tentacles slapped in at him, forcing his attention.

He was jerked out straight, yanked sidelong into the great maw, and he understood these newest slapping attacks to be merely diversions. Razor-edged teeth dug into his back and ribs, tore through muscle, and scraped against bone.

He punched out and grabbed a handful of slimy yochlol skin, twisting and tearing a hunk free. The creature did not react, continued to bite bone, razor teeth working back and forth across the trapped torso.

Aegis-fang came back to Wulfgar's hand, but he was twisted awkwardly for any hits against his enemy. He swung anyway, connecting solidly, but the fleshy, rubbery hide of the evil creature seemed to absorb the blows, sinking deep beneath the weight of Aegis-fang.

Wulfgar swung again, twisted about despite the searing pain. He saw Catti-brie standing free, the second drow lying dead at her feet, and her face locked in an expression of open horror as she stared at the white of Wulfgar's exposed ribs.

Still, the image of his love, free from harm, brought a grimace of satisfaction to the barbarian's face.

A bolt of silver flashed right below, startling Wulfgar, blasting the yochlol, and the barbarian thought his salvation at hand, thought that his beloved Catti-brie, the woman he had dared to underestimate, would strike his attacker down.

A tentacle wrapped around Catti-brie's ankles and jerked her from her feet. Her head hit the stone hard, her precious bow fell from her grasp, and she offered little resistance as the yochlol began to pull her in.

"No!" Wulfgar roared, and he whacked again and again, futilely, at the rubbery beast. He cried out for Bruenor; out of the corner of his eye, he saw the dwarf stumble out of a dark globe, far away and dazed.

The yochlol's maw crunched mercilessly; a lesser man would have long since collapsed under the force of that bite.

Wulfgar could not allow himself to die, though, not with Catti-brie and Bruenor in danger.

He began a hearty song to Tempus, his god of battle. He sang with lungs fast filling with blood, with a voice that came from a heart that had pumped mightily for more than twenty years.

He sang and he forgot the waves of crippling pain; he sang and the song came back to his ears, echoing from the cavern walls like a chorus from the minions of an approving god.

He sang and he tightened his grip on Aegis-fang.

Wulfgar struck out, not against the beast, but against the alcove's low ceiling. The hammer chopped through dirt, hooked about stone.

Pebbles and dust fell all around the barbarian and his attacker. Again and again, all the while singing, Wulfgar slammed at the ceiling.

The yochlol, not a stupid beast, bit fiercely, shook its great maw wildly, but Wulfgar had passed beyond the admission of pain. Aegis-fang chopped upward; a chunk of stone followed its inevitable descent.

As soon as she recovered her wits, Catti-brie saw what the barbarian was doing. The yochlol was no longer interested in her, was no longer pulling her in, and she managed to claw her way back to her bow.

"No, me boy!" she heard Bruenor cry from across the way.

Catti-brie nocked an arrow and turned about.

Aegis-fang slammed against the ceiling.

Catti-brie's arrow sizzled into the yochlol an instant before the ceiling gave way. Huge boulders toppled down; any space between them quickly filled with piles of rock and soil, spewing clouds of dust into the air. The chamber shook violently; the collapse resounded through all the tunnels.

Neither Catti-brie nor Bruenor still stood. Both huddled on

247

the floor, their arms defensively over their heads as the cave-in slowly ended. Neither could see amid the darkness and the dust; neither could see that both the monster and Wulfgar had disappeared under tons of collapsing stone.

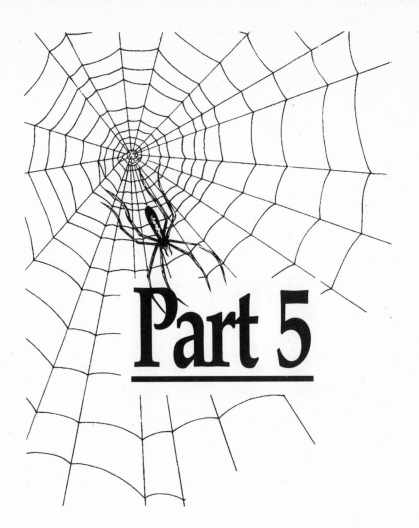

Part 5

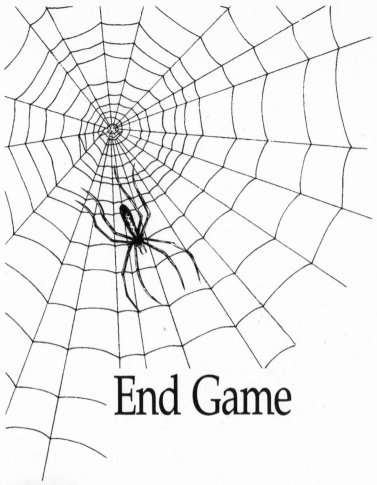

End Game

When I die . . .

 I have lost friends, lost my father, my mentor, to that greatest of mysteries called death. I have known grief since the day I left my homeland, since the day wicked Malice informed me that Zaknafein had been given to the Spider Queen. It is a strange emotion, grief, its focus shifting. Do I grieve for Zaknafein, for Montolio, for Wulfgar? Or do I grieve for myself, for the loss I must forever endure?

 It is perhaps the most basic question of mortal existence, and yet it is one for which there can be no answer. . . .

R. A. Salvatore

Unless the answer is one of faith.

I am sad still when I think of the sparring games against my father, when I remember the walks beside Montolio through the mountains, and when those memories of Wulfgar, most intense of all, flash through my mind like a summary of the last several years of my life. I remember a day on Kelvin's Cairn, looking out over the tundra of Icewind Dale, when young Wulfgar and I spotted the campfires of his nomadic people. That was the moment when Wulfgar and I truly became friends, the moment when we came to learn that, for all the other uncertainties in both our lives, we would have each other.

I remember the white dragon, Icingdeath, and the giant-kin, Biggrin, and how, without heroic Wulfgar at my side, I would have perished in either of those fights. I remember, too, sharing the victories with my friend, our bond of trust and love tightening—close, but never uncomfortable.

I was not there when he fell, could not lend him the support he certainly would have lent me.

I could not say "Farewell!"

When I die, will I be alone? If not for the weapons of monsters or the clutch of disease, I surely will outlive Catti-brie and Regis, even Bruenor. At this time in my life I do firmly believe that, no matter who else might be beside me, if those three were not, I would indeed die alone.

These thoughts are not so dark. I have said farewell to Wulfgar a thousand times. I have said it every time I let him know how dear he was to me, every time my words or actions affirmed our love. Farewell is said by the living, in life, every day. It is said with love and friendship, with the affirmation that the memories are lasting if the flesh is not.

Wulfgar has found another place, another life—I have to believe that, else what is the point of existence?

My very real grief is for me, for the loss I know I will feel to the end of my days, however many centuries have passed. But within that loss is a serenity, a divine calm. Better to have known Wulfgar and shared those very events that now fuel my grief, than never to have walked beside him, fought beside him, looked at the world through his crystal-blue eyes.

When I die . . . may there be friends who will grieve for me, who will carry our shared joys and pains, who will carry my memory.

This is the immortality of the spirit, the ever-lingering legacy, the fuel of grief.

But so, too, the fuel of faith.

—Drizzt Do'Urden

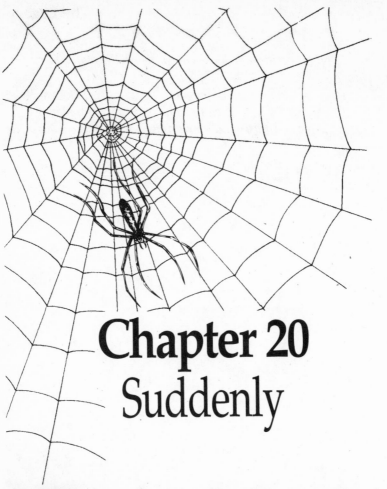

Chapter 20
Suddenly

Dust continued to settle in the wide chamber, dull-
ing the flickering light; one of the torches had been
extinguished beneath a falling chunk of stone, its
glow snuffed out in the blink of an eye.

Snuffed out like the light in Wulfgar's eyes.

When the rumbling finally stopped, when the larger pieces
of collapsed ceiling settled, Catti-brie turned herself about and
managed to sit up, facing the rubble-filled alcove. She wiped the
dirt from her eyes, blinked through the gloom for several long
moments before the grim truth of the scene registered fully.

The monster's one visible tentacle, still wrapped about the young woman's ankle, had been cleanly severed, its back edge, near the rubble, twitching reflexively.

Beyond it there was only piled rock. The enormity of the situation overwhelmed Catti-brie. She swayed to the side, nearly swooned, finding her strength only when a burst of anger and denial welled up within her. She tore her feet free of the tentacle and scrambled ahead on all fours. She tried to stand, but her head throbbed, keeping her low. Again came the wave of weak nausea, the invitation to fall back into unconsciousness.

Wulfgar!

Catti-brie crawled on, slapped aside the twitching tentacle, and began digging into the stone pile with her bare hands, scraping her skin and tearing a fingernail painfully. How similar this collapse seemed to the one that had taken Drizzt on the companions' first crossing of Mithril Hall. But that had been a dwarf-designed trap, a rigged fall that dropped out the floor as it had dropped out a ceiling block, sending Drizzt careening safely into a lower corridor.

This was no rigged trap, Catti-brie reminded herself; there was no chute to a lower chamber. A soft groan, a whimper, escaped her lips and she clawed on, desperate to get Wulfgar from the crushing pile, praying that the rocks had collapsed in an angle that would allow the barbarian to survive.

Then Bruenor was beside her, dropping his axe and shield to the floor and going at the pile with abandon. The powerful dwarf managed to move several large stones aside, but when the outer rim of the cave-in had been cleared, he stopped his work and stood staring blankly at the pile.

Catti-brie kept digging, didn't notice her father's frown.

After more than two centuries of mining, Bruenor understood the truth. The collapse was complete.

The lad was gone.

Catti-brie continued to dig, and to sniffle, as her mind began to tell her what her heart continued to deny.

R. A. Salvatore

Bruenor put his hand on her arm to stop her from her pointless work, and when she looked up at him, her expression broke the tough dwarf's heart. Her face was grime-covered. Blood was caked on one cheek, and her hair was matted to her head. Bruenor then saw only Catti-brie's eyes, doelike orbs of deepest blue, glistening with moisture.

Bruenor slowly shook his head.

Catti-brie fell back to a sitting position, her bleeding hands limp in her lap, her eyes unblinking. How many times had she and her friends come so close to this final point? she wondered. How many times had they escaped Death's greedy clutches at the last instant?

The odds had caught up to them, had caught up to Wulfgar, here and now, suddenly, without warning.

Gone was the mighty fighter, leader of his tribe, the man Catti-brie had intended to marry. She, Bruenor, even mighty Drizzt Do'Urden, could do nothing to help him, nothing to change what had happened.

"He saved me," the young woman whispered.

Bruenor seemed not to hear her. The dwarf continually wiped at the dust in his eyes, at the dust that collected in the large teardrops that gathered and then slipped down, streaking his dirty cheeks. Wulfgar had been like a son to Bruenor. The tough dwarf had taken the young Wulfgar—just a boy back then—into his home after a battle, ostensibly as a slave but in truth to teach the lad a better way. Bruenor had molded Wulfgar into a man who could be trusted, a man of honest character. The happiest day in the dwarf's life, even happier than the day Bruenor had reclaimed Mithril Hall, was the day Wulfgar and Catti-brie had announced they would wed.

Bruenor kicked a heavy stone, the force of his blow shifting it aside.

There lay Aegis-fang.

The brave dwarf's knees went weak at the sight of the marvelous warhammer's head, etched with the symbols of

256

Dumathoin, a dwarven god, the Keeper of Secrets Under the Mountain. Bruenor forced deep breaths into his lungs and tried to steady himself for a long while before he could manage the strength to reach down and work the hammer free of the rubble.

It had been Bruenor's greatest creation, the epitome of his considerable smithing abilities. He had put all of his love and skill into forging the hammer; he had made it for Wulfgar.

Catti-brie's semistoic front collapsed like the ceiling at the sight of the weapon. Quiet sobs made her shoulders bob, and she trembled, seeming frail in the dim, dusty light.

Bruenor found his own strength in watching her display. He reminded himself that he was the Eighth King of Mithril Hall, that he was responsible for his subjects—and for his daughter. He slipped the precious warhammer into the strap of his traveling pack and hooked an arm under Catti-brie's shoulder, hoisting her to her feet.

"We can't do a thing for the boy," Bruenor whispered. Catti-brie pulled away from him and moved back to the pile, growling as she tossed several smaller stones aside. She could see the futility of it all, could see the tons of dirt and stones, many of them too large to be moved, filling the alcove. But Catti-brie dug anyway, simply incapable of giving up on the barbarian. No other apparent course offered any hope.

Bruenor's hands gently closed about her upper arms.

With a snarl, the young woman shrugged him away and resumed her work.

"No!" Bruenor roared, and he grabbed her again, forcefully, lifting her from the ground and hauling her back from the pile. He put her down hard, with his wide shoulders squared between her and the pile, and whichever way Catti-brie went to get around him, Bruenor shuffled to block her.

"Ye can't do a thing!" he shouted into her face a dozen times.

"I've got to try!" she finally pleaded with him, when it became obvious to her that Bruenor was not going to let her back to the digging.

Bruenor shook his head—only the tears in his dark eyes, his obvious distress, prevented Catti-brie from punching him in the face. She did calm down then, stopped trying to slip past the stubborn dwarf.

"It's over," Bruenor said to her. "The boy . . . me boy, choosed his course. He gave himself for us, yerself and me. Don't ye do him the dishonor of letting stupid pains keep ye here, in danger."

Catti-brie's body seemed to slump at the undeniable truth of Bruenor's reasoning. She did not move back to the pile, to Wulfgar's burial cairn, as Bruenor retrieved his shield and axe. The dwarf came back to her and draped one arm about her back.

"Say yer good-byes," he offered, and he silently waited a moment before leading Catti-brie away, first to her bow, then from the chamber, toward the same entrance through which they had come.

Catti-brie stopped beside him and regarded him and the tunnel curiously, as if questioning their course.

"Pwent and the cat'll have to find their own way about," Bruenor answered her blank stare, misunderstanding her confusion.

Catti-brie wasn't worried about Guenhwyvar. She knew that nothing could bring the panther serious harm while she still possessed the magical figurine, and she wasn't worried about the missing battlerager at all.

"What about Drizzt?" she asked simply.

"Me guess is that th'elf's alive," Bruenor answered with confidence. "One of them drow asked me about him, asked me where he was at. He's alive, and he's got away from them, and by me own figuring, Drizzt's got a better chance o' getting clear of these tunnels than the two of us. Might be that the cat's with him even now."

"And it might be that he needs us," Catti-brie argued, pulling free of Bruenor's gentle touch. She flipped the bow over her shoulder and crossed her arms over her chest, her face grim and determined.

"We're going home, girl," Bruenor ordered sternly. "We're not for knowing where Drizzt might be. I'm only guessing, and hoping, that he really is alive!"

"Are ye willing to take the chance?" Catti-brie asked simply. "Are ye willing to risk that he's needing us? We lost one friend, maybe two if the assassin finished off Regis. I'm not for giving up on Drizzt, not for any risk." She winced as another memory flashed through her mind, a memory of being lost on Tarterus, another plane of existence, when Drizzt Do'Urden had bravely faced unspeakable horrors to bring her home.

"Ye remember Tarterus?" she said to Bruenor, and the thought made the helpless-feeling dwarf blink and turn away.

"I'm not giving up," Catti-brie said again, "not for any risk." She looked to the tunnel entrance across the way, where the escaping dark elves apparently had taken flight. "Not for any damned dark elves and their hell-spawned friends!"

Bruenor stayed quiet for a long while, thinking of Wulfgar, milling over his daughter's determined words. Drizzt might be about, might be hurt, might be caught again. If it was Bruenor lost down there, and Drizzt up here, the dwarf had no doubt which course Drizzt would choose.

He looked again at Catti-brie and at the pile behind her. He had just lost Wulfgar. How could he risk losing Catti-brie as well?

Bruenor looked more closely at Catti-brie, saw the seething determination in her eyes. "That's me girl," the dwarf said quietly.

They retrieved the remaining torch and left through the exit on the opposite side of the chamber, moved deeper into the tunnels in search of their missing friend.

* * * * *

One who had not been raised in the perpetual gloom of the Underdark would not have noticed the subtle shift in the depth

of the darkness, the slight tingling breeze of fresher air. To
Drizzt the changes came as obviously as a slap across the face,
and he picked up his pace, hoisting Regis tight to his side.

"What is it?" the scared halfling demanded, glancing about
as if he expected Artemis Entreri to jump out of the nearest
shadows and devour him.

They passed a wide but low side passage, sloping upward.
Drizzt hesitated, his direction sense screaming to him that he
had just passed the correct tunnel. He ignored those silent pleas,
though, and continued on, hopeful that the opening to the
outside world would be accessible enough for him and Regis to
get a welcome breath of fresh air.

It was. They rounded a bend in the tunnel and felt the chilly
burst of wind in their faces, saw a lighter opening ahead, and
saw beyond it towering mountains . . . and stars!

The halfling's profound sigh of relief echoed Drizzt's senti-
ments perfectly as he carried Regis on. When they came out of
the tunnel, both of them were nearly overcome by the splendor
of the mountainous scene spread wide before them, by the sheer
beauty of the surface world under the stars, so removed from
the starless nights of the Underdark. The wind, rushing past
them, seemed a vital and alive entity.

They were on a narrow ledge, two-thirds of the way to the
bottom of a steep, thousand-foot cliff. A narrow path wound up
to their right, down to the left, but at only a slight angle, which
offered little hope that it would continue long enough to get
them either up or down the cliff.

Drizzt considered the towering wall. He knew he could
easily manage the few hundred feet to the bottom, could
probably get up to the top without too much trouble, but he
didn't think he'd be able to bring Regis with him and didn't like
the prospect of being in an unknown stretch of wilderness, not
knowing how long it might take him to get back to Mithril Hall.

His friends, not so far away, were in trouble.

"Keeper's Dale is up there," Regis remarked hopefully,

pointing to the northwest, "probably no more than a few miles."
Drizzt nodded but replied, "We have to go back in."

While Regis did not seem pleased by that prospect, he did
not argue, understanding that he could not get off this ledge in
his present condition.

"Well done," came Entreri's voice from up around the bend.
The assassin's dark silhouette came into sight, the jewels of his
belted dagger glimmering like his heat-seeing eyes. "I knew
you would come to this place," he explained to Drizzt. "I knew
you would sense the clean air and make for it."

"Do you congratulate me or yourself?" the drow ranger
asked.

"Both!" Entreri replied with a hearty laugh. The white of his
teeth disappeared, replaced by a cold frown, as he continued to
approach. "The tunnel you passed fifty yards back will indeed
take you to the higher level, where you'll likely find your
friends—your dead friends, no doubt."

Drizzt didn't take the bait, didn't let his rage send him
charging ahead.

"But you cannot get there, can you?" Entreri teased. "You
alone could keep ahead of me, could avoid the fight I demand.
But, alas for your wounded companion. Think of it, Drizzt
Do'Urden. Leave the halfling and you can run free!"

Drizzt didn't justify the absurd thought with a reply.

"I would leave him," Entreri remarked, dropping his cold
glare over Regis as he spoke. The halfling gave a curious
whimper and slumped under the strong hold of Drizzt's arm.

Drizzt tried not to imagine the horrors Regis had suffered at
Entreri's vile hands.

"You will not leave him," Entreri continued. "We long ago
established that difference between us, the difference you call
strength, but that I know to be weakness." He was only a dozen
strides away; his slender sword hissed free of its scabbard,
illuminating him in its blue-green glow. "And so to our business," he said. "And so to our destiny. Do you like the battle–

261

field I have prepared? The only way off this ledge is the tunnel behind you, and so I, like yourself, cannot flee, must play it out to the end." He looked over the cliff as he spoke. "A deadly drop for the loser," he explained, smiling. "A fight with no reprieve."

Drizzt could not deny the sensations that came over him, the heat in his breast and behind his eyes. He could not deny that, in some repressed corner of his heart and soul, he wanted this challenge, wanted to prove Entreri wrong, to prove the assassin's existence to be worthless. Still, the fight would never have happened if Drizzt Do'Urden had been given a reasonable choice. The desires of his ego, he understood and fully accepted, were no valid reason for mortal combat. Now, with Regis helpless behind him and his friends somewhere above, facing dark elf enemies, the challenge had to be met.

He felt the hard metal of his scimitar hilts in his hands, let his eyes slip back fully into the normal spectrum of light as Twinkle flared its angry blue.

Entreri halted, sword at one side, dagger at the other, and motioned for Drizzt to approach.

For the third time in less than a day, Twinkle slapped hard against the assassin's slender blade; the third time, and, as far as both Drizzt and Entreri were concerned, the very last time.

They started easily, each measuring his steps on the unorthodox arena. The ledge was perhaps ten feet wide at this point, but narrowed considerably just behind Drizzt and just behind Entreri.

A backhand slash with the sword led Entreri's routine, dagger thrust following.

Two solid parries sounded, and Drizzt snapped one scimitar for the opening between Entreri's blades, an opening that was closed by a retreating sword in the blink of an eye, with Drizzt's attack slapped harmlessly aside.

They circled, Drizzt inside and near the wall, the assassin moving easily near the drop. Entreri slashed low, unexpectedly leading with the dagger this time.

Drizzt hopped the shortened cut, came with a two-chop combination for the ducking assassin's head. Entreri's sword darted left and right, worked horizontally above his head to block ensuing blows, and shifted its angle slightly to poke ahead, to keep the drow at bay while the assassin came back to equal footing.

"It will not be a quick kill," Entreri promised with an evil smile. As if to disprove his own claim, he leaped ahead furiously, sword leading.

Drizzt's hands worked in a blur, his scimitars hitting the deftly angled weapon repeatedly. The dark elf worked to the side, kept his back from flattening against the wall.

Drizzt agreed fully with the assassin's estimate—this would not be a quick kill, whoever might win. They would fight for many minutes, for an hour, perhaps. And to what end? Drizzt wondered. What gain could he expect? Would Vierna and her cohorts show up and bring the challenge to a premature conclusion?

How vulnerable Drizzt and Regis would be then, with nowhere to run and a drop of several hundred feet just inches away!

Again the assassin pressed the attack, and again Drizzt worked his scimitars through the proper, perfectly balanced defenses, Entreri getting nowhere near to hitting him.

Entreri went into a spin then, imitating Drizzt's movements in their previous two encounters, working his two blades like the edge of a screw to force Drizzt back to a narrower position on the ledge.

Drizzt was surprised that the assassin had learned the daring and difficult maneuver so completely after only two observations, but it was a move Drizzt had designed, and he knew how to counter it.

He, too, went into a spinning rotation, scimitars flowing, up and down. Blades connected repeatedly with each turn, sometimes lighting sparks in the dark night, metal screeching, green and blue mixing in an indistinct blur. Drizzt moved right by Entreri—the assassin reversed his spin suddenly, but Drizzt saw the shift and came to a stop, both blades blocking the reversed cut of sword and dagger.

Drizzt began once more, counter to Entreri, and this time, when Entreri again turned his rotation back the other way, the drow anticipated it so fully that he actually reversed direction first.

For Regis, staring helplessly, not daring to intervene, and for any of the region's nocturnal creatures that might have been watching, there were no words to describe the amazing dance, the interweaving of colors as Twinkle and the assassin's glowing blade passed, the violet sparkle of Drizzt's eyes, the red heat of Entreri's. The scrape of blades became a symphony, a myriad of notes playing to the dance, evoking a strange sense of harmony between these most bitter enemies.

They stopped in unison, a few feet apart, both understanding that there would be no end to that spinning dance, no advantage by either player. The stood like matching bookends of identical weight.

Entreri laughed aloud at the realization, laughed so that he might savor this moment, this many act play that perhaps would see the dawn, and perhaps would never be resolved.

Drizzt found no humor, and his private eagerness at the beginning of the challenge had flown, leaving him with the weight of responsibility—for Regis and for his friends back in the tunnels.

The assassin came in low and hard, sword darting, climbing with each strike as Entreri gradually straightened his stance, taking a full measure of Drizzt's defenses from a variety of cunning angles.

Entreri settled him into a parrying rhythm, then broke the melody with a vicious dagger cut. The assassin howled in glee, thinking for a moment that his blade had slipped through.

Twinkle's hilt had intercepted it cleanly, had caught it and held it, barely an inch from Drizzt's side. The assassin grimaced and stubbornly tried to push on as he came to understand the truth.

Drizzt's expression was colder still; the dagger did not move.

A twist of the drow's wrist sent both blades flying wide. Entreri was wise enough to push off and break the clench, to circle back and wait for the next opportunity to present itself.

"I almost had you," he teased. He hid his frown well as Drizzt in no way responded, not with words, not with body movements, not with the unyielding set of his ebony-skinned features.

A scimitar snapped across, ringing loudly through the breeze as Entreri brought his blocking sword in its path.

The sudden sound assaulted Drizzt, reminded him that Vierna might not be far away. He pictured his friends in dire trouble, captured or dead, felt a special twinge of remorse for Wulfgar that he could not explain. He locked stares with Entreri, reminded himself that this man had been the one to cause it all, that this enemy had tricked him into the tunnels, had separated him from his friends.

And now Drizzt could not protect them.

A scimitar snapped across; the other came slashing in the other way. Drizzt repeated the routine, then a third time, each movement, each ring of metal against metal, bringing his thoughts more in line with this task, lifting his emotional preparations, heightening his warrior senses.

Each strike was perfectly aimed, and each parry intercepted the attacking blades perfectly, yet neither Drizzt nor Entreri, locked through their staring eyes into mental combat, watched their hands through the physical movements. Neither one blinked, not when the breeze of Drizzt's high slice moved the hair atop the assassin's head, not when Entreri's sword thrust came to a parried stop a hairsbreadth from Drizzt's eye.

Drizzt felt his momentum building, felt the give and take of the battle coming quicker, strike and parry. Entreri, as consumed as the ranger, paced him.

The movements of their bodies began to catch the blur of hands and weapons. Entreri dipped a shoulder, sword lashing out straight ahead; Drizzt spun a complete circle, parrying behind his back as he flitted out of reach.

Images of Bruenor and Catti-brie captured by Vierna tormented the ranger; he pictured Wulfgar, wounded or dying, a drow sword at his throat. He imagined the barbarian atop a funeral pyre, a conjured image that, for some reason Drizzt could not understand, would not be easily dismissed. Drizzt accepted the images, gave the mental assault his full attention, let the fears for his friends fuel his passion. That had been the difference between him and the assassin, he told himself, told that part of himself that argued for him to keep his mind clear and his movements precise and well considered.

That was how Entreri played the game, always in control, never feeling anything beyond the enemy at hand.

A slight growl escaped Drizzt's lips; his lavender eyes simmered in the starlight. In his mind Catti-brie screamed out in pain.

He came at Entreri in a wild rush.

The assassin laughed at him, sword and dagger working furiously to keep the two scimitars at bay. "Give in to the rage," he chided. "Let go of your discipline!"

Entreri didn't understand; that was precisely the point.

Twinkle chopped in, to be predictably parried by Entreri's sword. It wouldn't be that easy for the assassin this time, though. Drizzt retracted and struck again, and again, repeatedly, willingly slamming his blade against the assassin's already poised weapon. His other blade came in furiously from the other side; Entreri's dagger turned it aside.

Drizzt's ensuing flurry, sheer madness, it seemed, kept the assassin back on his heels. A dozen hits, two dozen, sounded like one long cry of ringing steel.

Entreri's expression betrayed his laughter. He had not expected this wild an offensive routine, had not expected Drizzt to be so daring. If he could get one of his blades free for just an instant, the drow would be vulnerable.

But Entreri could not free up sword or dagger. Fires drove Drizzt on, kept his pace impossibly fast and his concentration perfect. To the Nine Hells with his own life, he decided, for his friends needed him to prevail.

On and on the offensive routine continued; Regis covered his ears at the horrid wail and screech of the blades, but the halfling could not, for all his terror, take his gaze from the fighting masters. How many times Regis expected one or both to pitch over the cliff! How many times he thought a sword or scimitar thrust had struck home! But they somehow kept on fighting, each attack just missing, each defense in line at the last possible instant.

Twinkle hit the sword; Drizzt's following strike from the other side was not parried but went in short as Entreri shifted his foot and fell back a step.

The assassin's dagger arm shot forward. Entreri released a primal scream of victory, thinking Drizzt had slipped up.

Twinkle came across from its high perch faster than Entreri expected, faster than the assassin believed possible, gashing his forearm an instant before he got the dagger to Drizzt's exposed belly. Back flew the scimitar, backhanding the sword away. Entreri leaped ahead to get in close, realizing his vulnerability.

His sudden charge saved his life, but while Drizzt could not angle the tip of his free blade for a killing thrust, he could, and did, punch out with the hilt, connecting solidly with Entreri's face, sending the man staggering backward.

On came the dark elf, blades flashing relentlessly, driving Entreri back to within an inch of the cliff. The assassin tried to go to his right, but one scimitar knocked aside his blocking sword while the other's maneuvering kept Drizzt directly in front of him. The assassin started left, but with his wounded dagger arm slow to react, he knew he could not get beyond the drow's reach in time. Entreri held his ground, parrying furiously, trying to find a countering routine that would drive this possessed enemy back.

Drizzt's breath came in short puffs as he found a rhythm to his frantic pace. His eyes flared, unrelenting, as he reminded himself over and over that his friends were dying—and that he could not protect them!

He fell too far into the rage, hardly registered the movement as the dagger flew at him. At the very last instant, he ducked aside, the skin above his cheekbone slashed in a three-inch long cut. More importantly, Drizzt's forward rhythm was shattered. His arms ached from the exertion; his momentum had played itself out.

On came the snarling assassin, sword poking, even scoring a slight hit, as he drove Drizzt back and around. By the time the ranger had regained his balance somewhat, his toes, not Entreri's, were squarely facing the mountain wall, his heels feeling the free-flowing emptiness of the mountain winds.

"I am the better!" Entreri proclaimed, and his ensuing attack almost proved his claim. Sword slashing and darting, he drove Drizzt's heel over the edge.

Drizzt dropped to one knee to keep his weight forward. He felt the wind keenly, heard Regis scream his name.

Entreri could have leaped back and retrieved his dagger, but he sensed the kill, sensed he would never again have a better opportunity to end the game. His sword banged down with fury; Drizzt seemed to buckle under its weight, seemed to slip even farther over the cliff edge.

Drizzt reached to his inner self, to the innate magic of his heritage . . . and produced darkness.

Drizzt dove to the side in a roll, came up several feet along the ledge, beyond the darkness globe he had created near Regis.

Incredibly, Entreri was still in front of him, pressing him wickedly.

"I know your tricks, drow," the skilled assassin declared.

A part of Drizzt Do'Urden wanted to give in then, to simply lay back and let the mountains take him, but it was a fleeting moment of weakness, one from which Drizzt recoiled, one that fueled his indomitable spirit and lent strength to his weary arms.

But so, too, was hungry Entreri fueled.

Drizzt slipped suddenly and had to grab for the ledge, releasing his grip on his blade. Twinkle toppled over the cliff, skipping down along the stones.

Entreri's sword slammed down, blocked by only the remaining scimitar. The assassin howled and jumped back, coming right back with a thrust.

Drizzt could not stop it, Entreri knew, his eyes going wide as the moment of victory finally presented itself. The twisted drow's angle was all wrong; Drizzt couldn't possibly get his remaining blade down and turned in line in time.

He couldn't stop it!

Drizzt didn't try to stop it. He had quietly coiled one leg under him for a roll, and he went to the side and ahead as the sword dove in, narrowly missing. Drizzt spun his prone body about, one foot kicking against the front of Entreri's ankle, the other hooking and slamming the assassin behind the knee.

Only then did Entreri realize that the drow's slip, and the lost scimitar, had been a ruse. Only then did Artemis Entreri realize that his own hunger for the kill had defeated him.

His momentum forward with the eager thrust, he pitched toward the ledge. Every muscle in his body snapped taut; he drove his slender sword through Drizzt's foot and somehow managed to catch a hold on the drow's impaled boot with his free hand.

The momentum was too great for Drizzt, still sidelong on the smooth ledge, to hold them both back. The drow was pulled out straight as he went over, right above Entreri, skidding down the stone, the agony in his foot fading as more pains, bruises and cuts from the jagged ride became evident.

Drizzt held tightly to his second scimitar, jammed its hilt into a nook, and found a grasp with his other hand.

He shuddered to a stop, and Entreri stretched out below him, over an inverted section that offered the assassin no chance of a handhold. Drizzt thought his entire insides would be ripped out through his impaled foot. He glanced down to see one of Entreri's hands waving wildly; the other clutched desperately to the sword hilt, a macabre and tentative lifeline.

Drizzt groaned and grimaced, nearly fainted from the pain, as the blade slipped out several inches.

"No!" he heard Entreri deny, and the assassin went very still, apparently understanding the precariousness of his position.

Drizzt looked down at him, hanging in midair, still well over two hundred feet from the ground.

"This is not the way to claim victory!" Entreri called to him in a desperate burst. "This defeats the purpose of the challenge and dishonors you."

Drizzt reminded himself of Catti-brie, got the strange sensation once more that Wulfgar was lost to him.

"You did not win!" Entreri cried.

Drizzt let the fires in his lavender eyes speak for him. He set his hands and squared his jaw and turned his foot, feeling every deliciously agonizing inch as the long sword slipped through.

Entreri scrambled and kicked, almost got a hold on Drizzt with his free hand, as the blade came free.

The assassin tumbled away into the blackness of night, his cry swallowed by the mourn of the mountain wind.

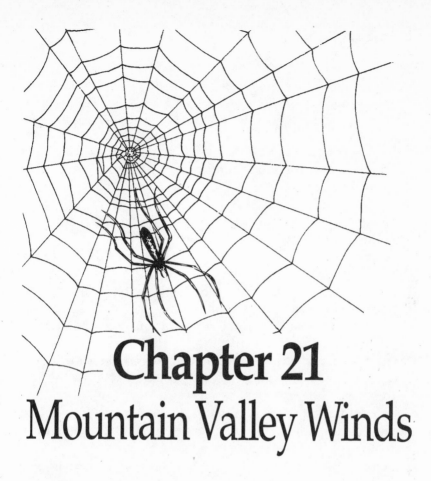

Chapter 21
Mountain Valley Winds

Drizzt slowly doubled over and managed to get a hand to his ripped boot, where he somehow stemmed the blood flow. The wound was clean, at least, and after a few tries, Drizzt found that he still had use of the foot, that it would still support his weight, though painfully.

"Regis?" he called up the cliff face. The dark shape of the halfling's head peered out over the ledge.

"Drizzt?" Regis called back tentatively. "I . . . I thought . . ."

"I am all right," the drow assured him. "Entreri is gone."

Drizzt couldn't make out Regis's cherubic features from that distance, but he could well imagine the joy the news brought his tormented friend. Entreri had chased Regis for many years, had caught him twice, and neither time had been a pleasant experience for the halfling. Regis feared Artemis Entreri more than anything else in the world, and now, it seemed, the halfling could put that fear to rest.

"I see Twinkle!" the halfling called excitedly, the silhouette of his arm coming over the lip in a downward point. "It's glowing down at the bottom, to your right."

Drizzt peered that way, but he could not see the bottom of the cliff since the stone sloped out directly beneath him. He inched his way to the side, and, as Regis had claimed, the magical scimitar came into sight, its blue glow stark against the dark stone of the valley floor. Drizzt cautiously considered this revelation for a few moments. Why would the scimitar, out of his grasp, flare so? Always he had considered the blade's fire a reflection of himself, a magically empathetic reaction to the fires within him.

He winced at the notion that perhaps Artemis Entreri had retrieved the blade. Drizzt pictured the assassin grinning up at him, holding Twinkle out as ironic bait.

Drizzt dismissed the dark notion immediately. He had seen Entreri fall, down across the face of an inverted slope with nothing to grab on to, the wall moving farther away from him as he plummeted. The best the assassin could have hoped for was a bouncing skid after a thirty- or forty-foot free-fall. Even if he was not dead, he certainly was not standing on the valley floor.

What, then, was Drizzt to do? He thought he should go back immediately to Regis and hunt on, to find out the fate of his friends. He could get back to the valley easily enough from Keeper's Dale when the trouble had passed, and, with any luck, no goblin or mountain troll would have scooped up the blade.

When he considered the possibility of battling Vierna's

charges once more, though, Drizzt realized he would feel better with Twinkle in hand. He looked down again, and the scimitar called out to him—he felt its call in his mind and could not be sure if he had imagined it or if Twinkle possessed some abilities that Drizzt did not yet understand. Something else called to Drizzt, too, he had to admit to himself if not to anyone else. His curiosity over Entreri's fate would not be easily sated. Drizzt would rest easier if he found the assassin's broken form at the base of the mountain wall.

"I am going for the blade," the drow yelled up to Regis. "I'll not be gone long. Cry out for any trouble."

He heard a slight whimper from above, but Regis only called, "Hurry!" and did not argue the decision.

Drizzt sheathed his remaining scimitar and picked his way carefully around the inverted region, catching firm handholds and trying as best he could to keep the pressure from his wounded foot. After fifty feet or so, he came to a steeply pitched but not sheer region of loose stone. There were no handholds here, but Drizzt didn't need any. He lay flat against the wall and slid slowly down.

He saw the danger from the corner of his eye, bat-winged and man-sized and cutting sharp angles in its flight along the mountain valley winds. Drizzt braced himself as it veered in, saw the greenish-blue glow of a familiar sword.

Entreri!

The assassin cackled with taunting glee as he soared past, scoring a slight hit on the drow's shoulder. Entreri's cloak had transformed, had sprouted to form bat wings!

Drizzt now understood the true reason the devious assassin had chosen to fight on the ledge.

The assassin made a second pass, closer, smacking the drow with the side of his sword and kicking out with his boot into Drizzt's back.

Drizzt rolled with the hits, then began to slide dangerously, the loose rubble shifting under him. He drew his scimitar and somehow parried the next passing strike.

"Have you a cloak like mine?" Entreri teased, cutting a sharp turn some distance away and seeming to hover in midair. "Poor little drow, with no net to catch him." Another gleeful cackle sounded, and in swooped the assassin, still keeping a respectable distance, knowing he held every advantage and could not let his eagerness betray him.

The sword, carrying the momentum of the assassin's swift flight, slammed hard against Drizzt's scimitar, and while the ranger managed to keep the slender blade clear of his body, the assassin clearly had won the pass.

Drizzt was sliding once more. He turned back to face the stone, clutched at it, put one arm under him, and hooked his fingers, using his weight to dig them deeply enough into the loose gravel to slow the descent. Drizzt seemed helpless at that awful moment, as concerned with holding his precarious perch as in parrying the assassin's strikes.

A few more passes likely would send him to his death.

"You cannot begin to know my many tricks!" the assassin cried in victory, swooping back toward his prey.

Drizzt rolled over to face Entreri as the killer dove in, the drow ranger's free hand coming up and out straight, holding something Entreri did not expect.

"As you cannot know mine!" Drizzt retorted. He sorted through the assassin's suddenly evasive spins and fired the handcrossbow, the weapon he had taken from the drow he had felled at the base of the chute.

Entreri slapped a hand against the side of his neck, tore the quarrel free just an instant after it had stung him. "No!" he wailed, feeling the poison burn. "Damn you! Damn you, Drizzt Do'Urden!"

He swooped for the wall, knowing that flying while sleeping would be less than wise, but the insidious poison, already coursing through a major artery, blurred his vision.

He bounced off the wall twenty feet to Drizzt's right, the

light of his sword dying immediately as it fell from his grasp.

Drizzt heard the groan, heard another curse, this one interrupted by a profound yawn.

Still the cloak's bat wings beat, holding the assassin aloft. He could not focus his weary mind to guide his way, though, and he flitted and darted on the mountain winds, hitting the wall again, and then a third time.

Drizzt heard the crack of bone; Entreri's left arm fell limp beneath his horizontal form. His legs, too, drooped, his strength stolen by the poison.

"Damn you," he said again, groggily, obviously slipping in and out of consciousness. The cloak caught an air current then, apparently, for Entreri soared off down the valley and was swallowed by the darkness, silently, like death.

Drizzt's descent from that point was not too difficult or dangerous for the agile drow. The hike became a reprieve, a few moments in which he could allow his defenses to slip away and he could reflect on the enormity of what had just occurred. His fight with Entreri had not spanned so many months, particularly by a drow elf's reckoning, but it had been as brutal and vital as anything Drizzt had ever known. The assassin had been his antithesis, the dark mirror image of Drizzt's soul, the greatest fears Drizzt had ever held for his own future.

Now it was over. Drizzt had shattered the mirror. Had he really proven anything? he wondered. Perhaps not, but at the very least, Drizzt had rid the world of a dangerous and evil man.

He found Twinkle easily, the scimitar flaring brightly when he picked it up, then its inner light died away to show the reflections of starlight on its silvery blade. Drizzt approved of the image and reverently slid the scimitar back into its sheath. He considered searching for Entreri's lost sword, then reminded himself that he had not the time to spare, that Regis, and probably his other friends, needed him.

He was back beside the halfling in a few minutes, hoisting Regis to his side and heading back for the tunnel entrance.

"Entreri?" the halfling asked tentatively, as though he could not bring himself to believe that the assassin was finally gone.

"Lost on the mountain winds," Drizzt replied confidently, but with no hint of superiority in his even-toned voice. "Lost on the winds."

* * * * *

Drizzt could not know how accurate his cryptic answer had been. Drugged and fast fading from consciousness, Artemis Entreri meandered along the rising currents of the wide valley. His mind could not focus, could not issue telepathic commands to the animated cloak, and without his guidance, the magical wings kept beating.

He felt the rush of air increase with his speed. He hurtled along, barely aware that he was in flight.

Entreri shook his head violently, trying to be rid of the sleeping poison's nagging grasp. He knew, somewhere in the back of his mind, that he had to wake up fully, had to regain control and slow himself.

But the rushing air felt good as it washed over his cheeks; the sound of the wind in his ears gave him a sensation of freedom, of breaking free of mortal bonds.

His eyes blinked open and saw only starless, ominous blackness. He could not realize that it was the end of the valley, a mountain wall.

The rush of air beckoned him to fall into his dreams. He hit the wall head-on. Fiery explosions erupted in his head and body; the air gushed from his lungs in one great burst.

He was not aware that the impact had torn his magical cloak, had broken its winged enchantment, was not aware that the wind in his ears was now the sound of falling, or that he was two hundred feet off the ground.

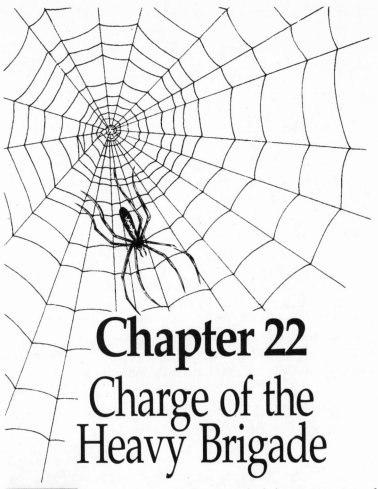

Chapter 22
Charge of the Heavy Brigade

Twelve armored dwarves led the procession, their interlocking shields presenting a solid wall of metal to enemy weapons. The shields were specially hinged, allowing the dwarves on the outside edges to turn back behind the front rank whenever the corridor tightened.

General Dagna and his elite cavalrylike force came in the following ranks, riding, not marching, each warrior armed with a readied heavy crossbow fitted with special darts tipped in a silver-white metal. Several torchbearers, each holding two of

277

the flaming brands out far for easy access to the riders, wandered between the tusked mounts of Dagna's twenty troops. The remainder of the dwarven army came behind, wearing grim expressions, different from those looks they had worn when they had come down this way to battle the goblins.

Dwarves did not laugh about the presence of dark elves, and, by all their reckoning, their king was in dire trouble.

They came to the side passage, clear once more since the darkness spells had long since expired. The ettin bones sat facing them, across the way, somehow undisturbed through all the tumult of the previous encounter.

"Clerics," Dagna whispered, a quiet call that was repeated down the dwarven lines. Somewhere in the closest ranks behind Dagna's elites, half a dozen dwarven priests, wearing their smithy apron vestments and holding mithril warhammer holy symbols tight in upraised fists, sighted their targets, two to the side, two in front, and two above.

"Well," Dagna said to the shield-bearing dwarves in the front rank, "give 'em something worth shooting at."

The blocking wall of shields broke apart, twelve dwarves stringing out along the wide intersection.

Nothing happened.

"Damn," Dagna pouted after a few uneventful moments, realizing that the dark elves had moved back to another ambush spot. In a minute, the battle formation was rejoined and the force tromped off, at a greater pace, with just a small group slipping down the side passage to make sure their enemies would not come out at their backs.

Grumbling whispers ran the length of the ranks, eager dwarves frustrated by the delay.

Some time later, the growl of one of the war dogs, leashed and held in the middle ranks of the army, came as the only warning.

Crossbows clicked from up ahead, most of the quarrels banging harmlessly off the interlocked shields, but some, coming from higher angles, soaring down to strike the dwarves in the second and third ranks. One torchbearer went down, his flaming brands causing minor havoc with the mounts of the nearest two riders. But the dwarves and their mounts were well trained and the situation did not deteriorate into chaos.

Clerics went into their chants, reciting the proper magical syllables; Dagna and his riders put the tips of their crossbows against the flaming torches; the front row counted in unison to ten, then fell straight to their backs, shields defensively atop them.

On came the cavalry, armored war pigs grunting, magnesium-tipped quarrels flaring to intense white light. The calvary charge took the dwarves beyond the area of torchlight quickly, but the clerical spells popped into the corridor ahead of them, magical lights stealing the darkness.

Dagna and every other member of his eager band whooped with delight, seeing the dark elves scrambling this time, apparently caught by surprise with the sudden ferocity and speed of the dwarven attack. The drow had been confident that they could outrun the short-legged dwarves, and so they could, but they couldn't outrun the sturdy, tusked mounts.

Dagna saw one dark elf turn and reach out, as if to throw, and, instinctively, the worldly and wise general understood the creature to be using his darkness ability, trying to counter the stinging magical lights.

When the magnesium quarrel lit up the inside of the drow's belly, his focus predictably shifted.

"Sandstone!" cried the rider right beside Dagna, a dwarven curse if ever there was one. The general saw his companion lurch backward, angling his weapon above. He jerked—obviously hit by some missile—but managed to fire his own crossbow before he tumbled from his saddle, bouncing along the stone.

The flaring quarrel missed, but it doomed the drow floating among the rafters anyway, serving as a tracer for the many dwarven foot soldiers rushing in behind.

"Ceiling!" cried one dwarf, and two dozen crossbowmen skidded to their knees, eyes going up. They caught a shifting motion among the few stalactites and fired, practically in unison.

More dwarves rushed by them as they reloaded, war dogs sounding anxious cries. Dagna's band charged on in hot pursuit, caring little that they had passed beyond the lighted area. The tunnels were fairly flat, and the fleeing drow were not far ahead.

One cleric stopped to aid the kneeling crossbowmen. They showed him the general direction of their quarry, and he put a light spell up there.

The dead drow, his torso ripped by a score of heavy bolts, hung motionless in the air. As if on cue to the revealing light, his levitation spell gave out and he plummeted the twenty feet to the floor.

The dwarves were not even watching him. The light in the ceiling had revealed two of the drow's hidden companions. These new dark elves worked fast to counter the spell with their innate powers of darkness, but it did them little good, for the skilled crossbowmen had picked them out and no longer needed to see them.

Groans and a scream of agony accompanied a frantic explosion of clicking sounds as the host of quarrels skipped and ricocheted off the many stalactites. The two drow dropped, one writhing about as he hit the floor, not quite dead.

The fierce dwarves fell over him, bludgeoning him with the butts of their heavy weapons.

* * * * *

The one tunnel became several as the riders, in hot pursuit, came into a region of snaking side passages. Dagna picked out his target easily enough, despite the growing maze and the gloom. Actually the dimness aided Dagna, for the drow he was chasing had been hit in the shoulder, the white-flaring magnesium serving as a beacon for the charging dwarf.

He gained with every stride, saw the drow turn to face him, the dark elf's shoulder glowing red when viewed from the front. Dagna dropped his crossbow aside and whipped out a heavy mace, angling the boar as if to make a close pass by the drow's wounded flank.

The drow, taking the bait, turned sidelong, getting his one working weapon hand in line.

At the last moment, Dagna lowered his head and veered the tusked boar, and the drow's eyes widened when he realized the wild dwarf's new course. He tried to leap aside, but got hit solidly, tusks catching him just above the knee, Dagna's iron helmet slamming his belly. He hurtled through the air for perhaps fifteen feet, and would have gone farther if the tunnel wall hadn't abruptly stopped him.

Crumpled in a broken heap at the base of the wall, the barely conscious drow saw Dagna pull his mount up before him and saw Dagna's mace go up.

The explosion in his head flared as brightly as the magnesium in his shoulder, then there was only darkness.

* * * * *

Bloodhounds led a large contingent of the dwarven army down to the left of the main chamber, into a region of looping, more natural caverns. Soldiers rumbled straight in, clerics among their ranks, while other dwarves, armed not with weapons, but with tools, went to work behind them and among the passages to the sides.

They came to the four-way intersection, the bloodhounds straining against their leads both left and right. The sneaky dwarves forced the dogs straight ahead, though, and predictably, more than a dozen dark elves slipped into the central corridor behind them, firing their nasty bolts.

The army swung about, the clerics called upon their spells to light up the area, and the drow, outnumbered four to one, wisely turned and fled. They had no reason to fear their way back blocked, not with so many tunnels before them. They had a good idea of the dwarven numbers and were certain that fewer than half of their options would be blocked.

Down the very first path they chose, they came to understand their error, though, running up against a freshly constructed iron door, barred from the other side. The dark elves could see around the edges of the portal—the dwarves hadn't had the time to fit it perfectly into the oddly shaped tunnel—but there was no way to slip through.

The next tunnel seemed more promising, and, by the hopes of the fleeing drow, it had to be, for the dwarven force, dogs barking wildly, was right on their heels again. Turning a corner, the dark elves found a second door, heard the hammers of the working dwarves behind it, putting in the finishing touches.

The desperate dark elves dropped spells of darkness on the other side of the door, slowing the work. They found the widest cracks along the jam and fired their crossbows blindly at the workers, adding to the confusion. One drow got his hand around and located the locking bar.

Too late. The dogs rounded the corner, and the dwarven force fell over them.

Darkness descended over the area of battle. A dwarven cleric, his powers nearly exhausted, countered it, but then another drow blackened the area once more. The brave dwarves fought blindly, matching drow skill with sheer fury.

One dwarf felt the hot burn as an unseen enemy's sword slipped between his ribs, slashing through his lung. The dwarf knew the wound would prove mortal, felt the blood filling his lungs and choking off his breathing. He could have retreated, hoped to fall out of the darkened area close enough to a cleric with curative spells to treat the wound. In that critical instant, though, the dwarf knew his opponent was vulnerable, knew that if he retreated, one of his comrades might next feel the dark elf's cruel sword. He lunged ahead, the drow's sword impaling him further, and chopped with his warhammer, connecting once, then again on his enemy.

He went down atop the dead drow and died with a grim smile of satisfaction splayed across his bearded face.

Two dwarves, driving in deeply side by side, felt their intended target dive between them, but turned too late to avoid a collision on the iron door. Disoriented but sensing movement to the side, each of them launched mighty swings with his hammer, each connecting on the other.

Down they went in a heap, and they felt the rush of air as the dark elf came back over them—this time at the end of a dwarven spear—to be slammed hard against the door. The drow fell wounded atop the two dwarves, and they had enough wits and strength remaining to grab on to the gift. They kicked and bit, punched out with their weapon hilts or with their gauntleted hands. In mere seconds, they ripped the unfortunate dark elf apart.

More than a score of dwarves died at the end of drow weapons in that narrow corridor, but so, too, did fifteen dark elves, half of the force that had stood to block the way into the new sections.

* * * * *

A handful of drow kept ahead of their pig-riding pursuers long enough to make their way into the back chambers, into the very room where Drizzt and Entreri had fought for the enjoyment of Vierna and her minions. The blasted door and several dead companions told the soldiers that Vierna's group had been hit hard, but they nevertheless believed their salvation at hand when the first of them leaped for the chute—leaped and got stuck on the webbing barring the way.

283

The stuck drow flailed helplessly, both his arms fully trapped. His companions, with no thoughts of aiding their doomed friend, looked to the room's other door for their salvation.

War pigs grunted; a dozen dwarven riders whooped in joy as they kicked their mounts across the blasted wooden door.

General Dagna came into the room barely five minutes later to see five dark elves, two dwarves, and three pigs lying dead on the floor.

Satisfied that no other enemies were about, the general ordered an inspection of the remarkable area. Grief stung their hearts when they found Cobble's crushed form under the conjured wall of iron, but it was mixed with some measure of hope, for Bruenor and the others obviously had hit the enemy hard in this place, and apparently, with the exception of poor Cobble, had survived.

"Where are ye, Bruenor?" the general asked down the empty corridors. "Where are ye?"

* * * * *

Sheer determination, pure denial of defeat, was their only strength as Catti-brie and Bruenor, weary and wounded and leaning on each other for support, made their way through the winding tunnels, deeper into the natural corridors. Bruenor held the torch in his free hand. Catti-brie kept her bow ready. Neither of them believed they would stand a chance if they again encountered the dark elves, but, in their hearts, neither of them believed that they could possibly lose.

"Where's that damned cat?" Bruenor asked. "And the wild one?"

Catti-brie shook her head, having no definite answers. Who knew where Pwent might have gotten to? He had flown from the chamber in typical blind rage and could have run all the way back to Garumn's Gorge by this time. Guenhwyvar was a different story, though. Catti-brie dropped her hand into her pouch, sensitive fingers tracing the intricate work of the figurine. She sensed that the panther was no longer about, and trusted the feeling, for if Guenhwyvar had not left the material plane, the panther would have made contact with them by this time.

Catti-brie stopped, and Bruenor, after a few steps, turned back curiously and did likewise. The young woman, on one knee, held the figurine in both hands, studying it intently, her bow on the floor by her side.

"Gone?" Bruenor asked.

Catti-brie shrugged and placed the statue on the floor, then called softly to Guenhwyvar. For a long moment, nothing happened, but just as Catti-brie was about to retrieve the item, the familiar gray mist began to gather and take shape.

Guenhwyvar looked haggard indeed! The panther's muscles drooped, slack from exhaustion, and the black-furred skin of one shoulder hung out, torn, revealing sinew and cordlike tendons underneath.

"Oh, go back!" Catti-brie cried, horrified by the sight. She scooped up the figurine and moved to dismiss the panther.

Guenhwyvar moved faster than either Catti-brie or the dwarf would have believed possible, given the cat's desperate state. A paw slashed up at Catti-brie, batting the figurine to the ground. The panther flattened its ears and issued an angry growl.

"Let the cat stay," Bruenor said.

Catti-brie gave the dwarf an incredulous look.

"Ain't no worse than the rest of us," Bruenor explained. He walked over and dropped a gentle hand on the panther's head, easing the tension. Guenhwyvar's ears came back up, and the cat stopped growling. "And no less determined."

Bruenor looked back to Catti-brie, then to the corridor beyond. "The three of us, then," the dwarf said, "beat up and ready to fall down—but not afore we take them stinking drow down under us!"

285

R. A. Salvatore

Drizzt could sense that he was getting close, and he drew his second blade, Twinkle, concentrating hard to keep the scimitar's blue light from flaring. To his delight, the scimitar responded perfectly. Drizzt was hardly aware of the halfling he still held at his side. His keen senses were instead trained in all directions for some clue that the enemy was about. He came through a low doorway into an unremarkable chamber, barely a wider section of hallway, with two other exits, one to the side and level, the other straight ahead, ascending once more.

Drizzt suddenly pushed Regis to the ground, fell back against the wall, weapons and eyes trained to the side. It was no drow that came through the side entrance, though, but a dwarf, possibly the most odd-looking creature either of the companions had ever seen.

Pwent was barely three running strides from the dark elf, and his hearty roar showed that he felt confident he had gained the advantage of surprise. He dipped his head, put his spiked helm in line with Drizzt's belly, and heard the little one lying to the side squeak out in alarm.

Drizzt snapped his hands up above his head, feeling grooves in the wall with strong, sensitive fingers. He still held both his blades, and there wasn't much to grab, but the agile drow didn't need much. As the confident battlerager barreled in blindly, Drizzt lifted his legs up, out, and over the spike.

Pwent hit the wall head-on, his spike digging a three-inch-deep gouge in the stone. Drizzt's legs came down, one on either side of the bent battlerager's head, and down, too, came the drow's scimitars, hilts pounding hard against the back of Pwent's exposed neck.

The dwarf's spike, bent queerly to one side, squealed and scraped as he dropped flat to the stone, groaning loudly.

Drizzt leaped away, allowed the eager scimitar to flare up, bathing the area in a blue glow.

"Dwarf," Regis commented, surprised.

Pwent groaned and rolled over; Drizzt spotted an amulet, carved with the foaming mug standard of Clan Battlehammer, on a chain about his neck.

Pwent shook his head and leaped suddenly to his feet.

"Ye won that one!" he roared, and he started for Drizzt.

"We are not enemies," the drow ranger tried to explain. Regis cried out again as Pwent came in close, launching a one-two punching combination with his glove nails.

Drizzt easily avoided the short punches and took note of the many sharp ridges on his opponent's armor.

Pwent lashed out again, stepping in behind the blow to give it some range. It was a ruse, Drizzt knew, with no chance of hitting. Already the veteran drow understood Pwent's battle tactics, and he knew the phony punch was designed only to put this fearsome dwarf in line, that he might hurl himself at Drizzt. A scimitar flashed out to intercept the punch. Drizzt surprised the dwarf by twirling his second blade above his head and stepping in closer (exactly the opposite course Pwent had expected him to travel), then launching his high-riding weapon out in a wide, arcing, and smoothly descending course as he stepped to the side, bringing the blade to bear at the back of the dwarf's knee.

Pwent momentarily forgot about his impending leap and instinctively bent the vulnerable leg away from the attack. Drizzt pressed on, putting just enough pressure on the dwarf's knee to keep it moving along. Pwent pitched into the air, landed hard on the floor, flat on his back.

"Stop it!" Regis yelled at the stubborn, fallen dwarf, who was again trying to get up. "Stop it. We are not your enemies!"

"He speaks the truth," Drizzt added.

Pwent, up on one knee, paused and looked curiously from Regis to Drizzt. "We came in here to get the halfling," he said to Drizzt, obviously confused. "To get him and skin him alive, and now ye're telling me to trust him?"

"Different halfling," Drizzt remarked, snapping his blades into their sheaths.

An inadvertent grin showed on the dwarf's face as he considered the advantage his enemy apparently had just given him.

"We are not your enemy," Drizzt said evenly, lavender eyes flashing dangerously, "but I've no more time to play your foolish games."

Pwent leaned forward, muscles twitching, eager to leap ahead and rip the drow apart.

Again the drow's eyes flashed, and Pwent relaxed, understanding that this opponent had just read his thoughts.

"Come ahead if you will," Drizzt warned, "but know that the next time you go down, you will never get back up."

Thibbledorf Pwent, rarely shaken, considered the grim promise and his opponent's easy stance, and he remembered what Catti-brie had told him about this drow—if indeed this was the legendary Drizzt Do'Urden. "Guess we're friends," the unnerved dwarf admitted, and he slowly rose.

Chapter 23
The Warrior Incarnate

With Pwent backtracking and leading the way, Drizzt was sure he would soon learn the fate of his friends, and would face his evil sister once more. The battlerager couldn't tell him much about Bruenor and the others, only that when he had been separated from them, they were being hard pressed.

The news drove Drizzt on more quickly. Images of Cattibrie, a helpless prisoner being tortured by Vierna, flitted on the edges of his consciousness. He pictured stubborn Bruenor spitting in Vierna's face—and Vierna tearing the dwarf's face

289

off in reply.

Few chambers dotted this region. Long, narrow tunnels dominated, some wholly natural, others worked in places where the goblins apparently had decided that support was needed. The three came into a fully bricked tunnel then, long and straight, angling slightly up and with several side passages running off it. Drizzt didn't see the forms of the dark elves ahead of him, down the long, dark corridor, but when Twinkle flared suddenly, he did not doubt the sword's warning.

The fact was confirmed a moment later when a crossbow quarrel zipped from the darkness and stuck Regis in the arm. The halfling groaned; Drizzt pulled him back and dropped him safely behind the corner of a side passage they had just passed. By the time the drow had turned back to the main corridor, Pwent was in full charge, singing wildly, taking hit after hit from poisoned darts but walking through them without a concern.

Drizzt rushed after him, saw Pwent charge right past the dark hole of another side corridor, and knew instinctively that the dwarf likely had wandered into a trap.

Drizzt lost all track of the battlerager a moment later, when a quarrel shot past the distant dwarf to hit Drizzt. He looked down to it, hanging painfully from his forearm, and felt the burning tingle as Pwent's countering elixir battled the poison. Drizzt thought of slumping where he stood, of inviting his enemies to think that their poison had felled him again, an easy capture.

He couldn't abandon Pwent, though, and he was simply too angry to wait for this encounter any longer. The time had come to end the threat.

He slipped up to the dark hole of the side tunnel, kept Twinkle back a bit so it would not fully give him away. A roar of outrage exploded from up ahead, followed by a steady stream of dwarven curses, which told Drizzt that Pwent's intended victims had slipped away.

Drizzt heard a slight shuffle to the side, knew that the battlerager had piqued the curiosity of whoever was in there. He took one deep breath, mentally counted to three, and leaped around the corner, Twinkle flaring viciously. The closest drow fell back, firing a second crossbow quarrel at Drizzt that nicked his skin through a shoulder crease in his fine armor. He could only hope that Pwent's potion was strong enough to handle a second hit and took some comfort in the fact that Pwent had seemed to be hit repeatedly during his corridor charge.

Drizzt pressed the crossbowman backward in a rush, the evil drow fumbling to draw his melee weapon. He would have had the drow quickly, except that a second drow joined him, this one armed with sword and dirk. Drizzt had come into a small, roughly circular chamber, a second exit off to his right, probably joining the main corridor somewhere farther along. Drizzt hardly registered the physical features of the room, though, hardly took note of the initial swings of battle, parrying aside his opponents' measured strikes. His eyes remained beyond them, to the back of the room, where stood Vierna and the mercenary Jarlaxle.

"You have caused me great pains, my lost brother," Vierna snarled at him, "but the reward will be worth the cost, now that you have returned to me."

Listening to her every word, the distracted Drizzt nearly let a sword slip past his defenses. He slapped it away at the last moment and came on in a flourish, scimitars swirling in a descending, crisscrossing pattern.

The dark elf soldiers worked well together, though, and they fended off the attack, countering one after the other and forcing Drizzt back on his heels.

"I do so love to watch you fight," Vierna continued, now smiling smugly, "but I cannot take the chance that you will be slain—not yet." She began a series of chants then, and Drizzt knew her impending spell would be aimed his way, probably at his mind. He gritted his teeth and accelerated the course of his battle, conjuring images of a tortured Catti-brie, putting up a wall of sheer anger.

Vierna released her spell with a glorious cry, and waves of energy rolled over Drizzt, assaulted him and told him, mind and body, to stop in place, to simply hold still and be captured.

Inside the drow ranger welled a part of him, a primal and savage alter ego that he had not known since his days in the wild Underdark. He was the hunter again, free of emotions, free of mental vulnerability. He shrugged away the spell; his scimitars banged hard against his enemies' blades, hard-pressing his two opponents.

Vierna's eyes went wide with surprise. Jarlaxle, at her side, gave an undeniable snicker.

"Your Lloth-given powers will not affect me," Drizzt proclaimed. "I deny the Spider Queen!"

"You will be given to the Spider Queen!" Vierna shouted back, and she seemed to gain the upper hand once more as another drow soldier entered the chamber from the tunnel to Drizzt's right. "Kill him!" the priestess commanded. "Let the sacrifice be here and now. I'll tolerate no more blasphemy from this outcast!"

Drizzt was fighting magnificently, keeping both his enemies more on their heels than on their toes. If the third skilled soldier came in, however . . .

It never got to that. There came a wild roar from the tunnel on the right, and Thibbledorf Pwent, head bowed in one of his typically frantic charges, plowed through. He hit the surprised drow soldier on the side, his bent helmet spike slicing through the unfortunate elf's slender hip, tearing into his abdomen.

Pwent's powerful legs continued to drive through until he at last got tangled in the impaled drow's feet, and both combatants crashed to the floor right before a stunned Vierna.

The drow thrashed in helpless desperation as Pwent pounded him mercilessly.

Drizzt knew he had to get to his peer's side quickly, understood the danger Pwent faced with Vierna and the mercenary having open shots at him. He brought Twinkle in a flashing downward cross, deflecting both his opponents' swords to the side, and he stepped right in behind the blade, coming with his second blade at his closest opponent, the one who had hit him with the crossbow bolt and who carried no second weapon.

The arm of the other drow shot across, dirk hitting the scimitar just enough to prevent a kill. Still, Drizzt had scored a painful hit on one opponent, slicing the drow's cheek wide.

Out came Vierna's snake-headed whip, the priestess's face an image of pure rage as she beat at the prone battlerager's back. Living snake heads darted about the battlerager's fine armor, finding gaps through which they could bite at his thick hide.

Pwent wriggled his helmet spike free, drove a glove nail through the dying dark elf's face, then turned his attention to his newest attacker and her wicked weapon.

Snap!

A snake head got him on the shoulder. Two others nipped his neck. Pwent threw his arm up as he turned, but got bitten twice on the hand, his limb immediately going numb. He felt his potent elixir fighting back, but he hesitated, near to swooning.

Snap!

Vierna hit him again, all five snake heads finding a target on the dwarf's hand and face. Pwent regarded her a moment longer, formed his lips as if to speak out a curse, then he fell to the stone and flopped about like a grounded fish, his entire body nearly numb, his nerves and muscles unable to function in any coordinated way.

Vierna looked Drizzt's way, her eyes burning with open hatred. "Now all your pitiful friends are dead, my lost brother!" she growled, something she sincerely believed true. She advanced a step, snake whip held high, but paused at the sheer and unbridled rage that suddenly contorted her brother's features.

All your pitiful friends are dead!

The words burned in Drizzt's blood, turned his heart to stone.

All your pitiful friends are dead!

Catti-brie, Wulfgar, and Bruenor, everything Drizzt Do'Urden held dear, were lost to him, taken by a heritage that he had not been able to escape.

He could hardly see his opponent's movements, though he knew his scimitars were intercepting every attack with perfection, moving in a precise blur that offered his enemies no openings.

All your pitiful friends are dead!

He was the hunter again, surviving the wilds of the Underdark. He was beyond the hunter, the warrior incarnate, fighting on perfect instinct.

A sword thrust in from the right. Drizzt's scimitar slapped down across it, driving its tip to the ground. Faster than the agile evil drow could react, Drizzt turned his blade completely over the sword and heaved high, throwing the drow back a step.

Across flashed the scimitar, severing the triceps muscles on the back of the swordsman's arm. The pained drow yelled but somehow held his weapon, though it did him no good as the scimitar came back across, squealing as it cut through the fine mesh armor, drawing a line of blood across the drow's chest.

Drizzt flipped the blade over in his hand in the blink of an eye, and the scimitar flashed back the other way, high. He flipped it again and sent it back a fourth time, and the only reason he missed the mark was that the head that had been his intended target was already flying free.

All the while, the scimitar in Drizzt's other hand had parried the other opponent's attacks.

Vierna gasped, as did the remaining soldier facing Drizzt, and Drizzt would have fallen over him just as easily. He saw Jarlaxle's arm pumping, though, from beyond the opening left by the fallen opponent.

Drizzt's next dance was pure and furious desperation. His first scimitar rang out with a metallic impact. Twinkle came across and batted a second dagger aside.

It was over in a mere second, five daggers knocked away by a dark elf that hadn't even consciously seen them coming.

Jarlaxle fell back on his heels, then began to circle, laughing all the while, amazed and thrilled by the stunning display and the continuing battle.

Drizzt's troubles were not ended, though, for Vierna, crying for Lloth to be with her, leaped ahead to lend support to the soldier, and her snake-headed whip presented more problems by far than had the dead drow soldier's single sword.

* * * * *

Regis huddled back into as small a ball as he could manage when he saw the dark shapes drifting silently past the opening of the side passage. The halfling relaxed when the group had passed, was daring enough to crawl nearer to the entrance and use his infravision to try to discern if these were more evil dark elves.

Those red-glowing eyes gave him away; a sixth soldier was moving behind the first group.

Regis fell back with a squeak. He grabbed a rock in his plump little hand and held it out before him. A pitiful weapon indeed against the likes of a drow elf!

The dark elf considered the halfling and the tunnel all about Regis, carefully, then entered, coming in cautiously. A smile widened as he came to realize Regis's apparent helplessness.

"Already wounded?" he asked in the Common tongue.

It took Regis a moment to sort through the heavy and unfamiliar accent. He lifted the rock threateningly as the drow edged in close, kneeling to Regis's level and holding a long and cruel sword in one hand, a dagger in the other.

The drow laughed aloud. "You will strike me down with your pebble?" he taunted, and he moved his arms out wide, presenting Regis an easy opening for his chest. "Hit me, then, little halfling. Amuse me before my dagger digs a fine line across your throat."

Regis, trembling, moved the rock in a jerking motion, as though he meant to take the drow up on the offer. It was the halfling's other hand which shot forward, though, the hand holding Artemis Entreri's dropped dagger.

The jewels in the deadly blade flared appreciatively, as though the weapon had a life and a hunger of its own, when it ripped past the fine mesh armor and sank deeply into the startled dark elf's soft skin.

Regis blinked in amazement at how easily the dagger had penetrated. It seemed as though his opponent wore thin parchment instead of metallic chain mail. The halfling's hand was nearly thrown from the weapon hilt as a surge of power coursed through the dagger, into his arm. The drow tried to respond, and Regis would have had no defense if he had brought either weapon to bear.

But the drow did not, for some reason could not. His eyes remained wide in shock, his body jerked spasmodically, and it seemed to Regis as if his very life force was being stolen away. His own mouth agape, Regis stared into the most profound expression of horror he had ever seen.

More vital energy surged up the halfling's arm; he heard the drow's weapons fall to the stone. Regis could think only of old tales his papa had told him of frightening night creatures. He felt as he imagined a vampire must feel when feeding on the blood of its victims, felt a perverse warmth wash over him.

His wounds were on the mend!

The drow victim slumped lifelessly to the stone. Regis sat staring blankly at the magical dagger. He shuddered many times, recalling vividly each occasion when he had nearly felt that weapon's wicked sting.

* * * * *

The two drow moved silently but swiftly through the
winding tunnels that would bring them to Vierna and Jarlaxle.
They were confident they had outdistanced the outrageous
dwarf, did not know that Pwent had sidetracked and had gotten
to Vierna first.

Nor did they know that another dwarf had entered the
tunnels, a red-bearded dwarf whose teary eyes promised death
to any enemy he stumbled upon.

The dark elves turned a bend into the tunnel that would get
them to the side room, parallel to the main tunnel. They saw the
short but wide form of the dwarf swing about, just a few strides
ahead of them, and charge in fearlessly, wildly.

The three opponents intertwined in a confused jumble,
Bruenor shield-rushing with abandon, whipping his many-
notched axe about him blindly.

"Ye killed me boy!" the dwarf bellowed, and though neither
of his opponents could understand the Common tongue, they
could discern Bruenor's rage clearly enough. One of the drow
regained his footing and slipped his sword over the emblazoned shield, scoring a hit on the dwarf's shoulder that should
have stolen the strength from that arm.

If Bruenor even knew he had been hit, he did not show it.

"Me boy!" he growled, slapping aside the other drow's
sword with a powerful swipe of his heavy axe. The drow
replaced the sword with his second sword, again pressing the
dwarf. But Bruenor accepted the hit, didn't even flinch, his
thoughts purely aimed for the kill.

He chopped his axe in a low swoop. The drow hopped the
blade, but Bruenor stopped the swing and turned it about. The
drow tried to hop a second time as soon as he landed, but
Bruenor's movement was too quick, the dwarf jerking the axe
around the drow's ankle and heaving with all his strength,
taking the drow from his feet.

The other dark elf came over the dwarf, trying to shield his downed companion. His sword slashed across, scarring Brue–nor's face, blinding the dwarf in one eye. Again Bruenor ignored the searing agony, bulled ahead within striking distance.

"Me boy!" he cried again, and he chopped down with all his strength, his axe blade cracking through the scrambling drow's spine.

Bruenor threw his shield up just in time to stop a sword thrust from the standing drow. Off balance and shuffling backward, the dwarf tugged repeatedly, finally tearing the weapon free.

* * * * *

Snake heads seemed to work independently of each other, assaulting Drizzt from different angles, snapping and coiling to snap again. Spurred on by the sight of Vierna fighting beside him, the male drow pressed Drizzt as well, sword and dirk working furiously, that he might score the kill for the priestess, for the glory of the wicked Spider Queen.

Drizzt kept his composure throughout the assault, worked his scimitars and his feet in harmony to block or dodge, and to keep his opponents, particularly Vierna, back from him.

He knew he was in trouble, though, especially when he noticed Jarlaxle, the devious mercenary, circling behind, finding an opening between Vierna and the male soldier. Drizzt expected another series of flying daggers, did not honestly know how he would escape their bite this time with Vierna's whip demanding his attention.

His fears doubled when he saw the mercenary point out at him, not with a dagger, but a wand.

"A pity, Drizzt Do'Urden," the mercenary said. "I would give many lives to own a warrior of your skills." He began to chant in the drow tongue. Drizzt tried to go to the side, but Vierna and the other drow worked him hard, kept him in line.

There came a flash, a lightning bolt, beginning just ahead of the ducking Vierna and the drow soldier. But there came, too, just as the mercenary uttered the triggering words, a flying black form, from behind Drizzt, that clipped the drow ranger's shoulder as it leaped past him and flew through the opening between Vierna and her male ally.

Guenhwyvar took the blast full force, absorbed the energy of the lightning bolt before it ever got started. The panther soared through its magical force, slamming into the surprised mercenary and driving him to the stone.

The sudden flash, the sudden appearance of the panther, did not distract the veteran Drizzt. Nor did Vierna, so filled with hatred, so obsessed with this kill, turn her attention from the furious battle. The other drow, though, squinted at the sudden flash and turned his head for an instant to look over his shoulder.

In that instant, when the drow turned back to the battle, he found Twinkle's deadly point already passing through his armor and reaching for his heart.

* * * * *

The flash had lasted no more than a split second, and it hadn't brought too much light into the main corridor beyond the entrance of the side chamber, but in that split second, Cattibrie, crouched farther down the hall to watch Guenhwyvar's progress, saw the slender forms of the approaching dark elf band.

She put an arrow into the air and used its silvery light to discern the dark elves' exact positions. Her face locked in a merciless grimace and the battered young woman rose behind the arrow's silvery wake to steadily begin stalking her enemies, nocking another arrow as she went.

Vengeance for Wulfgar dominated her every thought. She knew no fear, did not even flinch as she heard the expected reply from handcrossbows. Two quarrels stung her.

Another arrow went off, this one catching a dark elf in the shoulder and hurling him to the floor. Before its streaking light had dissipated, Catti-brie fired a third, this one screeching like a banshee as it careened off the worked tunnel's stone walls.

Still the young woman walked on. She knew the dark elves could see her every step, while she caught only silhouetted glimpses of the elves as her arrows streaked past.

Instinct told her to put an arrow up high, and she smiled grimly as it connected with a levitating drow, catching him squarely in the face as he rose, blowing his head apart. The force of the blow spun the body over, and it hung, motionless, in midair.

Catti-brie did not see her next arrow go off, and only then did she realize that the dark elves had put a globe of darkness over her. How foolish! she thought, for now they could not see her as she could not see them.

Still she walked, out of the globe, firing again, killing another of her enemies.

A crossbow quarrel hit the side of her face, scraped painfully against her jawbone.

Catti-brie walked on, jaw set, teeth gritted tightly. She saw the red-glowing eyes of the remaining two drow closing on her fast, knew that they had drawn swords and charged. She put the bow up, using their eyes as beacons.

A globe of darkness fell over her.

Terror welled up inside the young woman, but she fought it back stubbornly, her expression not changing. She knew she had only moments before a drow sword plunged through her. Her mind recalled the last positions in which she had seen her enemies, showed her the angles for her shot.

She put another arrow up, heard the slightest scuffle ahead and to the left, turned, and fired. Then she loosed a third and a fourth, using no guidance beyond her instinct, hoping that she might at least wound the charging dark elves and slow their progress. She fell flat to the floor and fired sidelong, then winced as her arrow soared away in the blackness, apparently not connecting.

Instincts guiding her still, Catti-brie rolled to her back and fired above her, heard a dull thump, then a sharp crack as the missile drove through a floating drow and into the ceiling. Chunks of rubble fell from above, and Catti-brie covered up.

She remained in a defensive position for a long while, expecting the ceiling to fall on her, expecting a dark elf to rush up and slash her apart.

* * * * *

He got his sword near the dwarf far more often than the dwarf's bulky axe came near to hitting him, but the lone drow facing Bruenor knew he could not win, could not stop this enraged enemy. He called upon his innate magic and lined Bruenor with blue-glowing, harmless flames— faerie fire, it was called—distinctively outlining the dwarf's form and presenting the drow with an easier target.

Bruenor didn't even flinch.

The drow came with a vicious, straightforward thrust that forced the dwarf back on his heels, then turned and fled, thinking to put a few feet between him and his enemy, then turn and drop a darkness globe over the dwarf.

Bruenor didn't try to match the drow's long strides. He brought his axe in, clasped it in both hands, and pulled it back over his head.

"Me boy!" the dwarf yelled with all his rage, and with all his strength he hurled the axe, end over end. It was a daring move, a move offered by the desperation of a father who had lost his child. Bruenor's axe would not return to him as Aegisfang had to Wulfgar. If the axe did not hit the mark . . .

It caught the drow just as he was turning the corner back into the winding side tunnel, diving into his hip and back and hurling him across the way to collide with the opposite corner. He tried to recover, wriggled about on the floor for a few moments, searching for his lost sword and air to breathe.

As his hand neared the hilt of his fallen weapon, a dwarven boot slammed down atop it, crushing the fingers.

Bruenor considered the angle of the sticking axe and the gush of blood pouring all about the weapon's blade. "Ye're dead," he said coldly to the dark elf, and he tore the weapon free with a sickening crackle.

The drow heard the words distantly, but his mind had shut down by that time, his thoughts flowing away from him as surely as was his life's blood.

* * * * *

Vierna did not relent as her companion fell dead, showed no signs that she cared at all for the battle's sudden turn. Drizzt's stomach turned at the sight of his sister, her features locked in the hatred that the Spider Queen so often fostered, a rage beyond reason, beyond consciousness and conscience.

Drizzt did not let his ambivalence affect his swordplay, though, not after Vierna had proclaimed his friends dead. He hit the snapping snake heads often, but couldn't seem to connect solidly enough to seriously damage any.

One got its fangs into his arm. Drizzt felt the numbing tingle and whipped his other blade across to sever the thing.

The movement left his opposite flank open, though, and a second head got him on the shoulder. A third came in for the side of his face.

His backhand slash took the nearest viper's head and drove the other attacking snake away.

Vierna's whip had only three heads remaining, but the hits had staggered Drizzt. He rocked back a few steps, found some support in the solid wall along the side of the entryway. He looked to his shoulder, horrified to see the severed head of the

302

snake still holding fast, its fangs deeply embedded.

Only then did Drizzt notice the familiar silver flashes of Taulmaril, Catti-brie's bow. Guenhwyvar was alive and about; Catti-brie was out in the hall, fighting; and, from somewhere far down the other corridor, the one along the right-hand side of the small chamber, Drizzt heard the unmistakable roar of Bruenor Battlehammer's litany of rage.

"Me boy!"

"You said they were dead," Drizzt remarked to Vierna. He steadied himself against the wall.

"They do not matter!" Vierna yelled back at him, obviously as amazed as Drizzt by the revelation. "You are all that matters, you and the glories your death will bring me!" She launched herself forward at her wounded brother, three snake heads leading the way.

Drizzt had found his strength again, had found it in the presence of his friends, in the knowledge that they, too, were involved in this fight and would need him to win.

Instead of lashing out or swiping across, Drizzt let the snake heads come to him. He got bit again, twice, but Twinkle split one viper's rushing head down the middle, leaving its torn body writhing uselessly.

Drizzt kicked off the wall, driving Vierna back in surprise. He worked his blades fast and hard, aiming always for the snakes of Vierna's whip, though more than once he felt as if he could have slipped through his sister's defenses and scored a hit on her body.

Another snake head dropped to the floor.

Vierna came across with the decimated whip, but a scimitar sliced deeply into her forearm before she could snap the remaining snake head forward. The weapon flew to the floor. The writhing snake became a lifeless thong as soon as the whip left Vierna's hand.

Vierna hissed—she seemed an animal—at Drizzt, her empty hands grasping the air repeatedly.

Drizzt did not immediately advance, did not have to, for Twinkle's deadly tip was poised only inches from his sister's vulnerable breast.

Vierna's hand twitched toward her belt, where twin maces, carved in intricate runes of spiderwebs, awaited. Drizzt could well guess the power of those weapons, and he knew firsthand from his days in Menzoberranzan Vierna's skill in using them.

"Do not," he ordered, indicating the weapons.

"We were both trained by Zaknafein," Vierna reminded him, and the mention of his father stung Drizzt. "Do you fear to find out who best learned the many lessons?"

"We were both sired by Zaknafein," Drizzt retorted, tapping Vierna's hand away from her belt with Twinkle's furiously glowing blade. "Do not continue this and dishonor him. There is a better way, my sister, a light you cannot know."

Vierna's cackling laughter mocked him. Did he really believe he could reform her, a priestess of Lloth?

"Do not!" Drizzt commanded more forcefully as Vierna's hand again inched toward the nearest mace.

She lurched for it. Twinkle plunged through her breast, through her heart, its bloody tip coming out her back.

Drizzt was right against her then, holding her arms in tight, supporting her as her legs failed her.

They stared at each other, unblinking, as Vierna slowly slumped to the floor. Gone was her rage, her obsession, replaced by a look of serenity, a rare expression on the face of a drow.

"I am sorry," was all Drizzt could quietly mouth.

Vierna shook her head, refusing any apology. To Drizzt, it seemed as if that buried part of her that was Zaknafein Do'Urden's daughter approved of this ending.

Vierna's eyes then closed forever.

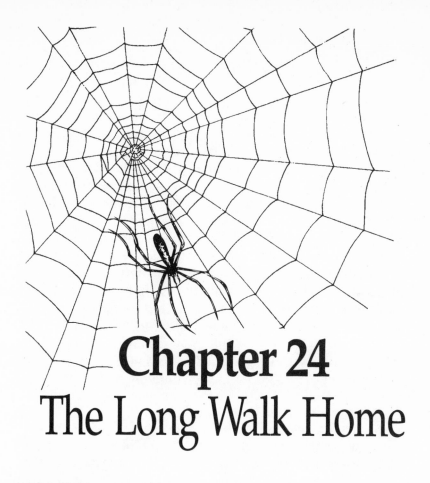

Chapter 24
The Long Walk Home

Well done." The words came at Drizzt unexpectedly, jerked him into the realization that while Vierna was dead, the battle might not yet be won. He jumped aside, scimitars coming up defensively before him.

He lowered the weapons when he considered Jarlaxle, the mercenary sitting propped against the chamber's far wall, one leg sticking out to the side at a weird angle.

"The panther," the mercenary explained, speaking the Common tongue as fluidly as if he had spent his life on the surface.

R. A. Salvatore

"I thought I would be killed. The panther had me down." Jarlaxle gave a shrug. "Perhaps my lightning bolt hurt the beast."

The mention of the lightning bolt reminded Drizzt of the wand, reminded Drizzt that this drow was still very dangerous. He went down in a crouch, circling defensively.

Jarlaxle winced in pain and held an empty hand up in front of him to calm the alerted ranger. "The wand is put away," he assured Drizzt. "I would have no desire to use it if I had you helpless—as you believe you have me."

"You meant to kill me," Drizzt replied coldly.

Again the mercenary shrugged, and a smile widened on his face. "Vierna would have killed me if she had won and I had not come to her aid," he explained calmly. "And, skilled as you may be, I thought she would win."

It seemed logical enough, and Drizzt knew well that pragmatism was a common trait among dark elves. "Lloth would reward you still for my death," Drizzt reasoned.

"I do not slave for the Spider Queen," Jarlaxle replied. "I am an opportunist."

"You make a threat?"

The mercenary laughed loudly, then winced again at the throb in his broken leg.

Bruenor rushed into the chamber from the side passage. He glanced at Drizzt, then focused on Jarlaxle, his rage not yet played out.

"Hold!" Drizzt commanded him as the dwarf started for the apparently helpless mercenary.

Bruenor skidded to a stop and put a cold stare on Drizzt, a look made more ominous by the dwarf's ripped face, his right eye badly gouged and a line of blood running from the top of his forehead to the bottom of his left cheek. "We're not for needing prisoners," Bruenor growled.

Drizzt considered the venom in Bruenor's voice and considered the fact that he had not seen Wulfgar anywhere in this fight. "Where are the others?"

"I'm right here," replied Catti-brie, coming into the chamber from the main tunnel, behind Drizzt.

Drizzt turned to regard her, her dirty face and incredibly grim expression revealing much. "Wulf—" he started to ask, but Catti-brie shook her head solemnly, as though she could not bear to hear the name spoken aloud. She walked near Drizzt and he winced, seeing the small crossbow quarrel still sticking from the side of her jaw.

Drizzt gently stroked Catti-brie's face, then took hold of the obscene dart and yanked it free. He brought his hand immediately to the young woman's shoulder, lending her support as waves of nausea and pain swept over her.

"I pray I did not harm the panther," Jarlaxle interrupted, "a magnificent beast indeed!"

Drizzt spun about, his lavender eyes flashing.

"He's baiting ye," Bruenor remarked, his fingers moving eagerly over the handle of his bloody axe, "begging for mercy without the begging."

Drizzt wasn't so sure. He knew the horrors of Menzo–berranzan, knew the lengths that some drow would travel to survive. His own father, Zaknafein, the drow Drizzt had loved most dearly, had been a killer, had served as Matron Malice's assassin out of a simple will to survive. Might it be that this mercenary was of similar pragmatism?

Drizzt wanted to believe that. With Vierna dead at his feet, his family, his ties to his heritage, were no more, and he wanted to believe that he was not alone in the world.

"Kill the dog, or we drag him back," Bruenor growled, his patience exhausted.

"What would be your choice, Drizzt Do'Urden?" Jarlaxle asked calmly.

Drizzt considered Jarlaxle once more. This one was not so much like Zaknafein, he decided, for he remembered his father's rage when it was rumored that Drizzt had slain surface elves. There was indeed an undeniable difference between Zaknafein

R. A. Salvatore

and Jarlaxle. Zaknafein killed only those he believed deserved death, only those serving Lloth or other evil minions. He would not have walked beside Vierna on this hunt.

The sudden rage that welled up in Drizzt almost sent him rushing at the mercenary. He fought the impulse back, though, remembering again the weight of Menzoberranzan, the burden of pervasive evil that bowed the backs of those few dark elves who were not of typical demeanor. Zaknafein had admitted to Drizzt that he had almost lost himself to the ways of Lloth many times, and in his own trek through the Underdark Drizzt Do'Urden often feared what he would, what he had, become.

How could he pass judgment on this dark elf? The scimitars went back into their sheaths.

"He killed me boy!" Bruenor roared, apparently understanding Drizzt's intentions.

Drizzt shook his head resolutely.

"Mercy is a curious thing, Drizzt Do'Urden," Jarlaxle remarked. "Strength, or weakness?"

"Strength," Drizzt answered quickly.

"It can save your soul," Jarlaxle replied, "or damn your body." He tipped his wide-brimmed hat to Drizzt, then moved suddenly, his arm coming free of his cloak. Something small slammed the floor in front of Jarlaxle, exploding, filling that area of the chamber with opaque smoke.

"Damn him!" Catti-brie growled, and she snapped off a streaking shot that cut through the haze and thundered against the stone of the far wall. Bruenor rushed in, axe flailing wildly, but there was nothing there to hit. The mercenary was gone.

By the time Bruenor came out of the smoke, both Drizzt and Catti-brie were standing over the prone form of Thibbledorf Pwent.

"He dead?" the dwarf king asked.

Drizzt bent to the battlerager, remembered that Pwent had been hit viciously by Vierna's snake-headed whip. "No," he replied. "The whips are not designed to kill, just to paralyze."

His keen ears caught the words as Bruenor muttered, "Too bad," under his breath.

It took them a few moments to revive the battlerager. Pwent hopped up to his feet—and promptly fell over once more. He struggled back up, humbled until Drizzt made the mistake of thanking him for his valuable help.

In the main corridor, they found the five dead drow, one still hanging near the ceiling in the area where the globe of darkness had been. Catti-brie's explanation of where this small band had come from sent a shudder through Drizzt.

"Regis," he breathed, and he rushed off down the hallway, to the side passage where he had left the halfling.

There sat Regis, terrified, half-buried under a dead drow, holding the jeweled dagger tightly in his hand.

"Come on, my friend," the relieved Drizzt said to him. "It is time we went home."

* * * * *

The five beaten companions leaned on each other as they made their way slowly and quietly through the tunnels. Drizzt looked around at the ragged group, at Bruenor with his eye closed and Pwent still having trouble coordinating his muscles. Drizzt's own foot throbbed painfully. The realization of the wound became clearer as the adrenaline rush of battle slowly ebbed. It was not the physical problems that most alarmed the drow ranger, though. The impact of Wulfgar's loss seemed to have fully sunk in for all those who had been his companions.

Would Catti-brie be able to call upon her rage once more, to ignore the emotional battering she had taken and fight with all her heart? Would Bruenor, so wickedly wounded that Drizzt was not certain he would make it back to Mithril Hall alive, be able to guide himself through yet another battle?

Drizzt couldn't be sure, and his sigh of relief was sincere when General Dagna, at the lead of the dwarven cavalry and its grunting mounts, rounded the bend in the tunnel far ahead.

Bruenor allowed himself to collapse at the sight, and the dwarves wasted little time in getting their injured king, and Regis, strapped to war pigs and ushered out of the untamed complex. Pwent went, too, accepting the reins of a pig, but Drizzt and Catti-brie did not take a direct route back to Mithril Hall. Accompanied by the three displaced dwarven riders, General Dagna included, the young woman led Drizzt to Wulfgar's fateful cave.

There could be no doubt, Drizzt realized as soon as he looked at the collapsed alcove, no doubt, no reprieve. His friend was gone forever.

Catti-brie recounted the details of the battle, had to stop for a long while before she mustered the voice to tell of Wulfgar's valiant end.

She finally looked to the pile of rubble, quietly said "Goodbye," and walked out of the room with the three dwarves.

Drizzt stood alone for many minutes, staring helplessly. He could hardly believe that mighty Wulfgar was under there. The moment seemed unreal to him, against his sensibilities.

But it was real.

And Drizzt was helpless.

Pangs of guilt assaulted the drow, realizations that he had caused his sister's hunt, and thus had caused Wulfgar's death. He summarily dismissed the thoughts, though, refusing to consider them again.

Now was the time to bid farewell to his trusted companion, his dear friend. He wanted to be with Wulfgar, to be beside the young barbarian and comfort him, guide him, to share one more mischievous wink with the barbarian and boldly face together whatever mysteries death presented to them.

"Farewell, my friend," Drizzt whispered, trying futilely to keep his voice from breaking. "This journey you make alone."

* * * * *

The return to Mithril Hall was not a time of celebration for the weary, battered friends. They could not claim victory over what had happened in the lower tunnels. Each of the four, Drizzt, Bruenor, Catti-brie, and Regis, held a different perspective on the loss of Wulfgar, for the barbarian's relationship had been very different for each of them—as a son to Bruenor, a fiance to Catti-brie, a comrade to Drizzt, a protector to Regis.

Bruenor's physical wounds were most serious. The dwarf king had lost an eye and would carry an angry reddish blue scar from forehead to jawline for the rest of his days. The physical pains, though, were the least of Bruenor's troubles.

Many times over the next few days the sturdy dwarf suddenly remembered some arrangement yet to be made with the presiding priest, only to recall that Cobble would not be there to help him sort things out, to recall that there would be no wedding that spring in Mithril Hall.

Drizzt could see the intense grief etched on the dwarf's face. For the first time in the years he had known Bruenor, the ranger thought the dwarf looked old and tired. Drizzt could hardly bear to look at him, but his heart broke even more whenever he chanced by Catti-brie.

She had been young and vital, full of life and feeling immortal. Now Catti-brie's perception of the world had been shattered.

The friends kept to themselves mostly as the interminably long hours crawled by. Drizzt, Bruenor, and Catti-brie saw each other rarely, and none of them saw Regis.

None of them knew that the halfling had gone out from Mithril Hall, out the west exit, into Keeper's Dale.

Regis inched out onto a rocky spur, fifty feet above the jagged floor of the southern end of a long and narrow valley. He came upon a limp figure, hanging by the shreds of a torn cloak. The halfling lay atop the garment, hugging close to the exposed stone as the winds buffeted him. To his amazement, the man below him shifted slightly.

"Alive?" the halfling whispered approvingly. Entreri, his

body obviously broken and torn, had been hanging for more than a day. "Still you're alive?" Always cautious, especially where Artemis Entreri was concerned, Regis took out the jeweled dagger and placed its razor edge under the remaining seam of the cloak so that a flick of his wrist would send the dangerous assassin falling free.

Entreri managed to tilt his head to the side and groan weakly, though he could not find the strength to form words.

"You have something of mine," Regis said to him.

The assassin turned a little more, straining to see, and Regis winced and pulled back a bit at the grotesque sight of the man's shattered face. His cheekbone blasted to powder, the skin torn from the side of his face, the assassin obviously could not see out of the eye he had turned toward Regis.

And Regis was certain that the man, his bones broken, agony assaulting him from every garish wound, wasn't even aware that he could not see.

"The ruby pendant," Regis said more forcefully, spotting the hypnotic gemstone as it hung low on its chain beneath Entreri.

Entreri apparently comprehended, for his hand inched toward the item but fell limp, too weak to continue.

Regis shook his head and took up his walking stick. Keeping the dagger firm against the cloak, he reached below the spur and prodded Entreri.

The assassin did not respond.

Regis poked him again, much harder, then several more times before he was convinced the assassin was indeed helpless. His smile wide, Regis worked the tip of the walking stick under the chain around the assassin's neck and gently angled it out and around, lifting the pendant free.

"How does it feel?" Regis asked as he gathered in his precious ruby. He poked down with the stick, popping Entreri on the back of the head.

"How does it feel to be helpless, a prisoner of someone else's whims? How many have you put another in the position you now enjoy?" Regis popped him again. "A hundred?"

Regis moved to strike again, but then he noticed something else of value hanging on a cord from the assassin's belt. Retrieving this item would be far more difficult than getting the pendant, but Regis was a thief, after all, and he prided himself (secretly, of course) on being a good one. He looped his silken rope about the spur and swung low, placing his foot on Entreri's back for balance.

The mask was his.

For good measure, the thieving halfling fished his hands through the assassin's pockets, finding a small purse and a fairly valuable gemstone.

Entreri groaned and tried to swing about. Frightened by the movement, Regis was back on the spur in the blink of an eye, the dagger again firmly against the tattered cloak's seam.

"I could show mercy," the halfling remarked, looking up to the vultures circling overhead, the carrion birds that had shown the way to Entreri. "I could get Bruenor and Drizzt to bring you in. Perhaps you have information that might prove valuable."

Regis's memories of Entreri's many tortures came flooding back when he noticed his own hand, missing two fingers that the assassin had cut away—with the very dagger Regis now held. How beautifully ironic, Regis thought.

"No," he decided. "I do not feel particularly merciful this day." He looked up again. "I should leave you hanging here for the vultures to pick at," he said.

Entreri in no way reacted.

Regis shook his head. He could be cold, but not to that level, not to the level of Artemis Entreri. "The enchanted wings saved you when Drizzt let you fall," he said, "but they are no more!"

Regis flicked his wrist, severing the cloak's remaining seam, and let the assassin's weight do the rest.

Entreri was still hanging when Regis slid back off the spur, but the cloak had begun to tear.

Artemis Entreri had run out of tricks.

EPILOGUE

Drizzt Do'Urden sat in his private chambers, considering all that had transpired. Memories of Wulfgar dominated his thoughts, but they were not dark images, were not flashes of the alcove wherein Wulfgar had been buried. Drizzt remembered the many adventures, always exciting, often reckless, he had shared beside the towering man. Trusting in his faith, Drizzt placed Wulfgar in that same corner of his heart where he had tucked the memories of Zaknafein, his father. He could not deny his sadness at Wulfgar's loss, didn't want to deny it, but the many good memories of the straight-backed young barbarian could counter that sadness, bring a bittersweet smile to Drizzt Do'Urden's calm face.

He knew that Catti-brie, too, would come to a similar, accepting mind-set. She was young and strong and filled with a lust for adventure, however dangerous, as great as that of Drizzt and of Wulfgar. Catti-brie would learn to smile along with the tears.

Drizzt's only fear was for Bruenor. The dwarf king was not so young, not so ready to look ahead to what was yet to come in his remaining years. But Bruenor had suffered many tragedies in his long and hardy life, and, generally speaking, it was the way of the stoic dwarves to accept death as a natural passing. Drizzt had to trust that Bruenor was strong enough to continue.

It wasn't until Drizzt focused on Regis that he considered the many other things that had occurred. Entreri, the evil man who had done grievous wrongs to so many, was gone. How many in the four corners of Faerun would rejoice at that news?

And House Do'Urden, Drizzt's tie to the dark world of his kin, was no more. Had Drizzt finally slipped beyond the grasp of Menzoberranzan? Could he, and Bruenor and Catti-brie and all the others of Mithril Hall, rest easier now that the drow threat had been eliminated?

Drizzt wished he could be sure. By all accounts of the battle in which Wulfgar was killed, a yochlol, a handmaiden of Lloth, had appeared. If the raid to capture him had been inspired simply by Vierna's desperation, then what had brought so powerful a minion into their midst?

The thought did not sit well with Drizzt, and as he sat there in his room, he had to wonder if the drow threat was ended, if he might, at long last, finally know his peace with that city he had left behind.

* * * * *

315

"The emissaries from Settlestone are here," Catti-brie said to Bruenor, entering the dwarf's private chambers without even the courtesy of a knock.

"I'm not for caring," the dwarf king answered her gruffly.

Catti-brie moved over to him, grabbed him by his broad shoulder, and forced him to turn and look her in the eye. What passed between them was silent, a shared moment of grief and understanding that if they did not go on with their lives, did not forge ahead, then Wulfgar's death was all the more pointless.

What loss is death if life is not to be lived?

Bruenor grabbed his daughter around her slender waist and pulled her close in as crushing a hug as the dwarf had ever given. Catti-brie squeezed him back, tears rolling from her deep blue eyes. So, too, did a smile widen on the vital young woman's face, and, though Bruenor's shoulders bobbed with unabashed sobs, she felt sure he soon would come to peace as well.

For all he had gone through, Bruenor remained the Eighth King of Mithril Hall, and, for all the adventures, joys, and sorrows Catti-brie had known, she had just passed her twentieth year.

There still was much to be done.

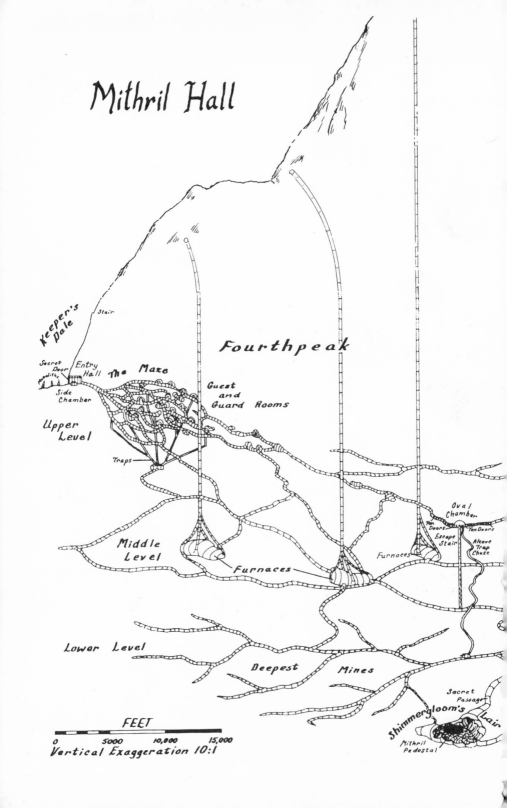

Mithril Hall

Keeper's Dale

Stair

Fourthpeak

Secret Door

Entry Hall

The Maze

Guest and Guard Rooms

Side Chamber

Upper Level

Traps

Middle Level

Furnaces

Furnaces

Oval Chamber

Ten Doors

Ten Doors

Escape Stair

Alcove

Trap Chute

Lower Level

Deepest Mines

Secret Passage

Shimmergloom's Lair

Mithril Pedestal

FEET

0   5000   10,000   15,000

Vertical Exaggeration 10:1